Gigi's Island Dream

Rosie Dean

ISBN-13: 978-0993472916

** *Spring* **

Chapter 1

Mostly it is loss which teaches us the worth of things.

Oh, boy. Never was a truer word spoken.

Through the soft-focus of drizzle, I watched a colourful huddle of people shuffling through the church doorway.

'Good old Nanna,' my brother, Freddy, commented, 'Una Gill rocking the funeral scene.'

Nanna – the matriarch, the keeper of family treasures, the cultivator of the family tree, the bestower of love, hugs and laughter. The woman who'd imparted her wisdom without preaching and who'd cared for us when our own mother had not. It was she who'd often spoken those words about loss, now printed on the funeral's Order of Service.

A bolt of panic lurched in my chest. I clutched Freddy's hand. Suddenly, I was twenty years younger and the brakes were failing on my bike as I hurtled down Station Road. Now I had the very same thought as I had then: *What am I going to do?*

My mother – bronzed from life in the south of France, and yet somehow ethereal in her magenta dress and floppy straw hat – clutched at her bag and frowned. 'Let's get this over with.'

You might be forgiven for thinking she was talking about despatching her mother to another realm, but I suspected she was referring to her forthcoming encounter with my father – the first after many years apart.

He stood by the church door, in his Savile Row suit, waiting for us.

My parents.

Two star-crossed individuals.

Two sets of gritted teeth.

The service was painfully long – a bitter-sweet pain – in which Nanna's friends delivered short, gracious eulogies about her kindness and her humour; her talent and her modesty.

As I watched the coffin lowered into the ground, I felt the pang of loss so keenly, it was all I could do not to scream. Flanking me were Freddy and Mum. Across the divide stood my father and Rupert, my boyfriend. I'd wanted him in the car with me, but my mother insisted on 'blood family' only. Ironic, considering she'd not set foot on the island for years.

Until today.

Today, Bluebell Farm, Nanna's home for the last fifty years, was hosting her wake. She had held many afternoon teas for charitable causes in that house but today's was *about* her and not *by* her. People were swapping stories and hooting with laughter, which is exactly how she'd have wanted it. She'd left strict instructions for mourners not to wear black. 'I don't like black,' she used to say, 'It shows a complete lack of imagination. I can't understand why artists insist on wearing it so dutifully. It's boring and makes them look like a bunch of old crows.'

As a mark of respect, I was wearing an aquamarine Pashmina over an apricot woollen coat and a pair of aquamarine, fringed ankle boots. Rupert studied me with a crooked smile on his face. 'You look like an exotic cocktail. You only need a pink paper parasol to complete the look.'

'Nanna gave me the Pashmina for Christmas.'

He tugged the paisley handkerchief in his top pocket. 'And me this.'

I was touched that he'd brought it and leaned up to kiss him. 'Thanks.'

Freddy reeled into view. His outfit was a vintage tailcoat in burgundy velvet, over an egg-yolk yellow shirt and mustard coloured chinos. In one hand he brandished a bottle of sherry, and the other, a cluster of cut-glass flutes. 'Who's for a little sherry – ladies?'

Half a dozen members of the Women's Institute heaved their bosoms and rustled their skirts eagerly. 'What, no gin?' said one of them, before grinning and winking like the cougar she probably wished she could be.

'This is just the aperitif,' Freddy explained, holding the flutes towards them.

'Go on then, and make it a large one. My HRT's not kicked in, yet.'

'Ooh, Ella, behave yourself!' one of her friends whooped, before watching attentively while Freddy filled her glass.

Rupe leaned towards me. 'Freddy should be good value, today.'

'Don't!' I studied my brother at work. 'It's just his way of hiding his feelings. I know he's going to miss Nanna, but he'll never say so.'

He reached for my hand. 'I liked Una.'

'Everyone did,' I said, as my father approached, smoothing his hand over the front of his jacket.

Everyone except Daddy. 'So, darling girl,' he said, 'What did the estate agents say?'

'I haven't contacted them, yet.'

'Well you should. Best do it while you're on the

island.'

'He's right,' Rupert added, squeezing my hand. 'I know it's hard for you to let go and all that but…'

'Daddy, can I talk to you for a moment?'

'You only ever call me Daddy when you want something,' he found this amusing. 'Go on, how much?'

My stomach pinched in anticipation. 'Nothing. No money. Can we go somewhere quiet?' I asked, loosening my hold on Rupert's hand. 'Sorry, Rupe. Back in a sec.'

Dad and I headed out to the courtyard. The drizzle had stopped but there was the threat of more. We stood on the old cracked path which led to the back garden. Dad puffed out his chest. 'Come on then, what's troubling you?'

I've never bungee-jumped out of an aeroplane but I suspect the anticipation wasn't far from how I felt right then. 'Daddy, I don't want to sell Bluebell Farm.'

He looked perplexed – at first. I'd inherited the farm, while Freddy had been left a cottage over on West Wight, which Nanna let to holiday makers. She'd made sure we were both looked after. 'Fair enough,' he finally said. 'We'll do it up and you can let it. Should provide a nice bit of extra income for you.'

'I don't want to let it. I want to live here.'

The face was blank.

And then he smiled. It was the smile he used before he delivered bad news. A practised smile. I'd seen it deployed many times at work. 'Don't be silly, Gigi. I need you in London. The business needs you on site. You can't possibly operate from over here.'

'I don't just want to live here, Dad. I want to work here. I want to leave the business and work on my sculptures.'

That did it. I've never seen a face fall so fast in my life. 'No, Gigi. That's not a good idea. You're clearly upset over your grandmother's death. You've not thought this through. At all!'

'I have, Dad. I can use some of my savings to convert the barn into a studio. The house just needs a bit of decoration...'

'Listen to me, I've worked bloody hard to establish Gill-Martin Property Holdings, I've done it for you and for Freddy. Don't you dare throw it all back in my face to pursue some madcap scheme.'

'I'm not throwing it back. I appreciate everything you've done for me.'

He grunted in disbelief.

'Dad, I just want to give this a shot. I'm lucky enough to have the property and the space here. Nanna always said I was talented and I should ...'

'Don't even say it! Just don't! It was bad enough your mother drifted off to "find herself". Look how that ended. What makes you think you'll do any better?'

He was referring to the day she'd walked out on him. On us. The day she'd put Freddy and me on a hovercraft to the Isle of Wight, where her mother would be waiting to take care of us. The day she, herself, had jumped on a cross channel ferry to France. I was seven and Freddy was four. She'd felt stifled by life in London; she hated playing hostess at my father's business dinners, and felt trapped by his relentless hunt for the next big deal.

Much as Nanna would have been very happy to bring us up, my father would have none of it. He'd considered she was the reason his wife had proved to be so flaky. No. We were his children, his responsibility and now, his project. His only concession was to allow us to spend our school holidays with Nanna. That had suited him. Boarding school and au-pairs of varying expertise had plugged the gaps.

'I'm not like Mum!'

'Really?'

'No, Dad, I'm not. I've spent the last five years working for you, I've worked bloody hard too – you know that. Don't you?'

He was glaring at me. He couldn't dispute the fact I'd given his company long days and my full commitment. After proving myself in the first three years, he'd given me a five percent share. Not massive, but it was on the understanding that my share would increase over the coming years, so long as I continued to pull my weight.

'Dad, I just want to do something else. Couldn't you get behind me on this?'

'It's a pipe-dream, Gigi. Nobody ever earns a decent living from the stuff you want to do.'

'Nanna did.'

'For heaven's sake! She was a botanical illustrator, two generations ago, pre electronic media. Good for Una!' He shook his arms in the air, like he was celebrating her success. 'But Gigi, you don't have a hope. Do you hear me. None!' He bellowed the last word and then checked himself. 'You have a good career at Gill-Martin Property. Excellent prospects. Especially now we're in the Spanish market.'

Oh yes. The Spanish market. I'd been back and forth over there last year, exploring properties and seeking out opportunities for development. I'd also encountered Jose de la Torre who smiled too much and was overly keen on stroking my arm at every opportunity.

'You know I'm not enthusiastic about the *Arboleda* development.'

'Based on what? I've been in the business for over twenty years, I know what I'm doing.'

We'd been here before. I backed away from the Spanish debate and tried another tack. 'Daddy, please think about it. I want to do this. You know how much I loved doing sculpture at college.'

'Another mistake. I should have pushed for a single honours degree – not bloody *Business Studies with Design*.'

'At least let me try.'

'Has your mother put you up to this?'

I sighed. 'Are you serious?'

'I can just imagine how she's going to gloat over this one.'

'I'm not the same as Mum, you know that. I might actually succeed.'

'You won't last a year.'

'Please, Dad. I'd much rather do this with your approval.'

His frown was as deep as I'd ever seen it. He was mulling it over. Hatching a plan. 'I tell you what I'll do. I'll help you refurbish the house, and the company will pay you your five percent of profit, each month, for one year and one year only. Look on it as a sabbatical. At the end of that, you make a choice – sell up and return to the business or cut loose. But I'm not going to spend the rest of my life, bailing you out over a wretched pipe-dream. Do you understand?'

'Of course. I wouldn't expect you to.'

'Good.'

'Thanks, Dad.' I leaned up to hug him.

He put an arm around me. 'But I mean it, Gigi. I'm only prepared to indulge you for twelve months. Got it?'

'Got it.'

As soft rain began falling, Nanna's favourite neighbour – Luke – appeared, from the back garden carrying a bucket of weeds. He was tall with dark, almost black, unruly hair and a beard like Rasputin. Even though he was a guest at the funeral he was still tidying up her herbaceous borders. He nodded at us. 'Excuse me, I promised Una I'd plant the salvias she grew from cuttings.' His accent was Canadian, I'd forgotten that.

'Thank you, Luke,' Dad said in an unnecessarily superior tone.

'Yes, thank you, that's really kind of you,' I added hoping to soften the tone.

He nodded again and headed over to the compost bin. The long ponytail tied at his nape with leather cord was quite a surprise. From the front, his naturally curly hair had just looked a bit unkempt, I had no idea it disguised another, longer batch at the back. Nanna had never mentioned this feature.

Dad went back indoors as Luke turned to me and said. 'I'll keep an eye on the salvias, make sure they take.' He brushed the dirt from his hands.

'I'd appreciate that,' I said. 'I'm going to be moving in, just as soon as we've done some work on the house.'

His body stilled and he looked at me for a moment. 'Okay, well, good to hear.' He nodded and raised his hand in a farewell gesture. 'See you soon.'

He turned and headed off down the drive.

I had salvias Nanna had grown from cuttings to nurture. Funny how something so small could suddenly give me such cheer. This was going to be my home and my future, and I was going to make it work.

** *Summer* **

Chapter 2

Stepping out onto the sunlit, newly-laid stone courtyard, I massaged hand cream between my fingers.

For the last two hours I'd been in my studio, gouging feathers into the wings of a clay angel. I was now a sculptor or 'sculptress' as my mother insisted on calling me. I'd decided I would model Morael – the angel of healing and of August – to mark the month I moved into my beautiful new home.

As I crossed the courtyard, I looked over the brow of the hill to the sea beyond and, for the umpteenth time that week, a contented smile lifted on my face.

I checked my watch. Any time now, Diva-1 and Diva-2 would be arriving for my house-warming party. Okay – their real names were Sonia and Fran but they were appropriately re-monikered by our crowd at university.

The phone in my pocket chimed into life. I pulled it out and checked the display. My brother was calling – from Tasmania. Since it was mid-afternoon here, that had to mean it was the middle of the night there. He was probably pissed.

'Hi, Freddy, what are you up to?'

There was a crackling of static. 'Gigi, are you there?'

I raised my voice. 'Hi, Freddy – yes, I'm here.'

'Listen, have you heard…'

More static and a click, followed by the void of

disconnection.

I waited a moment for him to call back. He didn't.

I tried his number. Nothing. I tried again. Still nothing.

Had I heard, what? Probably some dodgy joke about two Ozzies and a kangaroo.

My cats, Gaudi and Rodin, were curled together in the sunshine. It was their first day out of doors since we'd arrived, and I was praying they wouldn't scarper before I'd chance to shut them back in for the evening. Suddenly, the honk of a car horn jolted them awake, and me from my reverie. Gaudi peered across Rodin's back as we watched The Divas pull into the driveway in Fran's tomato-red sports car.

Sonia shrieked and waved both arms, at me. 'Gigi! We're here!'

You'd think I was blindfolded.

As I walked over, she threw open the car door and slid her Miu Miu clad foot out. It was a beautiful plum-coloured sandal; all shiny and neat with impossible-to-walk-in heels. Impossible for me, anyway.

'Pretty shoes,' I said. 'Are they comfy?'

'Christ, no!' she answered, 'I saw them in *Vogue* and just had to have them.'

'You're such a bloody fashion victim, Sonia,' Fran drawled from the driver's side, as she checked her face in the rear-view mirror. 'Take a leaf out of Gigi's book and get some biker boots.'

I wriggled my toes in my baseball pumps. 'Welcome to Bluebell Farm!' I said, holding my arms out to hug Sonia.

'Sweet name. So very Beatrix Potter,' she said over my shoulder. 'Where d'you keep Fluffy Bunnykins?'

Fran pushed herself off the driver's seat and strolled round towards us. '*Peter Rabbit*, you daft mare. Hi, babe. Roads over here are crap, aren't they?' she grumbled, leaning in to hug me.

'It's better after the school holidays,' I said.

'Really? Are you telling me they widen them out of season and shrink them for the holidays?'

'Stop whingeing, Fran,' Sonia flapped a hand at her, setting her twenty-plus bracelets jangling. 'Just because you drove full pelt at a hedge and scraped your precious paintwork.'

Fran shook her short, pixie-like blonde hair and ran her fingers through it. As much as Sonia was a fashion adventurer, Fran was a fashion classic.

'Champagne's on ice!' I grinned, knowing exactly how to divert them from one of their spats. 'Want some?'

Sonia winked at me. 'Natch!'

As they followed me into the house, Fran grumbled, 'Why do you have to say, "natch"? It's so pretentious.'

For the Divas to be scrapping so early, they must have had a lousy journey.

'Well!' Fran began, gazing up at the enormous kitchen clock, which was the size of a dustbin lid. 'This is gleaming with contemporary wholesomeness, isn't it? And I'm loving this old dresser. Where did you buy it?'

'That was Nanna's. It's Victorian oak.'

Sonia seemed less impressed. 'Didn't you want new?'

'She's got new,' Fran answered, indicating the hand-built kitchen units. 'This is fusion design – marrying old and new for an eclectic look. It works. It looks properly lived in.'

'Thank you, Fran,' I said, pulling one of twelve champagne bottles out of the double-fronted fridge-freezer.

She peered over my shoulder. 'What are you going to do with that great big pile of meat?' she asked.

'I'm hoping Rupe will man the barbecue.'

'So Rupe's still coming then?' Sonia asked, casually checking the kitchen table for crumbs before parking her linen-clad bottom on it.

'Of course. He's sailing over, right now.' Rupert was my boyfriend but I suspected Sonia rather hoped he could be hers. There'd been some doubt over whether our relationship would survive – what with me on the island and Rupe finishing off his architecture degree in Scotland. He hadn't visited the farm since Nanna's funeral. He'd thought I was mad wanting to keep it. But there was no way I was going to sell it. It meant the world to me. I'd spent some of my happiest times here and always considered it my special place.

After sharing a bottle of fizz on the terrace, I showed them my studio in the old barn across the courtyard. The massive wooden doors had been replaced by floor to lintel glass; there were windows at each end and skylights in the roof to allow even more daylight to penetrate. There was a heavy work table, hooks for my tools and shelves for my creations. Plus there were two new kilns – a small one for fine work and a kick-ass huge one for my major pieces.

Sonia passed a very cursory glance over it before saying 'Lovely' and heading back out into the sunshine. Which was a pity as I really wanted to explain what I had in mind for my first collection.

'I assume this is your shiny new Range Rover,' she said. 'Or is there some wealthy estate owner keeping your bed warm?'

'It arrived last week. Don't you just love the colour?'

'Burgundy and black – reminds me of vintage Zandra Rhodes,' she said.

My phone rang. It was Freddy again.

'Freddy. How's things. You okay?'

'No. It's a fucking disaster.'

'What is? What's happened?' I asked in vain, as an ominous click ended the call.

I yelled with frustration.

'What's up, babe?' Fran asked.

'It's Freddy. That's the second time he's called and got cut off.'

'What do you expect? He's probably in a jungle.'

'Yes but...' I stood up. 'I'm just going to get my iPad.'

I nipped inside, pulled my iPad from the dresser and opened it, immediately searching the internet for news on Tasmania. I could find nothing to worry me. Natural disasters aside, there must be some other problem.

Fran was hovering in the doorway. 'What's going on?'

'I don't know. Freddy's in some kind of trouble. I think.'

'Not got some native girl pregnant has he?' Sonia offered from behind her.

I could feel a tightening in my stomach. Freddy was on the other side of the world. If he was in some kind of trouble, how could I possibly help him? Please, I silently asked the Universe, please let him be okay.

'If I know Freddy,' Fran drawled, 'he's run up a massive bar bill and discovered his wallet's missing.'

I tutted and rolled my eyes. Freddy had a reputation amongst my friends. Oh, he was an absolute hoot to hang out with, never took anything seriously and was frequently found splashing the cash at some cool venue in town. But they all knew he could be a bit of a liability. I think when I was conceived, I inherited a double dose of responsibility, leaving none behind for Freddy.

'There must be something going on over there,' I said. 'He asked me if I'd heard something and then we were cut off.'

'Look, it can't be that tragic. When did he last tweet?'

I checked. 'Two days ago.'

'And?'

'He just says: Surfin' is sick.'

'Now you'll be worrying he's been attacked by a swarm of jellyfish.'

'Oh, God, is that possible?' I asked.

'Babe, he's phoned you twice in the last twenty-four hours. Did he sound like he was at death's door?'

I shook my head 'He sounded worried, though.'

'Gigi, he's a big boy now. He can look after himself.'

He was only twenty-four.

'I suppose…'

Fran put a hand on my arm. 'Has he been travelling for the last four months? Has he been having the best time, ever? Didn't he clear off just when you began your move to the island…?'

'Okay, okay!' She'd already told me Freddy could

have done the decent thing and helped me with the move, rather than clearing off on another of his hedonistic trips abroad. But that wasn't really Freddy's forte – he didn't engage in practical activities, he was more of a *bon viveur*: a sky-diving, rapid-shooting, bungee-jumping kind of a guy. He'd always had a very short attention span. That had been half the trouble with our au pairs. They could never hold his interest for long. Instead of being patient with him, and finding ways to keep him entertained, they'd shouted at him in frustration or shut him in his room. One used to pinch him on the soft flesh under his arm and make him squeal – until Dad found out and asked her to leave. We had so many au pairs, I can't remember them all.

'Have another drink, babe. He'll ring again, don't you worry.'

'When are the caterers arriving?' Sonia asked.

'Caterers?' I grinned. 'They're already here.'

'Oh?' she peered out of the window, probably expecting to find a mobile catering van tucked behind the barn.

Fran rolled her eyes. 'Oh, Christ. It's us, isn't it?'

'Don't worry. Marsha's Catering will be here soon to deliver loads of stuff. We'll only have to serve it.'

'What are your neighbours like?' Sonia asked, gazing out at a distant rooftop.

'I've met Luke, once or twice,' I said, pointing to Rookery Cottage. 'But I've never met the ones on the other side.'

'Hope they don't mind a bit of noise, there's bound to be a right old racket with the boys coming over.'

She had a point. Maybe it would be polite to invite

Luke to the party. In the last couple of years he'd helped her with the garden, so it might also be handy to introduce myself. The house-warming was a good excuse. I didn't expect he'd come but it could neutralize any hostility he might feel over the disturbance. Further along the road in the opposite direction, was a couple Nanna used to call 'The Pitbulls', chiefly because their name was Bull and they were short and stocky. At least I hoped that was the reason, I didn't fancy upsetting them and having one go for my throat.

'Drop them an invite,' said Fran. 'That way, they can't really complain if they choose not to come.'

'Good idea. You take your bags upstairs and I'll run off a couple of invites. You're in the blue room.'

Minutes later, I was at the Pitbulls'. There was no response when I rang the bell, so I slipped the invitation through the letter box and headed back up the road and on to Rookery Cottage.

I confess I approached it with some trepidation. The last time I'd seen Luke was at Nanna's funeral, when I was rowing with Dad. I didn't know him well, but I knew enough to think he might consider my moving in as a pain in the bum. The last time I'd seen his sister, Ava, was two years ago, when she had braces on her teeth and plaits. So when Freddy told me he'd had a 'thing' with her, last summer, I nearly choked.

Last summer had been my first summer away from the island, I'd been in Spain, scouting out properties for the business. So, I'd insisted Freddy go to Nanna's for three weeks, because I knew how much it meant to her to have us stay, and I couldn't bear to think of her spending an entire summer without one of us.

Now, of course, I deeply regretted missing her final summer, which was daft, really, because she'd been totally in favour of my trip to Spain.

Freddy had had an absolute blast; lounging around at the farm, occasionally taking Nanna shopping but mostly hanging out at the yacht club and bumming rides as crew whenever he could.

And corrupting Ava.

At least, that's what he called it.

'Ava?' I'd said. 'She's a school girl.'

'Nah.'

I'd tried to summon up an image of her – but all that manifested was a girl with one long plait down her back and wearing khaki shorts – looking about twelve.

'Totally in love with me,' he'd grinned. 'Cried when I left.'

'So, are you going to keep in touch?'

His horrified face answered my question.

Apparently, she'd sent him emails, she'd Instagrammed a whole catalogue of pictures of their summer together and had an album printed, specially for him. It was very sweet – any decent guy would have been touched. Not Freddy. He saw it as a trophy. She rang repeatedly and he hit the off button, every time – unless he was bored, when he would deign to have a convo with her.

Finally, I bawled him out. 'Don't be a complete bastard, Freddy. Guys like you break girls' hearts and twist their minds. Tell her you've moved on. Say you liked her but it's not going anywhere. Leave. Her. Alone!'

But it was Nanna who'd had the last word. She wrote Freddy a letter. He'd shown it to me with a guilty grin on his face.

In her shaky handwriting she'd written:

> *It has come to my attention you have been behaving with a complete lack of consideration and good breeding. I am so disappointed in you.*
>
> *Luke's sister is a very sweet, intelligent and polite young lady. You have apparently not been as gallant towards her as I would expect you, my grandson, to be.*
>
> *If you care anything for my feelings, and do not wish to blacken the family name and in particular, mine, then you will advise her that you cannot continue with any contact and end the affair completely.*
>
> *Luke is a very dear friend, and extremely kind to me. I will not have you play fast and loose with his sister. I don't issue many warnings, Freddy, but consider this one of them. And, in future when you visit, you will leave well alone.*

She had signed it, *Your disgruntled grandmother.*

Freddy hadn't visited her again.

So I could forgive Luke his understandable antipathy towards my brother, and... well... even for keeping me at a hefty barge pole's length.

The garden wasn't as tidy as I expected for someone who'd spent so much time on Nanna's shrubbery, but it had a rambling charm. From the open windows, I guessed somebody was home. As soon as I lifted the door-knocker, a deep woofing sounded from within, then it sounded from without and getting closer. I braced myself as a chocolate Lab bounded up to the side gate and woofed some more. There was a whistle, the dog looked over its shoulder and sat down. 'Good boy,' I heard Luke say before appearing, in battered shorts and a t-shirt. 'Hi,' he said.

'Hi. Luke, good to see you again.'

'Gabriella Gill-Martin,' he added, and reached over the fence to shake my hand.

'Yes!' I said, surprised to hear my full name. Everyone called me Gigi, except Nanna.

'Settling in okay?'

'Yes. Thank you.' I pushed the invitation forward. 'Look, I'm having a house-warming tonight, I wondered if you'd like to pop in? It's not much, just a few friends, maybe one or two of the workmen who did the renovation – Dan…erm…Dan, I don't know his name.'

'Dan Shaw.' He took the envelope.

'That's him!' I beamed. 'Would you like to come?'

'Afraid I'm busy, tonight. But thanks for asking.'

'That's a shame. I called on Mr and Mrs Bull too, but they were out.'

'They're touring Europe for the summer.'

'Right.'

'Nice people, though.' He followed this with a smile. Maybe he sensed my disappointment at failing to harness the support of my neighbours. 'It's a tranquil spot, this. Your grandmother always said she found it conducive to creativity.'

Maybe that was his way of saying *Keep the noise down*. 'She did. That's why I've always loved being here.'

'Understandable.' He had dark, inscrutable eyes and, at that moment, it felt like he was using them to weigh up just how much trouble I might cause, and if it would be on the scale of Freddy's shenanigans.

'What's the dog's name?' I asked. Anything to

bond with the guy.

'Chuck.'

'Is he friendly?'

'Sure.'

I moved forward and held my hand over the gate. 'Hello, Chuck. You're a handsome chap, aren't you?' Chuck sniffed my hand and nudged it till I stroked his ear. 'You're a lovely boy. Yes you are.' With no reaction from his owner, I squelched the enthusiasm and withdrew my hand. 'Right! I'll be off then. Lovely to see you again. Hope you have a nice weekend.'

He raised the envelope in acknowledgement. 'Enjoy your party,' he said.

'You must come over for coffee some time. Or a beer. See what we've done to the place.'

'Thanks, that'd be nice. You've got quite a studio over in the old barn, I see. I confess Dan did show me some of the renovations in there. It's impressive with those big windows.'

'Yes, it's fabulous, and I've already started working on something.'

'Good to hear.' he said before backing away and whistling Chuck to follow.

'Well?' asked Fran, when I came back. 'Any takers?' She was sitting on the swing-seat next to Sonia, who was busy tweaking her eyelashes in a crystal encrusted hand mirror.

'Nope. The Pitbulls are away and Luke has something else on.'

'Luke? As in, your gran's fancy man?'

I lifted my hands in mock alarm. 'He was Nanna's handyman'

'I'll bet he's pissed off she didn't leave him a wedge in her will. I'm always suspicious of people

22

befriending the elderly.'

'Nanna was a pretty savvy old bird. It wouldn't be like her to get taken in by a conman.'

'That's how the best ones get away with it – plausibility, darling.'

Sonia finally engaged with us and rolled her eyes. 'Who cares? The old bugger didn't get his hands on her loot and he won't be at the party. He'll have to find some other rich old biddy to fleece.'

I drew up a garden chair and sat down. 'Oh, he's not an old bugger at all. I doubt he's even forty.'

Sonia pulled a face. 'Euw! So he's a creepy conman.' She looked at Fran and wrinkled her nose with distaste.

My gaze drifted over to the terra-cotta tiled roof of Rookery Cottage and my stomach flinched with anxiety. 'He's not a conman!' I said in a harsh whisper. 'He's a good neighbour...I think. At least, he was to Nanna.'

'Good old Nanna. What say we pop another bottle and drink a toast to her.'

'What a sweet idea,' I said, a warm glow rushing over me. 'Thank you, Sonia. Nanna was a true gem.'

'Too right – leaving you a bloody lovely house like this. You're a lucky cow. What this world needs is more Nannas.' She dropped the hand mirror into her calf leather tote. 'It's probably time I took a trip up to Shropshire to see mine.'

'I thought you said she was a miserable old boot,' Fran challenged.

'She is. In any case, she'll probably leave her wedge to the Cats' Protection League.'

Fran shrugged. 'You should be alright then, darling.'

The catering van arrived and a guy began hefting trays of food into the house. Something the size of a small surfboard came out. It was the cheese selection, along with a garden trug filled with hand-made crackers and bread sticks.

We arranged disposable serving platters on the kitchen table, piled disposable plates on the counter and unwrapped tubes of disposable wine goblets and beer cups. I spotted Fran's nose wrinkling in disgust, but since I didn't have staff and none of us would relish doing the washing up, figured she'd get over it.

She surveyed the food in the fridge. 'Okay…so there's a heap of seafood, a whopping cheese board, stuffed courgette flowers…Any booze in this fruit salad? There's gallons of it.'

'I don't think so,' I said although I suspected that might soon change.

As the van drove away, we heard a voice holler from outside. 'Evening, campers!'

Fran slammed the fridge door, grabbed my hand and pulled me into the sunshine. Rupe had arrived and was grinning across at us. He was tanned from a day's sailing; his hair deliciously wind-blown and sun-bleached. He wore faded sailing shorts and battered deck shoes. In fact, he looked so tasty, I wanted to take him on a private tour of my estate, with a special stopover in my bedroom. But we had guests.

We hadn't seen each other for almost a fortnight but he was so polite, he greeted Sonia and Fran before treating me to a hug. As his sun-heated body pressed against mine, he murmured in my ear, 'What time's bed-time?'

Sonia who had arranged herself on the sun lounger was twitching with interest. 'Where are Simon and the rest?'

'Just walking up from the harbour,' he answered. He studied the view. 'Bit quiet around here, isn't it?'

He was still miffed at me leaving London. But since he'd be spending most of the year in Scotland, I couldn't see it mattered much where I was.

'I like it. It's tranquil,' I said, echoing Luke's appropriate description. 'And just think – you can all escape over here, any time you like.' Although I very much hoped they wouldn't.

'I trust you've set up a decent sound system?' he asked.

'Hey, no. Please – no loud music.'

'Are you mad?'

'We don't need loud music. In any case, I don't want everyone in St Helens and Nettlestone reporting me to the police before I've even put my name on the voting register.'

Rupe stepped back. 'You intend to vote…here?'

'This is my home, now.'

Rupe rolled his eyes. Just like Dad, he saw my move to the island as a whim, something I had to get out of my system. Maybe he was right. I'd tried getting a few things out of my system before; like that butterfly tattoo at the bottom of my back which I deeply regretted – chiefly because it was cockeyed. Then there were the classes I'd tried in classical guitar, astrology and conversational French – only because my mother lives in Biarritz. Needless to say, maybe, after a couple of winters on the island, I might realise how much I missed the pace of London. Maybe, my ideas for sculptures would dry up. But I was determined to give it a try. And, right now, I loved building my sculptures.

'Drink?' I asked to change the subject, and wandered back inside. 'There's plenty of beer in the barrel,' I called over my shoulder. I pulled a carton of blueberry smoothie from the fridge. 'Now, I'm going to grab a shower and tidy myself up.'

Rupe moved behind me. 'Can I scrub your back?' he asked, gently running a finger down my spine and nuzzling into my neck. 'Soap your shoulders, stroke your belly and in between your...'

'Rupert!' I giggled. I was feeling pretty frisky, myself.

'Babe, I was going to say, "in between your toes", honestly.'

I swivelled round and kissed him. His lips were warm and he tasted of beer over toothpaste. I could see where a touch of sunburn had caught the bridge of his nose. I looked up into his eyes. They were pale grey which, beneath his ragged mop of sun-bleached hair, looked more startling than they ever did in winter. 'How can I resist?'

Simon and Tully had arrived by the time we came back down. They had abandoned their rucksacks in my studio and were lounging around the courtyard on pink, candy-striped deck chairs. It was like a college reunion.

'Sweet place,' Tully said, getting up and giving me a hug. 'When's the party starting?'

'I think it already has,' I said. 'And it's so lovely having you all here.'

'I can imagine – it must be pretty bleak on your own,' he said, casting his arm around. Open fields and distant neighbours wouldn't do it for a seasoned metropolitan like him.

'No. I love it.'

He pulled his head back in surprise and quickly added. 'Well, of course, you artists need your space, don't you? It must be the ideal location to create wonderful…' he windmilled his hand, '…creations.'

Simon was helping himself to another beer from the barrel. 'Not a bad brew, this.'

'Right!' Rupert announced. 'Let's get this barby fired up.'

I heard my phone ringing in the kitchen. I ran in and snatched it off the table. 'Freddy, hi. Are you okay?'

'No. Have you heard from Dad?' he asked.

'No. Why?'

He groaned. 'So you don't know he's been arrested, then?'

'What? Are you kidding?' Freddy had always been a great leg-puller. I carried the phone into the sitting room and closed the door.

'I wouldn't joke about a thing like that.'

'Arrested?' I hissed. 'What's he done?' I was suddenly aware of my heartbeat.

'I don't have any details. Something to do with fraud.'

'Fraud? What's he told you?'

'He hasn't told me anything. I heard it from Jeff Atterbury.'

Jeff was Dad's accountant. 'When did you speak to him?' and why, I thought, hadn't Jeff called me?

'My allowance hasn't come through, and I've got this white-water rafting adventure to pay for; not to mention it's bloody expensive out here anyway. Dad wasn't answering his phone so I rang Jeff to see if he could shift some money across.'

'What did he say?'

'Basically, he said "No".'

'I don't mean about the money. What did he say about Dad?'

'Not much. Just that all his accounts had been frozen.'

'So where is he, now?'

'What, Dad?'

'Yes!' I was tugging so hard on my own hair I winced. 'Didn't you think to ask Jeff?'

'He didn't sound very happy to hear from me.'

'I'll see what I can find out.'

'I'll be in deep shit if I don't get my money through. Don't suppose you could transfer a couple of thou, could you?'

'What? No, I don't have that kind of money to spare, Freddy.'

'A few hundred then, something to tide me over till we can get hold of Dad.'

I had Freddy's account details, I supposed I could go online and transfer something, tonight. 'I'll try but I don't know how long it will take to get to you.'

'It's all electronic, Sis, it'll be here in minutes. You'll do that, yeah? Text me, yeah?'

'Okay.'

The call disconnected. I sank back into the ample cushions of my brand new Italian sofa.

Dad had been arrested.

It had to be a mistake. My father was a brilliant businessman. He never tackled anything and failed. He was like this great and all-knowing guru of the material world. Nothing phased him.

It must all be a mistake. A horrible mistake.

Chapter 3

After a moment, there was a tap on the sitting room door.

'Come in!'

It was Fran, looking concerned. 'Is Freddy okay?'

For a fragment of a second, I considered telling her.

'Yes. He's fine.'

'Let me guess, he was just calling to tell you his life was better than yours. I know how he loves to take the shine off anything you do.'

'No, he wanted to wish me a happy housewarming, that's all.'

'So what was all that "Have you heard" malarkey?'

Yes. Explain that, Gigi.

'Oh, that. He wanted to kid me that this area of the island was down for redevelopment – you know, building a theme park. "Have you heard, Disney is moving into St Helens!" He's such a plonker.'

She nodded but the look on her face said she didn't buy it.

'I hope your fridge can keep up with the demand for ice, tonight.' Fran now parked herself next to me. 'Sonia's drinking voddies on the rocks like she's training for some mad act on *Britain's Got Talent*.'

'So long as she's happy. It's a party, after all.'

'You do look a bit glum, babe. Freddy hasn't said something to upset you, has he?'

'Oh, no. Don't worry. I'm just tired and taking a breather.'

'Understandable. You were upstairs with Rupe for

an impressively long time.'

I smiled. That was an age ago. An age when I didn't have a care in the world. An age when snuggling into his strong, hot embrace had made me feel I could transcend from the mundane into blissful paradise. And, for moments of that time, I had. Blissful, rolling physical pleasure that we hadn't enjoyed for weeks.

I'd often thought how I might describe such feelings through sculpture. Figures in rapture was too obvious. Could I put a shape, a texture on the human orgasm? Was it a warm cloud, floating in the sky; was it a mellow, ebbing stream of fragrant beauty circulating around a central hum of music; could I freeze the climax in gorgeously vivid, explosive glazed spikes of colour?

'Wow, that good, hey? Earth to Gigi…'

'Sorry. Look, could you see if anyone's hungry? I just need to make a phone call.'

Fran gave me a look that said she absolutely knew I was hiding something but she'd wait till she could tackle me in detail. 'No worries. I think the answer to that will be a resounding, "Yes." You take as long as you like, babe.'

I didn't like phoning Jeff Atterbury but what else was I supposed to do?

'I was expecting your call,' he said. Why, I wondered for the second time, hadn't he phoned me? Had Dad instructed him not to?

'Is it true – what Freddy told me?'

'Your father has been arrested, yes.'

'What do they think he's done?'

I could hear Jeff moving around. He let out a sigh and I imagined him sinking into a large, leather armchair, whisky and cigar at the ready. 'Defrauded many people out of their hard-earned savings.'

There wasn't a hint of sympathy in his tone. 'How? Are you saying he took people's money and didn't invest it?'

'Exactly that.'

'Where is he?'

'Spain. I think he plans on calling you, tomorrow.'

'Jeff, do you think he's guilty?'

Jeff let out a very long sigh. 'I'm afraid so. Yes.'

A familiar sinking feeling weighed me down. Like the times before Mum left and they used to row. Only, this time, it felt like there were anchors on ropes attached to each of my limbs. I could imagine sculpting my body in rusted iron – an anguished look on my face. "Deeply Troubled" I could call it.

'If I need to speak to you again, can I?' The words didn't come out as smoothly as I intended.

'Yes. Although I very much doubt I will be able to help you. Financially, that is.' He added.

'Of course. I wouldn't ask.'

'No. Well, I think you need to make that clear to your brother, too. Do you understand? Nothing.'

'Of course. Thank you.'

'Goodbye, Gigi, and good luck.'

My body was responding in a way I recognized but didn't like; my heart was thumping, my scalp-tingling and there was a full body judder kicking off in my limbs. The primal panic of abandonment.

The first time I'd felt it, I'd been seven years old; handed to stewards on the catamaran and told by my mother to hold Freddy's hand until Nanna met us. 'If anything happens to Freddy, it will be your fault. So look after him.'

Keeping hold of a four year old Freddy would have been difficult for anyone. It was frightening and unfair but it didn't make it any less of a responsibility in my little head. So now, I did what I did then and started singing 'The Sun has got his hat on.'

I'd got through stuff before, I'd get through it again. After a few deep breaths, and a glance at Nanna's photo, I went out to see my friends, and I managed to keep it all together for the party. It wasn't fair to inflict my concerns on everyone else, particularly since they'd made the effort to cross the Solent to be with me. Then there were guys from the construction team and their wives, all celebrating their monumental efforts to transform the old farm and outbuildings.

I couldn't, however, keep it all to myself. Eventually, when the meat had been barbecued and everyone seemed to be settled in groups around the courtyard, I pulled Rupert to one side and took him around to the back garden. 'Rupe, that call from Freddy…'

'How is he? Wishing he was here?' He tolerated my brother when he had to. Freddy was like Marmite. Not everyone understood him.

I took a deep breath before spilling the beans. He listened with interest.

'Shit! That is big news.' He dropped back against the house wall as the news sank in.

'Dad has some excellent people working for him, though.'

'Let's hope that's all it takes.'

'Rupe, you're not exactly instilling me with confidence, here.'

'Sorry, babe.' He pulled away from the wall and

wrapped his arms around me. 'You've nothing to worry about. Thanks to your dear old Nanna, you have a roof over your head. This place is in your name, right?'

'Of course.' I looked up into his eyes. 'Why? Could they take this off me?'

'Not if it's legally yours.'

I slumped against him. It was definitely mine. I had the deeds in an envelope. I sighed. 'Poor Dad. He'll be so frustrated. He hates set-backs.'

'Gigi, this sounds like more than a set-back.'

'Not a word to anyone, okay?'

'Okay.'

Simon was organising team games. 'Bout bloody time!' he said as we came round from behind the house. 'We won't ask where you've been.' He pointed to two rows of people. 'Rupe, you're over there on Team A, Gigi, you're here leading team B. Jump to it!'

Hours later, I lay in the dark with Rupe who was breathing long and slow beside me, and wondered what I could do to help my father. I'd spent most of what was in my current account on soft furnishings. I'd just transferred £500 to Freddy's account – only after he'd rung to remind me – and that left me with a few hundred. My allowance would be... Oh, hell! Freddy's allowance hadn't come through so why would mine?

I slipped out of bed and reached for my bathrobe.

Downstairs, Gaudi was parked on the windowsill, busily washing his paws. Rodin was snoozing in the biscuit trug.

I unlocked the back door and wandered out into the courtyard. The moon was a sharp, silver crescent in the sky. A new moon. Excellent. A good time to meditate and set my intentions.

As I sat on the swing seat, the security light clicked on, flooding the courtyard. I let out three heavy breaths and closed my eyes.

Yesterday, my intentions had been to throw a great housewarming party, enjoy the weekend and, when everyone had departed, I would make a start on my first sculpture.

Today…today no amount of breathing, calming or clearing my head could banish the fear that my life was on a precipice. Dad was in trouble. Dad solved problems, he didn't face insurmountable ones.

I breathed in and out, imagining the breath as a pale mist swirling down into my lungs and further into my bloodstream.

Prison?

Was he in prison?

He must be or he would have called me.

It would all be okay.

Breathe.

It will be okay.

Breathe.

All is well.

I jumped as Gaudi pounced onto the seat beside me. He rubbed his head against my arm. I stroked him. He stopped, momentarily froze, and then shot off the seat and into the darkness. A mouse. It must be.

All is well, I reminded myself. The Universe will take care of everything.

So why was my heart thumping in my chest and why couldn't I steady my breath?

The security light clicked off.

I sat still in the pale moonlight.

Gaudi returned, triggering the security light again. A limp mouse hung between his jaws.

'Not here, poppet,' I said. I really couldn't stomach him feasting on this poor rodent.

He gave me a sidelong glance before trotting back into the house with it.

I closed my eyes again, waiting for the light to go out.

***

In Rookery Cottage, Luke had been unable to sleep through all the row from next door. Although it wasn't just the noise that bothered him, it was the disturbance of the peace by a bunch of spoilt, rich kids from London. DFLs, the locals called them: Down From London.

He'd had no desire to accept Gabriella's invitation and he was doubly glad his kid sister, Ava, wasn't here to join in. God knows, the sound of a party would have had her nineteen year old toes twitching and she'd have dragged him over to join in. The last thing he needed was Ava falling under the spell of Gabriella's brother. Again. He'd done enough damage, last summer.

Freddy Gill-Martin. What an irresponsible waste of space he was. And trouble.

He gazed at the watercolour painting of Compton Bay hanging above his desk. Una had given it to him in thanks for helping her with the garden. Work she'd paid for, anyway. But that was typical Una. 'I knew you'd like it. What fun is life if I can't treat the people I care about?' she'd asked.

Life carried on.

Life had carried on when his father had left, and again when his mother had died. It had carried on, just in a different way.

He sat at his computer, flicked it on and checked his geology website for any comments on his latest posting about the Wealden beds. Just one, from an ex-student, praising his latest theory.

He typed a quick response and then closed the site down and moved to check his email. The News window flashed a new headline: "Hertfordshire Man Implicated In Spanish Property Crash."

He shook his head. Greed. He'd seen it ruin lives before.

A couple of emails had come in from friends in Canada. He was planning a trip home with Ava at Christmas. The clock in the corner of his screen told him it was a little after three. He leaned back in his chair, hands behind his head. Across at Bluebell Farm the security light flared into life.

He switched off the computer, stood up and stretched. The farm's newly white-washed walls were brighter and the window frames were a fresh, eau de Nile. He had to admit, it was a cheerier aspect than the grubby, peeling white walls with dull black window frames he used to overlook.

The security light went out.

He left the study and wandered through to the kitchen, leaning into the fridge to find a bottle of juice. He flicked it open and leaned back on the fridge, to stare out across the garden, subtly lit by the moon until the farm's security light flared on again.

It was good to have life return to the farm, but just what kind of life would that be? He downed the juice and headed back to bed.

Chapter 4

I set the table for breakfast. There would be six of us.

I'd had a couple of hours sleep. The gang wouldn't be up for ages. There was fruit salad left from last night, plenty of cheese and part-cooked bread rolls in the freezer. That would do for breakfast. I'd planned smoked salmon and scrambled eggs but someone had left the salmon out and the cats had polished it off.

I moved a cardigan I didn't recognise, and hung it on the coat-rack

Around eleven o'clock, I heard stirrings from upstairs. Rupe was the first down. Bleary eyes or not, he still looked handsome enough to make me smile. 'Hi,' he said, wrapping his arms around me. 'I see you've been doing your Cinderella act.'

'Couldn't sleep.'

'No? I could barely wake up. Oh, damn. Your dad, I forgot about that. It must be very worrying for you.'

'It is.' I finally crumbled and gave way to a few snivels of self pity tinged with fear.

When Simon appeared, I sniffed hard. 'Please say nothing,' I whispered in Rupe's ear, as I stood up. 'Excuse me a mo,' I said and went outside.

'Wassup?' I heard Simon ask.

'Missing her grandmother,' Rupe replied.

An hour later, everyone was up and looking like extras in *One Flew Over the Cuckoo's Nest*.

'Who's on for a fry-up then?' Simon asked.

'Fry up?' I squawked. 'I don't have any stuff in for a fry-up.'

Simon pretended to look shocked. 'No worries,

there must be loads of cafés around here that do an all-day breakfast. We can fit in two cars.'

'Actually,' I said, 'there's Solent View about half a mile away. We could walk.'

Bloodshot eyes flickered around the table. Neither Sonia nor Fran were fit to drive. 'Walk?' Sonia dropped her head onto the table. 'Can someone call me a rickshaw?'

'You're a rickshaw,' drawled Fran.

So my plans for breakfast were parked and twenty minutes later, we were heading out. The sun was glaring out of the sky. I could feel my shoulders toasting through the thin cotton of my shirt. I have the kind of skin which tans the colour of Cherryade, before blistering and peeling.

We sat outside the café, at a large, wooden bench with a view of the ocean. All the guys ordered mammoth breakfasts – double everything, Fran went for just the single, while Sonia and I opted for toast. Although it has to be said, mine was the only lack of appetite which couldn't be blamed on a hangover.

Conversation was happening around me while my attention drifted like a rudderless dinghy.

'Gigi, you are very lucky,' Simon said. 'I've no wish to see my grandparents in the ground, yet, but I could bloody well use a place of my own, right now.'

Sonia agreed. 'And you've made it look really nice. I'd give anything to have all the stuff I wanted.'

Despite sitting on a bench, on a hillside, overlooking the sea, Dad's image was all I saw; Dad leaning back on the ropes as our little yacht tacked across the sea; Dad holding his face up to the sun and grinning; Dad helping me out whenever I needed it. We hadn't spent many times together, but they had been quality times.

'Gigi, love, what's up?' Fran's hand stroked my hot back.

'Nothing. Sorry. Nothing at all.' I stood up and hurried indoors to use the loo. It was engaged. Fran appeared behind me. There was a cautious frown on her face.

'Were you thinking about your grandmother?'

I nodded.

Fran's concern seemed to be churning my tears up and a new wave of them washed over my face. I gulped and hid the flood behind my hands. I don't do crying in public.

'Hey,' she said, in her softest voice as she gently stroked my shoulders.

More tears and a sob I had no control over. Bloody-hell, would I never get a grip?

She wrapped her arms around me and hugged me tight. 'Honey, it's okay. You can let it out. You'll feel better. Lots better. Go ahead, indulge yourself, I don't mind.'

I was so tempted to tell her the news about my father but I couldn't face the fallout. It wouldn't end there. It would be like lifting the lid off a flea circus and giving it a shake.

The sound of a flushing toilet cistern sobered me up. I drew a deep breath, right down into my abdomen, and let it out slowly. I sniffed noisily. A large woman sidled out of the cubicle, a grim look on her face. Fran ducked through the door and pulled out some loo paper. 'Have a good blow.'

I did. There was more snot than tissue, so Fran went back for more.

'Better?' she asked, as the storm of my emotions

39

subsided.

'Thanks.'

'No rush to get back to that lot. Take a breather while I have a pee,' she said, sounding more like the Fran I was used to.

Back at the table, everyone gave me warm, supportive smiles. Simon winked and Sonia blew me a kiss but Tully took the heat out of the situation by leaping up to help the waitress serve our meals. He was acting like a posh French waiter, even going back to the kitchen with her to carry out the remaining plates.

I glanced at my watch. In just a few hours, they would all be heading back to the mainland, even Rupe, who was working on a building project near Edinburgh for another couple of weeks. After that, he was scheduled to spend a whole fortnight with me. A whole fortnight when we planned to wallow in each other's company, have picnics at the beach, stargaze and reconnect. That would be tainted, now. The fortnight was destined to be overshadowed by my father's fall from grace. Unless, by some fabulous stroke of luck, his problems proved to be a mistake, and everything returned to normal. Which reminded me – why hadn't he phoned?

I waved The Divas off with a twinge of sadness. Only a couple of days ago, I'd been feeling just a tad smug – proud to show off my beautiful new home.

I'd also been glad I didn't have to face the daily commute into London, and inordinately grateful I wouldn't be returning to the mayhem of the city.

Well, that certainly taught me about humility. Yes, the Universe had lessons for us all.

As they sped off out of the driveway with a cheeky toot of the horn, what I felt at that moment was envy. At least they knew what they were going back to. Me? My stomach was in a huge reef knot as I tried to second guess what would happen next.

Freddy's phone was going straight to voicemail. Either he'd white-water rafted over treacherous rapids to certain death, or his phone was out of battery. He hadn't even texted to acknowledge receipt of the money.

I walked down to the harbour with the others. We took the scenic route, down through the wooded common to the old Duver golf course. Nobody's played golf there for over fifty years – it's a National Trust area now. I love it because you can walk in one direction to the beach, through the banks of buckthorn bushes, and in the other across the uneven tussocks of grass and thrift to Duver Marina.

On such a busy weekend, the boats were moored four deep – Tully's was on the far side. Half the owners were preparing to sail out on the evening tide.

We politely stepped our way across the other boats. There's a camaraderie in yachting – probably like there is in camping or caravanning. People nod and pass the time of day; share weather reports and offer a hand when needed. I guess you never know when you might need it – with the sea being so fickle.

Now on the boys' boat, Blue Goose, Rupe and Tully dropped their kit bags into the cabin. The evening breeze was warm, and around us we could hear bits of rigging clinking cheerfully. Sun sparkled on the water and the temptation to cast off with the guys and head out into the Solent almost made me cry. But that's all it would be – a fabulous evening sail, leaning out over the side as the boat cut through the sea; the thrill of each tack; the whole beautiful rhythm I loved about sailing. Simplicity. Nature. Beauty. Wind-lifted hair and salty spray. Usually, in my case, followed by sun-tightened skin if I'd forgotten to apply enough sun cream. I'd learned a few lessons about that in my childhood.

No. Tonight I would wave them off, climb the hill back to Bluebell Farm and seek the counsel of my cats.

Tully looked at his watch. 'Right then, Gigi, gotta love you and leave you.' He gave me a tight hug and a noisy kiss on the top of my head, before discreetly ducking below so Rupe and I could say our goodbyes. Simon was looking busy at the stern of the boat.

Rupe stroked stray strands of hair back from my face and looked into my eyes. Emotion welled up so I had to squeeze my eyelids tight to stem the tears.

'You'll be fine, babe,' he whispered. 'If I know your father, he'll have excellent counsel and probably a massive contingency fund tucked away in the channel islands. You wait and see.'

'I'm not worried about the money, I'm worried about him.'

'Like I said, he'll be okay. Sure of it. Come here.' He pulled me into his chest and wrapped his arms around me. 'I know you're worried, babe. But worrying won't help. Just focus on what you have to do and your dad will focus on what he has to do. Okay?'

I mumbled a reply.

'Now, give me a kiss to remember you by.'

It was hard to reconcile his lovely, warm kiss with the turmoil in my head and the prospect of two weeks alone. Oh boy, how I'd looked forward to some isolation. All that time stretching ahead of me to work. Now, it felt like I was heading for solitary confinement. That would certainly help me identify with Dad's plight.

'I guess that'll have to do,' he joked as I pulled back from him.

'Sorry, I can do better.' I kissed him again, trying hard to focus on my love for him and his for me. I'd get through the next fortnight. I had to. There wasn't any other option.

He groaned as he released me. 'Two weeks and I'll be back.'

'I know. And you can have me all to yourself.'

'I'm counting on it. Don't make any plans which don't involve exclusivity, okay?'

'Okay.'

'Good girl.'

He stepped back as Tully's head popped up through the hatch. 'Time to go, lovely people.'

Rupe handed me off the boat to the next one, and I made my way back to the pontoon.

I stood and watched as they motored slowly away. Tully was at the helm while Rupe looked busy. He waved a couple of times and blew me a kiss, which I took as his final gesture. He wasn't big on dramatic farewells.

I walked away, along the pontoon and out through the harbour gate. I turned right and made my way across the links, passing Attrill's workshops and on through to the beach, where the harbour opens out into the Solent. There was a steady file of boats heading out through the channel, back to the mainland. Another glorious weekend over. I watched as each boat meandered its way between the buoys.

On the opposite side, I could see people socializing on the sailing club balcony; sun glistening off their gold watches and gin glasses. A child's shriek made me jump. I looked around. A young boy was dragging a taller girl into the sea. She shrieked some more and her mother yelled, 'Tom! Not so rough!'

That could have been Freddy and me, a few years ago.

There was a shrill whistle from the channel. I looked across and saw Simon and Tully waving at me. I raised both my arms and wiggled my hands. Bless them for looking out for me. Rupe, looked up and waved too, then turned and stood gazing out at the horizon, with a hand stuffed inside his shirt front; it was his Horatio Nelson stance. I smiled and did the same.

Two more weeks, I thought. Two more weeks.

I walked along the promenade in front of the beach huts. I love beach huts; dinky little homes from home, all bright colours and rusting hinges. A family was on the beach below, cooking sausages on a disposable barbecue.

I kept checking the progress of Blue Goose heading to open water. They had a couple of hours of sailing till they reached Portsmouth. I turned and saw them starting to unfurl the main sail, soon it would be engine off and they would be underway. No hum of turbine or propeller, just the splash of water, the clink of rigging and the shush of air in the sail. Possibly the odd cry of derision from the other boats as they tried to out-psych each other or steal wind. I threw my hand up in a hopeful wave but they didn't see.

I walked away from the beach and up the hill,

stopping at the top where I sat on one of the benches under a large tree. The view over St Helens Common to the beach, the channel and Bembridge was one of my favourites. Nanna and I often used to sit there, enjoying an ice-cream and a chat. I glanced at the empty space beside me and imagined her savouring the view with me. There was still a stream of boats heading out of the channel but Blue Goose was hidden behind the trees.

They were there and I was here, Dad was a detainee in Spain and Nanna…who knew?

The phone in my pocket started to ring. Please let this be Dad.

Chapter 5

The phone number on the display said Blocked. I accepted the call.

'Gigi, it's good to hear your voice.' My heart lurched with gratitude.

'Dad, How are you? I'm really worried. What's going on?'

'I am absolutely fine. You don't have to worry about me.' He sounded calm but that wasn't surprising, he usually did.

'But Jeff told me you're in custody.'

'Not exactly.'

'What does that mean?'

'It's a bit of a mix up. We'll sort it out.'

'Dad, is this something to do with Jose de la Torre?' Like I needed to ask.

There was a pause. 'He's involved, yes, obviously,' he snapped.

'So have you broken the law or haven't you?'

'It's all to do with the land I was sold – there are debts attached which have just come to light – and it's possible that the permissions were illegal.'

'Possible? But you had legal advice, didn't you? Are you going to prison?'

'No but my passport is being held until I pay the debts.'

'And…can you?'

'It'll take time, and I'll have to move some funds around. But don't worry, I can clear this up. I'll have to.' I could tell he was thinking it was no concern of

47

mine, now that I'd left the business.

'Dad, do you need me to fly over and help?'

'No, Gigi. I'm absolutely fine. It's just a shame you're not in London to run the office.'

'Dad, I'll go if that's what you need me to do.'

There was a pause. 'No.'

'I will, Dad. Just say the word.'

'No. You stay where you are and finish your sabbatical. I can sort this out.'

'This sounds really serious, Dad.'

'Things are probably going to get a little tougher for you, I'm afraid, financially. I…You won't be receiving any profit share from the company for a while. So you'll just have to stand on your own two feet.'

'Don't worry, I'll get by. I'm not afraid of hard work.'

'I know. If you need anything, I'm sure your mother could help. I'm … it's just…'

There was another voice in the background. 'Sorry, I have to go. I'll be in touch.'

'Love you…'

The call was over. No protracted farewells just a click as the connection was broken.

I stared down at my dusty toes, aware of my abdomen rising and falling more quickly than normal. My mind was churning thoughts and ideas like a mechanical mixer. Will Dad be okay? Was I more like my mother than I realised – selfishly pursuing this dream of mine?

I lifted my head and took in the beautiful scenery. The early evening sun was casting long shadows. I pictured tall, carved hunks of wood, jutting from sloping stands, with tiny lights shining through them.

Large sculptural installations were probably a step too far for an artist like me.

Had Mum thought this way? For a moment I had a glimmer of understanding for the person she had been when she walked away from us.

I looked back down at my feet. The chipped nail polish needed replacing. I had a lovely red shade, the colour of ketchup. That would cheer me up.

As I walked home, the question pressing on my brain was, should I call Mum? And if I did, would it just stir up the hostility she already felt for Dad? My parents had never been reconciled. Theirs had been an attraction of opposites: he, the entrepreneur, the fast-thinking, practical whiz-kid; she, the beautiful, enigmatic artist. They'd fallen head-over-heels in love and she'd fallen pregnant. It had taken just seven weeks for me to be conceived and three more till they were married. He was driven to succeed and make his fortune; she was tortured by her need to be free to express herself.

My mother had had something to prove – to herself and to my father.

Truth be known, she was still trying.

If she hadn't met Pierre Longchamp, I'm not sure where she'd be now. He was fifteen years older, a little rough around the edges but loaded. Loaded as a result of his successful jewellery empire.

I should say 'apparently' loaded because it became evident that funds were dwindling. He had three children from two previous marriages and two ex-wives to support. They lived in a shabby-chic apartment in Biarritz, where Pierre encouraged Mum in all her artistic persuits. The shabby part was unintentional; the chic was exactly that; faded chic –

rather like the faded seaside glamour of Biarritz itself.

I loved Biarritz. If you'd ever been to the Isle of Wight, you could say Biarritz was like an upmarket Ventnor.

So, should I phone her and overlook the inevitable, 'Hah! Serves him right!' or keep quiet? As I wandered in through the farm gates, I decided it wasn't something I could keep to myself.

'Oh. How terrible,' she finally said. This was unexpectedly restrained for my mother. 'What er...' she must have been choosing her words carefully to avoid upsetting me. '...who knows? Is it in the papers?'

I told her the little I knew.

'What a fool,' she said quietly but loud enough for me to hear.

'That's a bit harsh, Mum.'

'Oh, Gigi, darling. Wake up! Your father is a very smart man – and arrogant with it. He just thought he could do one more big deal, didn't he? Well, he failed,' she added with hefty swipe of satisfaction.

'I'm not sure what I should do. What would you suggest?'

'Darling, make sure everything is nailed down!'

'What do you mean?'

'Your savings, your ISAs, any investment he's ever made for you. Check them all.'

'What? You don't honestly think he'd take my savings, do you?'

'Did you save them, Gigi? Or did your father open the accounts and invest money in your name?'

She had a small point. It wasn't like I'd been putting pennies in a jar for the last twenty-seven years.

'I'm telling you, Gigi, you need to make sure your investments are safe, or they'll be after those too.'

'Can they?'

'I don't know, if he put it in there…'

I could feel my heartbeat ramping up. Dad had given me account details and passwords, but I never went online to check them. They were just there, ready for when I needed them. And since I'd earned a good salary and bonus each month, I'd never had the need to dip into them. I was saving them for a rainy day. Well, I guess the heavens had just opened. Maybe I could use whatever was in there to help him out.

Hundreds of thousands, Jeff had said. I might not know what was in those accounts, but I was pretty bloody sure it wasn't anywhere near that ballpark; barely even in the approach road to the car-park of the ballpark.

'Okay. I'll check.'

'Do it now, Gigi. As soon as you put the phone down, check your accounts.'

'Okay.'

'I mean it. I wouldn't put anything past him.'

'You're talking about my father, Mum. You may not love him any more, but I do.'

'Yes. Of course, and so you should. But you don't have to trust him. Call me when you have some news.'

Typical Mum. She'd never say, 'Call me anytime, I'm always there for you.'

'I will. Bye.'

'Night-night, darling.'

It was Monday tomorrow. I would call Jeff, again.

I gazed out at the horizon, where the sun was still glinting brightly. I was fully confident that the money in my accounts would be safe. Freddy might love flashing the cash and milking life for everything it offered, but I'd always been more cautious, and Dad appreciated that. He used to joke I was the only person he wanted looking after him in his old age. 'You, Gigi, wouldn't sell your old man down the river, would you?'

The only sound in the kitchen was the ticking of the clock. My cats were out. Mum's words replayed in my head. 'Check your accounts.'

Five. Thousand. Pounds. That's all I had to my name. Two weeks ago, it appeared I'd had ten times that – sitting in shares and saving accounts but, just as Dad had put money in, so Dad had taken money out.

Really. I checked.

Fifty-two thousand pounds, in total, had been transferred out of my accounts.

'Dad!' I yelled. He hadn't given me the slightest warning. He must have believed he could put it back. He knew I wasn't active in those accounts because he used to hug me and say, 'Gigi, sweetheart, money's always safe in your hands, isn't it?'

Safe, yes. And I needed it to stay safe.

Although it pained me to do so, I elected to change the passwords on all the accounts. The last thing I needed was Dad, or anybody else, accessing the little money I had left.

Still, five thousand was more than many other people had. I could survive for months on that. I would shop carefully and find myself a part time job and, once my sculptures were done…yes, I'd be absolutely fine. I wasn't Freddy.

I also had the little paddock adjacent to the farm, which was rented out to Amanda Connell for two horses. Apparently, she paid quarterly, in cash. That would be something to rely on.

I'd always intended to eat more healthily by cutting down on processed foods and side-stepping red meat. 'Well, there you go, Gigi, the Universe has presented you with a gift. The opportunity and the motivation to eat better.'

Every cloud has a silver lining.

I decided to work out a monthly budget. It seemed the most practical thing to do. I pulled a notepad from the kitchen dresser and started a list. I could cut wine down to weekends only, that would be healthy and save loads. Red meat was out, hurrah! More money saved. Fish – I could buy locally caught, that would be cheaper, wouldn't it? And fresh produce from the market.

Note to self: where and when is the market?

Supermarkets had those bargain bins, didn't they? Prices knocked down when they reached the sell-by date. I'd read about people stocking up on those and freezing them. Great. I became unreasonably excited. I liked a challenge, and this was surely my biggest yet. It would be fun to test my creative culinary skills; I'd be like a contestant doing the invention test on *Masterchef*.

Just after eight, the following morning, I leapt from my bed at the sound of my phone. I snatched it off the cabinet. It was just Rupert, calling me from Southampton airport before he caught his flight to Edinburgh. 'How're you feeling, today, babe?' he asked.

The warmth of his voice made me close my eyes for a moment and imagine him beside me.

'Not too bad, thanks.'

'Still all torn up over your dad.'

'He rang me yesterday.' I filled him in on Dad's situation and the effect it had had on my finances. 'So, I've got things in perspective, and I'm going to be okay.'

'Gigi, your dad will be covered by insurance or he can declare himself bankrupt. There's absolutely no reason for him to plough into your savings. He shouldn't get away with this.'

'What am I going to do – sue? It's fine. I'm not totally penniless, and I could do bed and breakfast. I have three spare bedrooms.'

'Seriously?'

'Admittedly, a couple of the beds are a bit old, but the rustic look is in. I could whitewash the wooden headboards and tackle them with wire wool to create some aesthetic distress.' Thinking about it, Nanna's bed linens were still in the old blanket box. I could distress that, too. Distress was the order of the day. 'I just need to find a way to advertise my B&B and then I'll be on my way to solvency. There must be a website I could join.'

'You're seriously going to do B&B?'

'Sure. And I could run residential pottery courses, too. That's exactly the kind of holiday I'd enjoy. I mean, I know this isn't what I'd planned for myself, but needs must. Maybe this will be my true vocation – doing my own stuff while encouraging others to create theirs.' Saying this aloud, I found I liked the idea.

'Don't rush into anything, babe,' he said. 'Give it some thought.'

'Of course.'

I was good at thinking. I was an athlete when it came to thinking, which was why I needed to meditate.

I heard him stifling a yawn. 'Rupe, you sound exhausted. You should take it easy today.'

'No can do. I'm off to the client's site, this morning.'

'Well, you take care.'

I fixed myself some coffee in preparation for working on more plans for my future.

Seated at the kitchen table, I started a mind map with the central theme: Generate Income. My first branch was B&B, my second, residential workshops.

Each week I could have a little commune of kindred spirits modelling dreams out of clay and enjoying convivial conversation over shared meals at the kitchen table…

Actually, my culinary skills were pretty basic. I could manage salads, even simple pasta dishes. I was a dab-hand at ready meals from Marks & Spencer. I'm not sure that would pass muster with paying guests.

Perhaps I could employ Marsha's Catering to deliver savoury delights, and factor her charges into the price. Yes, that would work. I added *Phone Marsha* to the map and circled it vigorously.

I scoured the internet for similar pottery courses, so I could get a handle on pricing. Most creative courses were in Europe. Sadly, Britain didn't much feature. The dusky olives and mustard yellows of Italy said 'heat', 'romance' and 'escape'. Meandering rivers in French valleys said 'sunshine', 'vineyards' and 'ooh-la-la'.

The Isle of Wight said…coach tours.

'Think harder!' I said aloud, scribbling *Benefits* on a

new branch.

Think: no flight costs, no lurking in airports for hours, no deep vein thrombosis. Good.

Think: traditional English fare. (Courtesy Marsha's Catering.)

Think: no language barrier.

Think: only two double bedrooms and two single, minimum four guests – maximum six.

Think again…the summer's nearly over.

Not that I was limited to summer. Retired people went on holiday all year round.

On cruises and coach tours.

I was talking myself out of this.

Yoga. Maybe I could take a yoga teaching course and hold yoga classes on the terrace. At this, the sun disappeared behind a cloud and made the prospect less appealing.

I returned to simple B&B. How hard could that be? A bit of laundry and cooking breakfast. I didn't need qualifications for that.

Yes. I would make the farm work for me.

I pictured a display of my sculptures. If I could sell those, they would earn the most money but I could also knock out a few mugs and platters on the wheel.

'Ooh. More clay.' I said as I added another twig to the branch.

I didn't like wheel pottery. Churning out duplicate mugs was a discipline I found extremely tedious but I could grow to like it. I could grow to love it if it paid the bills.

My mind map was extensive and gave me a satisfying sense of purpose.

There was salmon in cheese sauce with a side of green beans and mange-touts in the fridge. Perfect. I popped it into the microwave and poured myself some of the remaining Sauvignon Blanc.

'Savour this, Gigi,' I told myself. 'Enjoy the indulgence while you can and look forward to the simple delicacies you have yet to discover.'

That wine tasted good. Infinitely better than the fizzy water I'd be drinking next week.

Recipe books. Thank goodness I'd kept a couple of Nanna's favourites – the ones with hand-written comments in the margin. As the microwave hummed, I pulled one out of the dresser and opened it. Cauliflower Cheese. Nanna had noted: 'Sprinkle with cayenne or paprika for more interest, and even some grated lemon rind.' Cayenne pepper and lemon – I remembered she added those to so many dishes.

I felt a thrill of anticipation. Cooking couldn't be too difficult. It was only following instructions, after all. If I could fire a kiln to 1250°C, I could sure as anything cook a meal in an oven at 200°C. A firing took two days – most meals took less than two hours.

Simple. The microwave went 'ping'. Although, some things were simpler.

I went to bed with an easier conscience and slept until the cats made their dawn visit.

Chapter 6

Luke pedalled to the summit of the hill, before free-wheeling down from Havenstreet to Ashey. Morning commuter traffic was starting to build. Two more big hills to climb. Having taken a few weeks off since the end of the ice hockey season, he was physically aware how out of condition his body had become. In the last few weeks, he'd spent too much time hunched over his PC.

Traffic was building but in no way did it compare with the lines of gas guzzlers filing into his old home of Ottawa during rush hour.

It looked like his contract at the college was good for another couple of years, so he wouldn't have to go back. Oh God. How he didn't want to go back there.

He cycled through Ashey and on towards the Downs.

He pressed into the pedals, choosing to marvel at the beauty of the fields around him rather than the tug and burn of his muscles. On he went, over Brading Down until it levelled out. He let up on the pedal power and scanned the view to his right over Sandown Bay, ahead to Culver and then left to the Solent. As he coasted along, seeing the landscape dropping away, either side, it was almost like flying.

Now he pedalled harder, feeling the rush of wind through his hair. He gained momentum to freewheel again, past the picnic bays and on down into Brading. He manoeuvred his bike slowly alongside the cars queuing at the traffic lights. The sun was fully up now and warming his face.

Then he pushed on up Marshcombe Shute towards Culver. A light aircraft buzzed overhead, making its way towards Bembridge.

Flying. He must learn to do that, one day.

Would he, though? That was just another in a long list of goals he wanted to achieve but, with Ava still reliant upon him, he'd have to put that off for a few years yet. Supporting her through Uni was costly enough without racking up his own expenses.

A small, sharp neural charge from his subconscious punched his brain. Learning to fly would have been well within his reach – once.

Remembered images of teaching Ava to ski in Banff were superimposed over the warm summer hillside. The luxury ski lodge had everything – sauna, hot tub and log fire. 'Luke, these are the coolest things!' Ava had said about the remote controlled curtains.

Who needed remote controlled curtains for heaven's sake?

Memories replayed through his brain all the way to the embankment beside Bembridge Harbour. A few more minutes and he'd be home. He would fix himself eggs on toast before taking a shower. Three eggs and maybe some beans. He'd worked up an appetite over the last twenty miles.

As he neared home, he saw Gigi outside the farmhouse gate. She spotted him and waved.

He hadn't spoken to her since he'd refused her invitation so, in the interests of neighbourliness, he carried on past his cottage towards her.

She was wearing mucky old decorators' overalls, torn off at the knee and sleeves hacked off above the elbow. She was in the process of repainting the

Bluebell Farm sign.

'Morning, Luke. I'm guessing, you haven't just been to the paper shop.'

He rubbed his sleeve over his face to remove any sweat and probably a few bugs. 'No. Havenstreet and back.'

Now he was stationary, he could feel the sweat trickling out from under his helmet and down his neck. He probably smelled pretty ripe, too.

'Lucky you.'

'You should try it some time.' Why had he said that? She'd probably no concept of cycling to the corner shop, never mind the undulating roads around the island. It was hardly surprising she was laughing.

'I could do it in the car but it wouldn't be the same, would it?'

He shook his head slowly as he thought, *Of course not. Dumb suggestion on my part.* 'You're making a good job of the sign,' he said, nodding to the now brilliant white board on which she was using royal blue to bring the words to life. 'Are you getting the creative juices flowing?'

'That would be handy.' She nodded to the sign. 'I want to make sure people can find me.'

He wiped his sleeve across the back of his neck.

'Luke…' she began, 'Do you know of any agencies on the island who promote Bed and Breakfast? I've found some sites on the internet but maybe you could recommend somebody who might send visitors my way.'

Bed and Breakfast? Gigi was thinking of doing that?

***

I could tell from the frown pulling his eyebrows

together, Luke didn't like the idea. It was hardly going to lower the tone of the neighbourhood, was it? The island being a holiday destination, and all. Maybe he didn't like the idea of increased traffic and noisy guests.

'I'll only be able to have a few guests, four, maybe six. It shouldn't affect you, I hope.'

He shook his head. 'I don't mind you having guests, I just hadn't imagined that's what you were planning on doing.'

'No, well…' I didn't need to explain, did I?

'Afraid I can't help you, there. Not really my field.'

'No. Not mine either.'

There was an awkward pause as my mind blanked. He probably had nothing more to say to me, anyway.

'I guess building up a body of work to sell will take time?' he asked.

'Yes.' I said, sounding surprised, which I was. 'A few months. I might be able to hold an exhibition around Christmas time.' I was banking on it. If I could sell some angel sculptures for the festive season, maybe the bigger ones to garden centres, I might make enough money to buy Rupe a nice present.

'Good luck with that.'

'Thanks.'

'Right. I need to get on,' he said, gripping the handlebars and reversing his bike away from me. 'Catch you later.'

As he trundled back along the road, he waved at an approaching car. Dan Shaw, the builder, was at the wheel, and heading my way. He turned off the road and pulled up just inside the gateposts. Perhaps it was his girlfriend who'd left the coral coloured cardigan on Saturday night. I walked around to the driver's door.

'Morning, Dan.'

There was something about the hunch of his shoulders and the dent between his brows which troubled me. 'Do you mind if we go up to the house to talk?' he asked, causing a bolt of concern to hit me in the gut.

'Sure. I'll make some coffee.'

Chapter 7

In the kitchen, I lifted the cardigan from the coat-stand. 'Did your girlfriend leave this?'

Dan stood with his arms folded. 'I don't know. That's not why I'm here, Gigi.'

'Oh.'

'I'm sorry to say this, but your father's last payment hasn't come through. He owes me eight grand.'

The world tilted. I steadied myself on the dresser.

'His mobile's turned off and, according to the bank, there are no funds available. I've got suppliers and workmen to pay, so I'd be grateful if you could settle up with me.'

'Of course. Absolutely, yes.' I opened the top drawer of the dresser and fiddled around. I only had one account with a cheque book and there was just over two thousand in there. 'Dan, I can give you a cheque for part of it, now. I'll have to transfer funds to make up the balance.' My heart was knocking on the walls of my chest. I didn't possess the full amount. I wondered how easy it would be to find a job.

'I'd rather have a bank transfer – for the whole lot,' he said, fixing me with a stern look.

'It will take a bit of time. I need to get it from different accounts.'

'I think transfers are done the same day, aren't they?' he said, and pulled a piece of paper from his pocket. 'Here's the invoice, and those are my bank details at the bottom. I'll give you until tomorrow.'

He thrust the paper towards me.

'Of course. I'm really sorry about this.' The lump in my throat made me sound like a Disney character.

He appeared to soften. 'So, what's going on?'

I shook my head and blinked a tear away. 'I think Dad said something about changing banks. Maybe your payment fell between the cracks.'

He didn't look convinced. 'Right. Well, I'll be checking my account for the funds. Don't let me down.'

'I won't.'

He nodded and made for the door, then turned back. 'Can I see that?' he asked, pointing to the cardigan. I handed it to him. 'Yeah, that's Hannah's. Thanks.'

And off he went, leaving me with more challenges on my plate and an unwelcome hole in my finances.

I hadn't known it would take so long to transfer money from one of my accounts to another. A couple of the accounts had penalties for withdrawing money without notice. I couldn't worry about that now. I needed to get all my funds and a purse full of somebody else's into my current account and over to Dan Shaw's.

These were desperate times. Despite the battle I knew I would face, my mother could bridge the gap until I got a bank loan.

She was less than sympathetic. 'Your father should be paying, not me.'

'Well that isn't going to happen, is it?'

'You do know I'll have to get it from Pierre, don't you?'

'Sorry. I don't know what else to do. I'll pay it back, of course.'

'Yes, you will.'

Quite how, I wasn't sure.

All the funds were finally through, and moved to Dan's account by three o'clock the following morning. I kept a regular vigil on my account for the money coming over from Pierre.

That was it. Done. I could finally go to bed.

I slept until mid-morning, when Gaudi pounced on me and began kneading my backside, while Rodin protested as he paced to and fro in the doorway. Maybe there had been slim pickings from their night-time safari, and undoubtedly supplies in the kitchen were out.

I buried my face back in the pillow and imagined the buttock kneading was a deep tissue massage. Rodin cried more loudly, leapt up onto the pillow and curled himself around the back of my head, flexing his claws on my scalp.

'Eurgh!' I rose from the mattress, bum first and continued up into Downward Dog which is possibly the easiest yoga posture after The Corpse. The action turfed Gaudi off but Rodin anchored himself by clinging to one of my ears. I shrieked in pain and nose dived back into the pillow to jolt him off.

'Enough, boys! I'll sort you out in a minute.'

With the cats both now pacing in protest, I performed a couple of cat stretches of my own before getting out of bed.

I heaped some food into their bowls and threw the switch on the kettle. Ginger tea would liven me up. I needed all the help I could get.

I'd sent a text message to Dan Shaw, asking him to text me when the funds landed in his account. They had. My slate was clean.

I just had to work out how to pay Pierre back.

So, overnight, my predicament had degenerated. New measures were in order. Outside, in the courtyard, my beautiful four-by-four sat gleaming in the morning sun. Although my car was an essential, I could make do with a smaller, older model. I would check out how much a two month old Range Rover was worth. It had hardly any miles on the clock, so it couldn't be much less than we'd paid for it. Correction – Dad had paid for it. Maybe I could find a dealership that would take it on. They would pay top dollar, wouldn't they?

Twenty grand, perhaps? I googled Range Rover.

Wow!

A new model, my model, was more than twice that! Hurrah! I was in clover. Once I'd cashed the car in, I could hunt for a second-hand one, and have plenty of loot to spare. Life was looking brighter already.

'How much?' The nearest dealership had just told me what they would give me for my car. 'I've only done about four hundred miles in it. There's a limit to the number of miles I can clock up over here.'

'You might do better if you return it to the dealership where you purchased it. Which one was it?'

I had absolutely no idea. Dad had arranged for it to be delivered to me.

'Sorry, I might be able to find out.'

'Do you have the paperwork?'

'I'm not sure.'

'Do you know the registration number?' His voice was showing signs of exasperation.

'Yes. Of course. One moment.'

I ran to the kitchen window and read the number

plate aloud.

'Thank you.' I waited while I imagined him scrolling through a database.

'According to our records, you are not the owner of the vehicle.'

My heart bumped. Dad was. 'Well, yes, that is correct. My father bought it for me.'

'Does your father own Poole & Reed Vehicle Leasing?'

'No,' I said in a swallow.

'Then, I'm afraid the car isn't yours to sell. Quite frankly, since you don't own it, you won't have the vehicle log book either, so I suggest you don't even try to sell it.'

'No. Of course. I wouldn't. I'm not a criminal!'

Although, there was a possibility my father was.

'Thank you for your help. Sorry to have bothered you.'

After banging my head on the kitchen table as the severity of the situation sank in, I decided to check out Poole & Reed. They were a London-based company. I called them.

'Yes, indeed, you have a Vogue model.'

'How long has it been hired for?'

'It's a two year lease.'

I heaved a sigh of relief, 'So it's mine for another twenty-two months?'

'Unless you choose to swap it for a different make.'

A cheaper make, I thought. That might be an idea. 'What's the cheapest make you do? Absolutely cheapest.'

He reeled off a couple of small hatchbacks. 'That would adjust your monthly payments to...'

'Monthly payments? I thought, you said it was mine for two years.'

'That's correct. There is a direct debit due on the 22nd of each month – as agreed with Mr Gill-Martin.'

Oh, Buddha! That left twelve days till Messrs Poole & Reed were the recipients of another bouncing payment. Twelve more days of independent transport and then I'd be on my bike – literally.

Crap! I didn't even have a bike. I had a pair of roller blades, which had had even fewer outings than the car.

'Thank you for your help,' I said. 'No doubt we'll be in touch again.'

I slumped in the chair.

The Universe had presented me with an opportunity to eat more healthily. Now, it seemed, I was destined to get fit too. Maybe I could double up with Luke and share his bike.

'Thank you, Universe,' I hollered at the ceiling. 'What's coming next?'

I stormed out of the kitchen and over to my studio.

My studio.

At this rate, I would be turning it into a bedsit. For me. And renting the house out.

I pulled a potter's knife from the tool box and stabbed it into a new bag of clay. It wasn't a violent act. It was an act of release.

I tore open the bag and plunged my hands in, tugging out two big clods of sticky, gritty clay.

Then I slapped the two clods together, slammed the lump onto the wooden table and screeched like Sharapova. I rolled it, I turned it, I made the familiar ram's head shape, again and again, until I was ready to

70

build.

Build what?

A car?

A magic flying saucer?

I leaned over the clay, hands sinking slowly into it. I could feel tears dripping onto my knuckles.

This was a waste of time. A complete and utter waste of time.

I sniffed.

The clay was ready to work but I wasn't. And I didn't trust myself to continue with the fine detail on Morael – I might decapitate the poor thing in this mood.

I tidied the clay into a ball. I pulled cling film from the dispenser on the wall and wrapped it around the clay, careful to ensure no air could get to it. Then I wrapped more cling film over the wounded bag; the last thing I needed was my clay drying out.

At least I knew this stuff was paid for – I'd used money from my own account.

I headed back outside and came face-to-face with Luke.

'You okay?' he asked, his concern evidence that I must be looking pretty scary.

'Oh, my goodness, yes,' I lied, bright and breeziness flooding my voice. 'Just having a bit of a moment. Coffee? Tea?'

'I heard you yell. I thought you must have injured yourself.'

'Sorry. No. Taekwondo.' I flicked my leg one way, my arms the other and yelled – just to confirm he hadn't been hearing things. 'I guess I need to be a bit quieter around here. Sorry, again.'

He looked bewildered. 'No worries. I'll know next

time.'

He glanced past me to the studio. 'You working on a sculpture?'

'Nearly. Just preparing some clay. I think tomorrow will be a better day for it.'

He looked up. 'Too hot, today?'

'No. I just don't feel fully aligned. Creatively speaking.'

'Right.'

'Coffee? Tea?' I repeated.

'Thanks but I need to get something finished.'

'Oh, I disturbed you. So sorry. Again.'

His face relaxed. 'Don't worry about it. Glad to see you're okay.' He studied me for a moment. 'Didn't have you down as a TKDist, though.'

'Huh?'

'Taekwondo student.'

'No. Not much. Now and again. I'm more of a yoga-ist. Yes, I like yoga.'

'Right. Well. See you around,' he said and headed off towards the drive.

A thought occurred to me. I trotted after him. 'Luke…' He turned. 'I've never really told you how grateful we are, as a family, for the help you gave Nanna. I know how much she appreciated what you did for her. She often mentioned you.'

His eyes softened. 'I was very fond of Una. She was a good woman.'

'She was. The best. I really miss her.'

'Me too.' AND THEN HE SMILED. It was almost a lens-shattering, eye-dazzling, toothpaste-commercial smile and proved he hadn't been botoxed. And believe me, I knew plenty of guys who had.

'She was the best person in my life,' I said, stopping short as I felt that tell-tale ache in the back of my throat.

'S'always good to have one of those,' he said, quietly.

I nodded frantically, swallowing back the tears and blinking rapidly. If I didn't get a grip, it would set off a chain reaction: crumpling chin, misshapen mouth and runny nose.

He raised his hand in a farewell gesture and turned away. He walked smoothly. He didn't bounce, he didn't swagger or toss his curly head in the cocky way some guys did. He just strolled comfortably down my drive and out between the stone gate posts.

'Taekwondo?' I muttered to myself. 'Where did that come from?'

I wandered inside to light some incense sticks in the hope they might lift my mood.

Chapter 8

Luke realised he didn't need to concern himself with Gigi's welfare in quite the way he had Una's. He'd become so tuned to Una's needs and looking out for her, that hearing a cry from over the neighbour's wall had triggered the instinct in him to rush round and offer assistance.

He would have to keep that in check or risk getting a name for himself. No-one liked a busybody.

He was grateful Una hadn't left the property to her grandson, Freddy. He'd met some dodgy people in his time but none to match Freddy. Freddy had all the surface charm of a real estate agent on the make, and no scruples.

Last summer, he had excelled himself. Not only had he played fast and loose with Ava's heart, Luke had caught Freddy trying to sell some of Una's possessions at a car boot sale on the village green. A Crown Derby china tea service, some silver egg spoons and a number of Georgette Heyer first editions. But the guy was an idiot. He'd have made more money selling them on e-bay or taking them to a dealer. Clearly he was out for a quick buck, because the prices he'd set for the items were laughably low – even for a boot sale.

It was the tea service which had drawn Luke's attention. He'd walked straight up to Freddy's stall – a large picnic table – and studied the goods on it.

Freddy had been shifting from foot to foot and tweaking the arrangement of cups. 'Morning,' he'd said politely enough, no doubt hoping Luke would walk on. He didn't.

'Selling this stuff for your grandmother?'

'That's right. Old stuff. Stuff she doesn't want any more. Thinks it'd be better going to a good home and the money given to charity.'

Luke nodded as he took this in. 'Which charity is that?'

'Lifeboats. Yep. She wants it to go to the lifeboat station in Bembridge.'

'You should have let them know,' Luke said, smiling, 'they might have given you a poster or a collection box. In fact, they might even have a stall up here – you could have saved yourself the table fee.' Luke looked around.

Freddy nodded vigorously. 'Thanks, I hadn't thought of that. I'm not much into marketing. You looking for something in particular?'

'Just going to buy a paper.'

'Right, well, hope you have a good day.'

Luke didn't budge. He scanned the table and totted up the prices. 'I'll give you a tenner for the lot.'

Freddy jerked his head back in contempt at the offer. 'Why not just make a donation to the lifeboats.'

'The RNLI.'

'Exactly. I mean, I stand to make a lot more for them if I sell everything here for the asking prices.'

Luke gave him a long hard look, and stroked his beard. 'How much have you made, so far...for the RNLI?'

'Not as much as I'd like, and certainly not with a rather economical tenner from you.'

'Either you take the ten pounds that I'm very generously offering you now, or I phone Mike Taylor from Ryde police station and report stolen goods.'

Freddy blanched a little. 'I told you, my grandmother…'

'Yes, I've heard your story. Odd that only a few weeks ago, Una was telling me she'd promised this tea service and spoons to her friend, Margaret, to sell online to raise funds for the hospice. And the books were going to be sold to raise money for under-privileged children.'

Freddy shot his chin forward and stood taller. 'Well, that may have been the plan then, but she's changed her mind.'

Luke shook his head. 'Your grandmother may be old but she's not stupid. She knew more money could be earned by selling them through the right channels. Which is why she asked me to look into it.'

He saw Freddy's eyes narrow as he tried to work out whether Luke was pulling a faster one than he was.

'One of these first edition Heyers could fetch thirty or forty on its own.'

Freddy's eyes widened and he ran a hand through his hair.

'You're lucky I'm offering you a tenner. I don't have to.'

'Then why bother?'

'Because if I don't you'll probably just pinch it from Una in some other way. And I'd hate any of the other stall holders to think no money had changed hands. I'm guessing the tenner will cover your table fee, right?'

Freddy was clenching his jaw. He had absolutely nothing to say.

'Right, so let's package this lot up and I'll make

sure they go the right people. That'll save you a job, won't it?'

Freddy's only answer was a huff of breath.

'Tell you what, I'll do this while you nip over to the Post Office and buy me a copy of *The Independent*, okay?' He handed Freddy a few coins. He didn't trust him a second longer with Una's treasures.

Freddy snatched the money from his hand and loped sulkily across the green towards the shop.

Luke would have to ask him for a lift home, too. He couldn't carry this stuff on his bike.

They packed the boxes on to the rear seat of Freddy's car. After taking one wheel off the bike, put that in too.

There was no conversation on the short run back to Rookery Cottage, and Freddy tossed the bike onto the patch of lawn in front of the house, before slamming the door. When he left, he deliberately executed a wheel-spin to churn up the gravel on Luke's drive.

Luke cursed quietly. Why would this boy, who had been given everything in life, still want to take more?

He couldn't help wondering whether Freddy and Gigi were tarred with the same brush. Yet that conversation he'd overheard between Gigi and her father, at the funeral, suggested she was much more ballsy. Ballsy and self-reliant. He smiled to himself. Yes, Una had thought so, too.

***

My car was on borrowed time – literally – and I had to decide how to make the most of our final hours.

Rupert still thought I was mad to stay on the island. 'What will you do without a car? You live in the back of beyond as it is.'

'I'll get one, eventually. People existed without cars for years.'

'But not you, my love. Not you. You're used to having tube stations on every corner.'

'We have public transport here, and taxis. I'll just have to mug up on the timetable and work around it. It's altogether more environmentally friendly.'

'Yeah, you're big on green issues, I know,' he said with heavy sarcasm.

'Actually,' I began rather haughtily, 'I'm going to start growing my own vegetables, too.'

There was a hefty snort from north of the border. 'What do you know about growing vegetables?'

'Not very much but I can learn.'

'Fair enough. Good luck with that.' There was a smile in his voice – affection more than mockery, I assumed. Although, as the conversation drew to a close, I did begin to think he found my situation rather amusing in an 'Oh, isn't she sweet' kind of way.

Well, I'd show him, and I'd show my dad.

And me. Yes, I was going to do this for me.

Another list was called for. If I were to make a go of this B&B malarkey, I must make sure I had everything I needed.

Who was I kidding? There were no significant funds left to purchase anything I was short of.

Pierre had actually loaned me a few hundred pounds on top of what I needed to pay Dan, so I had a small stash. What, I wondered, would be Freddy's plan? He had no job in Oz, and the money I'd sent over to him would be gone in a couple of nights.

Fran was right. He was a big boy. I had my own concerns without his on my plate, too. The best I could do was get him back home, where I could keep a close eye on him and help him out. On the other side of the world, he was much more vulnerable.

I thought about our mother's lack of maternal instinct. Even as a child, I'd recognised her abandonment of us as a selfish act.

She'd dressed it up as a holiday but I knew there was more to it than that by the edgy way she'd acted, the intense look in her eyes and the urgency with which she wanted shot of us.

To begin with, Nanna had been edgy too. I'm guessing behind the scenes she was busy battling it out with Mum and negotiating with Dad. Plus, how many women approaching their sixties would relish having to provide 24/7 care and protection for two little ones?

Freddy was still very much a Mummy's Boy but what four year old wouldn't be? Each time my mother made the effort to visit us, he would scream like a wild animal when she left. I think it was chiefly that which discouraged her from visiting us more often. She didn't like how guilty it made her feel. Sadly not quite enough to put us first, though.

No, she was living the Bohemian life of an artist in south-east France, following in the footsteps of her hero – Matisse. I think she liked his loose style because it was so different from her mother's meticulous botanical illustrations.

'She's always been a contrary madam,' I once heard Nanna say to my father.

'Not to mention deluded,' he replied.

'You don't know that, Max. Jennifer does have talent.'

'But for what?'

Contrary and deluded. Two new words for my

vocabulary. I hadn't been sure what they meant but they didn't sound complimentary. So when we were asked to write about our mothers at school, I knew better than to use those.

We'd spent a year in school on the island, because Dad thought Mum might return and settle there with her mother. He'd accepted she was through with his lifestyle, he just hadn't imagined she was through with us too. Mum insisted she was on the verge of something wonderful, he'd made arrangements for us to go to day school in Twickenham, and the first of the au-pairs was recruited.

Children can be unspeakably cruel when they spot weakness. Freddy's weakness was his absent mother: 'Did the policeman take her?' 'Does she hate you?' or 'Is she dead?' were questions he shouldn't have had to face. He always defended her passionately, even though he worried that any of these allegations might be true. And that gave him nightmares.

Parents don't know this stuff goes on but I did.

As he grew older, he came to realise she would only ever be a transient feature in our lives, and that's when he capped off his emotions, like a plumber caps off a pipe, and the hedonistic Freddy was born.

I checked the fridge and the cupboards. If I was very canny, I could survive on the contents for the next few days.

What could I afford to eat – rice, pasta, potatoes? I'd need the car to fetch those.

Catering packs – could I buy catering packs?

I spent the next couple of hours on the internet, researching suppliers and prices.

Excellent. I had a full tank of gas, my list, my satnav and funds to get me started.

Yay! I wasn't just a penniless sculptor. I was a resourceful business woman – almost. I could hear my Nanna's voice in my head, 'This might just be the making of you, Gabriella.'

I had Jack Johnson playing as I drove home after my excursion for supplies. The sun was popping in and out from behind the clouds and life was liveable.

Dad had always been such a good provider. He'd never let me down when it came to school trips, new shoes or holidays with my friends. 'And look how he helped me renovate Bluebell Farm,' I said aloud and immediately felt a little blip in my joy as I considered Dan Shaw's visit. More than a blip. 'Well, Daddy *intended* to help me.'

Intended to help me and then plundered my bank accounts.

I roared out loud. One of the benefits of driving around in an insulated box on wheels – above the obvious – you could bellow and scream without scaring the neighbours.

'Oh, Nanna,' I continued, 'Was Dad right? Am I going to wind up like Mum? A disappointed artist with hoards of work I can't sell?'

I slumped in the seat. To think I'd been congratulating myself on my ability to conquer all with a sack of spuds and a consignment of dried carbs.

Jack Johnson didn't sound quite so jolly, now. I turned him off and drove home in silence – contemplating my failings and asking the Universe to help me become a better person.

Under 'Budget Meals', Nanna's recipe book listed Cheese, Potato and Onion Mash. I could see why; it was easy and only used one hob ring. See – I was good at economizing.

Admittedly, it would have been nicer with a slice of gammon and a spray of grilled tomatoes but at least I wouldn't starve. Talking of tomatoes, on the way back from Newport, I'd seen a little stall outside a house on the main road, which was selling tomato plants for a pound each. I'd bought five. Nanna used to grow a few veg., so there was absolutely no reason why I couldn't. There were even some tools in her shed. Self-sufficiency had never been on my radar but needs must. I would be at one with nature.

I discovered courgette, carrot and bean seeds in the shed. I'd never grown anything before but it couldn't be that difficult. People had been doing it for centuries – long before the internet held all the secrets.

The internet was such a wonderful source of information. It told me how to sow and nurture all the good stuff for my diet. It also gave me some rather worrying data on the Spanish legal system and failed property investments.

Dad had sent a couple of texts to reassure me all was well, but other than that, he'd been worryingly quiet.

What a pity the landscapers had been in to lay Jerusalem stone over the whole courtyard and most of the back garden. And there were some spectacular shrubs developing in the borders. I went out front and stood on the drive between two large rectangles of lawn. 'Right, Nanna,' I said, 'I'm going to reclaim some of this and make a kitchen garden. How difficult can that be?'

Chapter 9

On Saturday morning, Luke stood by his landing window, gazing out over an amusing sight. Gabriella, once again in her hacked off overalls, was thrusting a spade – most ineptly – into the lawn and heaving out turf. By her side, in Una's rusty old wheelbarrow, was a growing heap of grassy sods. What on earth did she think she was going to put there? Was it a site for one of her sculptures, perhaps? Una used to have quite a spectacular dragon in her garden, which her granddaughter had created out of wire and gauze. He wondered where that was, now.

Gabriella howled as the spade hit something hard. She dropped the implement, shook her hand and then shoved it under her armpit. She shook it again, hugged it to her and paced away from the scarred lawn. After a moment, she stood on the drive with her fists on her hips and surveyed the excavation, before wandering back towards the house and out of view.

Probably gone to call Andy Winters, the landscaper, he thought. One square metre of digging and she'd given up.

He carried on downstairs and opened up his laptop. He had some references to add to his website. 'Damn!' There was a fold of paper in his wallet upstairs with the two references on.

He went back up, pausing to glance out of the window. Yep, just as he thought, Gabriella had given up.

He pulled his wallet from the bedside drawer and

fished out a scrap of paper.

At the top of the stairs he halted. Gabriella had reappeared, and this time was wielding a pick-axe. 'Jeez!' he muttered as she swung it at the ground. It penetrated a soft patch by several inches. She wriggled it free and threw it back into the ground. Another soft patch. With a third blow, she struck stone, let out an almighty yell, and threw the axe down. At this rate, she'd lose a couple of toes. He stuffed the paper in his pocket, took the stairs two at a time and headed off out to prevent an amputation.

***

'Shit and bollocks! It never looked this difficult on the internet.' My hands were throbbing from the totally unexpected resistance of what had appeared to be a lush and benign lawn. I looked up as I heard the crunch of feet on gravel. Luke was pacing up the drive towards me. Half of me wondered what he wanted while the other half considered offering him the spade and saying, 'Here, big boy, you finish it off.'

'Hi,' I said, resting my pulsing palms on my hips, then lifting them off and folding them in front of me.

'Hey, Gabriella, I don't wish to interfere but…what exactly are you trying to do there?'

Oh, hello – was he getting all territorial over a garden he used to tend or was he unleashing his inner caveman?

I frowned. 'The back garden's a botanical masterpiece, I thought this would be an ideal place for a few vegetable canes.'

'Vegetables, huh?'

'Yes. Will that be a problem?'

'Not for me.' He shook his head and stopped in front of me. 'But you'll need a JCB to clear that lot safely.'

'Why, what's under here, Atlantis?'

He huffed a small laugh. It was nice to know I amused him. 'Could be, though I doubt it. This grass only grows on poor soil. And that's exactly what you have just here. It's very stony. That's why Una had so many large planters for her shrubs and ornamental plants. If you want to grow vegetables, you need to build some raised beds.'

'I do?'

'You do.'

'Raised beds, huh?'

He nodded.

'I have no idea what raised beds are. Is that like soil heaped up behind a wall?'

'Can be. Or you can get some wooden boxes built. Fill them with good compost and sow your seeds in those.'

It sounded expensive. Still, if I could find some old timber, I wasn't averse to turning my hand to a bit of woodwork. I'd handled a saw and a plane at college. Compost couldn't be that expensive, could it?

'So, you wouldn't recommend carrying on with this, then?'

He looked straight into my eyes and didn't avert them for one second. 'Nope.'

I nodded. I was aware of the pile of hacked lawn lumps, now air-drying in the wheelbarrow.

'Do you think this stuff will take if I lay it back down?'

'Sure it will. I'd water it first, if I were you. Ground and er – turves.'

'Excellent. Thank you – and of course, thank you for intercepting when you did. I would have been here till midnight, otherwise.'

'D'you want a hand with this?'

'Oh no, I don't want to hold you up.'

He glanced around. 'Is the roll of hose-pipe still in the shed?'

'I expect so.'

'Okay, I'll fix that to the tap and we'll get some water on this.'

The corner of my lawn looked more crazy paving when we'd finished than Wimbledon Centre Court but Luke assured me it would rally. 'Keep it watered and in a couple of weeks, no-one will ever know it was patchwork.'

'Thanks Luke – you're a marvel.'

He laughed. 'That's exactly what your grandmother used to say.'

I smiled. 'It was, wasn't it?'

He gave me a sidelong glance as he took hold of the wheelbarrow and lifted it. 'Nature has a wonderful way of repairing itself, so long as you give it what it needs.'

'A bit like humans.' I stepped back to let him pass.

He shrugged. 'I guess.'

I followed him to the shed, which was behind my studio. He hung the tools inside and propped the barrow up against the wall. Something I imagined he'd done for Nanna, many times before.

'Cup of tea or a beer?' I asked.

'I'll take a small beer, thanks.' He sat himself down on a wooden patio chair, opposite the swing seat.

There were still half a dozen beers in the fridge. I wouldn't be replenishing those any time soon. I took one of them and went over to the tap to get myself some water. I looked out of the window at my guest, who was gazing over the more lush landscaping behind the house. What was his story? I wondered.

I went back outside and handed him his beer.

'Thanks,' he said before taking a long draught of it. 'You know, the landscaper could have built you some vegetable beds when he was here.'

'Ah, the wisdom of hindsight,' I said, sitting down. 'It never occurred to me I'd want to grow my own produce. But the more I think about it, the more it appeals.'

He nodded and took another swig. 'Gabriella, it's a very smart move, if you don't mind a little regular hard work.'

'Gabriella,' I echoed, 'Only Nanna ever called me that – or my teachers when I was in trouble.'

'Sorry. Gigi.'

'I don't mind. But it's a lot easier to say Gigi – half the syllables. Think of the energy you'll save.'

I'm pretty sure I spotted a smile twitch beneath his beard. I guessed I was quite a curiosity to him.

'I seem to recall Nanna telling me you're an archaeologist.'

'Palaeontologist.'

'Right, that's it. Like Ross in *Friends.*'

'That's the one,' he said through a sigh, like it was the only response he ever heard.

'What's your speciality?' I asked, hoping to redeem my stupid blonde comment.

'Right now, I'm writing a book on the dinosaur beds between Atherfield and Compton. They're called the Wealden Beds.'

'You're writing a book? Wow. I'm impressed.'

He shrugged. 'I don't bank on it being a bestseller.'

'Well, the important thing is, you're leaving your

mark on the world.'

'Is that what you're hoping to do with your sculptures?'

Was I? 'Possibly. Except my motivation is more about expressing myself but yes, you're right. Assuming every one of my pieces doesn't become landfill, then I'll have left a small mark or two on the world.'

'Una used to have a dragon in her garden, which she told me you made. I don't see it here now.'

'Oh, Gustav. No, Gustav's upstairs. He's a little weather-beaten so I brought him indoors to live out his old age. I made him when I was at school. He's survived pretty well, considering he's all wire and gauze and glue.'

'So, what do you make now?'

'Do you want to see?' I asked, leaping up, pathetically grateful someone was finally showing an interest in my work. The gang last weekend had been disappointingly cavalier about it.

'Sure.' He followed me into the studio. Most of my old pieces were still in boxes, but the angelic pieces I'd done for my final year show were on display in the corner. While he studied those, I carefully lifted the polythene and dampened muslin from my current angel, Morael, and waited for Luke to come and see it. After a few moments, he turned to me. 'They look kind of…capricious.'

'You think so?'

Capricious. I'd have to look the word up. If that described Moods of Angels then I could use it on promotional material. Most people thought they were garden ornaments.

'Yeah,' he continued, 'They're kind of whimsical,

unpredictable and other worldly.'

The guy was a walking thesaurus. 'Good, I like that. You have, of course, hit the nail on the head, that was totally my intention.'

He smiled again. He should do it more often.

Chapter 10

I'd been studying the *Job Vacancies* column of the *County Press* with some conviction but little success: Catering Supervisor, MOT Tester, HGV Driver, Experienced This, Qualified That.

There was a Washer Upper for the summer season, but that was on the other side of the island. A hotel in Ryde wanted a trainee kitchen assistant. That was surely within my reach so I rang them.

'Are you looking for a career in catering?'

Gah! 'Maybe…'

'You see, we really want to train someone up and have them take on more responsibility, over time. It's a career opportunity. My husband and I want to wind down a bit. If you understand me.'

'Of course.'

'So if that's how you see your future developing, we'd love to talk to you. You sound very nice.'

'Actually, perhaps this isn't the right choice for me. Do you have any bar work or waitressing?'

'No, love. Sorry.'

I looked at a Care Worker post. Thirty-five hour weeks for a third of the basic salary I'd been on in London. What? Thirty-five hours of potentially back-breaking work, hefting elderly ladies into the bath, would leave me with no energy in the tank to do my sculptures.

There had to be something part-time, surely?

Nothing in estate agency, which is closest to what I'd been doing for the last three years, and nothing in creative areas. Nothing.

The day arrived, as I knew it would, when Messrs Poole & Reed Vehicle Leasing came for the car. I probably should have let them know the payments would stop. If I was a truly decent human being, I would have offered to drive the beautiful beast back to their depot, but that would have, a) cost me money in diesel, ferry ticket and return travel and b) denied me any independent transport for a few extra days.

Forgive me, but I was playing the system.

It was one of those grotty summer days that feels like autumn. I was on my knees in the studio, sanding the old blanket box in preparation for painting and distressing it.

Movement in the courtyard attracted me. I looked up to see a man in a puffa jacket over jeans. I switched off the sander.

'Afternoon,' I called through the doorway, scrambling up from my position on all-fours.

He glanced at a piece of paper in his hand. 'Mrs Jill Martin?' He asked.

I nodded. 'Gill – the G is hard as in Gilbert.'

'Sorry. Mrs Martin. I'm here from…'

'The keys are in the car. Help yourself.'

He frowned back at me. 'I'm here to inspect your accommodation. I'm from Bide-a-while-on-Wight. You applied to be included on our website.'

'Oh.' I dusted myself off. 'I wasn't expecting you.'

'Sorry. I thought the office had emailed ahead.'

'Maybe they did. I've been having trouble with it recently.' I didn't want to offend him by saying I hadn't checked my Junk folder.

He was now perusing the slightly impressive

surroundings of my renovated courtyard and catching glimpses of the back garden, I approached him with a massive smile: charm offensive being order of the day when the prospect of essential business is in view.

'Not a problem. I'm Gigi.' I said, thrusting my dusty hand towards him.

'Kevin McHoy.'

'Kevin, lovely to meet you. I'm afraid I haven't had chance to dress the rooms – you're not planning on a photo shoot, are you?'

'Well, I could take a few, if the accommodation is up to standard but if you'd rather provide us with a set of your own pictures, that would be acceptable.'

'Absolutely. Or you're welcome to return and do the shoot yourself.'

'Let's see how we get on.'

I led him into the kitchen. I hadn't washed up since last night, and the table was a collage of crumbs, plates, sketches and one cat – Gaudi.

Cat food was crusted to the floor around their bowls and a tumbleweed of cat fluff rolled ahead of us in the draught from the door.

He saw it all, I have no doubt.

'Like I said, I wasn't expecting you and I've been a bit frantic with other work, recently.'

'Mm-hmm.'

The sitting room didn't look much better. A crumpled blanket was in a heap on the sofa, where I'd snuggled down last night to watch *One Day* and fallen asleep. A coffee mug, a half-eaten packet of supermarket digestive biscuits and a discarded bowl of yoghurt and muesli graced the coffee table.

'This is south facing, so it's wonderful in the summer. And of course, it overlooks my lovely garden,' I gestured to the landscaped borders and hoped he might forgive the detritus indoors.

'Dining room?'

'Yes,' I said weakly. 'But that's not been furnished, yet. I was planning on eating in the kitchen, it's more friendly.'

'Mmm-hm. Downstairs WC?'

'Yes.' That at least would have a flushed toilet, reasonably clean towel and…ah, a two-month old copy of *Grazia* on the floor.

'Mmm-hm.'

I should have sent him away and told him to come back after a magic squad of cleaners had been in.

I didn't show him my bedroom. It looked like a family of squatters had visited. Fortunately, the spare rooms were clean and devoid of fast-food containers, empty wine bottles or cat crap. Just furniture and unmade beds. 'If I'd known you were coming I would have dressed the rooms, really nicely. I'm quite creative. I'll make them look very pretty.'

My fists were clutching at invisible straws.

'No en-suites?'

'Yes. Well, no. I mean, there's one in my room but I was thinking of offering that as the superior room at a higher price. Otherwise, there's this bathroom…'

G-strings, bras and two t-shirts hung listlessly from a laundry rack over the bath. Recent rain meant I couldn't dry them outside, and I wasn't going to run up my electricity bill using the tumble-dryer.

'And you mentioned running pottery courses.'

'Yes!' My excitement was not sounding at all forced. 'Follow me.'

The studio, at least, was respectable. Nobody expects a pottery studio to be pristine. My angels were posed, benign and beautiful in a shaft of sunlight. Only a little of the dust I'd raised from the blanket box had settled in the folds of their hair.

'These are nice,' he said. 'Garden ornaments are very popular with some people, aren't they?'

'They are,' I nodded.

'Is this what you plan to make with your guests?'

He clearly had no idea how long these things took. Why would he? Although if someone fancied a four-week holiday to produce their own metre-high angel, I'd sign them up straightaway.

'Actually, I was thinking something on a smaller scale. Functional ware, perhaps – mugs and vases, or anything they fancied making, within reason.'

'Very good. Well, of course, if we were to accept you onto our site, your posting would be much better if you had some positive reviews to support it; satisfied customers, that sort of thing. Do you have any?'

'I used to give demonstrations at the Museum of Craft & Design – would a reference from them help?'

He made a squeaky noise in the back of his nose before saying, 'Not exactly what we're looking for. Do you have any courses imminent?'

'No.' My voice emerged pale and thin.

'Something to think about. Get a visitors' book, garner a few glowing reviews and then get back to us.'

He glanced over my shoulder, I turned to see what was distracting him. A taxi was at the foot of the drive.

Too much to hope this would be The British Tourist Board swooping in to snatch my business from the clutches of Bide-a-while-on-Wight.

'You have visitors, I'll be off.'

I thanked him for coming and followed him outside.

Striding up from the taxi was a bullet-headed henchman – he looked like Hannibal Lecter on steroids. Before he'd even got close, his voice ricocheted off the garden wall and bounced off the bonnet of Kevin's car. 'I'm from Poole & Reed Vehicle Leasing. Are you Gabriella Martin?'

I nodded but turned my attention to Kevin. I wanted him off the premises before Hannibal could stain my character even more than my sloppy, junk-filled home already had.

'Thank you again, Kevin.' I patted his arm in a familiar and possibly inappropriate manner. He nodded, sat in his car and fiddled about with some papers on the passenger seat.

Go! I was willing him. Go, before you witness something you might never forget.

Hannibal was fast approaching. I guess debt-collectors and the like need to be menacing from the outset. He probably had 'Don't Mess With Me' tattooed across his chest and kept a bag of raw meat in his pocket to chew on.

'I'm here for the vehicle.' He glanced at a file in his hand and across at the number plate of my lovely car.

I nodded.

Kevin still hadn't started his bloody engine, so I waved at him – an encouraging 'lovely to see you but clear off' kind of wave, before turning on my heel and marching up to the top of the drive where the vehicle in question stood.

I could hear the heavy thump of Hannibal's heels on the gravel behind me. The keys were on the driver's seat. I pulled open the door. The sooner he and it were gone, the better.

'It's all there; keys, satnav, seats, windscreen wipers. Nothing missing and no scratches,' I said, stepping away and folding my arms.

He walked slowly around it.

I'd given it a thorough washing yesterday, and polished it with the car-cleaning kit I'd found in the boot. The effort had been cathartic; every smear and smudge had been erased. It had gleamed like a jewel, till the rain came.

He sat on the edge of the driver's seat, started the ignition and checked the mileage.

He wrote something on his file.

'So, that'll be £2,100 final payment.'

I thrust my head towards him in shock. 'What? Why?'

He fixed his eyes on me. They were tired, whisky-soaked eyes set in a much younger face. He probably wasn't more than thirty, I managed to assess, despite my terror and disbelief.

'Premature cancellation of the lease agreement. You were contracted for two years and you've had it less than three months.'

'It's not my contract. It's my father's.' I said, Judas-like. 'Take it up with him.'

He chewed his lip for a moment – raw meat on tap. 'Contract says Gabriella Jill Martin.'

'Gill-Martin. It's double-barrelled! And I didn't sign the contract. My father did. He paid for it. Not me. It's not my responsibility.' I could hear my voice rising and starting to wobble.

Every penny I had was spoken for.

He stepped out of the vehicle and glowered at me.

I ploughed on. 'How do I know you're even who

you say you are? You could be a con-man, a bandit. Where are your credentials?'

He thrust the file towards me. Poole & Reed Vehicle Leasing was emblazoned across the top of the document. He stuffed a hand into his jacket, enough of a move to make me flinch but instead of a Magnum 45, he pulled out a plastic coated identity card.

I snatched it from him.

Tim Marsh.

I'd never met anyone who looked less like a Tim than he did.

'Well, Tim, I'm sorry. Speak to my father's lawyers.'

'You should have provided this information before. The company has sent correspondence to this address, hasn't it?'

I'd never read beyond the first paragraph. It was enough to know they'd scheduled repossession of the vehicle. 'Yes but...'

There was movement at the bottom of the drive. Kevin had finally gone.

'Miss Gill-Martin, either you pay this money now, or the debt will increase.' He held a hand up, 'And that's not me making threats, that's just the business I'm in. It's all in the contract, which I suggest you, or your father's lawyer, read.'

More money.

I was sure my father hadn't meant to be dishonest. He only wanted me to have a reliable car.

Tim continued. 'So, unless you want to ratchet up a whole load more expense, I suggest you find this money, or we'll have to send in the bailiffs, and that would mean seizing assets to the value of the debt.'

He looked around; his bleary gaze peering into my studio.

'But it's my father's debt, not mine.'

He studied the paperwork. 'According to this, payment is from an account in your name.' He came alongside and showed me the document. 'That makes you responsible for the debt. Do you have a lawyer?'

I sagged.

The paper blurred out of focus.

I had no lawyer. I couldn't afford a lawyer.

I didn't need one to tell me the debt was mine. All my cash had gone towards settling the account with Dan Shaw.

Suck it up, Gigi. Stick it on your credit card and rack up another debt. 'Please, wait here a moment.'

I walked with leaden feet over to the house and into the kitchen. I pulled my purse from the dresser, all the while thinking of further sacrifices I would have to make; another job I'd have to find; pieces of jewellery I might have to sell.

When I handed the card to Tim Marsh, he reached inside his jacket and pulled out a card-reader that looked like a chubby mobile phone. He peered at the screen. 'Not much of a signal round here, is there?'

My heart lifted a tad, maybe I could get a stay of execution...

'Ah, there we go. Should be enough of a signal to complete the transaction.' He shoved my card into the slot and tapped in some numbers before handing it to me.

'Your PIN please.'

With each beep of the device, another nail penetrated the coffin of my financial affairs.

'Thank you, Miss Gill-Martin. All being well,

that's an end to it.' He offered a hand to shake, which I'm ashamed to say I ignored. Instead I raised my hand dismissively, turned my back on him and headed indoors, unsure how much control I could maintain over my emotions.

I didn't watch the car drive away. It was only later, when I was peeling potatoes, that I saw how empty the view was across the courtyard.

Chapter 11

I thanked my lucky stars I had good friends in my life, and Rupert – lovely, funny, handsome, capable Rupert. I would phone him. I might not be able to snuggle into his warm and firm embrace but I could imagine it. Instead I could lie, snuggled into my deliciously cosy sofa, pull the cushions around me and pretend.

'Hi, Gigi.' He sounded distracted.

'Are you working?'

'Yep.'

'Fancy a break and a little bit of phone sex?'

'What, me and half the office? I could put you on speaker phone.'

'You're not at home, then?'

'Home? I've forgotten where that is. This project's taking all my time.'

'Poor baby.'

'Yeah. What d'you want?'

Well, not that attitude, I thought, as my eyes began to prickle. After a few seconds he said, 'Gigi? You there?'

I sniffed. 'Yes, I'm here, and I'm feeling … kind of low. I was just hoping for a little phone cuddle.'

'Sorry, babe. You've picked a really bad time. Let me call you when I'm not quite this snowed under.'

'Today?'

There was a heavy sigh. 'I don't want to promise you that, Gigi. But I will call as soon as I've got some time for you, and you alone, baby.'

'Okay.'

'And don't forget, I'm coming down in a couple of days. Gotta go. Love you.'

'Love you, too.'

After the click signalled his disconnection, I indulged myself in a few blubs of self-pity, before nodding off.

I woke with a jolt as the ceiling, which was crumbling above me, cracked and buckled beneath the weight of some prehistoric foot the size of a double-decker bus. 'No!' I yelled, and sat bolt upright.

The ceiling smoothed out and there wasn't a scrap of plaster dust around me.

I listened intently. Nothing.

I looked around and listened some more.

Still nothing.

The rain clouds had moved away and early-evening sunlight had warmed the carpet and was now kissing my bare feet.

The rain clouds had gone but the emotional cumulonimbus was hovering stubbornly over my head. The dream was a recurring one, when I would battle to secure the house from some looming threat. It was never the same house, and the threat was always unknown – but it was coming.

The prospect of rice and beans for dinner, with a smattering of chopped onion and chilli flakes, depressed me even further.

I lay back down and gazed across at the fireplace, where a colony of expensive, scented candles stood proud and luxurious. The last extravagance of my old life.

My. Old. Life.

No matter how much I wished things to be as they

were, every day reminded me that would never be the case – at least, not for the foreseeable future.

For me there was no way out. Some people take on challenges deliberately. Face their fears and go for it. I had no choice in this. All my plans, all my dreams for a blissfully tranquil existence had been side-swiped.

'This, Gigi, is it, and it's not going to get any better,' I told myself, pulling my cardi around me and sinking deeper into the squishy Italian cushions.

There was a buzz and a beep from my phone. Thank goodness I'd had the presence of mind to contact the mobile company and change the payment source for the contract, or I'd be totally out of communication.

I could see it was a message from Diva 1 – Sonia. I ignored it.

Moments later, it rang. Sonia was an impatient mare. I turned away. It stopped for all of twenty seconds then started again. I rolled over, grabbed it, ready to switch it off when I noticed MUM on the display.

She was calling me?

I may have been deep in the cavern of self-pity but my curiosity was piqued. 'Hello,' I said.

'Darling, you're there. Thank God.'

'Why?'

'I haven't heard from you in days, I was sure I would.'

My mother was worried about me?

'Sorry. I've been busy.' Keeping my head above water, I wanted to add. 'Everything okay?'

'Yes, we're fine. But what about you? I spoke to Julia Smithers, today. She's absolutely livid. She had money invested in your father's Spanish project and now it's not going through! Thousands she stands to lose. Thousands!'

Julia Smithers was one of my parents' old dinner party crowd – one of the few to stay in touch with Mum.

'And Julia is just one of dozens. Your father is ruining people's lives, Gigi. Ruining them!'

'Don't! I don't want to hear it.' It was bad enough I was living with the fallout.

'You can't go burying your head in the sand, Gigi. You'll have to face the music about your father, sooner or later.'

'Mum, they repossessed my car, today, they've cut off my land-line and, if I'm not careful, I might actually lose electricity next. That's enough music-facing for this week – wouldn't you agree?'

'Oh dear. Yes. Poor you. It's really quite a scandal. Has news hit the island, yet? Anything in the *County Press*? I mean, he's had connections there for some time, you know.'

'Of course I know but it's not like he was Lord Mayor, is it?'

'No, but…'

'Exactly. Now, d'you have any more words of advice because, quite honestly, I could do with some good ones.'

'Oh, darling.' There was a pause as she hunted around for something wise to say. Wisdom wasn't her forte. 'It's just a blip in your life, think of it that way.'

'Thanks, Mum. Now I need to go. I'm really tired.'

We said our goodbyes and I turned the phone off. I could see dust had gathered around the candles. I heaved myself off the sofa and wandered into the kitchen to find the feather duster. I might be a poor cow, I didn't have to be a dirty, poor cow.

As I rearranged the now dust-free candles, the doorbell chimed.

I could ignore it. There was no car on the drive, they would assume I was out. Good.

I continued to dust; defiant in my solitude.

There was a knock. Clearly someone who didn't trust the doorbell.

Tough.

I wasn't in.

Another thought struck me – journalists. Had my mother been right? Would there be people after my story?

My heart thumped.

No. Of course not.

I lowered myself onto the sofa and waited.

Would they come round to the back and peer through the window?

I shot around behind the armchair and hid.

I was hiding?

What the…?

How bloody dare they?

I jumped up again. Fired with indignation, I tore through the house to the back door and yanked it open.

Luke stood there with a box of courgettes and tomatoes. His hands were dry and dusty with soil.

'Bad time?' he asked, frowning.

Having been propelled to the door on a tidal wave of bile, it took me a moment to recover. I stared at his harvest offerings in preference to looking him in the face.

'No. Sort of. Sorry.' I stepped back, civility

returning. 'Hi, Luke. Come in.'

'It's been a good year for courgettes,' he said, heading for the table. 'More here than we need. They don't freeze very well but they make nice soup, and cake – if you're into baking. Una made a great courgette cake.'

He plonked them on the table, looked up and smiled. Voluntarily. No prompting from me. No cajoling, leg-pulling or joke-making.

I tossed the feather duster onto the work-surface, totally disregarding hygiene, and stood with my hands on my hips. 'You know, don't you?'

His mouth flattened as he pulled it tight. He glanced down and then fixed his gaze on me. 'About your dad? Yes.'

There was a tense, twanging kind of silence tightening between us.

He had come bearing gifts. Would that be the action of a nosy neighbour or a gesture of compassion? Worse even – charity?

My hackles were flexing – up and then down again.

He was watching me like a game hunter might watch his prey.

Would I bolt or would I lunge?

Undecided but mindful of good manners, I said flatly. 'Thanks for the veg.'

He shrugged; the hunter still hedging his bets on whether to approach or lay low.

'What do you want to know, Luke? Whether I'll be selling up to bail my father out?' It was the first time I'd voiced this idea aloud. I didn't much like it.

'No, Gabriella. Just offering the hand of friendship. I'm guessing this won't be an easy time for you.'

We watched each other some more.

'Anyway,' he hedged again, 'you know where I am.' He nodded and moved towards the door. 'Have a good evening.'

'Thanks,' I managed as he left. I could easily follow and spill all my misery. Is that what he expected? Or was he making a hasty getaway because, like most men, he'd rather not deal with the emotional fallout of someone else's torment?

The fragrance of fresh tomatoes began to soothe me. I picked one up and held it to my nose. They were large, like bunched fists. Nanna used to grow tomatoes like these. I bit into it and sucked the juicy seeds into my mouth.

Heaven.

As a child, I'd eaten tomatoes in preference to apples. But before I could finish it, the smell and the taste evoked wonderful memories, which compelled my troubled emotions to spill from my tear-ducts. Add to that, Luke's act of kindness, and I was awash.

I'd cried more in the last couple of weeks than I had in years – not counting soppy films and the occasional wildlife documentary. And it wasn't over. If my mother's concerns were spot on – then I was in for more challenges than a celebrity in the jungle. And crying 'Get me out of here!' wouldn't help.

After tarting up my rice and beans with courgette, chilli flakes, garlic and tomato, I managed to eat less than half of it. Even my food was on a par with jungle nosh. Never mind, I could put the rest aside and eat it tomorrow.

Rice salad. How healthy.

It wasn't even ten o'clock, but my bed was calling to me – chiefly because there was nothing to stay up for. I took three Nytol tablets to knock me out so I wouldn't have to lie in the dark worrying about the next financial catastrophe waiting to blindside me.

At least, not for a few hours.

Chapter 12

My father's brother – Uncle Charlie – once told me the early hours of the morning were the darkest hours; except he hadn't meant lack of moonlight. 'Darkest hours of the soul, Gigi,' he'd said, over his tumbler of whisky. I was beginning to see what he meant. I was developing a habit of waking early; somewhere between three and four o'clock, when it was dark, silent and often cold. Last night, I lay counting sheep, counting heartbeats, counting all the ways my life was falling apart until I was right royally sick of numbers. There was a heaviness pulling me into the mattress. 'Gabriella Gill-Martin,' I said out loud, echoes of Nanna in my voice, 'try counting your blessings instead.'

It didn't work.

I sat up, put the telly on and watched three minutes of a programme on teenage mothers. 'Glad that's not me, Nanna.'

At the adverts, I flicked through the channels to a Bollywood movie. It was subtitled but the music was jolly and everyone was beautiful. I totally lost myself in it and came up with a plan to model Indian-themed figures for my next project.

It wasn't long before soft daylight was filtering through the curtain folds. At last. I could get up without feeling I was on the nightshift.

Not that I'd ever done a night shift – the closest I'd come was stacking shelves in the supermarket one Christmas holiday, when we had to be in the store by seven in the morning. I actually enjoyed putting tins out on shelves. I delighted in turning all the labels to face the front, and rearranging the brands so they made more interesting patterns. It was my own special mosaic.

Norman, the section manager, nearly had a canary. 'You can't put those there!' he bawled, slapping the side of the transporter trolley and probably wishing it was me. 'They haven't paid the eye-level shelf premium.'

How was I to know? The finer points of product placement hadn't been considered crucial to my education. I offered to work overtime, for free, to make up for it.

His eyes had boggled, like I'd suggested blowing him at the wide aisle checkout. 'And get me fired for exploiting you?' he'd spluttered.

Like I say, blowing him in the wide aisle might have been preferable.

He huffed, puffed and called another temporary staff member to help me rearrange them in the correct locations. I'd considered my Christmas bonus was likely a goner.

The dawn chorus was tuning up, so I made my way downstairs for some coffee. Ginger and lemon tea would have been better for me but coffee and toast would cheer me up. Marginally.

I found a well-splattered recipe for Lemon Courgette Cake. It looked easy enough to make. I figured I should do the decent thing and make an extra one for Luke. I didn't believe he'd been dropping a hint last night, I was just feeling majorly guilty for getting the hump and snapping at him. I didn't have enough allies to go pissing off my nearest neighbour.

Nanna had several baking tins of different shapes and sizes, which I'd kept – mostly because of the same sentimental streak that had me clinging to Bluebell Farm.

I had everything except caster sugar, and I didn't think a handful of sweeteners or a bunch of brown sugar-lumps would work. I also didn't think nipping round to Luke's and asking to borrow sugar was an option.

Jumping in the car and popping to the corner shop was currently a wistful memory.

Jogging. I could jog to the shop. It wasn't raining. It would do me good. Physical exercise clears the head.

Just as I was about to spring over the threshold, I had the presence of mind to check the time. Six. It was six o'clock in the morning. The corner shop would be closed for at least another two hours.

On the table was last night's rice and beans. This morning, I was hungry.

I dipped a fork into it. It actually tasted better now. 'Waste not, want not,' I said, sitting on the table to wolf the remains down. Maybe that was the trick – hand it over to the maturing process. Yum.

I decided to clean the house to kill time. I might even do something decorative with the spare rooms, and take a few pictures for Kevin-of-Bide-a-While.

You can do a lot in two hours when you're trying to block thoughts out. Although I probably shouldn't have done so much after a belly-full of rice and beans. It seemed to have churned in my stomach and was causing all manner of gaseous eruptions.

A brisk walk to the shop would settle it down. The

idea of jogging had lost its attraction.

I set off. It was a good fifteen minute walk. No hardship at all, really. Who needed a car?

Well, of course, I did. After seeing the prices of supplies in the corner shop, the supermarkets would still be my first choice. I'd have to look into ordering on-line.

As I waited to pay, I noticed a tray of huge home-made scones on the counter. Normally, I would be tempted but today, my stomach was busy processing rice and beans, albeit not very efficiently.

'Hope you don't mind me asking, but aren't you Una's granddaughter?' the woman behind the counter asked.

'I am.'

'Recognised you from the funeral.'

'Of course.'

'We miss her, you know. I used to go to her charity tea parties. Lovely lady.'

'She was.'

'I'm Wendy, by the way.'

'Gigi,' I said, offering my hand to shake.

'Oh, Gigi is it? Hello.'

My stomach gave a monumental gurgle – the portent of a large and possibly smelly burp. I covered my mouth and swallowed it down. 'Scuse me,' I said. I was beginning to regret my unconventional breakfast.

She nodded and rang up the price of the sugar.

With another gurgle, my stomach clenched painfully. Who'd have thought wind could be so excruciating?

With a brisk 'Cheerio' I headed out into the fresh air. Unfortunately, it seemed every few steps, my stomach cramped a little more. I was beginning to sweat too. Damn. Maybe I should have chucked the rice away.

I began jogging, figuring I'd get home faster and it might just jostle the trapped air out of my gut.

I ran as hard as I could, riding waves of nausea and pain. Home was finally in sight. Another spasm nearly took my breath away and I doubled over.

Would I make it? Could I actually make it indoors before I threw up?

I had to. The indignity of vomming on the Queen's Highway was out of the question.

Swallowing, panting and jogging, I fixed my eyes on the gateposts. Home. Nearly home.

Nope. Too late.

At least I was barfing over my own drive.

If I could just catch a moment of calm, I'd fetch a bucket of water to clean up.

I shuddered and wiped my eyes.

'Are you okay?' a girl's voice asked.

Venus de Milo! I had an audience.

Still doubled over, I said, 'Fine. Thanks,' and waved dismissively, but it could have been mistaken for a greeting.

A hand rubbed my back. 'It's horrible isn't it, being sick?' she said. 'But you'll feel better for it.'

I hoped so. Right then, waves of sweat and chilly gusts were rippling over me like a tropical storm, and there was every indication my guts were building up for a tsunami. I just wasn't sure when.

'Would you like me to help you home?'

'I live here,' I managed.

'I know. I'm Ava, Luke's sister.'

I nodded and gasped a hasty 'Great,' then I

erupted again.

Eventually, my stomach stilled enough for me to straighten up and glance sideways at my neighbour. She looked a little different from how I remembered her. Like her brother, she was dark but neater. Her hair was now cropped short and her concerned eyes were framed by spiky black eyelash extensions, which matched the black of her t-shirt and leggings. Other than that she was fresh faced. She looked like an adorable pixie. I managed a weak smile.

'Let's get you a glass of water,' she said, giving my back a final stroke.

'Thanks.'

On legs like bungee rope, I made it up the drive. I fumbled in my pocket for the keys, apologising repeatedly for my state of health.

'Hey, we all get sick,' she said, a milder trace of Canadian in her accent than Luke's. 'Warm water's best if your stomach's upset,' she said. 'But if you'd prefer cold…?'

I shook my head. 'Any water's fine.'

After which, I was hoping she'd disappear and leave me alone with my gastric anarchy.

She warmed some water in the kettle. 'Any lemon?'

I pointed to the fridge. There were two wrinkly specimens in the vegetable drawer.

'Just a little lemon peel is good. The fragrance helps with nausea,' she added.

How did a child get to know so much? I studied her as she sliced the lemon. Adolescent. Older than twelve, I guessed.

'You should get to bed. Better still, lay on your duvet in the bathroom. D'you want a bucket?' She asked, a little too cheerfully.

116

'Actually, I need a bucket to swill the mess outside.'

'I'll do that.'

'You can't.'

'Duh, I can! You go to bed.'

I sipped the water. My stomach wasn't very welcoming and all I really wanted to do was sloosh my mouth out with it.

'Thanks,' I said, again.

'Hope you feel better, soon. I'll drop by later to see if you want anything.'

'Okay,' I said, feebly, before crawling upstairs.

The less said about the ensuing hours, the better.

Ava reappeared, mid-afternoon. Her gentle tap on my bedroom door stirred me from the welcome abyss of sleep. I looked up to see her elfin features peering in at me. 'How're you feeling?'

I blinked a lot as I assessed the state of my alimentary canal. 'Tender.'

'Ready to eat, yet? I could fix you some toast.'

I considered how it might feel to hit my system with scratchy toast. 'No thanks.'

'Are you warm enough?'

I'd opened the windows wide, to cool me down, before burying myself under my quilt when I'd started to shiver. 'Maybe you could close the windows.' I suggested.

I was very glad I'd spent two hours tidying up, this morning. At least she didn't have to scramble over a heap of dirty clothes to cross the room.

'Tummy bugs are usually done in twenty-four hours,' she said, full of encouragement.

'I don't think it's a bug. I ate some leftovers for breakfast. I'm pretty sure that did it.'

'You need to keep hydrated. I've brought some sachets of stuff over – they're full of magical things like salts and electrolytes to make sure you don't get all crampy and woozy-headed. I'll bring a jug up.'

'Ava, this is really very kind of you.'

'I bet you'd do the same for me. I know Una would've. She stayed over once, when I had flu and Luke had to go give a lecture.'

'Really?' I didn't recall Nanna mentioning it.

'Luke couldn't back out of the lecture because the money was already in the bank.' She sat on the chair in the corner, legs flayed like a colt. 'Am I talking too much? D'you want to go back to sleep?'

'No, it's nice having some company.'

'Good, it's really boring when the weather's like this. It's too cold for the beach and my best friend is away all summer. How old are you?'

'Twenty-seven. You?'

'Twenty in November.'

I resisted saying she looked younger. That's okay to say to someone in their forties but never at her age.

'What are you studying?'

'Astrophysics.'

Jeepers – what cauldron did she come out of? 'Wow. You must be brainy like your brother.'

She shrugged. 'We just have that analytical, scientific way of thinking. Mum was the same.'

'What did she do?'

'She was a research chemist.'

On cue, a chemical reaction within me emitted an ominous gurgle.

I sat up. 'Could we chat some other time? I need to go,' I said, swinging my legs out and feeling decidedly wobbly.

'Sure. I'll just go fix you that magic water and leave it by your bed.'

'Thanks, Ava. You're an angel,' I said, blowing her a kiss.

'Yeah, Luke said you're into angels. Neat. I'm looking forward to seeing them.'

'You will,' I said. 'Oh, and could you feed the cats, please? There's stuff in the big cupboard.'

'Sure.'

I heard her humming as she went down the stairs. She was such a cheerful little pixie.

I ate nothing out of respect for my over-stressed stomach. I did, however, work my way through the jug of magic water. It tasted like tears. I'd shed enough of those recently to know.

The toxins were kind to me, in that they forced my exhausted body into a long and undisturbed sleep until Rodin and Gaudi attended to my early-morning massage. Feeling hollow but stable, I started my day with a shower, followed by a generous application of my lightest scented body lotion. No longer did nausea have me wrinkling my nose at any pungent pong, so the fragrance actually added a little zing to my world.

I checked the sell-by date on a yoghurt before I ate half of it.

I wandered over to the studio to take a look at Morael. He was ready for a little burnishing, here and there, so I whipped the rubber kidney out of the toolbox and set to work. It's not especially arduous work but within minutes, I was huffing with exhaustion and my limbs trembled unhelpfully. So I had to wrap him up again and toddle back over to the house, where I flopped onto the sofa and hit the ON button for the TV. An hour of reality nonsense later, all seemed well in my stomach so I headed for the kitchen and finished off the yoghurt, and risked two mouthfuls of a banana.

Outside the kitchen window, Ava appeared. I beckoned her in. She had a couple of magazines with her. 'Feeling better?' she asked, parking the glossies on the kitchen table.

'Much, thanks. Can I make you a cup of coffee?'

'S'okay, I can't stop, we're going to pick my friend up in a minute.'

'Ah, the one from uni.'

'Briony, yeah. I just wanted to check you hadn't died in the night, or anything more sinister.'

'More sinister than dying – what did you have in mind?'

'I dunno, eaten by the cats, vaporised by aliens from Uranus.' She squeaked with laughter. 'Sorry, sick joke in the circumstances.' All the same she couldn't hold back another chuckle. For someone so cute-looking, she had a very gothic take on the world.

'As you can see, nothing so extraordinary.'

'Great. Well, come out with me and Bryony sometime. I guess you haven't really got into the social scene here, yet?'

'No, I haven't. Thanks, I might do that when I feel better.'

She gave me a double thumbs up. 'Cool.' Then she slapped the magazines and said, 'Hope you enjoy celebby trash, there's loads in these. See ya!'

And off she went, leaving a whiff of Patchouli in her wake.

The summer had not given up on us, after all, and sunshine was slanting through the window across the dresser. I took the rest of my banana and the phone outside to the swing seat and called my treasured other half. We'd only managed texts over the last twenty-four hours – chiefly because I didn't think the sound of barfing set the right tone for a romantic phone call.

My phone rang. 'Hey, babe,' Rupe said. 'Saw your text last night – how're you feeling?'

'Better. Thanks. How's the building of your dreams coming along?'

'Nightmare, babe. Nightmare. Planning department's proving tricky. Been a real strain.'

'Aw, that's a shame. You're coping though?'

'But it's a pain in the arse.'

I waited a moment, to give him chance to ask about my situation.

'You'd think that a planning department would have its rules laid down, wouldn't you? But d'you know what? The right hand doesn't know what the left hand's doing. One guy says "okay" the next says, "Ooh, no can do." It's a bloody joke.'

'Very frustrating.'

'You're not kidding. Anyway, how are you – how's the guts?'

'Better.'

'So, you're still as gorgeous as ever?'

'Yes,' I said through a sigh.

'Missing me?'

'Of course.' I could feel a lump building in my throat.

'But you're managing without me?'

'Only just. It's not easy.'

'Oh, babe. I hate to say this but…'

I was preparing myself for one of his corny McKenzie jokes, like, 'You'll have to put up with my constant advances for a whole fortnight.'

However, what he actually said was, 'I'm not going to make it down this Friday.'

I swallowed the lump. 'Why?'

'This project is a toughie.'

'But you had a fortnight booked.'

'I know but, thanks to the planning department, we need to rethink some fire exits and wheelchair access, and I have to be on site.'

'So, when will you be down?'

'I'm looking at the end of September.'

'What? That's four weeks away.'

'I've got Rory's stag do, remember?'

'Dublin.'

'Yeah. I wish I wasn't going. Apart from the expense, it's all that keeping up with the Beer-neckers I'll have to do.'

'Then don't go.'

'Like that's going to happen!' He let out a little laugh. 'No, I'll just have to go through with it.'

'Big personal sacrifice,' I grumbled. I was doodling on the notepad – a series of hard, square boxes casting dark shadows.

'Anyway,' he went on, 'Why don't you jump on a plane and come up here? You love Edinburgh. You can indulge in some retail therapy while I'm up to my bootstraps in Scottish mud.'

In My Old Life that would have been easy. Easy and fun. 'Rupe, I'm not sure they fly from the island to Edinburgh.'

'Go to Southampton, then.'

'I can't afford to.'

'What? Gigi, you can afford the flight, it'll be less than a hundred quid.'

'I can't.'

I'm not sure whether I heard a 'tut' at the end of the line, but there was definitely a sigh. 'D'you want me to buy you a ticket?'

I thought about the shopping I wouldn't be able to afford to do; the ready-meals I wouldn't be able to buy; my cats who needed looking after.

'No, but thanks.'

'Why not?'

'Rupe...' Emotion was surfacing as I tried to form a sentence that wouldn't sound too self-pitying yet I knew would be. Why hadn't he just asked about my dad, about my situation? 'My life's turning to shit in my hands,' I blurted out, followed by a checklist of all the debts, repossessions and uninvited misfortune recently visited on me.

Finally, he said as soothingly as he could, 'Okay, okay, okay. I didn't realize. You haven't said anything before.'

Hadn't I? I thought I'd at least hinted at it. Maybe he hadn't really believed it any more than I had.

'But the house is yours, isn't it?'

'Yes.'

'Well, sell that then. You don't need it. Sell it and move back to London.'

I knew he was being practical. And he was right. I didn't NEED the house but I WANTED the house. I wanted the future I'd planned out. I wanted to fulfil Nanna's dream for me. My dream for myself. She'd left me the house because I loved being there, and she knew I wanted to build a studio. She'd only needed the spare bedroom to paint in. She loved how I'd inherited the family's creative gene.

'I'm not going to sell it, Rupe,' I said quietly.

'There you go! Heart ruling head, as per... You get too emotionally attached to stuff, Gigi. Sell the house and buy something up here. It'll be cheaper than London and closer to me.'

It was sweet that he wanted me near him. Maybe he was right – why be so attached to bricks and mortar when my real attachment was to Nanna? If I sold the house, it was still her money I'd be using for my home, it would just be a different home.

The hard square boxes in my doodles had been augmented with pointy roofs, a central door and four windows.

'Are you suggesting we move in together?' I asked.

There was a pause. 'Ultimately, I suppose that's where it's going.' There was a clatter in the background. 'Morty, you plank!' he yelled at his flatmate. 'Sorry, babe, gotta go. Morty's just wrecked my model.'

I could hear Morty burbling apologies in the background.

'Oh...okay,' I said.

'Catch you later, right? Love you.'

Before I had chance to confirm what he meant by 'later' he hung up.

I pushed the scrawled notepad aside and studied the knots in the table top. They were oval, dark, swirling. I traced my finger round the largest one; around the outside first and then stirred around into the middle and back out again. Nature was remarkable in its subtle but effective designs for life, growth and survival.

At college, I'd been torn between pursuing wood as my chief medium and clay, but had settled on clay because it was more malleable, more at my mercy.

With wood, you need to go with the flow, follow the grain, not fight it. Yet I loved the feel of wood. I loved working with it, and giving in to the call of its structure. When I worked in wood, it surprised me. I surprised myself. I felt more at one with nature when I worked with wood but with clay I felt in control of nature. I'd never considered myself a control freak but if I wanted to create the image in my mind's eye, I knew how to make clay work for me.

What a pity I didn't have the same grasp over my life.

Chapter 13

'Luke, are you ready?' Ava called to her brother as she eyed the kitchen clock. 'Briony will be getting off the cat in precisely eighteen minutes.'

'Right,' he said, tossing his car keys in the air.

'Can I drive,'

'No way. Not if you're in a hurry. Those L plates stand for Learner not Loony.'

On the way, he decided to broach a subject he suspected might be a sticky one. 'I don't mind you making friends with Gabriella but be careful. It's only a matter of time before Freddy turns up, and we don't want a repeat of last summer. At least, I hope you don't.'

'You needn't worry. I'm over him.'

'Good.'

'He taught me a great lesson.'

'He did?'

'Love at first sight is a load of B.S. right?'

'You thought it was love?'

She shrugged. 'I did at the time. I thought he was perfect: funny, enthusiastic, good-looking.'

'Next door…'

She laughed. 'Exactly.'

'So you're not still waiting for him to come back?'

'One hundred percent NO!'

'Any cool guys at UCL?'

She smiled. 'Maybe.'

'Maybe, huh?'

'Don't worry, I'm not gonna throw myself at any

of them. That's another thing I took from my experience with Freddy. From now on, I'm taking things slowly.'

Luke smiled to himself. That was music to his ears.

The catamaran had already docked when they arrived. Ava left her brother parking the car while she watched out for Briony. Despite everything she'd just said, he couldn't help wishing Freddy would stay right away from the island.

'Wow!' Briony declared, as Luke drove slowly down the old wooden pier. 'This is different. Are we really over the sea?'

'Neat, isn't it?' Ava said, proudly.

'And there's even a train!' Briony trilled, watching the carriages on the parallel pier travelling along. 'How cool is this?'

Luke nodded. 'Gotta admire those early engineers.'

'It must be, like, a hundred years old.'

'Try two hundred.'

Briony clutched Ava's arm. 'Is it safe?'

'Nope. Could collapse at any time.'

'You're kidding, right?'

Luke glanced in the mirror and smiled. 'Don't worry. It's safe.'

Briony settled back in her seat. 'Any sign of Freddy?' she asked Ava.

Luke's jaw clenched. Ava answered, 'No. I'm so over him but...that doesn't mean I wouldn't like to ram his balls into a nuclear reactor and hit Ignition.'

'Euw – nice concept.'

***

I'd not baked for years but it all came back to me as I lined loaf tins with greaseproof paper. Nanna and I used to bake when I was little – biscuits or butterfly

128

buns mostly, but sometimes date and walnut loaf or banana bread.

Who first thought to put courgettes in cake? I wondered as I grated them down. They're hardly up there with chocolate chips or glace cherries.

My phone rang. I grabbed it and hit speaker. It was Rupert.

'How's the light of my life?' he asked.

'Good thanks, much better.'

'You sound a long way off, where are you?'

'Sorry. I'm baking courgette and lemon cake.'

'You're baking?'

'Yes.'

There was a funny sort of noise from him. I couldn't see his reaction but I sensed a look of disbelief crossing his face; possibly underscored by disapproval.

'It's quite a common past-time. People have been doing it for years.'

'Just not you, babe. You're not following in your old Nan's footsteps and doing charity teas, are you?'

Like that would be a small crime. 'D'you know, Rupe, it's not a bad idea. Networking. Getting my name out there as a sculptor and guest house...thingy.'

'Landlady,' he offered, sounding distracted. 'Look, what are we doing over Christmas?'

'Christmas?' Unlike most families, who gather together for the festive season, come what may, we – the Gill-Martins – were a fragmented bunch. Some years Mum wanted to see us, some years she didn't. The years she did, we had to fly out to Biarritz and endure at least one drinks party a day with her arty friends. I didn't mind but Freddy was easily bored.

She wouldn't come back to the island. She and Nanna, despite both being creatives, were not what you might call 'bonded'. Mum had always been a little rebellious and Nanna didn't approve of her selfishness.

These days, Dad liked to spend his Christmases skiing with two old buddies, or sailing somewhere exotic, which suited me, as my preference had always been to spend it with Nanna – but at Christmas, you don't always get what you want. Last year, before she became so weak, I'd already agreed to spend it in Glencoe with the McKenzie clan – a rowdy bunch. I'd regretted it too. Other people's Christmases are never the same as your own.

'How d'you fancy skiing in Verbier? Simon's booked a chalet for twelve. It'll be great.'

Skiing. One of the most expensive holiday options on the planet, after a Virgin flight to Mars. And over Christmas it would cost twice as much.

'Can I think about it?'

'Think about it? Why – do you have a better idea?'

I drew a very deep breath and stared at the wind-chimes outside, as they swayed in the sunshine. 'I'm sorry, Rupert, I just can't think that far ahead.'

'Right, well I'm going to say yes for both of us.'

'How can I pay for it?'

'That's what my trust fund's there for, babe. We'll have a great time. Better than last year.'

I couldn't be bothered to argue with him. Last Christmas had been a full-on, alcohol-fuelled McKenzie Christmas – booze in everything and at all times of the day and night. Booze led to frayed tempers and unspeakable rows, which generated more boozing. Fourteen Scots and twelve Assorted-Others, living cheek-by-jowl in a rented castle. Hardly a moment of the day passed when somebody wasn't airing their opinion or defending somebody else's.

And they loved it!

I confess, I'd originally thought it might be rather nice, celebrating with a big party in a remote highland castle – all heather enhanced walks with the possible chance of snow.

Wrong.

The rain had been relentless and frequently horizontal. And the central heating was on the blink.

Instead of relishing a festive Scottish carnival, I missed the tranquillity of Bluebell Farm. I missed Nanna's Christmas Eve soirée for her local friends. I missed snuggling around the fire, with mulled wine, to watch *The Sound of Music* – yet again – and singing all the songs at full volume. I missed walking along the lane to Midnight Communion, followed by sherry and cheese scones served from a trestle table at the back of the church. Most of all, I missed doing Nanna's annual Christmas jigsaw puzzle. Once the turkey and beef lunch was over, the dining table would be cleared and the year's jigsaw puzzle box cracked open. The dining room became the jigsaw room until the last piece had been popped into place. All other meals were eaten in the kitchen or around the fire. I spent many a calm and happy hour, poring over a jigsaw with Nanna.

Yes, those were the best Christmases.

'So, I'm putting our names down, okay? The break will be good for you. It's something I thought you might actually look forward to, for heaven's sake.'

There was no messing with the bold, strong McKenzies.

'Okay. I will. Thanks.'

'Good. Now, take care of yourself. I'm going to need you in fine fettle when I next come down. And you need to get that house on the market and move up here. Pronto!'

'Ho, ho.'

As I stirred the cake mix, all I could think about was Christmas at Bluebell Farm. Now the prospect of a skiing holiday loomed expensively in the future, all I wanted to do was make Christmas here – with Rupert. Even Dad and Freddy. Maybe Fran would come over, too. Perhaps Luke and Ava would like to join us. I already had visions for how to decorate the table. And the tree would go in the hallway, like it always did. Nanna's collection of beautiful glass baubles was still in the loft. Some of them, she'd painted herself.

But it wouldn't happen would it? No Nanna. No Dad. Rupe wanted to ski and Fran probably had plans of her own. Assuming my neighbours were busy, that would leave me and Freddy – unless Freddy was still abroad. Hell! It might just be me and the cats.

I sighed. It was a million miles from anything Rupert would ever want to do.

The cakes turned out well. I added juice from one of the puckered lemons to the icing and smeared it over the top. Hard to know if they were up to Nanna's high standard but my helpful neighbours were getting one, anyway.

I peered out of my bedroom window and saw Luke's car was there.

Good. I just had to deliver my peace offering and then I'd be re-planning my future – with or without Bluebell Farm. I grabbed a cake, wrapped it in foil and wandered round to Rookery Cottage.

I could see Luke was packing a cool box into the back of his car while his sister stood beside him with some sandwich boxes. She looked up and grinned at me. 'Hi, Gigi. Feeling better?'

'Loads better, thanks. I made you some cake.' I looked at Luke. 'It's to say thank you for the veg. you brought me, and to you, Ava, flying in like the Red Cross. I really appreciate it.'

Luke smiled. 'You didn't have to.'

'I wanted to. I also wanted to apologize for being such a moody cow when you came round. I'm not usually like that. It's just that it's been…'

'S'okay. Don't worry about it. And thanks for this.' He took the cake off me.

'Can't promise it'll be as good as Nanna's.'

Ava moved alongside him and said, 'We're going over to Compton Bay to watch the sunset.'

'How lovely. It's a great night for it.'

'Wanna come with us?' she asked, waving the boxes. 'We've got a picnic.'

'Oh, no, you're okay. I wouldn't want to intrude.'

'You won't be. It's an invitation,' she continued.

'I was going to do some ironing.'

'Are you kidding? Dump the ironing. Come with us. The more the merrier, hey, Luke?'

Luke smiled. 'Sure. We've room for another one and plenty of food.'

I did have ironing to do, and I was pretty tired.

'We've chilled the Pimm's,' she added. 'Please come. I've got my friend Briony with me, so you can keep Luke company.'

He huffed out a laugh. 'What an offer! Take your time deciding, Gabriella.' He headed back to the house, taking the cake with him.

'Come on, Gigi. You know you want to.'

'If you're sure?'

'No. You're right, you clearly need domestic chores to brighten up your day. Duh! Of course I'm sure.'

'Okay. I'll just grab a few things and lock up. See you in a mo.'

Chapter 14

Luke saw Gigi trotting down the drive. He was carrying a pair of beach chairs under one arm and a bunch of mint in the other hand. His sister was grinning at him. 'What's so funny?' he asked.

'Nothing. Gigi's coming with us.'

'You didn't give her much choice,' he said, lifting the chairs into the back.

'I was just being neighbourly. It'll stop you feeling like the odd-one-out.'

'I was feeling just fine, Ava.'

'She's very pretty, and she's the right age for you.'

'Is that so? And with a boyfriend all of her own.'

'I know. But he lives in Scotland and I doubt he owns a private jet. So he won't be around much.'

Luke shook his head and smiled. 'What kind of person are you, young lady, trying to come between a girl and her boyfriend?'

'I'm only thinking of you,' she stressed. 'We've been here three years and you still haven't had a proper girlfriend.'

'I never said I was looking for one.'

'All you do is work and play ice hockey. That's hardly the activity of a well-rounded human being.'

He ignored his sister – he'd heard it all before – and went back for two more beach chairs. When he returned, she was leaning against the car. 'Are you still in love with Crystal?' she asked, placing a hand on his arm.

He looked at her for a moment. 'No, Ava. I am

not.'

'Sure?'

'Positive.'

Briony trotted out from the house with a huge inflatable beach ball and some badminton rackets. 'Are we taking toys?' she asked.

Luke grinned. 'Why not. My sister's very good at playing games.'

'Briony, in fifty years time, my brother is going to end up perched on a rock, grey hair down to his knees and chomping his gums. They'll call him Old Man Luke – or more likely, The Old Fossil.'

'If you don't button it, Ava, you'll be lucky to make it to fifty yourself.'

'I'm so looking forward to this picnic,' Briony said, pushing the ball on top of the hamper. 'Sitting on the beach, watching the sunset – what's not to like?'

'Exactly, Briony.' Luke glanced at his watch. 'Right, well, if we don't set off in the next half hour, we'll be eating this lot in the dark.'

***

What a reprieve! One less night on my own, fretting. What on earth could I donate to the picnic? There was no chance of me passing cat food off as rustic pâté – not on this occasion. Simon had tried at a Freshers' Week party and been thrown into the river for it. I peered in the fridge and pulled out the last unopened box of cheese. I'd been saving it for a special occasion. This would be it, then.

Ava and Briony piled into the back of the car, which left the front seat for me.

The girls were very chatty, which kept me from thinking thoughts I'd rather not think. I seriously didn't want to have those thoughts to think.

'Why do you want to live here, and not in London?' Briony asked. 'I'm from a little town in Norfolk and I couldn't wait to get into a city. There's so much more going on.'

'That's the trouble,' I said. 'In a city, there's so much going on, it clouds my mind. I can't think. Here I don't have to try and block out the noise and the mayhem. It's peaceful here. I like it.'

Plus, it was full of lovely memories and happy times; my most settled times – even if they came in short spurts. There was a lurch in my stomach as I remembered my future days here could be numbered.

'I hear what you're saying but I'm with Briony,' Ava chipped in. 'There's loads more to experience over on the mainland.'

'Agreed.'

'Luke loves the island, don't you?' she added.

He glanced at her in the rear-view mirror. 'It suits me because my work is here. I'm not really a big city guy.'

'Ever lived in a city?' I asked.

'We used to live just outside of Ottawa.'

'Big change – from Ottawa to St Helens.'

He nodded, and focused on the summer-heavy traffic heading out of Newport.

The girls in the back had suddenly gone quiet, with their heads down, studying their mobile phones. In the silence, an image of Dad whirled into my mind. I saw him urgently trying to sort out his finances; pacing the floor of some Spanish legal office; hanging his head in despair.

'So, the island is good for palaeontology but where could you go next, I mean, when your work finishes here?'

'I think I'll stay put, for a while, although South Africa would be interesting.'

'Too hot,' said Ava.

On we travelled, into open countryside, between fields which curved like huge velour cushions on either side of the road.

'Don't you feel there's something very safe about the island? Like nothing bad could happen here?' I asked.

Luke glanced across at me, his dark eyebrows heavy over his eyes, and then returned his gaze to the road. 'I can see how it might give that impression.'

Briony chimed up from the back, 'Yeah, I can't imagine it being a big draw for terrorists.'

'No. It's already been colonised by the Saga-louts!' Ava added and they both snickered with laughter. 'Hell's Grannies on prescription meds.'

Ava put her hand on Luke's shoulder, 'Don't succumb, big bro. Don't give in to the temptation of garden centre teas and rambling with the over sixties. Stay young!'

He looked at her in the mirror. 'I didn't hear you complain about that slab of chocolate cake, the other day.'

'That's the trouble, temptation is everywhere, Luke. That's how they reel you in. But at least I know I'm going back to London in a few weeks. They won't come after me, there.'

I laughed. 'I love London, too, but whenever I come here, it's like all my planets line up. After a few hours, all my emotional kinks and energy wrinkles seem to iron out.'

'Wow! You do like it.' Briony said.

Luke spoke, 'You kids have no appreciation of the

finer things in life.'

'Speaking of which, Luke, I'm planning a cocktail and sushi party for Ava's birthday. Will you come up for that?'

'Sure, if you can bear the Old Fossil turning up.'

''Course we can.'

He inclined his head towards me, 'They're hoping I'll pick up the bill.'

'We are sooo not,' Ava protested. 'We're all dibbing in.'

After a moment, some peculiar urge gripped me so I asked, 'How old are you, Luke?'

'Not as ancient as he looks,' Ava piped up.

'Twenty-nine.'

Bloody hell! Ava was right. I stole another good look at him. His skin was pretty weathered. I guessed it was from all the beach combing he did. But it was the beard, in fact, the total lack of personal grooming which aged him.

The shock stymied any further questions from me, and I settled back into the seat to watch the scenery roll by.

***

Luke stepped out of the car and inhaled the fresh evening air. He thanked his lucky stars he'd found a job in this fabulous microcosm of the British Isles. His sister didn't get it yet, might never get it. But the island had been exactly what he'd needed.

What Gigi had said struck a chord: the island was a place of safety. Although that must surely be a recent viewpoint. Didn't the throb of city life course through her veins?

Interesting.

They each carried stuff down the wooden steps to

the beach and made camp over to the left. There was a bunch of other people, scattered across the sand, some barbecues were already alight. It was a balmy evening. Any breeze that had existed earlier was gone. Charcoal smoke hung in the still air, along with sausage and burger smells.

Gigi gamely joined in with the banter as they set up their pitch but there was something detached about her. She smiled when spoken to and she responded enthusiastically but there were moments when she looked stiff with anxiety. And, when her phone rang, she snatched it from her pocket before pacing several yards away to take the call.

'Damn,' said Ava, 'bet that's the boyfriend.'

Luke gave her a deadly look and sat down. Moments later, Ava whispered, 'Looks like the lovers have finished. She's obviously devoted to him. Never mind, Luke, there's somebody out there who'll just love your weird, free-spirited take on life. You might even find one who likes your beard...not.' She coughed the last word. Briony giggled, while Luke raised his sunglasses and looked at his sister beneath lowered lids.

'What?' she said, innocently, as Gigi joined them. 'Tell me, Gigi, what's your opinion on beards?'

'Oh-oh.' Gigi looked from Luke to Ava and back again. She smiled at him. 'Something tells me you're in the firing line.'

'Just my sister being a pain in the butt, as usual.'

'I'm serious,' Ava protested. 'It's a perfectly acceptable question to ask a person. Some people like beards, some people don't.'

'And some don't care,' Luke answered, lowering himself onto one elbow.

'Hey,' Gigi said, holding her hands up. 'I'm happy to answer.'

Ava sat up straight, eager to hear her opinion. Luke wafted a fly away from the food in front of him and looked up at Gigi.

'I think a beard is an expression of personality. It can be a fashion statement, it can be like camouflage or maybe...' she tilted her head as she studied Luke, 'an act of rebellion.'

Luke allowed a slow smile to lift behind his beard.

His sister let out a groan. 'But would you want to snog a guy with a beard – and I'm not talking goatee, here, I mean that kind of fuzz – like...honestly?'

Gigi sat between the two siblings. 'Honestly, Ava?'

'Yes.'

She grinned, 'Honestly, I think you're being very unkind to your brother, who's brought us all the way over here to enjoy the sunset.'

'That's such a cop-out.'

'Ava...' Luke's tone had a warning in it. He didn't mind a bit of leg-pulling, he was used to it, but he objected to his sister being impolite to their guest.

Gigi leaned across to pick up the box of cheese she'd brought along. 'To be perfectly honest, Ava, I've never kissed any man with a beard so for all I know, I could be missing a spectacular sensual experience.'

That was one in the eye for his sister.

As Gigi took the lid off the box she recoiled instantly. 'Pwhoar! This Stinking Bishop cheese is really whiffy. Who wants some?'

Chapter 15

It was a beautiful sunset. In all the years I'd visited Nanna, I had never made this journey to West Wight to witness the spectacle. Nanna considered a trip to Newport, only ten miles away to be a bit of a trek. Compton would have been an expedition.

We four sat lazily on the beach, watching the light fade. Ava and Briony nearly missed the event, absorbed as they were in social media, while Luke and I became comfortable in the silence.

I so wanted to fully immerse myself in the experience of being bathed in the sun's final rays, but the topic of my father's predicament rather eclipsed it. I deliberately didn't chatter through the final moments, wanting to soak up as much of the atmosphere as I could. Ava, on the other hand, created quite a drama out of capturing the image on her camera to share with the world. She captured it several times, and none of the attempts was up to scratch. 'Duh! This camera's crap!'

'Ava, just find a professional shot on the internet and tweet that,' said Luke.

'Not the same. This is Instagram.'

He sighed. I felt like sighing myself.

She turned her attention to taking snaps of us, instead.

Luke looked at me, a wry, older brother look on his face. 'Wanna help me bury her in the sand – like, six feet down?'

'I think I'd rather bury the cheese.'

He chuckled.

All too soon, we found ourselves sitting in near darkness with a suddenly chilly south-westerly upon us, which was whipping up my shorts and under my collar.

'Time to go, girls,' Luke announced, standing up in one, neat and fluid movement.

We each gathered stuff together and trudged on up the beach to the steps.

'Luke, can we borrow the car on Wednesday to go to see the new Zac Ephron film?'

'Not Wednesday, no. I'm going training.'

My ears pricked up. What, I wondered, did a palaeontologist need to train for? Or was he training other palaeontologists?

'Tuesday, then?'

'Okay.'

Nosiness got the better of me. 'Are you training students?'

He glanced across at me. 'No. I play ice hockey. The season's over but I like to keep up with my training.'

'Ice hockey? I've never seen a game of ice hockey.'

He and Ava gasped in mock horror.

I grinned. 'What?'

'It's practically a religion in Canada,' Ava explained.

'The season starts in September. You could come and watch with Ava, before she goes back to Uni.'

'Thugs on ice. You'll love it.' Ava said.

He countered with, 'It's fast, it's noisy and it's great to watch.'

'Right. I look forward to seeing my first game, then.' And I did – if only to see this quiet, beachcomber speeding around an ice rink.

The darkest hours of the soul seemed to be a frequent feature, now. Except instead of watching the Insomniacs TV channel, I'd started pursuing every opaque avenue and cul-de-sac of my soul; every fear was examined and polished until I realised it would never shine.

Gloom. Gloom. Gloom.

Tired of the gloom, I'd put music on and fold back into my pillow, hungry for more sleep.

Eventually, I'd drop off and sleep through the dawn chorus, most days, and wake up with a heavy cloud over my head.

Money. I needed to earn some money.

When I was a student, friends of mine had done temp jobs at numerous stores and offices around London. It seemed if you were prepared to do anything clerical or practical, and could count, you were in.

Not so, it appeared, on the island. I'd rung a temp agency, first thing on Monday.

'I can type a bit, and I'm good with people,' I told Suze who was dealing with my enquiry, and had already listened to a run-down of my qualifications.

'Okay. And what about driving, do you have a car?'

'Not at present, but I have a licence.'

'HGV?'

'No.'

'Any NVQs in care work or catering?'

'No.'

'Did you say you've temped before?'

'No.'

'Any experience in legal offices?'

'No.'

'Have you been CRB checked?'

'No. Do I need that for office work?' I added, so as not to sound like a parrot with a one word repertoire.

'To be fair, we don't have a lot of temp jobs in clerical fields.'

'Really?'

'Over here, jobs are a more finite commodity than on the mainland. People tend not to move around so much. They get a job and stick with it.'

'Don't they go on holiday or get sick?'

'Yes, but you often find other staff take up the slack. And, of course, we have our regular temps – ones who've been on our books for years – and our regular clients often ask for them by name.'

'I see.'

'Why don't you drop by the office some time and have a chat?'

I didn't want a chat. I wanted a job. I suspected she only asked me to 'drop by' so she could check I didn't have two heads.

'I will. Thank you,' I said in my very best receptionist's voice, 'It's been a pleasure talking to you, Suze.'

I hung up and bit the top of my phone in frustration.

Fran, love the very bones of her, was coming down for the weekend. She'd called, to check up on my state of mind and, after hearing Rupert wasn't coming, insisted on visiting me instead.

'Are you sure? Wouldn't you rather I came up to

London?' I'd asked weakly, since I didn't really have the funds for transport. 'You've already made one trek over the Solent, this summer.'

'Loved it, darling, loved it! Anything to escape London in the heat. You know they're forecasting a scorcher? I'm bunking off Friday lunchtime. Thought I'd get the train rather than sit on the motorway. I downloaded the latest Marian Keyes to read. You can pick me up off the boat, can't you?'

I hesitated.

'Is that okay?'

'Yes. Definitely. Text me when you get into Portsmouth Harbour.'

A taxi couldn't be too expensive, could it? Bloody hell. The fallout from my father's shenanigans certainly made life complicated.

Not only that, Freddy was beginning to worry me, he was begging for money. When I explained I was in exactly the same boat, he'd said, 'Fuckit! I'll have to come home, then.'

'Like that's so bad?'

'Duh! What do you think?'

'I don't know. If the idea is so abhorrent to you, find a job out there and stay.'

'Find a job?'

'Bar work. Labouring. Lifeguard.'

'Accountant, Lawyer, Doctor. You sound like a parent.'

'That's not what I meant.'

'I could start flogging off my organs. Why not?'

'Freddy...'

'Forget it!' he'd snapped and hung up.

Today, after three days of silence, he was back on to me. Following his initial indignation and disbelief,

147

he was showing signs of panic.

'Rupe says I should sell the cottage.'

He'd spoken to Rupe? It seemed my one-and-only was pretty keen on selling the Gill-Martin property portfolio. He should join the family firm and become an estate agent.

'Don't sell it!' I snapped.

'It's called liquidating my assets, Gigi.'

'I know what it's called. But it is an asset. It earns you money.'

'In the holiday season.'

'Then let it out through the winter. You'll more than cover costs.'

'I don't want to be a landlord.'

'Then come home and live in it. Set up your music studio. You've always wanted to do that.'

'I don't want...' he paused. 'Actually, you've given me an idea.' There was a moment's silence at the other end of the line, then, 'Cheers, Gigi. Be good.' And he was gone.

I stared at the phone for a moment. What idea, I thought with a pang of concern, did Freddy have in mind, this time?

I spent the rest of the week phoning after every job vacancy I might qualify for, and suffering rejection at every turn. And my visit to the temp agency hadn't raised my hopes much further, either.

I also rang all pubs within a three mile radius. It would mean an hour's walk each way, possibly a taxi home but I was pretty desperate. Finally, one said, 'We could do with someone at weekends. Take the pressure off the rest of the team. Summer's our busiest time, you know.'

I did know. 'I've done bar work before,' I said,

eagerly crossing my fingers.

'Okay. Can you pop in and see us?'

'Certainly, when would be good for you?'

'Pop over now? I'm here till half-past three.'

I looked at the clock. Usain Bolt at full sprint would struggle to make it, and there was only one bus an hour.

'I don't have any transport, today. Are you there this evening?'

'Okay. Six-thirty, before it gets busy. I'll give you a trial, if you like.'

'Fantastic! I'll be there.'

I hung up, feeling grateful and triumphant. It was a beautiful day and I fancied a late afternoon walk – it should only take an hour, and I'd catch the bus home.

At twenty past six, I limped into the pub, wondering why on earth I'd not worn socks in my pumps. They certainly looked better on my feet, beneath the dove-grey cropped trousers but my poor toes had been rubbed raw.

'Alright, love?' asked Bill, the owner, as I hobbled up to the bar. 'You look like you could do with a sit down.'

'Thanks,' I said, parking myself on a bar stool.

'What can I get you?'

'We spoke earlier, about a job. My name's Gigi. I'm here for my trial.'

'Oh. Right.' He studied me for a moment – all manner of questions running through his head, no doubt, but chiefly: where had I left my crutches? 'So, what experience do you have?'

I rattled off a list of jobs I'd had as a student and, of course, one summer season at the yacht club.

'Excuse me for asking, but what have you done to

your back?'

'Oh, it's not my back. It's just my feet. I walked here,' I said, boldly raising them and looking down. Patches of blood were seeping through the canvas. I lowered them rapidly before he could see.

He looked at me dubiously. 'It can be tiring work, this. On your feet all night. Are you sure you're up to it?'

'Absolutely,' I lied. My feet were bloody killing me. What wouldn't I give for a bowl of warm water, a box of plasters and a large drink?

'Okay, well let's have you round here and we can go through the ropes. Prices are on labels by the taps and optics, okay?'

Much against my body's wishes, I stepped boldly off the stool and marched smartly round to join Bill, ignoring the screams from my feet. I made a big show of smiling and making eye contact. 'So lovely to meet you, Bill, and thanks for this opportunity.'

'No worries. Right. Let's see you pull a pint,' he said, nodding to the nearest tap.

'Sleever glass or jug?' I asked, keen to impress him with a bit of industry jargon.

A smile twitched on his face. 'Most of our customers like a straight glass.'

I took one from the shelf and slipped it under the spout, angled it so the beer poured down the side and pulled the tap. Slowly, steadily, the brown liquid filled the glass until I began to close the tap to restrict the flow and, with a final flourish, formed a froth on the top. Perfect. I'd done a good job.

With a customer-friendly smile, I lowered the glass onto the counter and looked into his eyes. He looked back into mine. And down to my feet.

My bloody feet.

'Oh, don't worry about those,' I said, grinning. I looked down. Yikes! My previously white but slightly grubby pumps were now mottled like toad skin. Why was I grinning? He'd think I was some sad masochist.

'I think you should do something about those. Wait here while I get the first-aid kit.'

It wasn't nice parting the canvas from my ruptured skin. Three toes had blisters which had burst, rubbed and bled; my right heel had another blister and the tongue of the left shoe had slipped and caused chaffing on the top of my foot.

That was a pair of shoes I'd struggle to resurrect – unless maybe I could dye them?

Bill was no paramedic so didn't minister to my therapeutic needs. He left me with the plasters and wandered off to sample the beer I'd just pulled. Maybe he didn't like the sight of blood.

'All done,' I said, finally. My feet felt slightly more comfortable once they were protected. I'd prised them back into the shoes with caution, and was horribly aware of the throbbing in a couple of toes. 'What next?'

Bill scratched his head. 'To be honest, love, I think you'd be better off at home with your feet up. I can't have you working behind this bar in that state. It wouldn't be right.'

'Oh, I don't mind. I'm robust. Honestly.'

'Sorry, love. I can't. It's probably against health and safety or environmental health or, I don't know, employment standards.'

'Right. I understand. Thanks anyway.' I turned to leave.

'Hang on a minute, you're not planning on walking

151

home, are you?'

'No, I can catch the bus.' I looked at my watch. The next bus was in fifty minutes.

He sighed. 'You go and sit round there for a bit. When Valerie gets here for her shift, I'll run you home.'

I didn't see the point in arguing. 'Thanks, that would be great.'

On the way home, I asked, 'So... do you think there's a chance of some work for me?'

'To be honest, no.'

'Oh.'

'I wasn't absolutely sure when you rang but when you turned up with bleeding feet, well... let's just say it wasn't a good sign.'

'Oh.'

'Nothing personal.'

'Of course.'

So, back to *Situations Vacant* for me.

The rest of the time, I was working on my latest angel – Peniel – who rules Friday, my favourite day. I've always loved Fridays because that's when the weekend starts. They used to be particularly special when I was heading off to the island. Those Fridays held much more promise than casual, down-the-pub Fridays.

I allowed myself to think back to the last Friday I'd spent with Nanna. I'd rung her just before I set off. 'Okay, Nanna; gin, tonic and cucumber – I've got it. No wine?'

'No wine, sweetheart,' her voice crackled down the phone.

'And you have plenty of food in the fridge?'

'Luke did a big shop for me, before he left.'

I smiled to myself. She didn't ask him to buy the booze, I'd noticed. 'Right. I'm catching the two-thirty ferry, so I'll be with you soon after.'

'I'm looking forward to it, Gabriella.'

'Me too. Love you heaps!'

We'd had a great Friday, too, pouring over the family album she'd built up over the years; Photos, certificates and newspaper cuttings. The Gill family archive in one huge lever-arch file. 'You ought to computerize this,' she'd said.

'But Nanna, this is much more special.' And it was – labelled beautifully in her spiky, italic writing, with entertaining little asides about the characteristics of my ancestors.

The following morning, I'd come down to a chilly kitchen, and no sign of Nanna. I'd found her in her bedroom – pale, panting and clutching her chest.

'It's just a touch of angina,' she'd said.

I didn't think angina would make her look so grey. 'Okay, Nanna, I'll make you a cup of tea.' And I had, but only once I'd phoned for an ambulance.

Yes, my last Friday with Nanna had a special place in my memory.

Thank heavens Fran was coming down, this Friday.

I told her to catch the train from Ryde Pier to Brading. 'You'll love it,' I said. 'I'll pick you up at Brading.' This wasn't strictly true. I'd booked a taxi to meet us at Brading. I'd done my research, it was a couple of quid cheaper from Brading to St Helens, and it was a nice walk across the fields for me. An hour's walk, to be precise. With socks.

The Met Office had been accurate in their

forecast. It must have been the hottest day of the summer, I arrived just minutes before the train pulled in, my t-shirt clinging to me like a second skin.

Fran appeared marginally less clammy than I did, with what looked suspiciously like a designer backpack slung over her shoulder and a sunhat the size of Texas. She stepped onto the platform, peering out from under the hat brim and grinned. 'Hello Island Person! This is so much more exciting than going to Berkshire.

I ducked under the hat brim to hug her.

She smelled as she always did, of Mitsouko. There was something so comforting in that, I could feel a lump swell in my throat. I really could. I needed to get a grip.

'Lovely seeing you, babe,' I said, before sniffing and pretending to block a fictitious sneeze. I stood back and gestured grandly towards the exit. 'This way. We have a car waiting.'

When she saw the taxi-man holding a card out of the window with my name on, she said, 'Where's your car?'

'Long story. I'll tell you later.'

Once in the refreshingly chilly interior of the taxi, Fran reached out and gave my hand a squeeze. 'So good to see you without the rest of the mob.'

I agreed. She and Sonia might as well have been joined at the hip since Freshers' Week. But after entering the real world, it was clear Fran had been growing away from her. I glanced across as she watched the scenery flickering by, and noticed sunlight casting shadows beneath puffy eye-bags, which she'd artfully smoothed over with concealer. From this I deduced her motive for visiting might have less to do with my problems and more to do with hers.

Of course, I'd told her all about Daddy's bit of bother in Spain. She was the one friend I trusted to keep it to herself. Sonia would have engineered an Oscar award-winning dialogue out of the situation, with an Oprah confessional spin-off. And probably a compassionate photo-montage in *Hello* magazine followed by a 'Day-in-my-life' article at the back of one of the Sunday supplements. Hell, with the right connections she'd try for a true-life TV series on a reality channel.

Typically, when we arrived home, Fran was most insistent about paying for the taxi. I confess, I let her. I would have done the same for her, had the Louboutin been on the other foot. Finally, as we sat on the swing seat, and the first, velvety mouthful of Merlot had passed over my tongue, Fran said, 'Let's not beat about the bush, Gigi, you are in the throes of a crap-fest. A crap-fest compounded by a shit-storm.'

'Fran, you are so right,' I said, taking another swallow of wine. After a moment I added, 'Tell me honestly, what do you think about my plans? You think I'm wasting my time, don't you?'

'No, I don't. I just know how long it takes to build up a new business. You'll have to keep a really tight rein on the finances. Ever run a set of accounts – like, a spreadsheet?'

I shook my head.

'It's astonishingly easy. I'll show you how. More wine?' she asked waving the bottle over my glass.

Looking at the world through Merlot tinted lenses, the edges blurred and the focus softened. I could do this, I thought. I would survive.

'Where shall we go for dinner?' Fran asked, rising off the swing-seat and stretching backwards till something clicked.

'I was going to do a pasta bake.'

Her eyeballs slid sideways. 'Save that for another night. Let's go out. Somewhere lively. My treat.'

An hour later, we were stepping out of the same taxi I'd ordered earlier, and heading into Olivo's Italian restaurant in Ryde.

'A bottle of Prosecco, please,' Fran requested before we'd even sat down.

I could feel my conscience blanch. Weeks ago, I'd have done the same. Now, I measured the cost against my budget restrictions. Even though I knew Fran didn't mind paying, and even though she was doing it to treat me and to make the weekend fun for us both, it didn't quite sparkle the way it was meant to.

But it wasn't just my conscience at work here. There was a false jollity to Fran's mood. I really wanted to know what dynamic was at work but since we had two more days together, I could hold off on quizzing her. For tonight, I'd let her cheer me out of my stupor. So I forced my own jollity and chinked glasses; reminisced over wild nights we'd shared through the years and urged her on in her mission to buck my spirits up.

Tomorrow, I would turn the spotlight on her.

It's never a good idea to start the day with a hangover. But Fran and I had reputations to maintain. I was brewing coffee when she sauntered into the kitchen, wearing a lime-green kimono. 'Coffee?' I suggested.

She nodded, dragging a limp strand of hair behind her ear. She still managed to look gorgeous, in a just-tumbled-out-of-bed way. Although her eyes seemed more clouded this morning, and it wasn't just the wine. 'Eugh,' was all she said, as her eyes took in the chef on TV, trussing a partridge.

I fixed coffee while she flicked through the channels, finally settling on a Little Miss Gorgeous beauty pageant. 'Ghastly,' she croaked, at a five-year old from Ohio in a copper-coloured sheath dress.

'Gross,' I added.

Rodin stretched his body along the windowsill before his head popped up and he peered out. I heard footsteps and headed over to open the door. 'Good morning, Luke,' I said, deliberately alerting Fran to check out my neighbour. A mug clunked on the table behind me as I assume she craned her neck for a better look.

'Hi,' he said.

I turned to introduce him to Fran, who cocked an interested eyebrow and formed her lips into a gentle crescent shape.

'Luke, Fran – Fran, Luke,' I said.

He nodded, 'Good morning, Fran.' Today, he was looking bulky in a check shirt and cargo shorts.

'I just wondered if you could use some wood – for the raised beds? Maybe some firewood for the winter? I'm helping a friend clear some timber. I could probably get you a load, half-price.'

I wanted to ask how much was half-price but instead gushed, 'Of course. Great idea. Thank you so much.'

'You're welcome, I'll drop it off later this week.' He turned back to Fran. 'Nice to have met you.'

I followed him out into the courtyard. 'Thanks, that's so thoughtful of you. I really do appreciate it.'

He nodded, just the ghost of a smile softening his face. 'No worries,' he said and set off down the drive.

Fran had moved from the table and was peering out of the window. 'What is that guy, a hermit?'

'He's just a free spirit,' I said. 'Not every man wears Alexander McQueen.'

'Evidently.' She sat back down. A gloom hung about her like a storm over the Alps. Maybe I was more sensitive to the signs, since I'd been doing so much of it myself – staring broodily into the mid-distance and suddenly brightening when asked a question.

Once I was fuelled with fresh coffee, I began. 'Fran, are you going to tell me about your own personal shit-storm?'

She looked at me warily.

'I can sense it, Fran. I think both of our vibrations are at an uncommonly low frequency – for all we know, we might be triggering an earthquake in Indonesia.'

She rolled her eyes.

'Come on, Fran. Talk to me.'

'Okay,' she said quietly. 'This is strictly between you and me. I haven't told another living soul.'

'Of course.'

She blew out a lungful of air, like she was preparing to weight-lift a hundred kilos. After a moment's pregnant silence, she said. 'I'm having an affair with someone at work. They're married.'

I felt a sense of relief that it wasn't a terminal illness. 'Okay. And I'm guessing you're in deeper than is good for you, right?'

She nodded, running her finger along the wood grain. 'Profoundly so.'

'Does he have kids?'

She didn't answer.

'Are you pregnant?'

She looked up and shook her head. 'No but she is.'

'His wife?'

Fran's hands spread in a gesture of resignation.

'Not plain sailing, then.'

'Oh, so not.'

'Who is he?'

'It doesn't matter. The odds are stacked massively against us – against me.' She ran her hands through her hair. 'So that's my shit-storm. I'll get over it.'

'Is that why you wanted to come away?'

She shrugged. 'Kind of. It helps that you live in a totally other dimension.' She smiled and leaned across to clutch my hand. 'Thanks for letting me visit.'

'Fran, you're welcome any time. Leave a toothbrush here. It can be your home from home. Leave clothes, if you like.'

She squeezed my hand.

'And if you ever want to…you know…bring him over for a quiet weekend, away from prying eyes…'

'Nope.' She shook her head fiercely and released my hand. 'No, that won't be happening. We won't be coming down here or going anywhere together. Flying solo is the way it's going to be. Till it's out of my system.'

'Is he showing any remorse?'

'Gigi, if it's okay with you, I'd rather not dwell on this, okay? I don't want to talk about it because it's never going to happen, so the less said, the better.'

'You will recover.'

'I know.'

I desperately wanted to know how she was going to cope at work, seeing him every day. I wanted to know how long it had lasted and if he'd given her a load of bullshit about leaving his wife. Had the wife deliberately got pregnant to hang on to him? All of the above. But I knew Fran well enough not to press her now. She'd tell me, when she was ready.

'I won't tell anyone, I promise.'

'I know you won't. That's why I'm here. You're one of the few people in this world I trust. Maybe the only one.'

With all the emotion stirred up in my life recently, it was hard not to blub at this declaration so I pulled a broad smile and refilled the coffee machine.

That was something else shortly to be denied me – decent coffee. Once this bag of coffee was gone, I'd be drinking hot water. That was okay, it was healthy, cleansing and totally without toxins.

I would be radiant.

Penniless but glowing.

'Today looks like a beach day,' Fran said. 'Okay with you?'

'More than okay. I haven't had a laze on the beach since I moved in.'

'Kidding!'

'Fact. I've got trashy mags,' I said, nodding at the glossies Ava had left, 'and at least thirty books on my kindle that need reading.'

Fran's brow puckered. 'I only meant a few hours, babe, not the rest of my life.'

Chapter 16

That evening, it was Ryde Carnival. Fran stumped up for a taxi. We were aiming for the bus but missed it – chiefly because we were having too much fun reminiscing and devouring the pasta bake. Since the bus only went once an hour, it was find a taxi or miss the parade.

'We can't miss it,' Fran said. 'You've been banging on about this bloody carnival for years.'

I felt a smidgeon of guilt. 'Fran, it's not exactly Rio de Janeiro but it is the oldest illuminated carnival in Britain.'

'Where's that taxi number. Buggered if I'm staying in on a Saturday night when there's a carnival on offer.'

The town was buzzing with people, and all the restaurants and bars were full. We hung around in the courtyard by Yelf's, drinking Pimm's and waiting for darkness to fall.

'They're on their way,' someone yelled, waving their phone in the air.

We all began shuffling out onto Union Street. In the distance, came the toots and whistles of the parade as it drew nearer. All eyes were on the top of the hill, waiting to see the first lights of dancers and floats.

It wasn't Rio but it was fun. 'The rest of the island must be empty,' Fran said, as floats full of people in elaborate costumes came by. Dancers, firemen, musicians, children. They were all out for the last carnival of the summer.

Finally, in the distance, we heard a foot-tapping beat advancing; drums, sticks, whistles. 'Yay! It's the Samba Band, I love these guys,' I said, grabbing Fran's wrist and pulling her further out see them. 'This is the best bit!'

Like every year when I'd seen them, the approach of the samba band stirred something in me. The band of men, women and children were giving it their all in search of percussive excellence. Deep bass notes were pulsing behind syncopated drum beats and cowbells. It was electrifying – Fran clearly thought so too, as she stepped from foot to foot. Then her shoulders joined in – her head loose on her neck. It was hard not to dance. The beat worked its way into my veins – possibly even my marrow. Yep, my hips were going counterpoint to my shoulders. And the hands followed. Fran began stepping around me, grinning madly. It was infectious. Two younger girls next to us joined in, along with an old guy with skin like crumpled brown paper.

Soon they were alongside us. They were the rear guard of the formal procession. Behind them were crowds of people who'd tagged along and followed them down the hill. A couple more sharp whistles and the band leader was crashing the beat out on his snare drum. Whoo! Another tranche of drummers joined in, followed by bells, sticks and more whistles.

So good.

So exhilarating.

I felt totally wired by life. Something I'd not felt in a very long time.

So much fun to be had – and it was free.

We were in the throng, moving down the hill. Out onto the esplanade we went and then, as I knew it surely would, the band leader rapped the edge of his snare drum a significant few times and it was all over.

'No!' Yelled Fran. 'Is that it? I want more!'

I was still bouncing, like the vibrations were continuing through my bloodstream. 'I so want to join that band,' I said.

'Go do it!'

'Not now.'

'Why not? Go speak to the main man.'

'I can't.'

'Why not? Ask him,' she said, steering me through the crowd.

'What if he wants me to audition?'

'D'you wanna join in or not?'

'I suppose I can just ask about how to join. That isn't, like, committing myself, is it?'

She propelled me towards the guy with the whistle. Head Honcho of Samba Central – the Ubergrupenführer of Beat – Man In Charge of Music. I stopped. I couldn't do it.

Fran pushed.

I could do it. And I did.

'Hi,' I said.

He didn't hear me above the hubbub.

Fran accosted him with a firm arm grip followed by a darkly beautiful smile. 'Hi, my friend here really wants to join your band. Can she?'

Dragging his eyes from her hypnotic gaze, he looked at me. 'Sure, why not? Sign up on the website.'

'Really?'

'Give it a go!' he said, smiling pleasantly before being distracted by half a dozen members of his crew.

'See, that's all there is to it!' Fran said.

'Thanks for making me.'

'You wanted to.'

I did. It remained to be seen whether I'd be any good or not.

Sunday dawned bright and clear but with a chilly pinch in the breeze. It felt like summer's last push before autumn set in. No hangover, thankfully.

'Where can we go for a walk?' asked Fran. 'Preferably somewhere that doesn't involve sand.'

'We could go over the fields to Seaview, or we could walk along the old railway line towards Bembridge.'

'Over the fields sounds hilly, we'll do Bembridge. I need to get my ten thousand steps in but I don't have to kill myself to do it.'

The old railway line was a good choice, we were shielded from the breeze by banks of grasses and brambles on either side. I pulled a carrier bag from my pocket. 'Blackberries!' I announced. 'It's only right to reap Mother Nature's hard work.'

Fran gave me a look. 'That's your Nanna talking, isn't it?'

I grinned. 'Sorry.'

'I don't mind but won't they get a bit soggy if we're carrying them around for hours?'

'You have a point.' I stuffed the bag back in my pocket. 'Okay, we'll do it on the way back.'

'Speedwalk?' she suggested, although I'm not sure a refusal would have been well received.

'Absolutely,' I agreed. Thanking the heavens my feet had recovered.

Off she set, pumping her arms like a boxer and I fell into step beside her.

I'd never made it to Bembridge so fast on foot.

Gratefully, I dropped onto a bench at the top of Ducie Avenue. The sun was fully up now, and the breeze had dropped. I could tell by Fran's refusal to sit, she was up for another mile or two of yomping. She knocked back half a bottle of water and handed it to me – Gigi, equipped for blackberrying and little else.

'We could get some fresh orange juice round the corner,' I suggested.

She glanced at her step-checking device. 'We've done just over five thousand, we're walking the same distance home. Okay.' She flopped down next to me.

We sat, our chests rising and falling like bellows. 'I think I'm getting fitter,' I said. 'All this walking has to be beneficial, doesn't it?'

'I bloody hope so.'

My phone rang. It was Dad's number. 'What's happening, Dad?'

'Well, we've got to the bottom of the debts, and I'm in the process of sorting out my finances so that all the investors can be paid.'

'Doesn't that finish you off?'

'Not entirely. It'll be tight but not unmanageable.'

'Are you sure?'

'I'm fine.' I could hear background chatter and I imagined him sitting at a small table in the shade of a street café. 'Nothing to worry about.'

'So you'll be home soon?'

'Once the debts on the land are settled, I'll get my passport back.'

'How are you going to manage that?'

'It'll come out of the business.'

'And Jose de la Torre?'

There was a pause. Dad had always ignored my

qualms about Jose. 'He's somewhere near Santander, I believe.'

I resisted saying, So the creep's done a runner, then? 'Right. Well, let me know when you're coming home.'

After the call was over, Fran turned to me. 'That's cheered you up – not.'

I leaned my head on her shoulder. 'Dad and I used to be much more in tune.'

'I think I know how you feel – like your world's just a little bit more likely to spin out of orbit?'

'Exactly. How did you know?'

'My dad's business went tits up when I was doing my A levels.'

'I didn't know that.'

'Luckily, one of his old school friends had some good connections and introduced him to the company he now works for. But for two months, Mum kept phoning me at school, every night – full of histrionics, doom and gloom – not exactly what you need when you're trying focus on your exams.'

'No.' Poor Fran. I'd never regarded her as having had a troubled ride through life.

'Come on then!' she said, nudging me off her shoulder. 'You mentioned orange juice, take me to it.'

We didn't just have juice because there was a very tempting tapas menu on the table. Fran scanned it. 'It'd be rude not to, don't you think?'

My mouth watered at the choices. 'What about the calories? Wouldn't that undo all the good work?'

'It's the weekend, darling, and I'm at the seaside, which makes it a holiday.' She ran her finger down the list. 'We'll walk back even faster with a few little treats on board.'

Something about my courtyard had changed. Stacked neatly by my back door, were about twenty lengths of timber. Not firewood, but straight planks of wood. Not new wood, either, they'd been used before. Luke, the wood nymph, had been busy.

'I'll have to go and thank him later.' I told Fran, who looked singularly unimpressed by the ramshackle load.

'Watch out – he might bring you more.'

'Good. What I don't use for vegetable beds, I'll save for winter.'

'Vegetable beds? This is news.'

I explained my moderate plans for self-sufficiency. 'Whatever floats your boat, Gigi,' she said with a smile and, possibly, some amusement. As she wandered out of the kitchen I heard her add, 'Gabriella Gill-Martin – next stop, Chelsea Flower Show.'

Fran booked herself a taxi to Ryde. 'You stay here and chip your seeds, or whatever it is you have to do. No, wait, maybe that's just peonies.'

'Get you! "Chipping seeds," indeed. What's that all about?'

'I'm a closet *Gardeners' World* viewer.'

Tidying up after Fran's visit, I had plenty of time to dwell on things. Fran was right, my world did feel uncomfortably unstable. First Nanna had gone and now Daddy was teetering on bankruptcy – possibly worse.

When I made it up to Fran's room, to strip the bed, I found a little gift-wrapped package on the pillow. 'Aw, bless,' I said, plopping onto the bed and feeling tearful. There was a note with it too. I opened

167

that first:

> *Thought these would really piss Sonia off.*
> *Even more appropriate now I know you're going to be*
> *a proper farmer.*
> *Thanks for being there.*
> *Love you to bits.*
> *Fran xx*

I pulled at the ribbon on the parcel and gently teased open the paper. It was a pair of earrings – bucket and spade earrings, to be precise. I smiled through my tears. Sonia would absolutely hate them.

Eventually, I tidied Fran's room and changed the bedding. I was determined to keep the bedrooms guest-ready. It was all part of my positive outlook – setting my intentions for the business ahead.

I glanced at my watch. It was nearly eight, Luke should be at home. I could pop round and thank him for the wood. Yes. I should do that.

Chapter 17

Chuck heard me coming and issued a few barks of greeting. I tapped at the front door, although it was a redundant gesture after Chuck's welcome. The dog bounded around to the side gate. He was soaking wet and shook himself enthusiastically – water droplets radiating out from his body. His hind legs lifted momentarily from the floor as he completed his routine, and panted happily up at me. Next came Luke.

Luke in damp cargo shorts and...well, that was it. Luke in damp cargo shorts and carrying an old towel, which he used to mop the rivulets of water coursing down his chest. A fine chest it was too.

'Hi,' he said. 'Sorry, just been washing the sand and salt off him.'

I nodded. Of course he had. I didn't imagine he stripped to the waist and dowsed himself with water for anything other than a practical reason.

Eat your heart out, Michelangelo, I thought. You missed this one.

He was fit. Seriously fit. What a waste, as Sonia would say: 'All buffed up and no-one to shag.'

An odd sort of clicking noise came out of my throat as I attempted a cohesive selection of words. I think what emerged was, 'NnGahenthanx.' I could be wrong. But that's close enough.

He continued to mop his moistened chest and peer at me.

I stared into his face, noting how dark his eyes

were – brown, almost black with tar-black eyelashes. 'The wood.' I said.

There.

Two words, and a gesture in the general direction of my home.

He nodded. 'It's just some old pallets. Thought you could use them for your raised beds.'

'Absolutely. Great stuff. Just wanted to say thank you.'

'You're welcome.'

'Thanks. Again.' My heart was beating uncommonly fast. 'Is Ava about?' I asked, I fancied a dose of her bizarre optimism.

'No, she's over on the mainland. She's gone to some Minecraft convention.'

'Really?' I didn't hide my surprise very well.

He smiled. 'Yeah, beats me, too. So all's quiet here.'

Exactly how he liked it, I imagined. Before I could think of something to say, he asked, 'How's things with your father?'

'Moving slowly.' I folded my arms. 'Yep. Slowly.' How could I describe my deepest fear that Dad could lose everything he'd ever worked for?

'And you?'

'Oh, I'm doing okay.'

'Una always said you were a strong girl.'

Not trusting myself to speak, in case my mouth contorted out of shape and my voice cracked, I managed a nod and possibly a wiggle of eyebrows.

He continued, 'Yep, what was it she used to say? "Gabriella's a lot like me, tough in gruelling situations." That was it.' He smiled, looking satisfied to have remembered.

Hearing Nanna's words, and imagining her saying them, whacked my already tender emotional core so hard, I gasped, and clenched my jaw to hold it all in and hugged myself even tighter.

I nodded, mute, and stared into the middle distance.

'Hey, wait there,' he said, wheeling round and heading back behind the house.

I hauled a few deep breaths into my lungs and leaned over the gate to fuss Chuck's soft ears. The only reason I was still there was to avoid a dramatic and conspicuous exit.

I sniffed quickly but it wasn't enough to stem a stream of tears trickling over my face. I wiped them away and sniffed again. I so didn't want Luke catching me like this.

***

Shit! He hadn't wanted to upset her. He'd thought repeating her grandmother's words would have bolstered her. Instead it looked like he'd scored a direct hit on a raw nerve.

And now he didn't have time to hang around and put it right. He had to be in Shanklin. Roy was waiting for him. He grabbed his t-shirt off the table and pulled it on. Heading down the hall, he had a moment's pause while he considered his next action.

'Right,' he said, opening the front door. Gigi was bent over the gate, fussing Chuck. 'What are your plans for this evening.'

'Oh, well, um…'

'Good. I've gotta go over to Shanklin. Why not come along for the ride?'

'I don't know…'

He knew. He knew she was upset and he wasn't

going to leave her in a state he was partly responsible for. 'Come on, I could use the company,' he said, almost laying an arm around her shoulder and thinking better of it. Instead he patted her shoulder with the back of his hand, saying, 'It's too good of an evening to stick around indoors. Come on.'

She followed him to the car. 'If you're sure you don't mind. You must have spotted I'm not at my sociable best, right now.'

'You and me both. This should be a blast,' he joked.

Focusing on the car, all she said was, 'Okay.'

He held the passenger door open for her, and noticed the watery eyes and pink nose. Maybe it would be best to park conversation for a while. 'I'll just make sure Chuck has enough water.'

As they drove through Bembridge, she suddenly said, 'I see your hockey stick's in the back. When's your first game?'

'Next weekend.'

'Cool.'

'You should come – if you're not busy,' he added.

'Yes. Maybe I could.'

There was a long pause. 'What's your sport?' he asked.

'I did a bit of gymnastics at school.'

'Yeah? Hence the Taekwondo and yoga. It's important to do something active, huh?'

She didn't reply but he noticed her head nodding very slowly.

It was a busy evening in Shanklin. The school holidays were finished but coach parties and holiday-makers would be heading over on the ferry for weeks, yet.

As Luke drove through the Old Village, Gigi rallied. 'This place always reminds me of holidays with Nanna. She used to bring us here as a treat. She called this The Resort.' Luke was pleased to hear a smile in her voice. 'Oh, and Shanklin Chine!' she said, pointing off to the left. 'We always saved that till the end of the holiday. We'd come down about nine o'clock in the evening, when it was all lit up. We'd walk down to the bottom, then she'd buy us chips, which we'd eat on our way back up. She said it was bad manners to eat whilst walking along the road, so we should make the most of it while we were young because we mustn't do it when we were older.'

Luke smiled across at her – this was better. He drove a little further before taking a left turn. 'Roy lives down here. I just need to drop some samples off before he goes over to the mainland.'

Roy lived in an old Colonial style Victorian house, with a glass-roofed veranda running along the front of the property. He came out of the front door as Luke pulled onto the drive. He looked like an ageing boy scout, in his khaki shorts and shirt with button-down pockets. He greeted them with a raised arm and a cheery, 'Hello, both!'

Luke stepped down from the old Jeep, and went to open the back door. 'They're all labelled,' he said, handing a large box over to Roy. 'There's a memory stick with the photos and database, too.'

'Excellent. Excellent. Just the job.' Roy stepped back. 'Sorry can't offer you a drink. Need to be off. Ferry's in an hour.'

'Do you mind if I leave the car here for a while? Thought we'd take a walk into Shanklin.'

'Absolutely! Park here any time you like. Most welcome. Most welcome.'

Luke went back to the driver's door and peered in at Gigi. 'Jump out. We can do the chine before it closes. No point coming all this way and missing it.'

'Oh. Okay,' she said, pulling on the door handle.

Luke introduced her to Roy as Una's granddaughter and his new neighbour.

'Jolly good. Jolly good. Met Una a couple of times. Smart lady. Yes, very smart.' He began backing towards the house. 'Enjoy your walk. Lovely evening for it. Lovely.'

As they set off, Luke said, 'You happy to do the chine, tonight, or would you rather just go for a drink?'

'Definitely the chine. I would never pass up the opportunity to do the chine. I love it.'

'Alright then. Let's do the chine.'

***

I hadn't visited Shanklin Chine for the last three summers. Nanna had become too frail to manage it, and I hadn't found any reason to go there. Silly really, it was only a short drive from the farm.

I always enjoyed the approach down Chine Hollow, it's a narrow lane, overhung with branches, leading down to the upper entrance. I must have visited it a dozen times during my life but it still gave me a magical sense of anticipation.

Luke paid for our tickets. There was no point in arguing since I had no money on me.

After a warm day, the chine was smelling green and brown; foliage and earth that had simmered gently in the late summer heat supported by a background theme of flowing water.

I walked down to the first wooden balustrade, and looked down into the chine. In amongst the lush vegetation, lights of different colours glimmered, reflecting off the glossy leaves and casting deep and contrasting shadows.

Luke came and stood beside me, his hands braced on the railing. I breathed in the musty air and let out a sigh. He said nothing – just took in the view as I did. After a few moments, I headed off down the path, which turned a couple of times before we reached the next viewing platform. We paused again. I said, quietly, 'I know man has been through here and installed electricity and lights but it still feels special; still feels secret and natural – just like it must have done all those years ago, when smugglers used to haul their loot through here.'

'Yep. Nature can be awesome.'

'You must see some wonderful things, doing palaeontology, don't you?'

'Sometimes I do. A lot of the time it's quite mundane but there's always the promise of something amazing.'

'The promise of something amazing. I like that.'

I looked up at him, just as he looked down at me. A little woosh of electricity passed through me; the kind that momentarily causes your internal lights to flare and your circuits to throb – albeit ever so briefly. Then you leap away from the source and move to a safer distance – or in this case, head off down the path. I stopped as I saw, in amongst the plants the wooden sculpture of fox. It nestled there, not quite naturally. 'Sweet,' I said.

'I bet you'd love to see one of your angels in here, wouldn't you?'

'I would. I'd love it.' I looked around. 'Now you've started me thinking.'

'What?' he said, smiling. 'What's going through your head right now, Gabriella?'

Right then I was thinking how nice it sounded when he called me Gabriella. I seemed to be developing a little crush on Luke. I'd have to be careful, it was three long weeks since I'd seen Rupert and it was screwing with my libido. 'I was wondering if there was one perfect location for an angel. Just a discreet placement – somewhere you had to really look to see it. I'd hate to turn this place into some pseudo celestial theme park.'

'Glory Hallelujah Gardens viewed through the Pearly Gates,' he suggested.

'Exactly! How vulgar would that be?' I looked around. 'People seem to think I'm making my angels as garden ornaments. I'm not but maybe I should.'

'Does it matter how people see them? Does an artist get any say in where someone hangs his pictures?'

'No.'

'What did you have in mind when you created them?'

I shrugged. 'I just wanted to depict their grace.'

'I think you do.'

'Thank you.'

It was there again. The look. The look that sparked my inner circuitry. And off I shot, off down the path and across a little bridge and on to another viewing platform which looked out to the ocean, now a steely grey, as the moon had arrived for the nightshift.

Dad was across the water, somewhere. Trying to sort out his life. Nothing I could do would help him. I really missed him – not that I'd ever seen much of either of my parents. Boarding school had made sure of that. But, after working together, Dad and I seemed to have formed a much closer bond. I came to understand the world he inhabited and by association – him.

'Would you like to walk down to the bottom and eat chips, or walk back up to the top?'

I smiled. 'Chips sounds good to me.'

'Me too.'

'But I have no money on me.'

'Forget it. It's a sad day when I can't stand a friend a bag of chips.'

'Thanks.'

He nodded in response and looked out to sea. With his long, curly ponytail and beard, he might have been a pirate. A pirate with the most intense and fascinating eyes. I think the beard accentuated them – like a picture frame can draw your attention to the focus of a painting. Another spark activated my system, and he wasn't even looking at me.

'When we were little, as soon as Nanna said, "It must be nearly time for chips!" Freddy and I used to race down to the bottom gate. I always won until Freddy shot up and grew longer legs. Chiefly cos he used to push me out of the way before I'd hit top speed!'

Luke grunted at that. He wasn't Freddy's biggest fan. He turned and began making his way down the path.

'Boys don't like to be beaten by their sisters, do they?' I asked.

'Depends if it's done fair and square. I'd have no problem with Ava beating me at something.'

'Ah, well that's because she's your little sister. You'd be proud of her, wouldn't you?'

'What's Freddy's long term plan?' he asked, a slight judgemental tone in his voice.

I sighed. 'Good question, I wish I knew the answer. But I think he'll be coming home, soon.'

'Home – to you?'

'No. I hope not, but possibly back to the island.'

'Una's cottage?'

I nodded. 'The holiday lets will be winding down, soon.'

'Then what's he gonna do?' There was a distinct sneer in his delivery. Freddy's conduct had been a lot for Luke to swallow.

I stopped walking and turned to him. 'Luke,' I started gently, 'I realise Freddy doesn't always make the best decisions, and he can be…a little self-serving…'

Luke really huffed at that.

'But he isn't a bad person. He had a much tougher time as a kid than I did.'

Luke's face looked grim. Now he was a mean pirate, I thought. He'd cheerfully run Freddy through with his cutlass.

I continued, 'Freddy isn't…' I halted. 'He's not quite as tuned in to other people's needs as he is to his own.'

Luke didn't react, at all, but I had a feeling there was a lot going on inside that darkly thatched head. A lot of words he didn't want to say. I couldn't blame him. He'd only seen one side of my brother and, if I'd been a big brother responsible for a little sister's welfare, I might have had similar thoughts myself.

'I know he acted like a complete shit to Ava.

Nanna knew it too. She nearly cut him out of her will, she was so angry.'

I noticed Luke's eyebrows move a fraction.

'Honestly. She was seriously pissed off with him.'

'I imagine she was.'

'Didn't she tell you she was?'

'Your grandmother was a very diplomatic lady. She was like royalty; I seldom heard her criticise anybody. That's one of the things I admired about her. If she didn't like a situation, she wouldn't complain, she'd do something about it.'

'You're right.'

He was so right. I'd never heard a word of complaint from her about my mother and how she treated the family. Nanna had just rolled up her sleeves and got on with the business of looking out for us.

He fixed me then with an intense look. 'She was quite an inspiration and a friend worth having.' There was a real warmth in his tone, a warmth which touched me intimately, yet in a platonic way.

'That's such a lovely thing to hear,' I said and spontaneously reached up and pecked him on the cheek. 'I'm glad you were her friend, too.' I stepped back, suddenly analysing whether kissing him might have sent out the wrong signals. If it had, he didn't show it.

'Then we're in agreement on that,' was all he said.

'Excellent,' I said, and set off down the path.

Nanna always used to take us along the seafront to a little café that did take-away chips. Luke suggested we eat at the pub at the bottom of the chine. 'I could eat some seafood, how about you?' he said.

'Good idea. Nanna wouldn't approve of us hiking

179

up the hill eating chips at our age.'

Chapter 18

We sat at a table outside, looking over the beach. We chose a seafood platter to share. 'With chips,' Luke added, 'let's keep with tradition.'

I learned about how Luke and Ava had lost their mother six years previously.

'That's really tough,' I said. 'How did you cope?'

He shrugged. 'You just do. Fortunately, I was working and Ava carried on with school.'

'But financially?' I asked – hitting on a subject very close to my own heart.

'My mother was a bright lady. She had a good job and put money into trust for us, and took out a good insurance policy.'

'And your father.'

Luke's eyebrows flickered. 'He wasn't really a family man. He first left when I was two, then he came back when I was eight. He took off again after Ava was born. Mum gave up on him after that.'

'I don't blame her, poor woman.'

He shrugged. 'I'd say she was glad to see the back of him. He was…' his eyes narrowed, '…let's just say, he was a bit of a bad lot; full of charm but totally unreliable.'

The antithesis of his son, it seemed.

'Where is he now?'

'Don't know and I'm not about to start looking.'

'Is he the reason you came to England?'

His response wasn't immediate. 'I came to England because the Wealden beds fascinate me, and the lecturing job was right up my street.'

'Right,' I said, not entirely convinced it was the only reason but happy to accept it. 'What did you do in Canada?'

'I worked in the petroleum industry.'

I was shocked and, I'm guessing, didn't hide it well, as he went on to explain, 'Exploration and analysis is pretty crucial for interpreting what's in the earth, and whether it's worth drilling.'

'Dinosaurs and oil – that's a weird combination.'

He tilted his head and looked at me in an inscrutable way. I was being dumb, obviously. 'Not entirely, if you take into account I wasn't actually studying dinosaurs at the time, but microfossils.'

'Tiny, ancient organisms?' I was catching on.

'Exactly. I was involved with biostratigraphy – which is how we look at fossils in layers of rock to give us a clue to the age when they were laid down. Once you know that – then you can analyse the potential for finding oil or gas.'

'But here you're into dinosaurs, right?'

He smiled. 'That's my passion. I teach more general palaeontology.'

At that moment, the seafood platter arrived. It was vast: crab, crayfish, squid and mussels.

'These look like they could have been around for millions of years,' I said, feeling smart, then spotting the look of dismay on the young barman's face. 'As a species,' I added quickly. 'He studies fossils for a living.'

'Ah, cool,' the guy said. 'Plenty of those around here. My granddad had a fossilised turtle shell from Bouldnor Cliff.'

Luke nodded. 'Interesting site. Not had access to

it, myself.'

'Yeah. I don't think he dug it up himself. He used to show it to me when I was a kid.' He thought about it for a moment. 'Yeah. Okay. Good stuff. Enjoy your meal.' And he retreated back into the pub.

I hadn't eaten since the tapas at lunchtime, it was all I could do not to grab the platter and run. Instead I deliberately watched what Luke had and took the same: a squid ring for him, and one for me; a scoop of crab for him, a scoop for me. God, he was eating slowly! Maybe I could distract him for a second and scoff a mouthful of chips. How did it go? 'What's that over there, Luke?' SCOFF! 'Can you see those girls skinny-dipping in the sea, Luke?' SCOFF! SCOFF! 'Look, Luke, they want you to join them...' SCOFF! SCOFF! SCOFF!

After a few moments of matching him, mollusc for mollusc, he sat back and gestured at the tray in front of us. 'You carry on.'

I looked from Neptune's finest to him and back again. Had my greed been that obvious? I could feel guilt flushing heat through my cheeks.

'Honestly,' he added, 'I ate earlier.'

'You did?'

He nodded.

'But there's loads here.'

'I'll have anything you can't manage. I'm just not that hungry.'

Given the green light to tuck in, it took a lot of self-restraint not to appear like the Guinness World Record Holder for the most seafood shovelled into one mouth in under a minute. So I indulged my appetite at a very modest pace, coohing my appreciation intermittently and pausing to remark on the bliss of late-summer evenings by the sea.

When Luke wasn't gazing out over the ocean, he threw the odd glance in my direction. I couldn't decide if he was impressed by my methodical attack on the banquet before me or amused. Exercising massive self-control, I left three squid rings, one crayfish, no crab and six chips. 'All yours,' I said, pushing the plates towards him.

I detected a slight tremor of his eyebrows. 'Sure you don't want any more?'

'Nooo,' I lied. 'I've eaten far too much already, it's so delicious. And such a treat. You go ahead.'

He squeezed a little more lemon juice over the squid rings, picked one up and folded it into his mouth, before sucking the juice off his fingers.

I dragged my eyes away.

Not because I wanted that squid ring, believe it or not, but because I suddenly found Luke unutterably intriguing.

As I stared over the darkened sand, I replayed tiny snapshots from the evening in my head: his chest glistening with water; his taking charge of my evening when I was feeling so low; the twinkle of his smile; the flicker of his eyebrows...

Rupert! Think of Rupert. Rupert and his tousled blonde hair – he looked pretty scrummy after a shower too. Yes, a couple more weeks and I'd be locked onto Rupert like Lego. Lego? I thought. No, like a limpet...a Clingon...a leech...

'Would you like anything else?'

The vision of my limbs wrapped around Rupert quite wickedly transferred to Luke.

As coolly as possible and without looking at him, I said, 'I'm fine, thank you. But you go ahead.'

'No, I'm done.'

I side-glanced his way, he was scrunching up his napkin which he then pushed into his empty glass.

Good. We'd be on our way home, now, and I could take my sex-starved body out of temptation's way. Apparently, it only took three weeks of abstinence to turn me into a twitching nympho. Who knew?

'Right,' he said, 'you ready for the climb?'

'Ready,' I said, rising off the bench and surveying the selection of other males on offer – just by way of research, you understand. I needed to know if I could be persuaded to hump anything with a pulse.

Nope. It was just Luke. Seemed I was pretty discerning after all.

We started off up Chine Avenue at a steady pace. It had become evident Luke wasn't hot on small-talk.

An ice-cream van was approaching slowly. The driver gave his *Greensleeves* chime a blast as he advanced on us. I don't think I drooled and I certainly didn't cast my eyes, doe-like in Luke's direction but his words, 'Fancy a 99?' was right on the money.

I grinned. 'That's a proper holiday treat.'

'Why not?'

He hailed the near-stationary van and I watched, in childish delight, as he ordered two 99s.

The Whippy man was feeling generous, judging by the heap of soft, swirling ice-cream he pumped onto our cones. Just the one chocolate flake each, though. He was generous, he wasn't slashing profits.

We carried on up the hill in friendly silence. Passing a family on their way down, we both stepped off the pavement and bumped into each other as we did so – Luke's warm arm firm against mine. 'Oops, sorry,' I said and deliberately did it again when we crossed the road a little farther up. My hormones were on auto-pilot.

But of course, he didn't react. He didn't barge me and laugh like he might have done had we been teenagers. There was no side-long, eye-holding flirtatious gaze.

I blushed at my shameful and misguided behaviour and walked briskly on, leaving at least half a metre between us.

Get a grip, Gabriella, my conscience grumbled.

'How're your business plans going?' Luke asked, once we were driving home.

'So-so. The Bide-a-while website has finally approved me and added a page for the farm. And Fran submitted a glowing reference. It probably didn't hurt that she's the Honourable Francesca Fforbes-White.'

'I guess that would impress some people,' he said.

Not him, I observed.

'I'm also thinking of harnessing the energy of social media.' And I would, once I'd tuned into the library's Wi-Fi, or possibly the pub's. I could see Rookery Cottage's router from home, but without Luke's password I couldn't take advantage of it, and I didn't think it polite to ask. If I were in London, I could connect easily to free Wi-Fi or 4G but the reception around Bluebell Farm suggested technology hadn't progressed much beyond two soup cans and a piece of string.

'You could also try proper person-to-person networking. Una had quite a crowd of friends and acquaintances you could tap into.'

'I know. I did wonder if I could hold a tea-party,

186

like she used to. Invite a few group leaders. I'm sure they're all burning to know what I've done to the farm, and I could use it as an opportunity to tell them my plans; give them a business card with the web address on.'

'Why not? Like they say – it's not what you know…'

'Exactly. Can't hurt, can it?'

Afternoon tea. I was guessing a Hob-Nob poked into the saucer wouldn't quite cut it with the chairpersons and secretaries of local societies. It would have to be finger sandwiches with the crusts cut off and scones.

Luke turned the car into my drive. I could have easily walked from his cottage but he had a kind of old-fashioned chivalry which I'd learned not to question. I quite liked it. Although if he'd seen some of the roads I'd walked in the early hours around Clapham, he might not have been so concerned about me negotiating the short distance from his gate to mine.

'Thanks for taking me with you,' I said, 'and for dinner. I really appreciate it. And you must come over here some time – I do a great pasta-bake.' And I did. It was becoming my speciality – 101 ways with pasta, veggies and herbs. It was astonishing how lemon and cayenne pepper could really zhoosh up a dish. Good old Nanna.

'You're welcome. And if you need a hand with furniture for your afternoon tea, I know the drill.'

'There's a drill?'

'Una used to borrow stuff from the church. I'm sure they'd be happy to help her granddaughter.'

'Ha! I never knew that.'

'Yep. We'll get you fixed up.'

I pushed open the door before jumping down. 'I'll hold you to that,' I said, grinning back at him.

He nodded. 'I'll just wait till you're safely indoors,' he said.

'Thanks.' I slammed the door and headed for the house, still smiling. The Universe was working for me again.

Chapter 19

One of the things Luke most enjoyed about life on the island, was the peace it offered. Peace, quiet and an unhurried life. A couple of nights later, he was sitting on his back lawn, watching condensation trickle down the side of a beer can, while Chuck lazed a few feet away, soaking up the last of the evening sun.

This little patch of English countryside was a far cry from the vast and rugged expanses of Canada. Yet recently, he'd been reminded more and more of home. Not the scenery but the emotions; emotions he'd locked down.

Emotions and disappointment.

He'd made a concerted effort not to think about Crystal. Crystal was the first and last great love of his life. Poised and intelligent, she'd been a cut above the girls of his neighbourhood. Her smile was beyond any smile of the girls he'd grown up with – a smile with an air of challenge and mischief. Confidence – that's what Crystal had; confidence and composure. How could he not have been hooked, that first meeting?

Every summer, his employer – Black Rock Energy – held a summer games meeting at the sports complex they sponsored. Luke, two years into his first job for the oil company, was competing in the javelin event. They were all amateurs. A few had travelled from neighbouring counties to be there but Luke had won by a metre on his final throw. Crystal, local beauty and daughter of Black Rock's Chief

Accountant, had been enlisted to present the medals; the chief exec shook hands, but it was Crystal who draped the purple ribbons around the necks of the winners.

In that brief moment, the hot flash of recognition when Luke's eyes had met hers, had triggered a mutual attraction.

'Congratulations, that was some achievement,' she'd said, her hands smoothing the ribbon over this collar bones.

'Thank you.'

'Just a metre short of Olympic standard, they say.'

'I don't know about that.'

'You're obviously a natural athlete.' She'd tugged gently on the medal to make it sit properly on his chest. 'How are you at squash?'

'Not played in a long time.'

'I was top of my league in school...' she began. He could've just bet she was, in more ways than one. 'Fancy a game, next week?' she'd asked, that challenge in her eyes.

He'd nodded. 'Why not? I've never been thrashed by a woman in any sport .'

'Excellent. How does Tuesday at six-thirty sound? Lakeview Club.'

'I'll be there.'

With a brief tap of her fingernail on the centre of the medal, she'd smiled, turned away and walked back to the medal table, smoothing her long blonde hair over one shoulder as she went.

Luke had stood, momentarily swaying, as if she'd punched him in the chest.

Tuesday. It couldn't come soon enough.

Crystal, like Gigi, had led a privileged lifestyle;

private education, expensive holidays, skiing from the family's lodge at Mont Tremblant. Yes, Crystal had moved in all the right circles and had all the fun money could buy. It hadn't appeared to turn her into a monster though, just given her a taste for the good things in life and imbued her with self-assurance.

She hadn't thrashed him at squash but it had been close. He'd had to draw on all his power and guile to win, 10-8. 'Damn!' she'd said. 'You really made me work.'

'Fun, though?' he'd asked, through a smile.

'Best fun I've had in ages.'

'Me too.'

'Then let's not leave it on the squash court,' she'd said advancing on him with a delicious sense of sexual menace. 'How about we get cleaned up and go out for dinner?'

Result! He'd arranged a sleep-over for Ava with a school-friend, on the off-chance this might happen.

Crystal had suggested a newly opened Greek restaurant, where they'd shared Mezze and laughter, talking through the evening till their final shot of Retsina.

He'd driven her to her apartment in the heart of town, where they'd kissed, many times, before she finally let herself out of the car. 'Call me,' she'd said.

It was only as he drove home, he realised he didn't have her number so he'd driven back, pressed the buzzer on the entry-phone and waited. When her voice purred through, she was dictating her number. 'I hope you're writing this down,' she'd said.

'Got it!' he'd answered, carving it into his palm with a sharp stone. 'I'll be in touch.'

He lifted the beer can to his lips and drained it, before crushing it in his fist.

'C'mon, Chuck! Let's go for a run before it gets dark.'

The dog's head jerked up in surprise. Three walks in one day was quite a treat.

Chapter 20

The night of my first samba band practice had arrived. Nico, who was head honcho, spotted me and wandered over. 'Good to see you. Follow me and I'll get you a tamborim.'

He handed me a dinky little drumlet – which looked like a tambourine without cymbals – and a small stick. I was quite relieved not to have anything bigger or noisier. I wasn't one for drawing attention to myself. In fact, now it came to it, I was starting to wish I'd kept my trap shut at the carnival. He showed me how to hold it, and how to hit it – and I can tell you, it wasn't as easy as it looked. When I'd mastered the technique, he said, 'Good. Just follow what the others next to you are doing.'

He introduced me to a girl around my own age – if I could still be considered a girl at twenty-seven. She had about her a healthy bloom, like she drank smoothies for breakfast, ate nuts for lunch and tofu for dinner. 'Megan knows the ropes,' he said. 'She'll keep an eye on you.'

'Great,' I said. Keen not to appear half as fazed as I felt.

'Enjoy yourself,' Megan said quietly as he walked away. 'It's the best fun you can have with your clothes on.'

I did hope so.

Nico blew a few sharp blasts on a whistle to gain our attention. 'Come along then, let's start with a warm up.'

The group had gathered in a large circle around the room, with him in the centre. Damn! I was hoping to hide in the shadows at the back. Stood there, anyone could see when I made a right, royal cock up. My heart was doing a percussive beat all of its own.

I quickly gathered that whatever beat Nico bashed out, we had to echo with our instruments. The beats increased in speed and intensity. It was fun!

'All good!' Nico said. 'Now, for the benefit of Gigi, a reminder of the beat patterns for tamborims. This one,' he said, making a gesture like the Y of YMCA, 'goes like this: "I can play the tamborim nicely," got it?' And so he went on, making a series of weird body shapes or gestures to describe the actual phrase beat.

I gulped. So long as I could remember which phrase went with which funny face, I'd be in clover.

'Let's see if we can get through it without too much difficulty,' he said, raising his hands aloft. 'Listen to the silence, guys. Listen and prepare.' He gave us a look that said, 'Ready?' Then he drilled out the beat and we were off.

Finally, after nearly two hours of concentration and liberation, Nico uttered the magic words, 'Right, that's it for tonight. Thanks for all your hard work.'

'Wow! That was full on.' I said to Megan.

'What did I tell ya?'

'The best fun. At least, when I stopped over-thinking it.'

'Exactly. Will you be here next week?'

'Try and stop me. I'm not sure I can wait a whole seven days.'

'You will. It's quite a workout.'

'I can believe it.'

I beat the air with my stick. I was full of energy. Nico grinned. 'So, how was it for you?'

'Brilliant. Loved it. Wish I'd started years ago.'

'You've got natural rhythm. It helps.'

I could feel my cheeks glow with pride.

'Good, then we'll see you next week.'

'Looking forward to it already.'

He nodded and left me buzzing with the energy the last two hours had generated.

'Are you coming for a drink?' Megan asked.

'Oh…' I hadn't factored this in. 'I have no money with me. Sorry. Next time.'

'No worries. I'll stand you a soda water. I'm only having one, anyway, gotta pick my little boy up.'

A handful of us went to the pub but Megan and I stuck together. 'D'you drink wine?' she asked.

'Not at present. I'm detoxing,' It wasn't strictly true but, by virtue of the fact water was the only liquor quenching my system I was, by default, detoxing. 'Water will be fine. Tap water, even.'

She turned to the barman. 'Finest Vectis tap water, please,' she said before turning to me, 'with a slice?'

I nodded.

'Ice and a slice in that, and I'll have a small white wine, thanks.'

'How old's your little boy?'

'Two. Here…' she showed me a picture on her phone.

'He's super cute.'

'Wouldn't be without him.'

'Are you a full-time mum or do you have a job?'

'Both. I'm a full-time mum in that there's no dad on the scene and I'm a hairdresser.'

'Where?'

'At home or I go to people's houses. That way, I can fit it in around Mackay.'

'I could do with some work on mine.' I thought about the scrappy mess my hair had become when it wasn't harnessed by a scrunchy.

'Sure. My rates are very reasonable.'

'Great.'

'So Gigi,' she began, 'Tell me about you. What's your story?'

After much apologetic prevarication, largely punctuated by half-sentences I finally managed to say. 'I'm a sculptor.'

Her eyes widened. 'For real?'

I shrugged. 'I'm not making any money at it though, so I don't know if it counts.'

'Hey – Van Gogh only sold one painting in his lifetime. One! Imagine that.'

I laughed. 'Me and Van Gogh – I'm liking the association.'

'Mad as a hatter, mind,' she said with a grin.

'Understandable. I'd be pretty pissed off myself if I couldn't sell my work.'

'What do you sculpt – is that even a word?'

'It is.' I probably bored her for several minutes on my passions but she acted like she was genuinely interested, which is always a plus in my book, and earned her a slew of bonus points.

'I want to come and see them,' she said. 'Art was my favourite subject at school but I'm an academic numpty.'

'Who cares? It's what you're good at that's important.' I'd often said that to Freddy. 'Hairdressing's a kind of sculpture, isn't it? So we're in the same business.'

'Cheers to that!' she said, raising her glass.

'Are you okay to come and give me a trim?'

'Absolutely.' She pulled out her phone. 'Let me check my calendar and we'll fix a date.'

I think I had a smile on my face, all the way home. Megan was like a whirlwind of positive energy. I'd booked her to return my hair to silky, flaxen normality in time for Rupert's visit.

Chapter 21

Megan's comment about Van Gogh had me thinking. Not, I hasten to add, along the lines of severing my ear and gifting it to a farmer's daughter. No. More along the lines of getting my work noticed.

I went to the library and made a list of all the galleries on the island. It wasn't exactly an exhaustive list. Then I researched how to put a website together – somewhat easier than I'd expected. Why did web developers make it sound like some dark art?

I set about uploading all my degree show pictures, and individual shots of my sculptures. Just as soon as I could fill and fire up my kiln, I'd have more to shoot. Finally, by the end of the week, I rang each gallery to see if anybody had space available in the New Year.

Dovetailed with this activity, I was firing off phone calls and letters to Nanna's afternoon tea crowd, who were delightful. Her address book was in a box in the loft, which I'd labelled, 'Sentiment and Nostalgia'. Nobody minded me contacting them at all. In fact, they sounded positively thrilled to be invited back to Bluebell Farm.

The days shot by and I didn't even mind that Rupert was stuck in Scotland, doing his thing. I was doing mine and it was all positive – creative in its own way. I was building my future, and it felt good.

'Wanna come watch the ice hockey with me, this weekend?' Ava stood in the studio doorway. She was head-to-toe in black: leggings, sloppy vest over tight t-shirt, platform boots and nose-ring. I think the nose-ring was new, judging by the pink glow beneath her pale foundation.

'I'd love to.'

She wandered over and peered at Peniel, who was receiving a final grooming before he went in the kiln. 'Who's this?' she asked.

'Peniel. The angel with care and responsibility for Fridays.'

'Cool.'

'Do you go to all Luke's games?'

She wrinkled her nose, quickly moved her hand to cover it and shook her head. 'No. I'm not a fan, exactly, but when I'm over here I like to go and show my support.'

'You have a really good relationship with him,' I said, knowing I would do the same for Freddy, but not sure he'd do the same for me.

'I guess. He's like a parent as well as a brother, which can be a real pain in the ass, but I know he has my best interests at heart.'

'At least you appreciate that.'

'I'd be pretty stupid not to,' she said, fiddling with her nose ring.

'New piercing?' I asked.

'Yeah. Sore as hell, right now.'

'What did Luke say?'

'He thinks it's hilarious. Says he'll clip a lead to it and take me for walks with Chuck.' She rolled her eyes. 'I'm going back to uni in two weeks, would you mind keeping an eye on him for me?'

'Chuck?'

'No. Luke.'

'Why, what d'you think's going to happen to him?'

'Nothing. I just worry about him being lonely. He's not exactly the world's greatest mixer.'

'Maybe he likes it that way.'

'That's what worries me. He's all work and ice-hockey. Boring.'

I thought about how my dad used to be a workaholic – and he didn't play ice hockey. Then there was Rupert – no, he knew how to party.

'Isn't that just ambitious men?'

'You think?' She chewed her lip for a moment. 'He didn't used to be. Back home. He was much more fun.'

'Then he's maybe just focussing now. He told me he's pretty obsessed by this project of his.'

'Duh! Obsessed? Possessed more like.'

'Don't worry, I won't ignore him. I'm probably going to need his help with my vegetable garden. No – I will need his help. I haven't a clue.'

'Brilliant! That's just what he needs.' She brightened enormously at this news. 'I'm so glad you moved in. You're kinda like family. We regarded Una as family, so when she died it was...you know...'

I smiled. 'I do. She was fond of you guys, too.' Ava nodded but looked thoughtful. 'Ava,' I began. She looked at me expectantly. 'I'm really sorry Freddy was so awful to you, last year.'

She waved a hand. 'Forget it. I was probably a right royal pain in the ass.'

'No. I'm sure you weren't. Freddy just isn't very good at being affectionate.'

'Yeah, I get that,' she said, raising her eyebrows, and again reaching for her nose.

'Come with me,' I said. 'I've got a bag of frozen

peas that might help.'

'Thanks. The affects of an Aunt Bessie's Yorkshire pudding has worn off, now.'

'You had a Yorkshire pud on your nose?'

'It was in a plastic bag.'

'Okay.'

'We only have a little freezer. It was that or a leg of lamb.'

I hadn't expected the ice hockey match to be such a show. I thought I was going to sit passively in the cheap seats, watching twelve guys belting round the ice and whacking the puck into the goal. That was only a part of it. The announcer was like a warm-up comedian, psyching the audience into a frenzy of excitement. Music pumped through the speakers. It was like being in a *Rocky* movie. A roar went up when the players finally hit the ice.

'Which one's Luke?' I asked – since I'd have had difficulty recognising *myself* in all the gear they were wearing.

'Over there,' she pointed, 'number eighteen.'

Of course. The ponytail hanging down his back beneath the helmet was a bit of a giveaway. I watched him briefly. I didn't want Ava thinking I only had eyes for him. Although, to be perfectly honest, I did. I was fascinated to see how this usually laid-back guy behaved on the ice. He was fast. He was fast and strong. He was fast and strong and agile. They all were.

When the horn sounded to start the game, the power in the room went up a notch.

Part-way through the first half, I turned to Ava. 'This is fantastic! I can't believe how fired up I am.'

'Yeah?'

I neglected to say exactly in what way I was fired up. Watching Luke charging across the ice, attacking the goal like a warrior, added a whole unexpected layer to his personality. I found I was contemplating the guy in a very different light. 'They're all so energetic and aggressive – in a positive way, I mean.'

'Man at his brutal best.'

'And there's the vibe of the crowd, the noise, the excitement. I've never, ever been to see a game like this. It's thrilling.'

'Great!' she said, clutching my arm. 'Then will you go to all the home games and support Luke for me? Hey – you could go to the away games too, if you can hitch a ride with one of the others.'

That was a little more commitment than I could promise but I really did want to see another game.

Later, after they won twelve-nine, we stood in the bar waiting for the guys to come out. 'So this game is big in Canada, right?' I asked.

'Huge.'

'Do you miss living there.'

She wrinkled her still-pink nose. 'Sort of. But Luke thought it best for both of us if we left.'

'Because of your father?'

She looked away before she answered. 'I guess he was part of the reason. It was a shame, cos Luke had such a good job over there.'

'He mentioned working for an oil company.'

'He had fantastic prospects, but…'

At that moment, Luke appeared. His hair, which was damp from the shower, hung in ringlets where it hadn't been captured by the leather cord at his nape. His face was flushed from the exercise and I'd even go as far as to say there was a gleam in his eyes. Perhaps his sister wasn't such a good judge of how much fun her brother needed in his life.

'Hey, bro, you were great, and Gigi loved it so much, she's going to come again. Aren't you?'

'I definitely want to come again… some time.'

'Fantastic. We need all the support we can get. Did you follow the rules?'

'Hey, Luke, I'm just high on the atmosphere and inhaling testosterone – who cares about the rules?'

He laughed. It took years off him.

'You'll pick them up,' he said, clearly believing his sister's take on my enthusiasm for the game. I knew I was destined to disappoint them both.

'I played hockey at school – but we had more players,' I said.

'Jeez, twenty-two guys going for it out there would be carnage,' he said with a look of fake panic.

A couple of his friends joined us – Ryan and Grant. Ryan was tall, like Luke, but Grant was shorter – they were both thick set. I wouldn't want to be mown down by either of them travelling over the ice at speed.

I happily listened to the to and fro of banter, with Ava nudging in the odd jibe herself.

'So, here's to your next year at uni,' Luke said, raising a glass of beer to his sister.

'Cheers to that!'

'And here's an early birthday present,' he added, pulling an envelope from his pocket.

'Wowzer! You're giving me a thousand pounds in cash?' she joked.

'Funny girl. Open it.'

She pulled a travel folder out and studied the

contents, a smile spreading across her face. 'We're going to Canada for Christmas?!'

'Yeah, I meant to say, it's your Christmas present too.'

'Luke, you are the man!' she threw her arms round him, slopping half the beer out of his glass. I could see from the way his eyes crinkled deeply at the corners, this was the reaction he'd been hoping for. After hugging him hard, she stepped back and wrapped her hand around his beard. 'Does this thing have to come with us, too?'

'Hey, watch it, young lady. I can still get a refund on those tickets.'

She studied them again. 'This is sensational. I can't wait.'

After the excitement had died down, and Luke was busy analysing the game with his mates. I asked her, 'Will this be your first time back to Canada since you left?'

'Yes. Though I have to admit,' she added quietly, 'I'm kinda scared I'll be disappointed. I'm remembering it through a teenager's eyes.'

I smiled. She was still a teenager, if only for a few weeks. 'Why do you give your brother such a hard time over his beard? Ever considered he keeps it just to piss you off?'

'Yeah, I guess he could,' she said, rolling her eyes. 'Thing is, he's not shaved since we left Canada.'

'Wow, that's pretty symbolic.'

'Exactly. Maybe going back there, he can lay a few ghosts; one in particular.'

Leaning closer, I whispered, 'Are we talking love interest?'

She nodded. 'I don't know exactly what happened,

he won't ever say, but she broke his heart. For sure.'

'So that's why you left.'

She shrugged. 'Gotta be. He makes out the job over here was perfect for him. I mean, the island's one enormous fossil, right? And he said it's a really safe place to bring children up – me a child? – so it was the best opportunity for both of us. Like, really? Here, after Ottawa? No. It's heartbreak.'

'Do they keep in touch?' I asked, nosiness getting the better of me.

'Don't think so. But I have a theory,' she pulled me slightly to one side. 'I'm good with theories and they're hardly ever wrong. That beard is his emotional armour – it's his way of keeping women at bay.'

'Not if she has a beard fetish.'

She shook her head. 'Gigi, don't underestimate the power of that beard. It's charged with all his defensive energy. It's like a force field. The longer it gets, the more power it emits. He generates this special current for repelling women. If one of them tried to get close… Pow! She'd be thrown back a couple of yards – eyebrows scorched, lips blistered.'

I grinned.

'Seriously, if we could plug him into the National Grid, he could pay for these tickets in a week. And I've never seen him charge his mobile phone at night, he just sleeps with it nestled in his beard.'

'Stop!' I was laughing now, and she was really getting into her stride.

'He's like Sampson on battery acid. If only we could just get close enough to cut it all off…'

'Oooh, no. He'd be much too vulnerable,' I was joining in the fantasy, now. 'He has to do it himself.'

'Exactly. And when he does – watch out ladies!'

I hadn't enjoyed an evening quite so much in ages. I swear the cats exchanged looks of incredulity when I breezed into the kitchen singing *Hit Me Baby One More Time.*

And that night, I slept.

Properly slept – like seven hours straight.

Chapter 22

I'd never attended one of Nanna's teas, although I had been to Claridge's a couple of times. My budget was so tight, I was tempted by a box of Family Selection biscuits but I could feel Nanna's disapproval pressing in on me.

So in the third week of September, Bluebell Farm was open for business ... well ... tea.

I opted for simplicity – egg and cress sandwiches and cream cheese with cucumber. I cut the crusts off in the interests of style but saved the bits in a plastic box. Tomorrow I could dip them in beaten egg and make French Toast fingers. I splashed out on some watercress garnish to add a little greenery.

Tesco had cherry cakes on a two-for-one offer, not as impressive as home made but half the price and far less trouble. At least the fluorescent vermillion of the cherries livened the things up. I worked like stink to get the house looking smart. My wish-list of accessories and fittings from Italy and France had been parked, for now. When my fortunes changed and funds returned to normal – as I felt sure they would – I might revisit it. For the moment, I had to make do with the shabby-chic of Nanna's old bits and a couple of impressive flower arrangements... well... hedgerow arrangements really, with later flowering blooms from the garden strategically poked in amongst the twigs and ivy.

Usually, when you throw a party, people don't turn up till way past the start time. It's never fair to panic the host by being punctual. We all know, if the start time is eight o'clock, two minutes beforehand, the hostess will be belting upstairs to yank off her food-splattered dressing gown, before spritzing herself liberally with cologne, then she's stepping into the dress that's been hanging on the wardrobe door. It is at this point she discovers she has no tights without visible ladders and her legs need waxing. With a toothbrush in one hand and a razor in the other, she deftly coordinates scrubbing and shaving, before tackling her make-up. In her haste, she squirts foundation down her dress – which we all know is the kiss of death – and she resorts to her old faithful: slinky top and black jeans which cover up her newly sleek legs.

Or is that just me?

Whatever the case, it is, in my book, deeply rude to turn up on time.

It seems afternoon tea is different.

At two-fifty-seven (three minutes before the appointed start time) a car rolled sedately up the drive. I peered out of the kitchen window to check the visitor was a guest and not a bailiff. Yes, I was dressed, although still in jeans and crumb-encrusted apron. There were three in the car: two plump women and an even plumper chap. I glanced nervously at the trays of food and wondered if I had enough. I chucked my apron into the washing machine and said under my breath, 'Here we go, Nanna. Wish me luck.'

'Gabriella, how lovely of you to invite us,' a tall, fading blonde said, holding a potted cyclamen towards me and introducing herself. 'I'm Jane Cranham, chair of the WI, and this is Kate Mappen and her husband, Bob.'

No sooner had we all shaken hands than there was a skirl of gravel as a little sport scar swerved up the drive.

'Oh, and that's Ella Heap, widowed six months ago and loving every minute of it,' Jane added.

'Don't!' Kate said, with a note of disapproval but a wry smile.

I recognised Ella from Nanna's funeral – the cougar flirting with Freddy. I noticed Bob smoothing a hand through his grey thatch as he studied her parking technique.

Then another car appeared through the gates, this one with three women on board.

'Why don't you go through to the sitting room?' I suggested as each guest arrived. 'You all know where it is.'

I hadn't, for a second, anticipated so many welcoming gifts. There were plants, flowers, bottles of wine and pots of jam. As the dresser filled up with all these lovely presents, the daunting PR stunt for Bluebell Farm now felt like a proper house party with new friends.

The tea urn I'd borrowed from the church sat on the work surface, its sharp green light letting me know it was up to temperature. Cups and saucers from the same source were lined up beside it. I'd discovered Nanna's name opened doors in these parts.

By twenty past three, there were fourteen lovely people squashed into the sitting room; bums on every seat, chair arm and stool. I feared for the stool. It had seen much service over the years and creaked. It creaked a lot with Kate Mappen on it.

'Thank you all for coming. I know you were good friends of Nanna's – Una's – and I'm sure we'd all love for her to be here with us today but I like to think she's with us in spirit.'

There were chirps of agreement from around the room.

'As you know, she left the farm to me because of how much I loved it – still love it. I really want to make this my home but...'

What could I say: I need the farm to earn its keep? I'm utterly stony-broke and prospects for survival are decidedly grim?

'We understand, darling,' Ella Heap chimed up, tossing her exquisitely quaffed salt-and-pepper hairdo and waving scarlet-tipped fingers. 'Places this size take a lot to keep going. Very wise of you to start a little business. It's what the island relies on.'

There were mumbles of agreement.

'I wouldn't want any of you to think I was... cashing in. I need to earn a living and this seems like the best way to do it.'

'Don't you worry, Gabriella,' Jane Cranham said. 'Una always felt this place was too big for her, so I imagine she'd applaud your enterprising attitude.'

'I'm so glad you feel that way,' I said, as heads around the room began to nod.

I detailed my plans to offer accommodation and run pottery courses, which caused a little shiver of excitement from a couple of the women.

'I'd definitely come to classes,' said one. 'If you fancied teaching local residents?'

'Me too,' said another.

'You've certainly spruced this room up nicely,' Bob added. 'It's really quite stately in here.'

'Thank you. Not all rooms are up to this standard, yet but I'm working on it. Now, perhaps you'd like to wander around in small groups. The back garden has changed, as has the barn, which is now my studio. You're very welcome to look upstairs. Then please come into the kitchen for a spot of tea.'

A spot of tea. That's what Nanna used to say.

I nipped back to the kitchen and peeled cling-film from the trays of food and set them on the table. I poured myself a cuppa to check the strength – good – and waited.

I needn't have worried. There was praise for the new decor, wonder at my sculptures and optimism for my business venture. The kitchen buzzed with chatter and clatter as they balanced teacups and plates. A couple of ladies said they would sign up for pottery classes, and insisted I take their names, and Jane invited me to talk about my sculptures at the Women's Institute.

This could work, I thought to myself. Really work.

Their enthusiasm had so lifted my spirits, I was high on adrenalin. There's nothing quite like fearing something was heading for failure, and then foreseeing a whole new possibility.

Ella Heap, keen to get ahead in the pottery stakes, said she planned on trawling YouTube for videos on pottery techniques. 'Fail to prepare – prepare to fail!' she added.

Whilst I applauded her zeal, no amount of study would prepare her for the feel of the clay or its unique characteristics and limitations. But I kept my trap shut – no point tiddling on her strawberries right now.

Bob tapped his teacup with a spoon, calling the group to order. 'Right then,' he began, 'I'd like to

213

propose a toast to Gabriella and the success of Bluebell Farm.'

'Gabriella and Bluebell Farm!' they all chorused.

I beamed and raised my own teacup. 'And to all of you!'

'Cheers!'

'You've actually made me feel I can make this happen,' I said, my voice breaking over the unexpected lump that had formed in my throat. 'Thank you so much for your kindness. It really means a lot to me.'

A gentle hush settled on the kitchen. 'You're welcome, love,' Jane said softly. 'Una would be proud of you.'

As I sniffed, there was a crash behind me as someone hit the back door.

'Fuck-a-duck! Who uses a bloody boot-scraper, these days?'

I turned to see Freddy stumble through the door, his backpack hitting the floor with a thud. 'Afternoon,' he said grinning at the startled crowd. 'What's going on here?'

Chapter 23

After a shower, Freddy smelled considerably fresher than when he'd arrived. My guests had smiled then recoiled as he barged around the room, shaking hands. At first sight, Freddy was appealing. He had a ragged thatch of conker brown hair, a deep tan and, today, the haphazard tailoring of a middle-class back-packer. Highlight that with his dazzling smile, and he was quite a looker. Unfortunately, at arm's length, in week-old clothing seasoned with man sweat, he had an unpleasant pong about him.

On the upside, he emptied the kitchen of my guests faster than a bull with St Vitus's Dance.

'So,' he said, lounging on my sofa in a green and orange sarong, 'you seem to have quite a grip on our new pauper status. Making any money yet?'

I spotted the hopeful glint in his eye. 'No. I haven't even started.'

'Bit of a bugger, isn't it? You'd think the old man might have tipped us off – you know, given us chance to bank a bit of cash before they collared him; set us up, even; squirreled away some funds into off-shore accounts in our name; tipped us the wink.'

'Freddy, he's trying to do the right thing.'

'Course he is. Stupid man.'

Freddy had always found our father wanting. Dad was a strategic thinker who played his cards close to his chest, as opposed to Freddy who seldom planned anything, always acting impulsively and sometimes erratically. They had nothing in common. Freddy

215

irritated Dad, so commands like 'Freddy, go to your room!' or 'Freddy, leave me alone, I'm trying to think!' had peppered our childhood. I, on the other hand, seemed to draw Dad in. Around the house, I was usually to be found quietly making things like papier mâché puppets, Christmas decorations or painting blown eggs for Easter. Dad would watch me for a while, marvelling at my industry and saying, 'You are a clever girl,' before kissing the top of my head and retreating to his study.

Occasionally, Freddy would muscle in on the action, causing havoc and reducing my creations to trash. Not out of jealousy so much as an effort to emulate my creativity and capture a little of our father's admiration.

Sadly, Freddy has always been clumsy so his efforts only drew disapproval.

I did try to help him but he'd always blow it with some rash improvisation. Dear little Freddy, in his efforts to please he invariably screwed up.

'Freddy, Dad will do everything he can to clear this mess up. We just have to keep treading water till it's sorted out.'

'Gigi, you're just saying that. Truth is, we're fucked – or at least, Dad is, but d'you know what? I'm not a baby, any more.' He said this with an edge.

I nodded.

'So,' he continued, 'I'm going to start a business myself.'

'You are? You?'

'Willow View will be empty as of next week...'

'How come? You had holiday lets till mid-November.'

'The place is uninhabitable, due to a plumbing

disaster and flood damage.'

'That's awful. Are you insured?'

'Don't be a mug, Gigi. There is no flood damage, it's just what I told the agency to tell them. They've found alternative accommodation for the punters so nobody loses out.'

'Except you. No rent for weeks.'

He shrugged.

'So what now?' I asked.

He tapped the side of his nose. 'You'll see.'

'Freddy, unless you've won the lottery, you don't have any more money than I do.'

'But I have an investor.' He smiled smugly. 'That, Gigi, is the clincher.'

'Investor in what?'

'You'll see.' He tugged the sarong tightly around his legs as he swung them up onto the sofa and lay down.

I watched as he plumped one of the cushions under his head, making himself at home. As he closed his eyes, I asked, 'Where are you going to live?'

He snuggled into the sofa. 'Here, until next week, then I'll move into the cottage. You don't mind, do you?'

I'd certainly mind if he stayed longer. That would reduce my available accommodation – not to mention my potential income – by a third.

'Okay but then you're on your own, Freddy. Like you said, you're not a baby any more. We both need to look after ourselves, now.'

'Agreed. The Bank of Dad has ceased trading, defunct. It's just you and me, babe, you and me.' Then, with characteristic insouciance, he sank into the kind of sleep I could only dream of.

I went up to my room and rang Rupert. 'Freddy's turned up.'

'How is he?'

'Cagey. Reckons he's got some great business idea and even some investors but he won't tell me what.'

'Good for him. How did your tea-party go?'

'Really well, I think.' I related Freddy's spectacular entrance.

'True to form.'

'I wish I knew what he was up to.'

'Don't worry about him. You just concentrate on what you're doing.'

He didn't understand, I'd always worry about Freddy. 'So, you're off to Rory's stag, tomorrow, aren't you?' I asked.

'I am. It'll be good to get away for a break.'

I still felt miffed he hadn't made it down to see me. 'But next weekend…'

'Yes. That's ours. I'm flying into Southampton on Friday, and I've booked us a room at a lovely little boutique hotel. You'll absolutely love it – it's just what you like: pristine white bathrobes and baskets of free toiletries.'

I giggled. 'And, of course, undisturbed sex in an anonymous hotel bedroom, right?'

'Oh, most definitely.' His voice dropped.

For the first time in ages, we were having a conversation that didn't involve finances, family or town-planning.

'It'll be bliss. I can't wait.'

'Me too.'

Twenty minutes later, the glow of my romantic tête-à-tête with Rupert ended abruptly as I heard Freddy yell out. He was having a nightmare, he must be.

I ran downstairs and found him thrashing his head back and forth, as he yelled some more.

'It's okay, sweetheart. You're okay. Freddy, I'm here.' I knelt by the sofa and stroked his shoulder. His eyes opened and he scowled into the distance, studying whatever horrific images played across his mind. Eventually, he rolled towards me, took my hand and settled back to sleep.

***

Luke drove slowly up the drive of Bluebell Farm. This was the first chance he'd had to see how Gabriella's afternoon tea had gone, and he was here to help her take the tea urn and cups back to the church. He was puzzled and maybe a little put out that she hadn't been round to report on the tea-party before now. It had been such a major landmark in her plans for the business, that when she hadn't rushed round to fill him on the details, he feared it might have been a complete washout.

The kitchen door was open and Gigi's two cats sat in a pool of sunlight outside, watching his approach through slanted eyes.

He stopped the car and looked around. Gigi was in the studio, working on one of her angels. She waved before coming out to meet him.

'Hi,' she said, folding her arms. 'Want to see what I've done to Balthioul?'

'Balthioul? Sure.'

'Good. Come in.' There was something unusually clipped in her tone.

'How did your tea party go?'

'Good, thanks. Fourteen came. They were all really positive.'

She turned the angel towards him. 'See.'

Like all her angel sculptures, the body was structured to convey strength with compassion; the attitude of the figure noble yet full of grace. But it was the face that startled him. The brows were low over the eyes and the mouth was firm and pinched. 'Wow,' he said, 'what was Balthioul the angel of?'

'He has the power to thwart distress.'

Luke nodded. 'So, what's his story?'

'His story?' She looked puzzled – no – she looked like she wasn't really tuned into the conversation. She'd manoeuvred the angel so Luke could see it in the light from the window. Next she was nudging him towards it. 'His story, good question,' she continued. 'Can you tell what his story might be, just from looking at him?'

Luke struggled. Angels weren't exactly his field of experience. He was a factual man not a fantasist. 'He looks kinda pissed off, to me.'

'Right, right.' She stood opposite him. 'Yes. I know what you mean.' She frowned and glanced out over Luke's shoulder. Something was definitely distracting her.

'Hey, wassup?' asked an unpleasantly familiar voice.

Luke turned to see Freddy leaning against the door frame. He looked like he'd just rolled out of bed.

'Freddy,' Luke said flatly.

Freddy pulled a lop-sided smile. 'How's it going?'

Luke sensed Freddy's customary charm was failing him, as he laboured under the guilt of last summer's poor conduct. Quite right too. This was their first meeting since Luke had bawled him out over the car boot sale.

'D'you want something, Freddy?' Gigi asked quickly.

Now Luke understood why she'd been so preoccupied. How long had her reckless brother been back?

'Just thought I'd say hello.' Freddy tried his smile out on them both.

Luke wasn't humoured. The word *Sorry* might have been more appropriate, he thought.

'How's things?' Freddy continued.

Luke nodded. 'I'm doing okay thanks.'

'And the beautiful Ava, how's she?'

Luke acknowledged the guy had balls. No elephant in the room for Freddy. 'Ava's doing really well.'

'Good, glad to hear it.'

'Okay, guys,' Gigi chimed in. 'So, let's do this now – hatchets can be buried and olive branches thrown down.' She looked from one to the other. 'Freddy?'

'Yeah. Sorry I wasn't exactly the model of chivalry, last summer.'

That was an understatement. Luke was still trying to summon up an expletive-free sentence when Freddy pulled a hand from his pocket and held it out. 'No hard feelings?' he asked.

'Freddy, if you're back to help Gigi, then I'm prepared to draw a line under what happened.' He still had plenty of hard feelings where Freddy was concerned but Gigi's tension was charging the air around them.

As their hands met, Freddy said, 'Okay. I'll take that. Cheers.'

Luke stood full square in front of him and released his hand quickly. He might not be voicing his opinions but his body spoke volumes.

Freddy shoved his hand back in his pocket and pulled a taut smile. 'I'll leave you to it, then.'

Luke turned away and studied Gigi as she tugged the scrunchie off her ponytail and re-fixed it. He'd like to think Freddy was home to show solidarity but Luke was pretty sure the self-centred, hedonistic son-of-a-bitch had only come over to feather his own nest.

Maybe she already knew that. Maybe it accounted for her attitude right now.

Gigi coughed. 'The whole Ava thing, last summer... he knows he was a complete shit.'

'So does she. That's one thing I don't have to worry about.'

'Thanks for being so reasonable.'

'Hey, water under the bridge.'

Finally, she smiled. 'Good. I'd hate there to be an atmosphere. You're such a good neighbour, I wouldn't want Freddy's presence to...'

'Forget it. And just to prove my good neighbourliness, I've come to help you take the stuff back to the church. The warden's up there now.'

'Thanks, Luke. Let me put this under wraps and we can go.' She lifted a large, damp cloth and draped it over the sculpture. She wore a frown as grim as Balthioul's.

As they packed the stuff into the back of the car, Luke said, 'So, fourteen isn't a bad turnout for your first effort at promotion.'

'I know, and they were all very sweet.'

'And enthusiastic?'

'About the business idea, yes, maybe not so excited about my afternoon tea.'

'Tell me more.'

She stood rubbing her forehead with one hand. 'I should have made scones with jam and cream; possibly even a little glass of fizz to celebrate, and macaroons or hand-made chocolate truffles. That's how I wanted to do it,' she said, throwing her arms out in frustration. 'It's how I would have done it a few months ago. And I have a sneaking suspicion it was exactly what they expected. Nanna would never have served supermarket cherry cake, would she?'

Luke straightened up. 'Who cares? They were probably more interested in checking out the alterations at the farm. People are nosy. At least you've given them something to talk about.'

'Exactly: "Not up to Una's standards," is what they'll be saying.'

'Hey, you don't strike me as the self-pitying type. Don't start now or you'll be defeated before you make a buck. Onward and upward, Gabriella. Onward and Upward!'

She smiled.

'Sorry, *Gigi.*'

'I don't mind you calling me Gabriella. And you're right – no point me giving up before the fat lady sings.'

'Hell, no! Gag that fat lady!'

Gigi laughed. 'Keep that fat lady right away from me. I don't want to meet her, I don't even want to see her for a very long time.'

He pulled the driver's door open. 'Best you don't come into the church with me, then.'

'Why not?'

He grinned. 'It's choir practice.'

***

Maybe Balthioul was on my side, after all.

223

I'd been dreading Luke's first encounter with Freddy. The last thing I needed was losing my ally-next-door. They had, at least, been civil although Luke was obviously under the misapprehension that Freddy had come to help. Which was fine by me. Luke could go on thinking that as much as he liked.

Truth was, I didn't need Freddy's kind of help. Historically, Freddy had proven to be more of a hindrance in most things – love him though I did.

Talking of love, Rupe had messaged me from Dublin: a blurred photo of six naked male groins. Almost naked, I should say, their modesty protected by joke-shop plastic faces: black glasses, pink noses and black moustaches. I showed it to Freddy.

'What is it with guys and their willies?' I asked.

'Nice to know he's thinking of you, though,' he grinned.

'Yeah. Super thoughtful!'

A few days later, as I stood at the sink, scraping crusted food from the cat bowls, I got a call from Ramona who'd recently taken over managing Grenville's Gallery. 'I have a week to offer you in March.'

'Fantastic!'

'I know it's not the busiest time of year, and it's only five days but it's five days we didn't have available last time you called.'

'I'm grateful for any time. Thank you so much.' Showing my work was essential if I was going to make a name for myself.

'We should have been closed that week because the last manager was going on a cruise but now I've taken over... so...'

'Great!'

'I'll email you the details and the contract, okay?'

'Lovely!' Just as soon as I had those, I could start emailing reviewers, journalists and anyone else that knew me. Now I had something else to work towards. 'Go, Gigi!' I sang, as I shoved the phone back into my pocket.

From outside, I heard the rumbling sound of a large engine and through the window I saw a hulking great motor-home loom into view. I shot to the back door and stuck my head out to check the gate posts were still intact.

Had word somehow got out that Bluebell Farm offered camping facilities? I certainly wasn't going to let them park it on the paddock and upset Amanda Connell's horses. And I didn't want them in my courtyard either.

Hovering on the doorstep, I peered at the driver, waiting for some explanation. He pushed his door open and jumped down from the cab. He was short and balding but with hair down to his shoulders. He looked like a member of a seventies tribute band. Perhaps he'd taken a wrong turn looking for the holiday camp.

'Hello there,' he said, 'You must be Gigi.'

He had what can best be described as a well-practised smile; well-practised and well-used, probably to show off his expensive veneers. You see, in those few seconds, I already had him nailed down as a slime-ball on the make.

'I am, and you are?'

'Me, I'm Jason but you can call me Phil.'

'How does that work?'

'Long story. So where's Freddy, then – still in bed?'

Of course. It would be a Freddy connection.

Jason-you-can-call-me-Phil was alongside me now and surveying the surroundings. 'Sweet part of the world, isn't it?' he said.

'Did you and Freddy meet when you were travelling?'

'On a beach in Fiji. Very romantic.' He laughed, like there was some spectacular joke behind the suggestion.

'So, you're still travelling then – how does the Isle of Wight compare with the Pacific islands?'

'I'll let you know.' That smile of his, too big and too fixed, spread across his face.

I was about to suggest he might like a cup of tea while he waited for Freddy to surface, when another door, further back in the motor-home, opened and a tall and tanned man emerged. He wore a tight-fitting black t-shirt and jeans, with a suede jacket. He wasn't nearly so smiley, although he did manage a friendly nod in my direction.

'Gigi, this is Matteo.'

'But I can call him Steve?' I ventured.

'Ha! No, just Matteo – although sometimes we call him...' he paused and chuckled. 'Nah, just Matteo. He's Italian.'

Matteo came over to me and placed his hands on my upper arms, so he could cheek bash me on either side, as was customary. Unlike the British, who are inclined to hug and cheek-bash or sometimes squeeze and cheek-snog in a jolly fashion, Matteo took a very much more continental approach to it; stroking my arms with his thumbs as he looked down at me through glossy brown eyes, before turning to land a soft peck on each cheek. He smelled subtly fragrant

226

with cedarwood and spice. Nice.

Really, our boys could learn a thing or two from Matteo.

I was, however, glad Jason-slash-Phil hadn't presumed to wrap me in his oily embrace... yet. Probably didn't want to compromise his dental work.

'If you'd like to come in I'll put the kettle on. Freddy should be down soon.' Or he would be once I'd yanked the duvet off his carcass and subjected him to an interrogation.

Chapter 24

'They're here?' Freddy croaked, after I'd slammed the lights on over his bed.

'No, Freddy. I teleported into the future. They're due in an hour.'

He dropped his head back onto the pillow. 'That's what I thought.'

'Who are they?'

'Friends.'

'You do know they plan on camping out here, don't you?'

'Just till we move to Willow View.'

'You didn't think to tell me?'

'Chill out. It's only a couple of nights.' He pulled the duvet up around his ears.

I waited until he'd relaxed before I yanked the whole thing off the bed. 'Up, Freddy! They're your guests, you entertain them!'

He swore and scowled at me. I clutched the duvet and scowled back.

He groaned and I left, taking the duvet with me and plonked it on the blanket box at the top of the stairs. I barely had enough funds to feed the two of us. If Freddy expected me to cater for two more, we might come to blows.

By the time I returned to the kitchen, there was a woman draped decoratively on the corner of my table, stroking a purring Rodin.

She was very decorative, in a post-pre-Raphaelite way. She wore an oversized shirt and leggings; her long, magenta-coloured hair, was sleek with product and draped over one shoulder. Her huge, brown eyes, which were heavily lined with kohl, blinked – maybe once.

'This is Babette,' Matteo announced.

Babette tilted her head, lifted a hand from the cat and said, 'Hi.'

'Hi.'

She returned to stroking the cat.

'Is this your first visit to the island?' I asked.

The look she gave me was indescribably vague; which I judged either to be from the effects of recreational drugs or, if I were slightly less cynical, a lobotomy.

She shrugged, which I took to be her answer but it might have been involuntary.

'Kettle's boiled,' Jason-slash-Phil informed me.

Grudgingly, I dispensed instant coffee into mugs. Minutes later, Freddy joined us. He was visibly damp from the shower, and wearing a white collarless shirt tucked into his best jeans. I was glad to see the beach bum had taken a back seat.

Some over-enthusiastic man-hugging and back-slapping ensued. You'd think they were war veterans meeting up on Armistice Day. Babette lifted her hand from Rodin to stroke Freddy's face. They exchanged an incomprehensible greeting and I detected the likelihood of some former liaison.

Interesting.

'We'll take our coffees into the sitting room, is that okay?' Freddy studied me for approval.

'Fine. You carry on.'

Taking a sip from his coffee, he scowled at me for the second time this morning. 'Gigi, this is disgusting.'

He chucked his coffee down the sink. 'Where's the decent coffee? Sorry, guys.'

What a charade. He knew exactly why I hadn't made proper coffee. I threw my hands up in apology. 'It hasn't arrived yet, Freddy. I ordered it from Fortnum's the other day. Deliveries to the island seem to be slacker than in town.'

Matteo looked sympathetic.

Jason smiled. 'No worries. Tell you what, Freddy, there must be a café nearby, why don't we get out of your sister's way for a while?' This, I thought, was a surprising display of perception on his part – resentment must have been pooling around my feet.

Politely, Matteo gulped some of the instant coffee before emptying the rest down the sink and rinsing the mug. Jason, followed suit, and even rinsed Freddy's discarded one.

They departed then, leaving me feeling like a grouchy old battleaxe.

I didn't see much of Freddy and his mates after that. They only stayed one night in my courtyard, before they took Freddy off my hands and headed over to Freshwater. I truly hoped they weren't intending to hound out the occupants of Willow View. I'd overheard Freddy mention re-decorating, which suggested he still planned on selling the cottage despite earlier protestations.

Jason-slash-Phil was keen to check out the more wild and rugged coastline of West Wight. 'We might even catch a few crunchers, yeah?'

Freddy shook his head. 'You'll be lucky, Phil. Surf'll be messy today. Nothing worth riding,'

Whilst I could picture Matteo on a surfboard (and happy to do so) the image of his friend crouched amongst the waves was harder to invoke.

I still hadn't persuaded Freddy to confide his business plans to me. He'd always enjoyed mixing music; fancying himself a bit of a DJ after a few guest spots at nightclubs in locations as glamorous as Nice, Auckland and Guildford. But I couldn't see how anyone would want to invest in him doing that. He'd dabbled with music composition, too. He liked to play scenes from horror movies without the sound, and come up with dastardly music, overdubbed with stomach-churning sound effects. Now, if he'd managed to persuade someone to invest in his music composition, that would really be a coup.

In twenty-four hours, I would be with Rupe, thank goodness. This long distance relationship was proving to be an odd kind of challenge for me. Something in my brain was able to flick off. It's a bit like when you go away on holiday, you turn the water off at the stop cock because you'll have no use for it and hope to avoid disasters. Well, it seemed I had a Rupert stop-cock in my brain. I steeled myself not to pine for him. I switched from Couple Mode to Single. I focused on problems to tackle and solutions to meet them. Then, twenty-four hours in advance of his arrival, the waxing strips were deployed and all silk raunch-wear was aired and spritzed with cologne.

I was looking forward to this mini holiday. I hadn't known I needed one but, as the day drew nearer, I became skittish at the thought.

✱✱ *Autumn* ✱✱

Chapter 25

The hotel was within walking distance of the Southampton ferry terminal although, wearing my aquamarine, Saint Laurent fringed ankle boots, it might just as well have been a mile over icy cobbles. Who cared? I was feeling sexy – sexier than I had in ages – and he was worth it. The jade green mini dress wasn't quite up to a British autumn so I wrapped a scarf the length of an anaconda around my neck a few times.

Pitching through the revolving door, I caught sight of myself in one of the wall-to-ceiling, bronze-tinted mirrors. My hair was as flat and uninteresting as a fajita wrap – all the mousse and tong work had been deactivated by the damp air. Still, the dress made my waist look tiny and my legs look long so that would have to do.

'Babe!' I heard Rupert's voice over to my right. He was lounging on a leather couch with a beer in front of him.

I tried to fluff my hair but it flopped listlessly so I swung it forward over one eye and attempted to walk like Jessica Rabbit.

He rose up out of his seat in one movement and opened his arms to me.

I jettisoned all my sass and vamp by tripping up the shallow step I hadn't seen through my curtain of hair, and lurched into him.

'Whoa! Babe, are you pissed?' he chuckled as he steadied me against him.

'No. This is me sober.'

'Never mind, we'll soon change that. Here. Come and snog the face off me.'

Moments later, I looked up at him through a haze of lust. His summer frosting of blonde hair had been chopped away and replaced with a short, trendy cut. His tan had faded but there was a hint of stubble around his jaw. 'Liking the new style,' I said, running my fingers over his hair. 'You look hot.'

'Really hot?'

'Seriously hot.'

'Good. Let's find you a drink and we can go upstairs and sizzle.'

We emerged from our room in time for dinner. Rupe had managed to secure a cosy corner table. A bottle of champagne in an ice bucket was waiting for us. The waiter deftly popped the cork and left us sipping.

'You really know how to spoil a girl,' I said in a faux Hollywood accent.

'We're celebrating.'

'We are?'

'I've secured a post in a top class architects' practice.'

'Fantastic! Where?'

'It's one of the top practices – in the world.'

'Great. Where?'

'Dubai.'

I stared at him over my glass. We both knew where Dubai was.

'Gigi, this is such a brilliant opportunity. There's

an apartment thrown in, rent-free. And Dubai is such an amazing city. We'll have a ball.'

'You want me to come with you?'

'Of course I do. What do you think I'm going to do, commute? You can let the farm if you don't want to sell it.'

He was right. I probably could. It was a wonderful opportunity. Living in Dubai was supposed to be fantastic but the first thing springing into my mind was: *Is it what I want?*

'We won't be going till next summer, so there's plenty of time for you to get used to the idea.' He chinked his glass against mine. 'Think of it: day-long sunshine, sailing at weekends, brunches by the beach. Hell, I can even play all-night golf, it's floodlit over there.'

I smiled and sipped my champagne. Lots of new experiences indeed, but what about the pottery workshops I was setting up? Four people had already expressed interest. Bide-a-While-on-Wight had set up a Bluebell Farm page on their site. I'd used the paddock rental to pay for twelve months of advertising with them.

'Are you even a little bit excited?' he asked.

'Erm…I guess I will be, once it's sunk in.'

'You'll love it. And you just know all our friends will want to come and visit. Honestly, it's the best I could have hoped for.'

'How long is the contract?'

'Depending on how well I do – indefinite.'

I nodded. 'I wonder what the opportunities are like for someone with my skills. I'll have to start googling.'

He sighed. 'You could sound more excited.'

'Sorry. I'm still adjusting my brain. There's been

such a lot going on this year.'

'I know, babe. But this is something good, yeah? Something to look forward to.'

'What about my family? It's such a long way away.'

'It's only a seven hour flight, Gigi. We're not going to Mars.'

'I know, but…'

'Don't say "but". We'll be together.'

I studied his hand on mine; I followed the line of the tendon on his thumb as he stroked my fingers.

'Come on, Gigi, please don't go all glass-half-empty on me.'

I swallowed. 'You're right. It is exciting.' I raised my glass. 'Let's drink to Dubai.'

'Dubai!'

Dubai: a seven hour flight from home, from Dad, from Fran, from my lovely studio, from Freddy – although that might be the making of him – and from Luke.

Luke? Why had I thought about Luke?

In fairness, he'd probably welcome my departure – one less incompetent female to worry about.

All too soon it was Sunday and I was heading back along Town Quay for the catamaran to Cowes. Thin sunlight, the kind you get through an autumnal haze, was brightening up the old buildings and glinting off the halyards and shackles of yachts across in the marina. Gazing at the boats as they bobbed and clinked gently on their moorings, I asked God or whoever it is who runs the show, the all-embracing question…Why was life so complicated?

The only response was the sound of an almighty fog-horn ripping through the peaceful afternoon, as

236

the car ferry blasted its annoyance at some feckless seafarer crossing its path. The noise was immense; totally suited to its purpose of scaring the crap out of anyone and galvanising them into action.

Action. That's what my life needed – only the right action. I just had to work out what that was. A roar of engines heralded the Red Jet's imminent departure.

'Shit!'

I legged it into the terminal, fixing my eyes on the steward and defying him to close the doors without me. 'Here you go,' I said, thrusting my ticket towards him.

He looked at it and tutted, shaking his head. 'Can't travel on this.'

'What?'

'Pulling yer leg,' he grinned.

Oh. How I laughed.

I dropped into the first available seat, and contemplated my future, as the catamaran cruised swiftly over the Solent.

Once off the ferry and heading towards the chain ferry, I noticed grey clouds were gathering above and it was inevitable I would get wet. By the time I reached my bus-stop, drizzle was descending and the breeze was cranking up. I looked at my watch – fifteen minutes to wait. How grim was this – standing in the rain waiting for a bus? And it was only the first bus. I'd have another wait at Ryde for my connection home. But what choice did I have? My Bus Rover ticket was a fraction of the cost of the taxi fares. The drizzle turned serious. I wrapped my scarf around my neck and over my head.

At least in Dubai my chances of being caught in a rainstorm were slim to zero.

Yes. I could get used to the idea of becoming an ex-pat.

Possibly.

The rain was at full pelt as I stepped off the bus in St Helens. What wouldn't I give for a stinging-hot bath to lower my backside into? But the heating was off. My house would be cold and it would be an hour before the water was hot enough for a bath. I splattered along the road, towing my case behind me through the developing stream.

A fire. I would treat myself to a proper fire.

Two cars soared past, hurling filthy water over me. 'Bastards!' I yelled, dropping my head quickly against the driving rain. I heard another car approaching from behind. I turned towards the hedgerow, bracing myself for the next drenching. The car slowed.

'Hey, I'd offer you a lift but you look pretty wet already.'

It was Luke. I looked over my shoulder. 'Thanks. You carry on. I'll survive.'

He pulled slowly away from me, spray arcing up from his tyres as he headed towards Rookery Cottage.

I shivered and clenched my teeth against the chill creeping through my bones.

The house welcomed me with a nippy hug.

I've often thought it odd how we're warned not to leave candles burning unattended, or to stub cigarettes out fully, in case they smoulder and start a fire, yet try starting one in the grate, with dry sticks, paper and matches and the result is a complete flop.

Smoke. I could make smoke – choking clouds of it.

The smoke alarm screamed from the hallway. I ran about the place, trying to open windows that were locked. Bloody security. So I threw open the seldom-used front door and let even colder air in. I wafted smoke away from the alarm but still it screeched. I opened the back door too, in the hope a through draft would suck the smoke away. I found a bottle of barbecue lighter fuel under the sink. That would do the trick, and returned to the sitting room, shutting the door behind me.

I injected the greying heap of firewood with the fuel and threw another match at it.

Whooff!

We were in business.

As it crackled and soared, I gingerly added small logs, sat back on my haunches and watched in satisfaction as the fire took hold. Fantastic. Heat was hitting my damp thighs and making them steam. I would sit there and dry off.

At last, the smoke alarm stopped panicking. There was now another noise in the hall and the door was thrown open as Luke stood tall and concerned on the threshold.

'Everything okay?'

Oh, lordy. 'Yes. Sorry. Absolutely fine. Could you hear it over at your place?'

'No. I just brought a parcel round for you, it arrived yesterday.'

'A parcel?' I hadn't ordered anything. I stood up and felt damp clothes clinging to my limbs.

'It's in the kitchen. I knocked but I guess you didn't hear me over the alarm.'

'It's one helluvan alarm. I'm surprised my ears aren't bleeding. Or maybe they are – p'raps you should check.' I said as I approached him.

He smiled. 'I fitted that alarm for Una. She nodded

off a couple of times and let the saucepans burn. It has a ten-year battery. Should last you a good while yet.'

'Not me,' I said breezing past him. 'If all goes to plan, I'll be in Dubai this time next year.'

He followed me to the kitchen.

Parked on the centre of the kitchen table, and looking quite majestic, was a huge box marked 'F&M', which could mean only one thing.

I whimpered like a puppy spotting its mother after a long absence. 'It's a hamper from Fortnum & Mason.'

A large one.

I touched the box fondly.

Luke was standing beside me. 'What's this about Dubai?'

'Oh, yes, hang on…' I began scouting around for a pair of scissors to free the hamper from its packaging. 'Rupert's going there to work.'

Luke watched while I sliced the sticky tape. Inside was the most magnificent wicker basket. I tore the cardboard away from it. 'Oh, wow. This is Christmas come early. Look – port, chocolate truffles, pistachio biscuits…Luke, you must try one of these, they're the best.'

'Who's it from?' he asked – ever practical.

'Good point.' I found the card. 'It's from The Divas! Listen to this: "Sending supplies in advance of our visit." Yay! They're coming to see me.'

He smiled. 'Okay, well, I'll leave you to it.'

'No, don't go. Have a cup of tea,' I said, pulling out a box of F&M's finest. 'And one of these biscuits. Please, I can't possibly wait till The Divas arrive – and I don't imagine they really expect me to. I'll put the kettle on, you open the biscuits.'

I went straight to the kettle and filled it. Unless Luke had a ferry to catch, he couldn't possibly desert me now, not when I was celebrating my imminent return to the real world.

'Okay. I'll just check on the fire,' he said.

We sat in armchairs either side of the hearth; warmth on our faces and chill rolling down our backs. 'It takes a good couple of hours for this house to warm up in winter,' I said, my hands wrapped around my tea mug as I watched flames licking over the logs.

'Not something you need worry about in Dubai.'

'No.'

'So, tell me the story, how did Dubai come about. When are you off?'

I filled him in on Rupert's plans. 'His father has some amazing contacts. It's exactly the kind of posting he wanted, so he's really pleased.' Unfortunately, I wasn't but no need to tell Luke that.

Luke nodded. 'Glad it's worked out for him.'

'Odd isn't it? We just never know what's around the corner.'

'True. So what's going to happen about your sculpture work?'

'Oh, I'll work on those till I go, then I'll lock up the studio while I'm away. The tenants will only have access to the house and garden.'

'I meant, what about sculpting while you're away – what will you do? I'm guessing you won't be able to work when you're out there.'

'I am hoping to find a job. In the meantime, I can do lots of other things – read books, do touristy stuff, sketch. I might even build up a batch of ideas for new sculptures – it could inject an Arabic twist into my work.'

He nodded. 'So, do your plans for Bluebell Farm go on hold? The pottery classes, the B&B…'

'Not yet. I'll do everything up until I go. I can't deny I still need the money.'

'Good, well, I guess Dubai is the light at the end of your tunnel.'

'I intend coming back here – when the contract is up.'

'You think?'

'Why not?'

'Won't that depend on Rupert's work?'

I shrugged. 'That's probably a couple of years away.'

Luke nodded, glanced at his watch and then drained his mug.

'Have you planned what you'll be doing in two years, Luke?'

'Nope.' He stood. 'I'm just kinda surprised your plans have taken such a big swerve. You seemed so stoked on building your studio here.'

'I was. I am. This is just a small diversion. And it means Rupert and I will be together, finally.'

'Of course. Well, I wish you luck with it all.' He turned and headed towards the kitchen with his mug. I followed. 'Nice biscuits, by the way,' he said as he opened the back door.

They were lovely biscuits. A little taste of luxury. 'Thanks for delivering them!' I called after him.

He raised his hand as he passed the window.

I could feel something in my heart-space shrink.

Two years from now where would I be?

***

A 'small diversion', thought Luke as he jogged down

the drive away from the farmhouse. She would be travelling half-way round the world to a culture far removed from that of this small British island. Away from the very place she said she loved the most.

And what of her plans? She'd appeared so committed to building up the studio business, and making a go of marketing the farm to holiday-makers.

Typical of her type. Perhaps she was more like Crystal le Blanc than he'd first imagined. Crystal had been so positive – not full of self-doubt like other girls he'd dated. Such positivity had been a huge aphrodisiac for him.

Ava had liked Crystal too. With no mother around to listen to her girlie secrets, Crystal's openness had encouraged the young teen to relax in her company. This had taken a load off Luke's mind and his admiration and love for Crystal had rocketed.

He didn't have a lot to offer, back then, but he'd known he wanted to marry her. His prospects were good and, given a few more years in the company, he'd hold a position of some importance. Just as soon as Ava was off to university, he'd be happy to make a home with Crystal.

It just hadn't been soon enough for Crystal.

No. Crystal wanted the massive wedding with an exclusive spread in some glossy magazine. He'd seen her toes visibly twitching at the prospect of being a celebrity bride. She'd even gone ahead and signed up with the department store's gift service – despite the fact there was no ring on her finger and no date. It was a done deal, as far as she was concerned.

When Luke had broken it to her that things were moving too quickly, her reaction had been fast and cold. Two weeks later, when he was hoping he might broker a reconciliation, he'd spotted a story in the local paper about a charity ball, to which Crystal was 'escorted by Troy Oakley'. More than 'escorted' Luke had deduced from the way they were wrapped around each other.

Two things Crystal and Gigi did have in common: a privileged upbringing and money. Crystal had been given her first pony when she was seven, and a Mercedes coupé at seventeen. He didn't know what Gigi's first car had been, but he'd just bet it wasn't a second-hand Ford. With those kind of benefits in childhood, who could blame them for wanting more of the same throughout the rest of their lives?

Gigi was no more equipped to be patient or to tough it out than Crystal had been.

It seemed she wasn't the strong-minded woman he'd believed her to be.

Nope. It sure looked like Gigi was another spoilt little rich girl who liked the easy life. All it had taken was for Rupert to click his fingers and she'd thrown in the towel.

He shook his head at the disappointing inevitability of it.

It was only later, as he lay in bed staring at the ceiling, another thought hit him: Crystal hadn't felt the love or commitment for him, that Gigi felt for Rupert.

Gigi was different.

He wondered if Rupert appreciated that.

Chapter 26

Dubai or no Dubai, my finances were not about to miraculously recover but at least the money for Amanda Connell's horses was a constant. She'd handed over six hundred pounds at the end of September. The December payment would be even more welcome after Christmas.

Christmas. If I were to make any money from my wares as gifts, I would need to get a spurt on. Angels were my current passion but they took ages and should carry a very high price tag. Even if I managed to make half a dozen in time, I might not sell a single one. Knocking out mugs would be fast but tedious, yet the smaller the product, the more I could complete in a firing, which would be the most economical option.

Keeping with the angel theme, I came up with an Art Nouveau style wall plaque. Once I had the model complete, I would make Plaster of Paris moulds and make multiple plaques. I could add individuality at the decoration stage. If I struck just the right style, they might work indoors or outdoors.

On an even more commercial level, I would try making mugs. I couldn't rely on being able to produce sets of six identical mugs, so I decided on individual ones personalized with an initial letter. Named mugs would be too much of a gamble but if I made mugs with common names in mind, and applied a large letter 'A' or 'J' on the side, I stood a reasonable chance of selling those.

I aimed to build up a stock by the last week in November. Yes. Bluebell Farm Studio had merchandise to produce. I needed to buy more clay. It wasn't expensive, per se, but being low on funds, the question was, what could I go without? Scratch that, what could I sell? There was barely a rattle of loose change in my bank account and my credit card had been maxed out on the car.

Nanna had been a botanical illustrator. There were prints galore in the loft, a hangover from the days when she exhibited at local craft shows. Perhaps I could try those on e-bay.

E-bay.

I didn't have an account. Yet another thing for my To-Do list.

I had a full week to get underway with my work before The Divas arrived, and then I would kick back and have some well-earned girlie fun. I needed it.

Samba band practice was, I have to say, the best therapy on offer. Whilst getting my hands stuck into clay pacified my creative urges, thrashing my tamborim for a couple of hours a week did wonders for lowering my stress level. I'd walk in to the rehearsal feeling knotted up, and glide out with my nerves unkinked. Miraculous.

I had a ramble around Google where I discovered drumming actually promotes the production of endogenous opiates. Fact! I was high on samba.

Sadly, I didn't have a sound-proof room at the farm, and bashing a pillow with my tamborim beater didn't quite cut it, so by the time band practice came around, I was wide-eyed and twitching like a junkie.

Megan found this hilarious. 'Gigi, hun, ready to score?'

'You have no idea.'

'Think I do. Mackay has reached the Terrible Twos. I had to carry him, rigid, from the beach on Sunday. He wanted to fill his sand hole with sea water.'

'You didn't fancy waiting for the tide to come in, then?'

'No. Midnight's a cold and lonely place on Appley Beach.'

'Dubai!' exclaimed Sonia, the moment I let slip my new plans. 'You lucky mare! It's absolutely one of the best cities I've ever been to. The shopping – the beaches – the hotels – oh, and the GOLD. I'll be flying over to see you at least once a month.'

'If you didn't spend all that money on flights, darling, you could afford to shop in Bond Street,' Fran grumbled.

'Fran, I can shop in Bond Street anytime. Where's the fun in that?'

We were lazing on the floor in front of the fire, sharing a bottle of white wine and a bowl of mixed wasabi treats from the hamper, while my budget chilli con carne simmered on the stove; that's vegetarian mince, budget kidney beans and tinned tomatoes with heaps of chilli powder and onions, all enriched with a dollop of black treacle. Once we hit the bottle of red, they wouldn't care what they were eating.

'I don't mind how often you come to visit. I won't know a soul out there, apart from Rupert.'

'Well, if Rupe has any scrummy work colleagues you can introduce me to, I might end up in Dubai myself!' she grinned. 'I quite fancy a touch of the ex-pat lifestyle.'

'What about your job?' I asked.

She wrinkled her nose. 'Too many women. I need a change of scene.'

'I don't know why you're complaining,' Fran said. 'You've had more dates this year than half of Camden Town.'

'I like a busy social life.'

'What happened to that Malaysian Chiropractor you were seeing?' I asked. 'He sounded promising.'

'Oh…Tuan.' A wicked twinkle appeared in her eye. 'He was definitely flexible. I'm pretty sure he knew every position in the Kama Sutra.'

'Including the publisher's logo,' Fran added.

Sonia snorted with laughter. 'Trouble is, that's all there was. Plenty of activity but not much of a party boy. You know me, I like to mingle and mix.'

'You do.'

'Speaking of which,' Sonia continued, 'I don't suppose any of those lovely building chappies are coming over this weekend, are they? I could quite enjoy a bit of rough banter.'

I should have expected this. 'No, Sonia, fraid not.'

'What about Nanna's fancy-man – is he still around?'

'Luke – who happens to be a very clever palaeontologist – has been really helpful to me, actually.'

'He didn't get his hands on Nanna's dosh, he's probably hoping to get them on yours.'

'What dosh do I have?'

'P'raps he just wants to have his evil way with you, then.'

I pushed myself up off the floor. 'Sonia, I'll leave you to savour that tawdry little image, while I go and put the rice on.'

'Is there time for me to have a shower?' she asked.

'Now?'

'Yes. What's wrong with that?'

'There won't be enough hot water. It's not due to come on till six tomorrow morning.'

The way she looked at me, you'd think I'd asked her to fetch a bucket from the well.

'Oh,' she said in a very clipped manner.

'Sorry, I didn't think...'

'Suck it up, Sonia,' moaned Fran. 'You can shower in the morning.'

'I could put the emersion heater on, but it won't be ready for about twenty minutes.'

Sonia looked tempted, but Fran took her wine glass and refilled it. 'You're not getting laid tonight, darling, you can go to bed grubby. We won't mind.'

Fran followed me to the kitchen for another bottle. 'Aren't you a little bit sorry to be leaving this rural idyll for downtown Dubai?'

'Very funny, Fran.'

'I wasn't joking.'

'Really? Everyone thought I was mad moving over here – even you.'

'Not entirely.' I looked at her over the pan of rice. She continued, 'You've always been a bit different – dancing to your own Gigi gavotte. It's what I like most about you.'

I smiled. 'Aw, thanks.'

'You were sounding so fired up about your plans for the farm, especially the sculptures and the workshops. Last time we spoke you were buzzing.'

'I was. But it's really hard. And Rupert...'

'Can be persuasive.'

'No! Not that. We want to be together. If Nanna hadn't died, if I was still working for Dad... you know it would have been different. Now he's going to Dubai I don't really have a choice, do I?'

'I thought so.'

'What?'

'You're not as excited about going as you make out.'

Why was she judging me?

'Your point being...?' I glared at her.

She stared back at me for a moment before moving over to hug me. 'Sorry, babe. You've been having a crap time. Of course you want to be with Rupert.'

I sighed over her shoulder. 'I know it's not part of the plan, at least my plan, but it is an opportunity to do something different.' I stepped back and lifted the lid on the chilli to give it a stir. 'It's not for ever. My long-term goal hasn't changed. There's plenty of stuff going on for ex-pats out there. Who knows what opportunities might come up?'

'I like your attitude, sweetie.'

'How about your situation?' I ventured. Fran hadn't been very forthcoming on the phone about the affair with her boss. I was hoping, face to face, I might at least be able to assess how she was coping.

'I'm glad to get away from it this weekend.'

'It's still going on?'

There was a noise as Sonia headed our way.

'So, how long till we eat?' Fran asked, changing the subject.

'Fifteen minutes. Shall we eat in here?'

'Can't we eat off trays, in front of the fire?' Sonia asked. 'It's cosier. Oh – what's that bottle of Rioja doing there and where's the corkscrew? It won't have time to breathe before I get my lips round it.'

Fran grabbed the bottle. 'I'll whizz it up in Gigi's blender, that'll oxygenate it pretty bloody fast.'

Within minutes of dinner being consumed, Fran stretched and stood up. 'If it's okay with you guys, I'm off to bed.'

Sonia rolled her eyes. 'Lightweight.'

'Sorry. I got up at six.'

She certainly looked weary, but I put that down to the strain of her love life. 'Night, Fran,' I said, sitting up to hug her.

Minutes later, Sonia surprised me. 'Fran's really unhappy, and I don't know why. I can't shake her out of it. D'you think she's bi-polar?'

It wasn't my place to enlighten her. 'You know Fran – she's always been more grounded than us two. Perhaps she just takes life more seriously.'

'Well, she's seriously sad and I don't want her to be. I thought coming down here would cheer her up.'

'Give it another twenty-four hours. She just hasn't clicked in to the weekend groove, yet.'

'Maybe.'

We tuned back in to the telly. After a while, she said, 'Do you have any cheese?'

I went for the two packs included in the hamper, along with the crackers. By the time I came back, she was asleep. I fetched the duvet from her bed and draped it over her. I'd have had more luck rousing a flattened hedgehog than trying to wake Sonia in that state.

'We're walking how far?' Sonia croaked, through a mouthful of toast.

'Just a couple of miles. It's mostly along the beach,' I said.

'That doesn't make it any shorter.'

Fran was focussed on her phone; tapping out messages and waiting for the ping of a reply.

'No but it's more enjoyable.'

'Where are we going?'

'Seaview.' I looked at the clock. 'We need to leave in the next twenty minutes if you don't want wet feet.'

'Huh?'

'We need to do the walk during low tide.'

'It gets worse! I don't want to be marooned.'

'You won't be. Worst case scenario – we'll climb up through the woods at the back of the beach.'

She groaned. 'I'd like to retract my last statement. If I could be marooned on a Caribbean island with Aidan Turner, I wouldn't complain.'

Fran looked up. 'So long as there was a free bar and air conditioning.'

'Natch.'

From the Duver we made our way across the beach towards Priory Bay.

An easterly wind was pushing us along. 'Couldn't you have hired some of those beach kite thingies?' Sonia asked. 'You know, like skate boards with a sail on?'

'Sail-boards.'

'Exactly.'

'Watch out. Incoming!' Fran warned as a dog came bounding towards us. He thrust his soggy head into my welcoming hands.

'Hello, Chuck, you gorgeous boy. Have you been for a lovely swim?'

He dodged back and shook some of the sogginess

onto the rest of us.

Luke was a few feet away. The wind had whipped strands of curly hair from his ponytail, and was causing him to squint against the force of it.

'It's your neighbour isn't it?' Fran muttered.

'Yes.'

'Who?' Sonia asked.

'Morning, Luke,' I said as he approached. There was a throaty 'Aha!' from Sonia.

'Morning, ladies.' He nodded to Fran, 'Hello again.'

'Hi,' she said, offering her hand to shake. 'It's Fran.'

'Fran, I remember,' he said, shaking it briefly. 'I see the magic of the island has drawn you back.'

Sonia stepped forward. 'Bugger the island, we've come to see our darling Gigi.' She thrust her hand forward and fixed him with a penetrating stare. 'I'm Sonia,' she added with a challenging smile.

'Good to meet you, Sonia.'

Her default setting around men – regardless of age or class – was High Voltage Sexual Allure. Creating desire had long been a pastime of hers. Before she'd had chance to suck him into her force-field, he turned back to me, 'It's a great day for clearing the head, right?'

'We're walking to Seaview for lunch,' I said – not that I needed to.

'Looks like you should just about beat the rain.'

Sonia frowned at the sky. 'Are you predicting rain, Luke?' and transferred the frown to him.

'It's forecast.'

'Are you from the States?'

'Canada.'

'Oh really? Then a drop of rain won't worry you in the slightest, will it?'

He nodded. 'You mean, I'm usually up to my neck in snow, right?'

'That's what they say.'

Fran and I watched this exchange with mounting curiosity. Sonia spent her life surfing the breakers of society. She could engage anyone on any subject – no wonder she was a whiz in PR. Since we both doubted her desire to hook up with Nanna's Fancy-man, it was interesting to see where this was going.

'It's such a huge country, Canada. What draws you to a tiny island like this one?'

He looked at her for a moment, and I could see a vague flicker of amusement cross his eyes before he huffed a small laugh. He moved to pass us. 'No snow.'

'Touché.'

'See you ladies,' he added and was off, striding back towards The Duver.

'Nice try, Sonia,' I whispered as he went.

She winked at me before calling out. 'Hey, Luke!' He stopped and looked round. She did a girly run over the sand towards him. 'If you're not busy tonight, why don't you come out with us for a drink?'

'I'm playing ice-hockey tonight.'

'Great! Where do you go to drink after? There must be room for three gorgeous girls to join you?'

Luke glanced across at us. I shook my head and mouthed, 'Don't worry.'

With a smile for Sonia, he said. 'Sure. We'll be in Fowlers.'

'Blood and sand,' said Fran as she came back to us. 'D'you ever give up?'

'Hey, it's a night out with some ice hockey hunks and an opportunity to see what Nanna's Fancy Man is made of.'

'How do you know I didn't already have plans?' I asked.

Sonia looked suddenly guilty. 'Sorry, Gigi. I didn't think. What did you have in mind?'

'I thought we could go for a drink in Ryde.'

'Oh. So where's Fowlers?'

I hesitated. 'Ryde.'

'Ta-da!'

Together we linked arms and headed across the beach and round the rocks into Priory Bay.

'Are we there, yet?' asked Sonia.

'I'd say we were half-way.'

'Ugh. I hope they have taxis in Seaview. I'm not doing this in reverse.'

'You don't have to. We'll get a bus.'

'A bus?!' She changed her tone. 'Okay. That's sweet. This weekend's starting to remind me of school trips, and they were always fun.'

'Yeah, arranging to meet a bunch of strange boys in a bar sounds very familiar,' added Fran.

Chapter 27

For the second weekend on the trot I was glamming up. Not that I could be considered glam alongside The Divas. Let's just say I parked the trainers and overalls in favour of my best Marc Jacobs' top and jeans, with a string of huge gold and amber beads.

I folded myself onto the back shelf of Fran's sports-car. Okay, it's not exactly a shelf but neither is it a seat, unless you happen to be a Chihuahua.

Fran was looking ultra-cool in a grey woollen sheath dress that skimmed her narrow hips, while Sonia rocked the night scene in a crimson camisole and jacket – both trimmed with pearls – and skin-tight black jeans. Her blonde hair was fluffed and pinned high on her head, and I'm guessing the crimson lipstick came with the jacket. Fragrances of Mitsuko, Balenciaga and Cartier mingled to form a fragrant cloud over our heads as we strode into the pub.

But Ryde isn't Chelsea so there was no squirming and slithering through crowds of equally fragrant lovelies to reach the bar. No, that only happens in Ryde during the holiday season or New Year's Eve. Sonia didn't mind. She liked being conspicuous.

Luke and three of his hockey mates were already at the bar – hardly surprising, it was nearly ten o'clock.

'I thought you'd opted for a quiet night in,' he said as we joined them.

'Are we late?' Sonia asked, making eye contact with each and every one of them. She had a knack of shifting her body so her eyes moved in perfect unison with her boobs. She believed nobody should be denied her full charms. Sonia was very generous where her charms were concerned.

'I'd say you're just in time,' said one of them, fixing on Sonia like he was within two balls of a lottery win.

We were swiftly supplied with drinks and the night was underway.

I don't believe I was deliberately steering clear of Luke, I hadn't set out to, but it seemed a lot easier to talk to anybody but him. I hadn't forgotten the look of disillusionment which crossed his face when we'd discussed Dubai. He was, quite possibly, the only person outside our family who knew how much Nanna had wanted me to make Bluebell Farm my home.

I still would – one day – I was sure of that.

To add to my discomfort, Dan Shaw – a man I had every reason to avoid, following the earlier embarrassment of unpaid bills – was standing with him. I hadn't factored his presence into the evening at all.

Ryan – the guy hoping to hit the jackpot with Sonia tonight – was very entertaining. He was one of those laugh-em-into-bed types. Not that he needed to try particularly hard with Sonia. It was Saturday night and she was wearing her magic bra: under-wired for presentation, with the nipple patches snipped out for maximum impact. If he'd known how accommodating Sonia could be, he might have shelved his best material for her next visit.

I hung around for the laughs and there were plenty. Lord knows there'd been precious few in the recent weeks. There'd also been much less alcohol, so after a couple of large G&Ts, Ryan's jokes were sounding really funny. His mate, Grant, was very lacklustre but laughter's a great leveller so I forgave him his dullness and we chuckled companionably together.

But it was Sonia's night and Ryan was Sonia's prey. So when her flashing eyes began raising his temperature, I stepped away.

Followed by Grant who had a hungry look in his eyes.

Fran was holding court with Luke and Dan.

Shit. I didn't want Grant thinking I was this evening's take-away. I might be tipsy but I wasn't completely leathered. There was nothing for it, I'd have to latch on to Fran, so I rammed my arm through hers and gave it a squeeze.

'Hello, darling,' she said. 'We're just talking about Darwin.'

'Right. Evolution and all that. I imagine you have plenty of time to contemplate such things when you're examining fossils, don't you?' I looked up at a smiling Luke.

Dan Shaw chipped in. 'We were talking about Darwin, Australia. I've just spent three weeks in the Northern Territory.'

'Oh that Darwin.'

'That Darwin.'

'But named after Charles Darwin, as it happens,' Luke added.

'Well there ya go!' I was downright tiddly.

The bell rang for last orders. Fran, being designated driver, opted for coffee.

'Smart choice. Black coffee over here, too.'

Grant went to the bar, while I set about pretending

to be sober. 'Do you have a theory on evolution?' I asked Luke.

'Darwin was pretty much on the money. Look back far enough into the earth's sediment, and the types of plants and creatures you discover do evolve over time.'

I nodded slowly to show I understood.

'Did you know, birds are considered to be direct descendents of dinosaurs?' he asked, warming to his subject.

I thought for a moment. 'I could see that happening. They all have two legs with claws, don't they?'

Grant handed over our drinks and joined in the discussion. 'Do you believe all dogs are descended from wolves?'

'Could be.'

'So a Yorkshire Terrier and a Saluki are distant cousins? I just don't see it. A wolf mutates into a Great Dane in Germany, and a Bulldog over here.' He shrugged. 'Nah.'

Luke shrugged and said, 'If only we had a complete and comprehensive collection of fossils for every species.'

'Why don't we?' asked Dan.

'Because you need unique conditions…'

Later, as I finished my coffee, I looked around the bar. 'Fran, where's Sonia?'

'Gone off with Ryan.'

'I didn't see her go.'

'No. You were trying to impress Luke at the time.'

'I so wasn't!'

'You so were.'

'Is she coming back?'

'In time for lunch, I would think.'

'She's got her phone, hasn't she?'

Fran pulled her own out of her bag and flicked through to her tracking app and waited for it to synch. 'Yes, looks like it. She's heading west in pursuit of pleasure.'

'Do you want to go to a club?' Grant asked, as we placed our empty cups on the bar. If Sonia had been with us, the decision would most definitely have been made for us. I looked at Fran, Fran looked at me and I said, 'I think we'll probably pass.'

We headed outside, where wind was gusting off the Solent. It had been gathering pace all day. The sea air acted like a catalyst on the booze in my bloodstream, making my brain tip off-centre. I anchored myself between Fran and Luke.

'I see you've lost Sonia,' Luke commented.

'Not entirely,' Fran said. 'She's in Binstead.'

'Makes sense.'

'It's Ryan's lucky night,' I said, clutching them both. 'Sonia does Pilates.'

'Right.'

'Pelvic floor like a bulldog clip.'

Luke's laugh was as loud as it was surprising. 'Gabriella! What would your grandmother say?'

'She'd hoot with laughter and say, "Lucky old Ryan." '

The weather was clearly going to wreak havoc on the island. Fran had to dodge a large branch on the road, and there were twigs scattered everywhere, like vermicelli. I insisted she drive very slowly, and I watched every bend and dip for hazards. It was strangely sobering.

The house was cold again so we snuggled together

under my big duvet to drink hot chocolate and watch MTV.

After a while, I said, 'I know you find this difficult, Fran, but please tell me you're going to be okay over this affair you're having. I'm worried about you. Even Sonia's worried about you.'

'You haven't told her?'

'No, of course not, but she knows there's something wrong.'

Fran hutched her knees up under her chin. 'It's not a straightforward situation.'

'These things never are. But either he finishes with you or he finishes with his wife. He must know he can't have both of you. And you don't want to be second-best, surely? You're worth more than that.'

'It's not really down to him.'

'What? So it's you – you're the one keeping it going?'

I had visions of Fran doing a Glenn Close in *Fatal Attraction*.

'Like I said, it's not that straightforward. He…' she sighed. 'He isn't the issue.'

'It's the wife then, refusing to let go. Is she threatening him – threatening you?'

'No. She's lovely.' Fran tilted her head towards me and rested it on her knees. Her gaze was intense – like she was willing me to join the dots. A big tear welled in her eye and spilled out over her nose. 'I love her.'

The emphasis made it suddenly clear. 'Your affair is with the wife?'

A feeble smile twitched on her face.

'Oh, Fran.' I leaned over and hugged her.

Back at uni, while Sonia had been sampling male undergraduates from every faculty, Fran had embarked on her own odyssey and investigated all areas of her sexuality. She'd even flirted with me, once. But in her final year she'd appeared to 'settle' into heterosexual normality, as if the wild years had purely been experimentation.

'She's my boss's wife. She works in a different department.'

'What's her name?'

'Alissa.' She said it with pride and tenderness.

'Does her husband have any idea?'

She shrugged. 'He's still flirting with me himself, so I doubt it.'

'And the baby's his?'

'Well it isn't mine.'

We sniggered like schoolgirls. Fran wiped her eyes and sniffed.

'She's not leaving him, then?'

'Not leaving him, not telling him.'

'Even though he flirts with you?'

'It's just office banter.'

'Have you asked her to leave?'

'I've asked her to be honest.' Her voice rose. 'She says she doesn't want to end our affair because she loves me. But she refuses to tell him. Whatever happened to authenticity?'

'It's one thing to own up to having an affair, Fran, you're also asking her to tell the world she's not who they think she is.'

'This isn't the dark ages. We have same sex marriage now, you know.'

I let the mood settle for a moment. 'Fran, you're not completely out of the closet yourself, are you?'

She looked a little sheepish. 'You knew how I was at uni, and I did tell my parents I was bi.'

'Yes, but then you only took boyfriends home.'

'I didn't have many of those, did I? I'm not the settling down type. At least, I didn't think I was.'

'Till now.'

'The baby is why she's staying with Jeremy. He wants a family. Their parents want grandchildren.' She sighed. 'Oh, Gigi, it's a complete mess.'

I couldn't argue with that. What's more, I had no solution up my sleeve. Instead, I hugged her to me. 'Fran, Nanna used to say, "If something's worth having, it's worth fighting for." Maybe you have to decide if you're prepared to fight.'

She shook her head. 'You can't do battle with a pregnant woman.'

Outside, the windstorm was throwing an almighty tantrum. It was like a foreshadowing of the emotional cyclone in store for Fran.

We lay, watching music videos, until we fell asleep.

Hours later, a hammering on the front door jolted us awake. 'Why didn't she ask me for a key before she ran off with lover-boy?' I said grumpily and rolled out of bed.

At least the storm had passed and sunlight was slanting through the curtains.

I unlocked the door and pulled it open. Amanda Connell was on the doorstep. 'Sorry to wake you, Gabriella. The storm brought a branch down onto the stable. It's right through the roof.'

'Jeez! Are the horses okay?'

'No physical damage that I can see, but the roof needs repairing. Rain's forecast so you might want to get some tarpaulin fixed over it till then.'

'Of course. I'm so sorry about that, Amanda.'

'Not your fault.'

'I'll grab some clothes and come over.'

'No rush. We're going riding and the weather should hold till lunchtime.'

'Okay. Thanks for letting me know.'

I waved her off and leaned against the door.

'When is my life going to get easier?' I whispered.

Most of the damage was across the front corner of the roof – affecting the shelter above the stable doors, but the fractured beam and roof timbers continued over the supporting wall, exposing part of the stall to the elements.

Fran had come with me.

'Where am I going to get a tarpaulin, today?'

'Ring Dan Shaw, he's a builder.'

'On a Sunday – do you think I should? He'll be watching Match of the Day in his pyjamas and eating leftover curry.'

'That's pretty intimate knowledge, Ms Gill-Martin. Do you have something you wish to confess?'

I smiled at her. It was good to see she was more chipper today. 'No.'

It seemed I was not the first distressed island resident to call Dan for his professional services. Trees, fences and roof slates had been ripped up all over the place. 'Sorry, Gigi, I won't be able to get to you today. It's a timber roof, isn't it?'

'Yes.'

'Find some plastic sacks and nail them over the opening. That should be enough to keep the worst of the rain out. I'll come by tomorrow, if I can.'

Thank goodness I had a roll of polythene sheeting in my studio.

Between us, we managed to rig up a temporary roof across the corner and stood back to admire our handy-work.

'Who needs men?' asked Fran.

'Sonia.' I replied.

Chapter 28

Ryan dropped a satiated and smudged Sonia back to us in time for lunch, when we headed down to Ganders on the Green for Sunday roast.

I'd persuaded Fran she needed to tell Sonia about her situation because, in spite of a hedonistic attitude to life, Sonia really cared about Fran. Plus, I was convinced part of Fran's agony came from keeping everything bottled up. So, on our walk to the restaurant, it all came out.

'Thank God for that!' Sonia said, hugging her fiercely. 'I thought it was me.'

'No. Just me.'

'If you want my advice, you should withdraw your favours. Take away the sugar,' she suggested, unabashed. 'Or doesn't it work like that with women?'

'I don't know, Sonia. Does it even work with men?'

'Sometimes. But you're probably right, I'm not really qualified to advise on affairs of the heart, my expertise is further south.'

'Well, now you know my shabby little secret, I'd be very grateful if you didn't broadcast it to the rest of the crowd.'

'Cross my heart.'

I touched Fran's arm, 'It's not a shabby little secret, Fran. Alissa is who you love, and we're okay with that. The problem is, you've fallen for somebody who's married and that complicates things – whatever the gender.'

She stopped walking. 'I know.'

I glanced at Sonia who said, 'Either she loves you or she loves her marriage more. Sooner or later she has to decide.'

'That's the problem. She has decided and it's not me.'

'Then it's her who'll be living the lie, not you.'

I agreed. 'But you can't "out" her, Fran, it would be cruel. It'd be like shoving a reluctant swimmer into the deep end and watching them panic.'

'I wouldn't dream of it. Alissa's love for her baby has changed everything and I don't blame her. She wants it to have the stability of an untroubled home life. She wants Jeremy to be its father – fulltime not just weekends and holidays.'

'D'you think she'll ever tell him?'

Fran shrugged. 'Now this hormonal soup of motherhood has kicked in, she sees things differently. It's hard to reach her.'

'Did you know they were trying for a baby?' I asked.

'No.'

Sonia gave me a look of disapproval. I knew what she meant – Alissa hadn't been entirely honest with Fran, and she wasn't being honest with Jeremy either.

'Life can be so complicated,' I said, aiming for neutrality. 'Any mother might do the same.'

'Exactly. I just have to suck it up and move on.'

The restaurant came into view. 'Here it is.'

'Great. Let's have a good lunch. I need fortifying before that bloody journey up the M3.'

Moments later as we stepped inside, Sonia said – loudly enough for the staff to hear, 'What a darling little restaurant.' It was a trick she often used to encourage the best service. 'I love it!'

The knotty subject of Fran's private life was parked for now, and she very generously treated us to roast beef and Yorkshire pud, followed by Strawberry Pavlova.

The house was cold, quiet and empty with The Divas gone. A note from Amanda was on the doormat, thanking me for patching up the stable. I groaned to myself – having conveniently forgotten about the responsibility of repairing the roof. At least it would be covered by the insurance.

An icy blast of dread surged through me.

'Oh, dear God, let me be insured for this!' I roared, and rushed to the dining room. All my legal papers were in a filing box.

I pulled it open.

Don't go mad, I told myself. Approach this calmly. You are not in an episode of Eastenders.

Calm down. Breathe.

I read the household insurance papers carefully. I read some sentences at least twice in an effort to understand them.

I didn't.

In panic, I began skip reading, just looking for the word *Stable*. It wasn't there.

Outhouse? Nothing.

External buildings? Nope.

Field? Nada.

Paddock? Shit! 'There has to be another policy, obviously,' I told the house. A separate one, probably something to do with public liability.

I put the household papers on the table and dug around in the file.

I found the TV Licence – at least that didn't expire till April.

A faded brown envelope at the back said: Bluebell Paddock. 'Yessss!!'

Slowly, I took the papers out, begging for just one small break in my personal hell of insolvency.

It was, however, an invoice for the construction of the stable, dated 2007.

There was nothing else to read.

Dan's estimate for repairs rocked me back on my heels.

'It's not just a hole in the roof. The supporting wall and the beam are damaged. I could probably fit it in next week, if you want to go ahead.'

I barely nodded. Payment would boil down to whatever I could sell or whomever I could pester for help. Winter was on its way, I didn't have any option but to do it.

'Thanks, Dan. I'll give you a call in a couple of days.'

'Okay but don't leave it too long. The whole structure has been compromised by the damage.'

'I know.'

Amanda wouldn't want her horses endangered by any further dilapidation. I waved him off with another thought brewing. Perhaps Amanda would pay for the repairs in return for free stabling over the next year. Then, after twelve months, I would pay her back with interest. Jeff Atterbury could calculate that.

It was worth a try.

I paced the kitchen while I made the call. Immediately Amanda's reluctance trickled through the phone. 'It's not that I disagree in principle,' she said, 'it's more that I don't know if we'll be here for much longer.'

'Oh.'

'We want to move back to the mainland and John's already applying for jobs. So you see, I might be giving you notice in the New Year.'

'I understand.'

'You will keep an eye on the damage, won't you? Until it can be repaired? I looked this morning and it seemed to be holding up but if the wind gets up again…'

'Of course. Dan says he can do it next week.'

'Excellent. Thanks for the call, and sorry I can't help.'

She couldn't help and she couldn't promise there would be continued income for the paddock.

I sank into one of the chairs by the table and lowered my head onto my arms.

Maybe Rupert was right. I should sell Bluebell Farm. It was madness to think I could maintain this house on my own.

'Nanna, how did you cope?' I mumbled into the oak. 'Because I'm not doing very well, am I?'

There was a tap on the window. I looked up, saw Luke and waved him in.

'You okay?' he asked.

'I've been better.'

'Wassup?' he pulled the chair out next to me and sat down.

Did I really want to divulge all my concerns to him? I stared at the knots in the wood, now so familiar to me. He wouldn't want to hear about my financial worries.

He broke the silence. 'Dan told me about the

stable.'

'Did he?' I looked at him. His eyes were the darkest brown and I saw, for the first time, how his nose was perfectly shaped. There was an exquisite symmetry to the upper part of his face. I could only speculate on the outline of his jaw beneath that beard. Perhaps his face – clean-shaven – might make the ideal study for one of my angels.

'I have a suggestion. You might not like it, and I apologise if I'm interfering but...' he stopped and studied me, like he feared I might be too fragile to hear it.

'What? What on earth are you going to say?' I asked, bracing myself for another blow.

He sat back a little. 'I'd like to suggest I do the work for you. Dan will provide the materials and get me started. He knows I'm capable of doing it, and it'll save you the labour costs. Plus, I'll be doing him a favour. He's stacked out with other repairs.' The line of his mouth flattened, as he waited for my reaction.

He waited a few moments as I absorbed it. Labour costs formed the bulk of Dan's quote. Grateful tears welled up as his offer sank in. He *was* an angel. 'Are you sure?' I managed, conscious my chin was puckering and I had no control over it.

'Unless you had someone else in mind? Maybe Rupert's good with that kind of thing.'

'Rupert?'

'Architecture, you know, construction being his thing.'

'Oh, yes. No. No, Rupert isn't...well, he might be...'

I hadn't even thought to ask Rupert. Rupert was the kind of guy who found other people to get their hands dirty. He was more of a delegator, a foreman, the man holding the plans and wearing the hard hat. I wiped the tears away from my face and sniffed. 'I doubt Rupert will be able come down in time, anyway.'

'Okay, well, the offer's there.'

'Luke, you are a lifesaver.'

'No, just helping out,' he said, standing up.

I stood too, and followed him to the door. 'I haven't even offered you a drink. Would you like one?'

He hesitated. 'No, you're okay. I've things to do.'

'Thanks again, Luke. I really appreciate it.'

'I know. You take care.'

I watched him go and my eyes prickled again. 'Thanks, Nanna,' I whispered, and allowed myself a good sniffle.

I took my cuppa over to the studio and set about wedging some clay. Maybe I could turn out a dozen or so mugs before the monotony froze my grey matter. I always found churning out identical domestic pots a tad industrial for my creative brain, but needs must. Monogrammed mugs meant pennies in the bank – so long as I sold them.

I got stuck in, necessity driving me beyond boredom to a place of purpose. Two hours later, I had twenty acceptable mug bodies, which meant there were twenty handles to pull. I would do this. My fate was, quite literally, in my own hands. And I liked the feeling.

Chapter 29

Two days later, Dan delivered materials to the paddock and stayed an hour to get Luke started. Grant came along to help out. I'm ashamed to say, he didn't seem quite so dull when engaged in physical labour repairing my stable.

I popped out to see them with coffee and biscuits, and suggested they might like to stay for dinner. 'It's only vegetarian lasagne but it's home-made.'

Grant looked crest-fallen. 'I'd love to, but it's scouts tonight. I'm troop leader.'

'Ah, that's a pity. Well, not for the scouts, obviously. How about you, Luke?'

'Sounds great, if it's no trouble.'

I pointed at the stable. 'If I could repair that roof with lasagne, I would. You guys are doing me a MASSIVE favour. I assure you, it's no trouble at all.'

Later that afternoon, Gaudi was perched on the windowsill, languidly licking his hind leg as I spread garlic butter onto some crusty bread, ready to bake. The lasagne was releasing its delicious Mediterranean aroma into the kitchen and twilight was settling over the courtyard.

I smiled, counting myself lucky to have good friends around me. And in that moment, my phone trilled from the table. Rupert was calling, at last, although it wasn't unusual for us to go days without speaking. We were happy to give each other space. I wiped my fingers and picked up the phone.

'Hi,' he said, sounding tense. This final year of

study was a tough one. It was taking its toll on him. Or so I thought.

His first statement was a blow to the solar plexus when he said, very seriously, 'Gigi, you and I have a problem.'

'We do?'

'I don't really know how to say this…'

'Rupe, just say it. Tell me.'

'Freddy owes me money.'

My first reaction was: 'Is that all?' but the gravity of his tone stopped me. 'How much?'

'Four grand, plus interest.'

'Four grand? When? How? I mean…'

'I gave him some of it while he was travelling, before I knew your Dad was going to vaporise into oblivion. Freddy said he couldn't ask your Dad for money, because they'd had a falling out – which in fairness, Gigi, isn't unusual for Freddy is it? But he assured me, once the row had blown over, he'd be good for paying it back, and I believed him.'

'You said you gave him "some of it", when did you give him the rest?'

'The other weekend, when I was in Southampton.'

'What? When you were with me.'

'I saw him before you came over.'

'You never said.'

'No, well, it wasn't totally above board.'

'What? What are you talking about, Rupert, you're starting to scare me.'

'He had some…' There was a long gap punctuated by a couple of deep breaths, which sounded vaguely sinister across the ether. 'He had some goods to sell. I had some friends who were interested…'

'Shit! Rupe, are the two of you selling drugs?' I

hissed.

'Don't be ridiculous, Gigi. That would be illegal.'

'I know! So what are these "goods" you're talking about?'

There was another pause.

'It's just a few blue movies.'

I rolled my eyes. 'Oh, Rupert!'

'The goods were faulty.'

'What – you mean the DVDs wouldn't work, or the models weren't pretty enough?'

'I mean nothing was delivered.'

'Like – lost in the post?'

'No! They're delivered online but the site's disappeared. And so, it seems, has Freddy, with my money. He's not answering his phone or his emails. And I'm out of pocket, as are a whole bunch of my friends.'

'I don't understand, Rupe. How could a few blue movies cost so much?'

'It's not just the movies, I invested in his shady little business.' I could imagine his teeth clenching over the words.

I lowered the phone and stared at the wall.

'Gigi? What's going on?' I heard him snapping.

I lifted it back up. 'Rupert, this is insane. You are insane. I don't believe we're even having this conversation.'

'Well, we are, Gigi. And you'd better find that bent little brother of yours, and his bent little mates, and get my money back!'

He was gone.

'Or what?!' I yelled into the empty kitchen. 'What, Rupert? You think I'm going to ride over to Willow View, on one of Amanda's horses, with a shotgun under my arm?'

I rang Freddy. Voicemail. 'Nice one, Freddy!' I yelled, slamming the phone down on the oven gloves. At least I had the presence of mind not to smash it down on the work-surface.

I span round and continued berating the absent Rupert across the table. 'Since when did I become your bloody debt-collector?' I yelled. 'And as for Freddy – I stopped having any influence over him when his voice broke.'

There was a clatter as Gaudi made his getaway over the draining board and out through the cat-flap.

I yelled again and Rodin shot through from the sitting room, and straight out after Gaudi.

***

As Luke walked up the farm's drive, he could hear Gabriella's raised voice. One of the cats shot out across the courtyard, followed by a guttural cry from inside, and another cat.

He hit the gravel hard as he sprinted towards the house.

'Will you never give me a break?' he heard, loud and clear.

Through the kitchen window he could see her alone, arms thrown out like an evangelist preaching to the blank wall. 'I don't want to have to deal with this shit!'

He hesitated. If he entered now, he might get a saucepan round the back of his head.

'Raargh!' she roared again, before bringing her fists down and stamping her foot.

This wasn't the Gabriella he recognised. He doubted it was even the Gigi her friends knew. He just bet it had something to do with Freddy. That guy was trouble.

He watched as she dropped her head back and closed her eyes – like she was summoning up the courage to handle whatever had been dealt her. After a moment, she seemed to regain her composure. Then she turned and looked out of the window and directly at him.

He blinked, unsure just what exactly might develop. But he had no intention of leaving and he couldn't pretend he hadn't witnessed her outburst.

As he stepped towards the door, she beat him to it and yanked it open.

'Luke, I need a favour. Another favour. Sorry.'

'What's up?'

She was already back across the kitchen, and reaching for her phone. 'I need a lift to Freshwater.'

He was right. Freddy. 'Okay. I can do that.'

She reached for her jacket hanging on a wooden coat-rack. It appeared she meant to go right now.

'Dinner's on hold. Sorry. We'll have it later. I promise.' She raised her hand in apology, before grabbing the oven gloves, dipping down and pulling the lasagne from the oven.

'I'm not worried about dinner,' he said, despite his stomach feeling fully in the mood at the sight and smell of the bubbling, cheesy concoction.

He watched as the dish was parked on the stove, the control switched off and the gloves thrown back on the counter. 'Right. Let's go,' she said, her eyes wide with intent.

'Sure.' He stood aside to let her pass.

'Wait!' she span back round and headed for the dresser, pulling the top drawer open and grabbing some keys. 'Okay. Ready,' she said rushing past him.

He noticed her hand trembling as she locked the door.

There was a good forty minute drive between here and Freshwater. Plenty of time for her to relax and open up to him about whatever it was that had just hit the proverbial fan.

No sooner were they in the car than she said, 'You've probably already guessed this involves my brother.'

'Not another broken heart, I hope?'

'Cuh! If only.' He didn't appreciate this comment; Ava had been seriously cut up last summer but he held his tongue. 'Sorry,' she added. 'I didn't mean to be callous.'

Luke made no reply just drew a deep breath and waited for her explanation. He could hear her breathing too – rapidly – a sure sign she was trying to control her emotions.

But no clarification was forthcoming.

He felt a pang of sadness for her. She had a mother who'd abandoned her children, a father whose investments had ruined the family business, and now her good-for-nothing brother was pushing her to breaking point. Which brought another pang – this time of anger.

He thought of his old friend, Una. She'd been the glue that had held her family together. Now the stability of her presence was gone too.

Gabriella's head was turned away from him – he imagined she was either hiding her tears or looking for answers in the darkness.

After a while he quietly said, 'Would you like some music on?' Wondering if it might soothe her a little.

'Got anything loud?'

'Loud?'

'Yes. I don't want to lose this anger. I think I'll be more effective if I stay wound up. Heavy metal would work. Something head-banging.'

He raised his eyebrows. 'Surely, head-banging's just gonna help you let off steam, isn't it?'

He could feel her gazing at him. After a moment she said, 'Luke, you don't have anything head-banging, do you?'

'Not exactly in that ball-park, No.'

'What about Hard House? I really hate Hard House. Maybe that'll piss me off enough to say what I have to say when I get there.'

'Nope. Sorry.' He heard her sigh. 'Hey, maybe I could just piss you off all the way over the island by not playing any of the music you want. Would that work for you?'

He thought he heard her sigh again, but realised it was almost a laugh, as she said, 'You don't even look like a guy who plays Hard House.'

'I'm kinda relieved at that.'

She was silent for a while. 'The truth is, I'm not good at confrontation. I never have been. And I'm afraid that when we get over to Freddy's, I'll just…bottle it.'

'Well, you've got time to prepare. Think about what it is that's making you so mad, and think about what needs to be said to put it right.'

'Trouble is, Luke, it's going to take more than words to put it right.'

'Maybe so, but whatever it is, I'll bet Gabriella Gill-Martin isn't to blame, is she?'

'She may not be to blame but she still has to sort it out.'

They were coming down the hill into Newport now. 'Okay. Well, if you want to run anything by me, I'm happy to help, but you don't have to say anything if you don't want to.'

'Thanks.'

She settled back into her seat and said nothing. He negotiated his way through the town and out onto the Calbourne Road, where the street lights gradually dwindled to nothing, and countryside again took over.

Through the silence of the rest of the journey, Luke ran through a whole brainstorm of possible misdemeanours that Freddy's guilt might be saddled to:

Theft? He certainly had previous, but who had he stolen from?

Selling up? It was clear Freddy had no sentimentality when it came to his grandmother's belongings; had he perhaps put the cottage on the market and was also planning to abandon Gabriella?

Screwing with his father's business? That was only a slim possibility; he doubted old Gill-Martin would trust his son with access to those finances. For now, it remained a mystery but judging from Gabriella's reaction, he was pretty sure the transgression was either illegal or immoral.

Willow View Cottage was on the outskirts of Freshwater. Luke had only been a couple of times before, to carry out small jobs for Una, and it saddened him to think on this occasion he was there under wholly different circumstances. He pulled over before they reached it. 'Are you ready, Gigi?' he asked, feeling awkward using her pet name, but figuring it might put her more at ease.

She nodded. Her focus appeared to be on the

glove compartment in front of her. 'It's got to be done.'

'Would you like me to come in with you?'

She looked at him. The only light came from the moon and the dashboard so he couldn't fully read her eyes but he sensed part of her wanted to say 'yes'.

'Thanks, Luke, but I think you know your presence will only make things worse. You and Freddy aren't exactly…close.'

'True. I'll be here for you if you need me.'

She took a deep breath. 'Let's get it over with. I'll try not to take too long.'

'Good idea. Say your piece, state your conditions and leave.'

She nodded. He shifted the car away from the verge and headed down towards the cottage.

There was a motor-home parked in the drive.

Gigi sat forward and her anger resurfaced. 'Shit! I might've known.' Pushing her way out of the car, she slammed the door and ran around the motor-home towards the cottage.

Luke switched the engine off, and stepped out of the car.

She might not want him to follow but at least here, he could listen for any trouble.

***

Seeing that motor-home had done the trick; fired me up again to tackle Freddy.

Of course Jason-call-me-Phil was in the blue-movie trade.

Don't get me wrong, I'm no prude. I'd done a project on erotic sculpture at college, which had been most enlightening, not to mention a little – what shall we say – stimulating? And I wasn't averse to spicing

283

up my one-on-one time with Rupert by sharing fantasies and the occasional erotic short story. But Phil was slippery – and not in a sensual way.

My brother, on the other hand, was a mug with poor judgement but it would be Phil who'd capitalized on that, I had no doubt.

There were lights on inside the cottage but the door was locked. I used my key to let myself in. I rather liked the element of surprise. If I'd made contact earlier, Freddy and his oily chums would have had time to create their defence or, worse, scarper.

A dense whiff of after-shave over curry hung in the air. My stomach churned; hunger exacerbated by stress. I could hear a slight murmur of voices from the back of the house. The room at the front was unoccupied. I looked around and marvelled it could be so tidy with three men on site. There was even a velvet and satin throw on the sofa, with matching satin cushions.

Advancing on the main room at the back, I hesitated outside the door. I knew exactly what I had to say. It was time to say it and leave.

My hand closed around the doorknob.

I bit my lip, shut my eyes and quietly asked the Universe for strength.

It didn't answer.

But someone did.

'That's it, honey. Oh, yeah. That's where I like it. Right there.'

Chapter 30

It was all going on in Willow View Cottage: spotlights, reflector screens, cameras – both fixed and hand-held, with Phil shouldering the hand-held. He was also sporting an enormous hard-on that bobbed enthusiastically through his opened trouser zip.

Matteo, in riding boots, stood legs akimbo, looking very much like an Olympic three-day-eventer who'd just won gold. Before him, the magenta-haired, spray-tanned Babette was getting busy with his manhood.

I saw all this in the seconds it took for Phil to clock my entrance through the camera lens. 'What the…?' he said, lowering the camera a fraction, sadly not enough to conceal his nodding pecker.

I'm guessing my entrance in jeans and sweatshirt, with a face on me like an old boot, would hardly mesh with their storyline.

There was a clatter from the kitchen area. I turned to see Freddy, who was sitting by a laptop which showed the performance from each camera angle.

At this point, my hands were parked firmly on my hips to simulate – I hoped – a strength that might be convincing. 'Frederick, this is too much! I don't care what you get up to in your own time and in your own home, but not if it means screwing up things between me and Rupert. Do you hear me?'

I could hear myself and it wasn't pretty.

Freddy vigorously gestured me to leave the room.

'No, Freddy. We'll have this out now! I don't care if your…' I waved my hand, '…actors and crew hear it, since they're pretty much part of the problem too.'

Freddy was out of his seat and moving towards me, his eyes urging me to back off.

'You owe people money. All of you!' I extended my indignation to the others. The camera was still pointing in my direction and I noticed Matteo was watching me with interest. The lovely Babette had abandoned her task and was leaning sulkily back on her elbows,

'Gigi!' Freddy took hold of my arm. I shook him off.

'No! Rupert wants his money back. I'm not leaving till you've sorted it out.'

Jason-call-me-*Fill* cut in with a smarmy smile. 'Good idea, young lady. Stay as long as you like.'

I rolled my eyes.

Matteo ran one hand through his hair and the other over his erection – no doubt keen to maintain its vitality. Which was, I confess, mighty impressive.

'Can't you guys put your cocks away for now?' I said, testily.

Freddy's eyes were flicking from me to the others. Quietly he said, 'Sis, please, let's go outside and discuss this.'

'No. I want this put to bed...so to speak. And then I'm going to try and get some semblance of normality back into my life.'

In a display of uncharacteristic machismo, Freddy tightened his grip on my arm and pulled me away from the supercharged tableau before us. 'This is going out live,' he said through gritted teeth.

'Live?' I quacked. Resisting his pull, I focussed on Phil's camera which was focussing on me.

I looked towards the static camera still trained on Matteo's eager wedding tackle. 'Why not join us,' his silky Italian accent invited me. 'It's a pity to waste the opportunity.'

I turned and stared down the lens of the other camera now advancing on my face. The words, 'Hello, Mum,' sprang to mind but I swallowed them down. This wasn't a joke. We were actually broadcasting across the internet; beaming into candle-lit bedrooms and shadowy garden sheds.

I'd never imagined my fifteen minutes of fame, as predicted by Andy Warhol, would amount to this.

I closed my eyes, spun on my heel and belted into the hall followed by Freddy.

The door had hardly shut behind us when the sounds of two erotic performers, making the most of a bad situation, resumed.

We stood facing each other in the front room. Its similarity to a Victorian bordello had escaped me before. Freddy didn't look half as shamefaced as he deserved to. Instead his eyes pinched as he said, 'You do realise you've fucked up that broadcast, don't you? People have paid for that service. I'm supposed to be doing the live edit.'

'Well I'm glad to hear you're actually taking money. That must mean you can pay Rupert back.'

'No it doesn't. The money's gone on kit. I told him it was a long-term investment.'

'Well that's not his story. All his mates have been logging on, todgers in hand, for a bit of vicarious stimulation, only to be met by a blank screen and an error message. He and they are not happy. And now, because he's made it my problem, neither am I.'

'He'll get his money, I swear. We've only gone live a couple of times and we've already got repeat customers. This is a goldmine.'

'Really? You think?' I gazed around the room, hoping to spot something we might sell. There was a selection of false beards hanging behind the door. 'Is that the extent of Matteo's wardrobe – boots and beards?'

Freddy glanced across. 'They're not beards, they're merkins.'

'What?'

'You know…women wear them. Down there.'

'Fanny wigs?!' I exclaimed, inspecting them from a safe distance. 'Holy Shoot! I missed that section in *Vogue*.'

Freddy sighed. 'Are we done?' he asked, keen to get back to his equipment.

I stared at him for a moment. 'Four thousand pounds, Freddy. Plus interest. That's what Rupert wants. Your bloody business is affecting my relationship. And, as ever, I'm running around picking up the pieces after your mistakes. I can't keep doing this, Freddy. And I won't. Sort it, before next weekend. Sell something. Anything. Start with the furniture. But pay Rupert back!'

There were a couple of antique chairs in the cottage. I doubted they'd fetch four grand, but they might fetch enough to placate Rupert's friends and, in turn, Rupert.

'Oh-kaaay!' he said, sounding like a little brother with a guilty conscience.

'I mean it.'

'I get it!'

'Good. Now go!' I said, with a dramatic sweep of my arm. Anything to feel like I was actually taking control.

He paced out of the room and left me gazing in

wonder at the tutti-toupees.

Outside, I drew a massive lungful of fresh autumn air, the kind suffused with smoky, musty smells that put you in touch with the earth. Relief at the completion of my task washed over me.

Luke was leaning against the bonnet of his car. He unfolded his arms and stepped forward. 'How'd it go?'

Yes, how did it go, Gabriella? Do tell all.

'I think I got my point across.'

'Good. And he's going to sort things out?' He was right in front of me, now, hands on hips and legs apart – a sort of New Age Matteo.

I nodded, and discovered I was fighting a smile.

'Okay. You certainly look happier than when you went in.'

'Do I?' I could feel my smile broaden.

'Sure. Must have gone well.' The puzzlement on his face was a study.

I broke into a laugh. Hysteria, possibly.

He smiled – what else could the poor guy do?

I walked round to the passenger side, still chuckling, and climbed in.

He sat beside me and started the engine. 'D'you fancy a drink before we go back?'

'Oh, boy, yes. A big one.' The last phrase had me cackling like a mad woman.

'Okay,' he said, reversing out of the drive, 'then a drink you shall have.'

I'd calmed down by the time we reached the pub. I wasn't sure if that was a colossal disappointment to Luke or a blessed relief. My instinct was to order a very large spirit of any denomination – possibly a bottle of gin with a straw – but sanity steered me towards wine. 'Red, please.'

When we were seated at a table, he studied me with a soft but constant gaze, which I kept avoiding.

Did I owe the guy an explanation? I wondered.

For the sake of his loyalty to my Nanna, I supposed I did.

'So, my brother has entered into business with someone who I instinctively don't trust.'

Luke nodded gently in an understanding way.

'To enter into that contract, he borrowed some money. Unfortunately, he hasn't honoured the terms of the loan. As a result, the people he borrowed from aren't happy.'

Luke nodded again. No comment. Just nodded.

'I'm guessing none of this comes as much of a surprise to you, does it? I know your opinion of my brother's probably at ground level most of the time. Subterranean, even.'

He shrugged. 'Maybe not that low.' There was the vaguest twinkle of a smile in his response. 'I'm used to finding really interesting things by digging below ground level. The question is, Gab… Gigi, did you manage to resolve the issue?'

My turn to shrug. 'Freddy knows what he has to do.' I lifted my wine and savoured it. It was mellow and warming.

'So what is this business young Freddy's invested in?'

I studied the lights shimmering on the surface of my Merlot. 'Video production.'

'Wow. That sounds like a major investment. Does he have experience?'

'He's dabbled in home movies, now and again.'

'What kind of videos are they –music, small features, weddings?'

I peered into the wine for an answer. Something about my hesitation must have given the game away, because he leaned across the table and whispered, 'Something athletic but not for family viewing?'

I winced.

He threw his head back with laughter. 'No, for real?'

'He says it's a goldmine.' My voice cracked with humour before I finished the sentence.

God, it felt good to share the joke with someone. Except it wasn't a joke at all.

We chortled together for a few moments.

'My timing was impeccable,' I said. 'Straight in for the live show.'

'Geddaway! You actually caught them at it?'

'Better than that – I was an unpaid extra.'

His eyes lost a little of their sparkle, so I hastily added, 'Bystander, really. I just happened to enter the scene at an angle the cameraman couldn't avoid.'

He smiled again. 'They'll edit you out.'

'They might when they archive it. Today's performance was going out in real time.'

'Don't tell me…your brother's chief stud?'

I shook my head. 'Well, not today, at least. He's the editor.'

He huffed out a small laugh, shook his head and took a swig of beer. I followed with a sip of wine. As we placed our glasses down, we made eye contact. I don't know how long it lasted – maybe two seconds or ten – but in those moments I relaxed. Truly, it was like the laces had been snipped on my corset of anxiety.

Okay, so the problem hadn't gone away but I was grateful I didn't have to deal with Luke's judgement. He hadn't sneered or preached. He hadn't given me a list of actions to take. He'd just listened and been supportive.

What was it George Orwell said? 'Happiness can exist only in acceptance.' In those few, delicious moments, I felt happier than I had in a long time.

Half my wine had gone. I stifled a yawn.

'Should we eat here?' Luke asked.

Guilt collided with my complacency. I owed the guy a meal, he must be starving. 'No, of course not. Let's go.' I downed most of the remaining Merlot, spilling some in my haste. I caught it with my hand and wiped it on my sweatshirt. I'm nothing if not practical.

'Hey. Easy there. No rush.'

'No. You were promised lasagne hours ago. Drink up!' I commanded. It seemed Jack-booting around Willow View had given me a taste for power.

'Won't it keep?'

'Yes but...' I thought for a second. 'You're starving now, right?'

'They do great cheese-burgers here.'

I salivated at the mention of it. 'Luke, I have no money on me.' Or anywhere else, for that matter.

'Forget it.' He stood up. 'Let me get a menu.'

'Don't. Cheese-burger sounds great – really great. Thanks.'

I cradled my head in my hands while he went to the bar. I was indebted to Luke in so many ways I was beginning to feel much like Freddy. Assuming Freddy felt anything.

I sometimes wondered.

After eating the burger and downing another red wine, it was a given that I would conk out on the way home. I have a vague recollection of passing Yarmouth Harbour. The next thing I knew, tyres were scrunching over the gravel of Bluebell Farm's drive and Luke was bringing the car to a halt.

A dull thump in my head reminded me I'd been out of regular wine-drinking practice. I peered across at Luke. 'You are a star, Luke. An absolute shining member of the galaxy that is the human race. The lasagne is yours. All of it. It's the least I can do.'

'You think I can eat a whole lasagne?' he asked.

I frowned. 'Possibly not in one sitting.' Another thought occurred to me. 'I know! You can invite Grant over to help you. He won't be scouting tomorrow, will he?' I opened the door and lurched out. 'Wait here. I'll get it.'

Eventually, I managed to line up the key with the lock and let myself in. I grabbed the lasagne, now torpid and cold, threw a clean tea-towel over it and headed out. 'Bon appetit!' I chimed, as I parked it on the passenger seat. 'Sorry there isn't any meat in it. I think it'll be quite tasty, though.'

'Thanks.'

'No, thank you-ou. Thank you, Luke, Star of St Helens. You are the best. Super. A super-nova. Yes. A super-nova.'

At that, my inner censor slapped a virtual sock in my over-active mouth. I saluted him and slammed the car door. He saluted back, making me feel another wave of acceptance, before he reversed out of the way and back to normality.

'A super-nova?' I asked myself. 'Do I even know what one is?'

Gaudi sauntered into the courtyard and threw me a glance of disapproval. How do cats do that? He was bang on the money though.

I spotted my phone lurking in the recess beside the toaster. In my haste to grill Freddy, I'd left it behind. There was a message from Rupert. His tone was snarky. 'Nice one, Gigi. Thanks for broadcasting my name across the internet. Subtle, really subtle.'

'You ungrateful pig!' I snapped back. It's not like I'd given his full name and national insurance number, had I?

I switched the phone to silent. I'd had enough of being told what I was doing wrong while trying to do something right. That phone would stay silent until I chose to switch it on again.

Chapter 31

It was becoming a habit – this waking up during the dark hour of the soul malarkey. Silence and darkness hung around me like an ominous presence – added to which was the knowledge that Rupert and his friends were after money from Freddy, which I deeply suspected wouldn't materialize as quickly as required.

My head thumped in the aftermath of my red wine consumption.

The prospect of Insomnia TV lowered my spirits even further.

Twenty-past four.

I stared at the shadows on the ceiling and thought about Luke.

He had been brilliant.

As always.

He'd never let Nanna down and now, it seemed he was proving just as stalwart for me.

It wasn't fair – on him. Nanna had been elderly, physically weak, and he had been a good neighbour. Whereas I was just needy. Too needy.

The world was falling about around my ears and I was making it Luke's problem, and I was wrong to. He didn't need dragging into my warzone – however willing he might be or however much he felt he owed it to Nanna. I was taking advantage of the man's good nature and, sooner or later, he'd resent it. People did.

I thought about the lasagne I'd handed him, last night, and shuddered. It was a feeble offering and what's more, I'd suggested he eat it with Grant. Like he'd want to invite Grant round for dinner. Who was I to tell him how to spend his evenings?

'Gabriella, you plonker!'

I quaked at the humiliation of it. From now on, I needed to brace up and sort these problems out on my own. The last thing I wanted was to become some kind of 'project' for Luke to worry about.

I hauled myself out of bed into the chill of my unheated room, pulled on several layers and went downstairs to make some tea.

With a steaming mug in my hand, I headed across to the studio. It was warm from a recent kiln firing. Seventy-two mugs were sitting in that kiln, along with twelve angel plaques. I wouldn't know how successful the firing had been until I could open the kiln tomorrow.

In the meantime, I would plough my hands into more clay and get busy on another consignment.

I'd already decided it was worth trying to sell my pots on-line. That way, all the profit would be mine. Yes, the garden centres and craft shops would be local clients but they were looking for rock-bottom prices. And, without a car, it was difficult for me to make deliveries. Whereas, any sales I made on-line could be carted to the post office in Nanna's trusty wheelbarrow, at no significant cost to me at all.

I'd managed to bring my productivity level up to between twelve and fifteen mug bodies in an hour. That didn't include trimming them, pulling and applying handles or decoration. If I put in a four hour shift, I might achieve twenty-five bodies and handles.

Then I had a batch of recycling to do – a lovely messy job hauling clay slops out of a bin and onto a plaster slab.

Following that, I had three dragons I was working on. A long way from angels, I'll admit but Gustav – the dragon Luke remembered from Nanna's garden – had inspired me. If I made a few small dragons, they might appeal to gardeners or lovers of fantasy. And they exercised my creativity in a more entertaining way.

For elevenses, I made jacket potato with beans, and ate it intermittently while I carved scales on the backs of the dragons. Multi-tasking was going well until I shoved the modelling tool into my spud.

I wiped it on my overall and carried on.

Afternoon tea was toast and jam. I gave myself a break from the studio and ate it leaning on the kitchen counter and staring at the table – still laid for last night's abandoned supper. The cats were snuggled together for warmth on one sheepskin cushion. A withering glance from Rodin told me what they thought of my economy drive. I'd have invited them into the studio to sit by the kiln, but experience had taught me their natural curiosity could jeopardize production. One sweep of a paw or one nudge of a snout might undo of hours of painstaking work.

My phone still rested silently by the toaster. It could stay that way.

Even though the problem was not – officially – mine, I couldn't seem to stop myself from running through possible ways to pay Rupert back. Nothing viable came to mind. I could sell my new furniture but why should I? I'd already planned to sell some of Nanna's prints online, but they wouldn't fetch enough to cover the debt and might not sell for months anyway – years even.

I could take out a loan from the bank and generate

more debt. Not a thrilling option either.

No. This was between Rupert and Freddy. I had to stop fighting my brother's battles. And for that matter, Rupert's.

'Bloody men!'

I arched my back to even out the kinks, and stretched my arms above my head, wind-milling them round to loosen up my aching shoulders.

'Freddy,' I said into the ether, 'You can find something to sell. Meanwhile I'm getting back to work.'

In the warmth of the studio, the mugs had dried enough to have their bottoms turned. If I could get those done, and their handles attached tonight, I'd have twenty-five mugs ready to dry out for another firing.

I fixed the first cylinder to the wheel, hunched over and began.

Two hours later, I was busy attaching a handle, when the courtyard lamp flicked on in the twilight. I looked up to see Luke outside. I waved him in.

***

Luke had seen the lights on in Gabriella's studio from his landing window. He'd seen them on at five in the morning, when he'd got up to use the bathroom. They were still on when he went downstairs for breakfast and they'd been on when he'd come home from college.

'Looking busy, there,' he said as he entered the studio.

'Yes. If I can hit the same rate of production tomorrow, there's a good chance I can do another firing in a few days.'

'Been working all day?' he asked, not wanting to

own up to knowing that she had. She'd probably find that creepy. And it would be – spying on the movements of your neighbour was creepy. But keeping an eye on Bluebell Farm had become something of a habit for him.

'Most of it.' She didn't look up from the mug.

He wondered if her reluctance to chat was merely down to concentration, or did she have some other reason?

'Gabriella, I don't want you to think I'm interfering but...' What? What did he want to say? 'I'm aware you're up against it right now, there's no doubting that, and I don't want you to feel awkward about it...awkward about me knowing what's going on. I won't tell another living soul. It's your business and I'm not the kinda guy that gets involved with gossip. So please don't worry that I might.'

She was working a tool around the base of the mug's handle as she said, 'I don't.'

He imagined she'd finish it soon and turn her attention to him. He looked around at the fruits of her labours. She'd been busy.

Eventually, she stepped away from the wheel and placed the mug on a board.

'Looks good,' he said.

'Thanks.' She sat back and pulled her head down towards her shoulder, stretching the tendons of her neck.

'How much for a set of six?'

She frowned at him. 'Why? You don't even know what they're going to turn out like.'

He'd never seen her so touchy before. 'I didn't say I wanted to buy any, I'm just curious.'

'Oh.' She fidgeted with the pottery tool. 'Sorry. I'm

not sure. I'm thinking maybe ten pounds a mug.' She stood up and carried two of them over to a shelf.

Eventually, he said. 'What's up? Has something else happened?'

'Luke, I'm fine. I've been in better situations but I'm fine. I can handle this. I am handling this.'

'Okay.'

She paused and fixed him with an intense look. 'I'm really grateful for everything you've done, and I appreciate your concern but please…you don't have to feel responsible for me. I'm tougher than I look.'

So that was it. Now her detachment made sense.

He studied her for a moment. 'I don't feel responsible for you, Gigi. Not at all. But I know if Ava were living alone and found herself in the kind of pickle you're in, I'd hope some concerned neighbour would look out for her. I like to think of it as paying it forward, so to speak.'

She looked away briefly and then nodded. 'Thanks.'

To put her mind at rest, he added, 'I don't need that kind of responsibility, I promise.'

'Of course. Sorry. I'm just a bit…'

'Forget it.'

'But you have been very kind, Luke. Don't think I don't appreciate it.'

He huffed her comment away. 'Yeah, well, that's not the only reason I'm here. I was hoping you might be able to help me out.'

Her face relaxed. 'Really? Of course. Anything.'

'Well, you being into ceramics and all, I thought you could maybe retile my bathroom for me.'

After a moment's pause, she said, 'Sure. Absolutely. Why not?' She wiped her hands on her

300

overalls. 'I'm pretty good at DIY.'

'Glad to hear it. It's quite a big job. Especially round the shower cubicle.'

'Okay.'

'Cutting tiles can be pretty tricky, but I guess you know that.'

'Right. But I don't have a tile-cutter, do you?' There was a worried wrinkle between her brows.

He'd love to keep this going but hadn't the heart. He grinned. 'I'm just kidding. There is no tiling.'

'No?'

'Truth is, I'm reheating this massive lasagne and Grant's got a date. I was hoping you'd help me eat it.'

'Luke! You big fat fake!' She was smiling now.

'I know. Couldn't resist. D'you want lasagne? I hear it's very good.'

She looked around at the remaining pots. 'Will it wait twenty minutes?'

'Sure. And come as you are,' he nodded at her overalls, 'I don't have any napkins.' He grinned and headed out.

For a moment there, he'd thought Gabriella had been ready to pull up the drawbridge and retreat into her own little fortress against the world. That, he decided, would make for a very lonely place.

***

I'd say the lasagne had just about survived its second visit to the oven, although it was a bit on the stodgy side. I apologised for it and Luke just shrugged like he hadn't noticed. 'Tastes great to me.'

We sat in front of the telly, eating off trays and watching a re-run of *Grand Designs*. The room was painted in a cool dove grey, with a three piece suite in faded blue denim. He had photos of what I guessed to be Canadian landscapes – all mountains and pine forests. There was a wooden tryptic photo frame above the fireplace – in the centre had to be his mother. Her hair was dark but greying at the temples – wavy hair, like Luke's but cut short. She had a lively look about her. To the right was a picture of Ava taken a couple of years ago, with one long plait hanging over her shoulder. The third was of the three of them, I assumed, standing by a lake. From that distance, I could tell Luke was pre-beard. Damn, it was too far away for me to check him out but maybe I could get up and take a closer look later.

Yes, I'd do that. I was very curious to see how he looked without it.

After fifteen hours in the studio I was so pooped, I kept nodding off, finally waking with a jolt as the end credits rolled.

'It's okay,' Luke said after I apologised again. 'You don't have to stay and entertain me.' He came over and took the tray from me and smiled. 'Take yourself off home and get a good night's sleep.'

Like that was going to happen. The prospect of waking again at Doom O'clock made me want to curl up on the sofa, right there, and doze through till morning. Then, perhaps, Luke would wander in with a steaming mug of fresh coffee and a plate of hot buttered toast.

'I'll go in a minute,' I said, yawning rudely before slapping a hand over my mouth. 'Sorry,' I repeated to his departing back. I dropped my head onto the cushion and rested my eyes a moment longer. Just a moment.

Chapter 32

I became aware of the muffled rumblings of air being breathed over soft tissue.

Rupert doesn't usually snore, I thought. He was rather hogging the bed, though, with his bum pressed into the back of my knees like that. I stretched my legs and he moved. He moved with a peculiar whine, like a dog yawning.

Followed by a snuffle.

I lifted my head. The bedside drawers and lamp had gone, replaced by a coffee table with a bottle of water on it. I looked down at my sleeping partner, Chuck, who was curled up between crook of my knees and the back of the sofa.

Luke's sofa.

There was a duvet over my shoulders and I still had on my work clothes.

Looking about me, I saw everything was tidy, illuminated by the hallway light shining through the partially open door. The clock on the wall said six-thirty. Was that evening or morning?

Chuck sat up, turned to look at me and stepped over my legs to get off the sofa, like his work there was done. Then he sauntered over to bless me with a morning kiss – a little tentative but nonetheless tender – right over my nose, eyes and forehead. Then he performed a perfect yoga down-dog stretch before trotting out to the kitchen to slurp a bowl of water, very noisily.

Six-thirty. The first signs of daylight were starting

to frame the curtains.

I'd slept maybe eight hours. Eight hours straight.

I sat up and stretched.

Chuck padded back in, presented his head to me for a stroke. He'd be the perfect partner if only he made coffee.

I needed a pee. That meant going upstairs and possibly disturbing Luke, or else I could go home like a normal person and use my own bathroom.

I really should do that.

Go home, make instant coffee and feed the cats.

Luke wouldn't expect me to hang around for breakfast. Truth be known, he was probably hoping I'd already gone.

I folded the duvet and draped it over the back of the sofa. I plumped the sofa seat to remove the body dent. Just before I tiptoed out to the kitchen, I had the presence of mind to take a peek at the third photo. Wow! This was a very different Luke from the Robinson Crusoe I'd come to know. They were all dressed for a special occasion. Ava looked to be about thirteen, which would have put Luke around twenty-two. He was clean-shaven with a sleeked back hairstyle, which made him look more corporate than castaway, not to mention youthfully handsome. Because they were all laughing, I couldn't help but smile too – smile and yet feel sad, for this family unit had been fractured by his mother's premature death; probably not long after this picture was taken. Luke was still young, fresh-faced and without a care in the world, it seemed.

I stepped away, feeling vaguely guilty for studying the picture in his absence, and headed out to the kitchen, followed by Chuck. The gleaming coffee machine was sitting empty and cold on the side, and so desperately in need of a large scoop of Brazilian Arabica.

No time to do that, my bladder was crying out for relief.

I should go – go home but leave a note first.

I was just hunting around for a pen and paper when Chuck hurried out of the kitchen as the stairs creaked – signalling the imminent arrival of Luke.

Crap. I must look crap. I hadn't washed my hair yesterday and my clothes had been slept in. I shot a look at the back door.

Too late.

'Morning,' Luke croaked through a bleary smile. 'Sleep okay?'

'Yes. More than okay. I don't know what happened there,' I said, trying not to study his shoulder muscles through the loose t-shirt he wore over jogging bottoms, or the random texture of his hair, only just caught at the back of his neck with cord. 'Sorry. I was just about to go home.'

'No coffee?' he asked, unhooking the water pot and heading for the tap. I sensed he wasn't much of a morning person.

I squirmed on the spot as my bladder became more insistent. 'Mind if I use your loo?'

'Nope.'

I sprinted up the stairs and tried the first door, it must have been Ava's room – all purples and blacks – then the next; Luke's, judging by the warm manly smell and rumpled duvet, then the next. Hurrah!

Startled by my hideous reflection, I nearly wet myself.

Finally, thudding onto the loo seat, I relaxed and

considered my predicament.

My life was a minefield; I never knew when or where another shit-storm might detonate. My already fractured family was on the verge of collapse – with my father God alone knew where and potential law suits stacking up like driftwood in a dam. Then there was my brother in league with Profligate Phil, careering towards that tabloid destination known as Infamy.

What's more, my boyfriend was pissed off with us both. Actually, since I hadn't spoken to him in over thirty-six hours, he was probably roaring bloody angry right now.

And where was I?

Peeing in my sexy neighbour's loo, after spending the night on his couch in clothes that hadn't been washed for days.

Sexy neighbour, did I say? Where did that come from?

I replayed the image of him in the kitchen; the triangular outline of his upper body just concealed by the thin fabric of a battered old t-shirt. His long, curling black hair held together with leather cord as it hung down between those finely toned shoulders. Did he sleep with it tied up? I wondered dreamily. But it wasn't just the shape of him, it was the comfort of being around him; the way he so easily coped with the stuff of life and quietly took charge. I thought about the wonderful way he cared for his sister and looked out for her. Yes, a girl like me could get used to a little more of that.

'This is one shit-storm you don't want to unleash, Gigi,' I told myself quietly as I stood up. 'Just cos your life is a warzone, right now, you don't have to throw your morals down the toilet like the world is about to end.' I hit the flush and stared at my pale face in the mirror. 'Look at you, Gigi. Be honest, he'd have to be pretty desperate.'

I washed my face and rubbed it vigorously with a towel.

'And so would I.'

I ran back downstairs. The smell of fresh coffee nearly floored me but I was resolute. 'Okay, Luke,' I said, watching him putting away the dinner plates. 'Thank you for letting me sleep last night. I so needed it.'

'You sure looked like you did.'

'Now, I'm going to leave you to it. I've a lot to do.'

'You don't want coffee?' he asked, studying me in an unnerving way.

I paused.

I so wanted a decent cup of coffee I was nearly drooling. Desperation must have been written all over my face. 'Would it be very rude if I took one with me?'

He smiled and reached for a mug. 'Not rude at all.'

My house was several degrees cooler than Luke's. The cats stepped around my feet, mewing with disapproval. I set down some food for them and replenished their water bowl.

Next to the toaster, my phone waited patiently for me to bring it back to life. My existence was relatively peaceful with it turned off. It meant I didn't have to listen to intense messages from Rupert or pathetic excuses from Freddy. I liked it that way. I cradled the mug of hot, strong coffee and thought how much simpler life could be.

After my shower, I bit the bullet and checked the phone.

There were six missed calls from Rupert but only one message and a text, which read: ANSWER YOUR BLOODY PHONE!!

I clicked the button to hear the earlier message. Rupert's voice sounded calmer than the text suggested. 'Gigi, why are you and your brother being so elusive? Is it a family condition – this tendency to disappear? Please call me, babe.'

He'd left that message before the shouty text. I'm guessing he wasn't worried I might be ill, or handcuffed and gagged over at Willow View, then. No concern for my welfare at all.

With a heavy heart, I called him.

He answered quickly. 'Finally!' he said. 'Where've you been?'

'Working in my studio.'

'Why couldn't you answer your phone?'

'I could have done. I chose not to.'

'What? Why?'

'Because I'm fed up running around after Freddy – and you for that matter. I didn't ask you to get involved with Freddy's business, did I? That was entirely down to you. I went over and delivered your message. The rest, quite frankly, is your problem, Rupert.' My heart was beating unnaturally hard.

'Oh, well thanks for that, Gigi. Good to know you're on my side.'

'Right now, Rupert, I'd like to know who's on my side. I'm struggling to keep my head above water, here, but I'm determined I will.'

'You know the solution. Sell up.'

I glared at the floor. 'I don't want to sell up. I want

308

to try and make a go of it down here.'

Rupert tutted and sighed at my inconvenient state of mind. 'Gigi, I've had enough of this. It's quite obviously time you knocked this Isle of Wight nonsense on the head.'

'Nonsense?'

'If you don't, then it's clear to me you have no vested interest in our future.'

'What?'

'You'd even choose that crumby farm over Dubai, wouldn't you?'

'Rupert, you didn't even consult me over Dubai. You just went ahead and planned it.'

'Yeah. And you're going ahead and planning a future on the island without me.'

'We did talk about living on the island. You were all for it. You said it would be a great base for sailing.'

'One day. I didn't think you'd settle down there, right now. I thought you'd get tenants in. Make it pay. That would be the smart move.'

I could. Perhaps. But I didn't want to. 'Rupert,' I began quietly. 'I think you said it right when you said I'd choose the farm over Dubai. I don't want to go to Dubai. I'd hate it – the heat, the opulence, the massive gap between those with money and then the rest…'

'For crying out loud! Get real, Gigi.'

'Real, Rupert? I am being real. There's nothing more real than counting every penny like I've had to these last few months.'

'Then sell up and you won't have to.'

'No!' There was a pause before I said. 'Rupert, I'm really sorry but this is over between us, isn't it?'

'Can't you think of one compromise, Gigi – a way

of having what you want and me having what I want?'

I couldn't. It was bad enough being at opposite ends of the UK, without being on different continents. 'Rupert, I didn't mean for this to happen. We...' a lump came to my throat. 'We had such a lovely weekend when you came down.'

'I know, Gigi. We're good together. Are you really giving up on us?'

Despite the turn of events, my heartbeat had steadied and I felt calmer. 'Maybe it's just bad timing.'

I could imagine what he was thinking: *Maybe if you just came to Dubai this wouldn't have to happen.* 'Then I suppose there's nothing much more to be said, is there?'

'Rupe, I do still love you.'

'Not enough, apparently.' He let out a heavy breath before he said, 'See ya.'

He was gone. Gone in a way I hadn't anticipated.

Tears followed – not surprising, really. We'd been together nearly two years. Although, I have to say, the sadness was tinged with relief. Relief I didn't have to battle with him any longer over the future.

The sun was fully up now and glinting off the studio windows. 'Right,' I said, blowing my nose on some kitchen paper. 'Let's get that kiln open and see what's in there.'

I threw myself into work. I didn't give Freddy's financial predicament much thought. Well...I thought about it but I didn't feel obliged to do anything. That's not to say I take the attitude Every-Woman-for-Herself but it was his business and his debt. Freddy was doing what he always did and not thinking things through. If Freddy wanted to screw up his own life, that was his choice. Sooner or later, he had to face the consequences. I couldn't afford to face them for him any longer.

My stock of ceramic goods was building nicely. I started photographing them for the internet. I even drew up a price list and a stock list. If I could just sell everything on-line, and all profits came to me, I'd have a tidy three thousand pounds to see me through Christmas and into the New Year. And that didn't include my large pieces. Of course, that was only if I sold everything. Full price.

Dream on, Gigi.

After emailing pictures to several shops on the island, four agreed to take some on sale or return. It was better than nothing, but it would deplete my ready stock. It also meant I had to hire a car for a day to distribute them, eating into any future profit I might make. But – speculate to accumulate – I reminded myself.

Luke was bewildered when he learned about this. 'You could have used mine. Why didn't you ask?'

'Because you use yours and I didn't want to impose.'

'Next time, just ask,' he said.

Word had reached London about me and Rupe. I hadn't told Luke yet, though. It wasn't a conversation I felt comfortable broaching, not while it was still so raw.

Fran and Sonia both rang to commiserate. Fran's take on it was, 'That's you and me out on the town, then, babe.' While Sonia favoured, 'What will Rupert do, now?' Friend or not, she'd always fancied him.

Truth was, I actually felt more upset over Rupert's emotional distance from me than our split. It's true what they say, you discover who your friends are in a crisis.

I also believe that when the going gets tough, you have to roll your sleeves up and work hard. I'd definitely been doing that recently.

Luke dropped round, one afternoon, when I was photographing some dragons. 'These are great,' he said, studying the dragons. 'Can I buy one for Ava? She'd love one, I'm sure.'

'You can have one. I can't sell you one.'

'No, Gigi. I'll buy one or I won't have one at all. That's the deal,' he added, very firmly.

I didn't argue. He asked which was my favourite and bought that.

'Does he have a name?'

'Well, Ava might want to christen him, herself.'

'True, but what would you call him?'

'I think he looks like a Boris.'

'Boris, huh?'

'I see dragons as northern European – unless they're Chinese. Chinese dragons are a totally different species – much more difficult to tame.'

'Right. I guess you're the expert.'

I grinned back at him, and he smiled back, briefly before scanning the rest of the products. 'You've done really well, here. I hope they sell for you.'

'Thanks. I am pretty pleased with myself.'

'You should be.' He studied the dragon for a moment. 'Nice work.'

He stuck his hand in his jacket pocket and pulled something out. 'I found this today.' He handed me a fossil that looked like a ram's horn. 'It's an ammonite.'

'Oh, that's beautiful,' I said, tracing the texture with my finger. Is it rare?'

He chuckled. 'Not very. Not over here. I just cracked this stone on a rock today, it split open and that was inside.'

'Amazing. To think it's been there for, how long, thousands of years?'

He smiled. 'Oh, many thousands. More like sixty-five million.'

'Yikes! That's incredible,' I said, gazing with renewed admiration at the fossil. 'To think it's been in the ground all that time.'

'Speaking of which, you might want to start picking some of those carrots, now.'

'I will. Absolutely.' If it weren't for Luke, my home-grown veggies would be fossils themselves, one day.

'Right, well I'll leave you to it. Good luck with the sales.'

I watched him go. All the while, a little thought was niggling at my brain: what did he think about me? When I first moved in to Bluebell Farm, I had the distinct impression he didn't really approve of me. It was an absolute certainty he didn't like my brother – and no wonder. I was certain his view of me was tainted by association. He'd seen me trying to excavate the front garden with a pick-axe; he'd witnessed my hapless attempts to grow vegetables, and he'd been right there when I'd lost my rag over Freddy's dodgy business scheme.

Now, however…now I definitely sensed I had his approval. There'd been a subtle but satisfying tone of admiration regarding my work, and I think he respected what I was trying to achieve.

Somehow, that brought a little glow to my existence.

Luke studied the dragon. He thought it was extraordinary how much detail and personality Gabriella could bring to such an object. It had beauty of form, charm and humour.

Not unlike its creator.

This fantasy animal was in many ways like some of the ancient fossils he'd seen; the skeletal structure, the wings, the scales across its back. A composite of prehistoric creatures imbued with a unique Gill-Martinesque persona.

Maybe she could apply her talents to bringing some of the fossils in his collection to life – a three-dimensional artist's impression would be so exciting. He imagined how much fun it would be to work with her on something like that, more than fun…

A smile had formed on his lips as he entered the cottage. 'Chuck, I've had a great idea.' The dog approached him, wagging his tail so excitedly, his pelvis swung back and forth. Luke placed the dragon carefully on the kitchen work-surface. 'This is Boris.'

He pulled a beer from the fridge and wandered into the sitting room. 'Yep, I'm working on a great idea,' he said as he flopped into the armchair, still smiling.

Chapter 33

Why is it that just as you fall into a welcome and satisfying sleep, the phone rings or, as in this case, the Gestapo comes tolling on the doorbell? Okay, so it wasn't the Gestapo but it might as well have been, judging by repetitive buzzing that dragged me from my slumber. I stuck my head out of the window to look for a car. There was none.

More buzzing.

'Hello?' I called, as quietly as I could. I didn't need to jettison poor Luke from his bed, too.

The security light around the corner was on. Stepping into the edge of its beam came Freddy.

'Let me in, Sis.'

'Shhhh.' I hissed. 'Of course I'll let you in.'

He shot back around the corner to wait for me.

As I opened the back door, he pushed past me into the kitchen and dropped his rucksack on the floor, closed the kitchen blind and said, 'Lock it!'

'What the..? Freddy...'

He sat at the table but he was far from relaxed. I hadn't seen him this agitated since the time he'd smashed three of Nanna's Lladro figures when he was practising keepy-uppies with a football – in the sitting room. He'd been ten at the time.

'Freddy, it's five-thirty in the morning, what are you doing here?'

'Surprise!' he said, forcing a laugh.

'Not surprise, Freddy. Shock – an unmitigated, unexpected reaction to an unscheduled visit by my brother. What's going on?'

He shook his head. 'Not much. Nothing to worry about.'

'Good. Then I'll unlock the door and open the blinds again.'

'No!'

'Do you want a cup of tea?'

'Scotch.'

'No scotch, I'm afraid. Tea.'

He let out a sigh. I didn't have much control over my little brother but just now and then, he lacked the energy to give me an argument.

I made tea without any further discussion. I was too busy thinking up a litany of questions to interrupt it with chit chat.

He curled up in one of the armchairs. I glared at his dusty trainers, fearing for my Italian chenille. He didn't notice. I passed him his mug which he lifted to his mouth but put it down on the side table, without taking a sip.

I kicked the footstool towards his chair and sat on it. It put me lower than Freddy – my customary position when I wanted him to talk to me. I'd always figured I was less intimidating to him like this.

I didn't press him for information. I'd learned the best way to elicit the truth from Freddy was to smother him with silence. His only escape, right now, was to vault over me to reach the door, trapped as he was between the wall, the side table, the log basket and me.

'I'm in trouble,' he said, eventually.

This was no surprise. 'What kind of trouble?' I asked.

He looked at me like he didn't know who I was.

'Four hundred grand.'

Three words. One number. One extremely large number.

'How?' was all I could manage.

'Gambling debts.'

I was fully awake now. 'Who spends that kind of cash gambling, Freddy? Where did you even get the money from?'

'Macau. Earlier this year.'

'But you haven't been in Macau since July.'

'They caught up with me.'

'Caught up with you?!' my mind was juggling one thought after another. And just as I studied one idea, another popped into the mix.

'Sis, if I don't come up with the money, they're going to kill me.'

'Matteo and…'

'No! Not them. They've gone. The other guys.'

'What other guys?'

'From Macau. Well, Southwark I think, judging by their accents.'

'I still don't understand. You gambled nearly half a million? You were only there a few weeks.'

'It's complicated. I got involved in some syndicate. It's my name on the papers.'

'So it's not really your debt?'

'That's just fucking semantics!' Freddy yelled. 'My name is on the papers! My head is on the block! You don't screw with these people, Gigi. You just get screwed by them. I've been screwed and there's no way out unless I pay up.'

'Then you have no choice, Freddy, you have to sell the cottage.'

'They've already got it.'

'What?'

'They're there, now. I escaped.'

'Let me get this straight – some gangsters from Macau are sitting in Willow View, right now, ready to kill you – and doubly pissed off because you've run away?'

'Unless I pay up.'

'Nobody can get their hands on that kind of money overnight.'

'They have Willow View. They're prepared to wait for the rest.'

'Have you signed it over to them?'

'Pretty much. They have the deeds and a dodgy lawyer's on the case.'

'Freddy!' No wonder I hadn't heard from him. I'd thought he was busy playing Hollywood with the Horny Brothers.

'If only our father hadn't…'

'Stop it, Freddy! He didn't sign up to some shitty gambling syndicate – you did. But just like him, you're in debt too. You're more like him than I ever imagined.'

Freddy huffed. 'Ironic, isn't it? Dad would be so proud.' He looked around. 'Are you sure you don't have any scotch, brandy, anything but tea?'

'No.'

'They will kill me, Sis. If they don't kill me, they'll cut my arms off. I heard they did that to another guy.'

Blood chilled in my veins. 'We have to tell the police.'

For the first time in my life, he actually gave me a look of contempt. My little brother was suddenly wiser than I was. 'You don't understand how it works. They'd kill me or maim me anyway they choose, and slip away in the night. This is an underground gang, Gigi. It's not a bunch of thugs from Cowes.'

I swallowed.

'We can't tell anyone. We just have to pay them.'

I put my tea down.

'Still want that drink?' I asked.

He gave me another look of disdain. Of course he did.

There was a quarter of a bottle of Limoncello in the back of the cupboard, left over from God knows when. It was disgusting. I hated it. But it was alcohol.

We've all heard the saying 'between a rock and a hard place'. Well I was right royally wedged in there. My nose was rammed into the crevice of a granite cliff, marked, 'Sacrifice Freddy' and my back was crushed by a boulder marked, 'Sacrifice Bluebell Farm'.

Like there was really a choice?

Limoncello might be disgusting, but it put me out for a couple of hours until first light, when I hauled myself out of bed, pulled on some harem pants and a fleece. If only I'd had a car, I'd have driven off into the wilds of the island and treated myself to a blast of yelling therapy. I could have driven round, roaring my head off and swearing like a trooper with Tourette's.

Not today.

I looked towards the studio. How futile would that be – building sculptures I might not have time to finish and fire?

I pulled the hood up on my fleece and ventured out into the cool, autumnal morning. I jogged down the drive, out past Luke's cottage and on towards Node's Point. My feet pounded the road. Maybe I could pulverise the anger from my system, let it dissipate into the surroundings and leave me cleansed and sanguine.

Down through the near-empty campsite I ran, picturing tents and camper-vans of summers past. Memories. That's all I'd have to hang on to. Memories.

And Freddy.

Memories of Freddy too – screaming himself awake and boys bullying him for wetting the bed. Didn't they know bullying would only make him worse?

Maybe they did.

I ran down onto the beach where the tide was out, and jogged across the firm sand and vaulted the groynes wherever I could. A man was hitting tennis balls into the sea with a golf club, while his dog gleefully bounded into the water to retrieve them.

My legs were tired, now but the pain was something to hang on to. Physical pain was oddly preferable to the other kind.

Back along the concrete path by the beach-huts. A blister was forming on my toe, I had no doubt. Good.

Jeez, the hill up was a killer. My thigh muscles were burning. 'Suffer!' I told myself. 'Suffer!'

As I made my way back home, I could see Luke heading towards me on his bike. 'Hi!' he called, slowing down for a chat.

'Can't stop. Sorry.' I waved and kept up my momentum. 'Catch you later!'

Bluebell Farm was going on the market.

Freddy and I had talked for hours, choking back the Limoncello, trying to come up with an alternative but there was none. Dad's position was clear, and

Pierre would never come up with that kind of cash – even if he had it.

We were out of options.

Not only that, my opportunity to prove to Dad that I could succeed as a sculptor was threatened beyond anything I could have predicted.

The entire Gill-Martin fortune was accelerating towards a cliff – totally lacking the chutzpah of *Thelma and Louise* but facing an identical and inevitable outcome.

Yep, we were fucked.

Chapter 34

The estate agent, an earnest girl called Tess, thought the farm would most likely sell in the summer. 'But you never know – it might be exactly what someone's looking for, right now. We have a mailing list of clients with quite specific requirements,' she said.

'We don't mind dropping the price for a quick sale,' Freddy countered eagerly.

Her eyes flashed with interest. 'Leave it with us.'

'Great,' he said, pacing about like a cat on a hot barbecue. 'We need to sell it. This week.'

'Freddy!'

He glared at me. 'It's got to be soon.'

Tess twitched in sympathy. 'I see. To do that, we'll have to drop the price immediately, generate interest.'

'Do it.'

I realised this was out of my hands.

Everything I'd looked forward to, everything Nanna had intended for me, was spewing down the drain. My only consolation was the body of work I'd managed to produce over the last few weeks. I'd proven to myself that I could do it. I just needed to prove I could sell it too. Then, at least, I might have a future.

Freddy was massively keen to flee the island in an effort to safeguard his limbs and his life. Whilst this was totally understandable, it would leave me equally vulnerable. It wouldn't take long for the assassins to discover my whereabouts and hold a machete to my throat. So, forgive me, I found his passport and hid it.

Plus, if he went, how could I be certain he'd negotiate the deal with his creditors? No, I needed him around to make sure this was sorted, signed and sealed.

Then, perhaps, we could get on with our lives.

For now, he assured me, nobody knew I was on the island.

'Except Matteo and Phil,' I said.

'I told you, they're gone. They legged it as soon as the heavies turned up.'

'They could still tell them where I am. And it wouldn't be difficult to find me through social media, would it? Freddy, you have to let these thugs know you're getting the money.'

'How? I'm not going back there.'

'Phone, email, tweet. I don't know Freddy. You ran away, you must have had some plan.'

He chewed on his lip for a moment. 'Okay. I'll phone Leopard.'

I didn't ask who Leopard was.

Later that afternoon, a man in a van turned up to fix the For Sale sign.

A twinge of disappointment squeezed my chest as I watched from behind the carrot bed. My carrots were long and slim and wholesome looking. They'd done well. What a pity I wouldn't be here to harvest the Japanese onions, next year.

For Sale. How ironic that Rupert and I were no longer an item. I dreaded to think what his reaction might be when he found out.

Still, not my problem any more.

Who needed problems like that when I had the Macau Mafia hunting my baby brother?

Once I'd saved his life, there was still the knotty

problem of packing up all my belongings and finding somewhere to live.

A job would be handy, too.

And I'd thought my earlier problems were huge.

It was no surprise to see Luke appear in the driveway. I'd anticipated this. He would be shocked, possibly saddened but understanding. Of that I was sure.

His face was a study in disbelief as he approached, his arms outstretched as if to say, 'What's going on?'

'I know,' I began. 'I'm afraid it's been on the cards for weeks. It's just too hard to keep this place going on my own. I have tried.'

'But what about your work; your plans for doing bed and breakfast?'

I shook my head. 'It was a lovely idea. But not realistic. This way I can focus on my future with Rupert. Dubai is only a few months away. Hopefully I'll have it all sorted by then.' For the sake of my grandmother's memory, I didn't want him knowing just how feckless Freddy had become. Much better he believed I was selling up and marching on into a brand new future with Rupert.

Luke nodded as he took it in but he was still frowning. 'I guess you just have to do what's right for you. It's a shame though. I thought you were really making a go of it.'

'Smoke and mirrors, I'm afraid.'

He looked around at the newly disturbed soil in the raised beds, and up at the house. 'I shall be sorry to see you go, Gabriella, but I wish you luck.'

'Thanks.'

He loitered in front of me. I couldn't invite him in. He'd see Freddy – who was in no fit state to be seen by anyone – and then the truth would be much harder to conceal. Luke thought little enough of Freddy as it was. I held up the carrots. 'These are a success, aren't they?'

'Sure,' he moved over and took hold of a bunch. 'They'll be lovely and sweet with some butter and parsley over them.'

Now he was in my personal space, I felt the pressure of my guilty lie. If only he'd just back off and go home.

'Take them.' I said, with what I hoped was a tone of finality.

'No. You enjoy them. Blanch and freeze them, they'll keep.'

'Good idea,' I said.

He handed the carrots back to me. 'Did the estate agents give you any idea of the state of the market?'

'Buoyant, for a house like this.'

'Hey, that's good news.'

'Yes.' I gave him a nod of dismissal. I didn't want to continue this conversation, couldn't he see that?

His head tilted slightly. 'Okay, well, good luck with the sale and if there's anything I can do to help, you know where I am.'

'Thanks but you've done enough. Hopefully it's all plain sailing from here. The future's bright!' The force of my will was pushing him down the drive. I wanted him to go so badly and yet the feeling was utterly conflicted by my desire for him to stay. Before my inner turmoil became evident, I turned my back on him and headed for the kitchen. 'See ya!' I called out, waving the carrots' leaves over my head like a cheerleader's pom-pom.

Smoke and mirrors, I'd said. There'd be plenty

more of those before I scrambled out of this mess.

'We have to tell Dad.' I announced to Freddy. 'This isn't the kind of thing we can hide – it's not like that flower-bed you destroyed with your home-made bomb.'

'How did you know about that?'

'Saw it from my bedroom window.'

It had been a curious sight – two rose bushes jumping up in a cloud of soil, then settling back down. I'd watched him clear the whole mess up afterwards. He'd left it looking really tidy. Nobody need ever have known anything untoward had occurred. Except the following day, the bomb's ingredients – weed-killer and sugar – took effect.

'You were at piano practice,' he said.

'I was skiving.'

'Blimey.' He paused for a moment, then grinned. 'Funny though.' He gestured with his hands, 'Dooff!'

'Yes, well, we can't laugh this off, Freddy. This is the loss of the family estate.'

He frowned. 'Dad can hardly stand in judgement though, can he? Considering the losses he's facing, right now.'

'It's still going to hurt.'

He appeared to slump even further into the sofa. 'Better get it over with, then.'

Our father sounded surprisingly upbeat when he answered the phone. 'Do you want to hear some good news?' he said immediately.

'Of course we do.'

'We've got our passports back. We're free to leave whenever we want.'

'Then it's all sorted?'

'I still have some investors to pay off but the Spanish debts are settled.'

Freddy leaned forward and wrapped his arms over his head as I continued. 'That's great news, Dad. We're so pleased.' And I was, very pleased. It was such a pity his balloon was about to burst.

'Is Rupert with you, then? How's he doing?'

'No. Not Rupert, Freddy.'

'Freddy?' the tone of his voice instantly cooled. 'So, the wanderer returns. Is he there?'

Freddy lifted his head. 'Hi, Dad.'

'Where've you been – on the moon? It'd be nice to hear from you, once in a while, you know.'

'Sorry. I've been travelling.'

'Not according to Jeff. He tells me you've been back in the UK for a while.'

'Dad,' I cut in. 'Freddy and I have something to tell you.'

'Oh. What?'

I took a deep breath but it was Freddy who started. 'Dad, you won't be surprised to hear that I've cocked up, good and proper.' There was a slight murmur from the other end. 'When I was travelling, I got mixed up with the wrong sort of people – you'll understand that, having put your trust in Jose de la Torre...'

I think my mouth dropped open at that point, to hear Freddy couching his story in the same frame as Dad's.

'...So I'm in exactly the same boat as you. I owe people money. I've got to sell Willow View.'

'Jeez! How?'

'It doesn't matter how, Dad, it's a debt. Just like yours.'

We heard a heavy sigh. 'Well, I suppose I should be glad you've got the decency to face the consequences,' he said rather grimly. Freddy looked at me.

I leaned towards the phone. 'I'm selling up too.'

There was a pause before he asked, with heavy suspicion, 'Why?'

Freddy held up his hand. 'Gigi's helping me out. My debts were more than the cottage was worth.'

'Oh, good God! What on earth are you playing at, Freddy?'

'I made a mistake, Dad. A bad investment but I've learned my lesson. It won't happen again.'

'Of course it won't! You've got nothing left to invest.'

'Dad,' I cut in, 'We're sorting it out, please don't worry. And don't be angry, it's just money. We're both okay.'

'But...' he sighed again. 'Clearly I'm not going to get the full story over the phone, am I? Once everything's wrapped up over here, I'll be home, and then I want a full briefing. Do you hear?'

Freddy flopped back and rolled his eyes.

'Looking forward to seeing you, Daddy. Love you.'

With the house on the market, and my life teetering on the brink of failure, I needed to talk to Fran. She was the only person I trusted – both in terms of not over-reacting and keeping it to herself.

I went to my bedroom, wrapped the duvet around me and made the call.

'I don't know what to say to you, Gigi,' she said, in an uncustomary nonplussed way. 'Freddy's life is actually in danger?'

'Apparently.'

I could hear her breath. 'Look, I don't want to add to your worries, but are you absolutely sure about this? Could Freddy be pulling a fast one – you know – trying to get his hands on your share?'

'No. Definitely not. Freddy's done some daft things in his time, and yes, his judgement is often poor but he'd never do that to me.'

'And you're sure he's not on drugs?'

I thought for a moment. 'He might smoke the odd spliff.'

'Because if he's been taking something hallucinogenic…you know…'

'Fran, he's not out of his mind. Well, other than being terrified.'

'Have you met these guys?'

'No.'

Fran was evidently thinking hard about what to say next. Finally, she said, 'We all know Freddy, and we all know he can be a bit of a loose cannon. Just be careful you don't give up your birthright for some hair-brained scheme of his.'

I didn't have a ready reply. I was too busy wondering if she might be right. I hadn't seen a gun at Freddy's head, and there was no threatening letter. I just had Freddy's word. Could he be capable of that?

'Gigi, are you still there?'

'Yep. Just trying to wrap my head around the whole thing.'

'I'm not surprised. It's pretty frigging big.'

'Yep.'

'Poor Gigi.'

I sighed. 'Don't. It could be worse.'

'You're right, though I can't think how.'

'How's you? How's things with Alissa?'

It was her turn to sigh. 'No change but I'm adjusting to the idea. Instead of perching on my high moral horse about being true to yourself and all that righteous stuff, I've realised that if she thought I was truly worth changing her life for, she'd do it.'

'You are worth it!'

'No, yes, I mean I'm not worth it in her eyes. I want someone who's prepared to make a stand for me, to want me unconditionally. Alissa says she loves me but her need to bring up her baby with its loving father – which I'm sure he would be, he's a nice guy – is greater. If I force her hand in this, it'll be like winning an argument – which is no win at all. Is it?'

I thought about Rupert, how he'd tried to persuade me to sell the farm – to suit him not me. He might have persuaded me too, but I would have given it up with huge reluctance and a side order of resentment. Now I was selling it to save Freddy. I was sad but I had no choice and saving your brother's life isn't something you can ever resent.

'I wish I fancied you, Fran. We'd be perfect for each other.'

'My mother would never approve.'

'I'm not having a sex change to suit your mother.'

'Ah, we have made progress there. I leapt from the closet last weekend.'

'Wow! Good for you. How did it go?'

'Surprisingly well. Dad said very little and Mum said, "Well, we did wonder," and was quite upbeat about it. She still wants me to marry a doctor or a lawyer, though.'

'Good luck with that.'

We chuckled. For a few lovely moments I was

331

soothed by her voice, and the knowledge that while some things change, good friends are always there for you.

There was the roar of an engine outside, and gravel parting beneath spinning wheels. I threw off the duvet and shot over to the window. A black motorbike throbbed in the courtyard, under a man in black leathers. He flexed the throttle and the bike roared some more.

Fran's voice came over the phone. 'Gigi, what's happening? What are you swearing about?'

'Fran, I'll have to call you back. Sorry.'

Freddy appeared in my doorway, terror working on his features. 'It's one of them. He can't find me here.'

'Attic.'

'Don't let him in.'

'Now!' I pointed to the ceiling hatch. Then I headed downstairs, pressing 999 on the phone keypad. I wouldn't hit 'Call' yet, I just wanted to be sure the number was dialled in.

Chapter 35

Nanna had a great saying – well, several actually – the one that sprang to mind, right then, was: 'You can catch more flies with honey than vinegar.'

I walked towards the back door with the phone clutched in my cardigan pocket, I settled my face into a kindly smile. 'Okay, here goes.' I announced as I went outside.

The revving subsided.

I stopped a couple of feet ahead of the front wheel, tilted my head to one side.

I could feel my smile twitch so pulled it even tighter.

He turned the engine off. Good. Less chance of him running me over.

He pushed his visor up. Dark, slanting eyes peered out at me – not smiling.

'Hi,' I repeated. 'Are you looking for accommodation – bed and breakfast?'

The eyes narrowed. 'I'm looking for Freddy.'

I acted like this was news. 'He lives in Freshwater. Let me give you the address. It's about half an hour…'

'He's not there and you know it.'

'Oh.' My frown was now as forced as my smile had been. I was seriously over-doing it. I'd always been rubbish at acting. I pulled it back quickly. 'Maybe he popped over to the mainland. Did he know you were coming? Shall I ring him?' I asked obligingly, and took the phone from my pocket.

He ignored me and looked at the upstairs windows. The attic had a retractable ladder, Freddy should be in there by now. There were heaps of cases and boxes to hide behind.

No shotgun, though. Nanna's old shooting stick was the nearest we had to an assault weapon.

He dismounted and kicked the bike stand into place.

'I'm Gigi,' I said, holding out my hand. 'Did you meet Freddy travelling?'

'No,' he said, ignoring my hand and walked past me towards the house.

'Excuse me,' I said, indignation superseding common sense. 'Where are you going?'

'Like I said, I'm looking for Freddy.' He walked straight into my kitchen.

'And like I said, he lives in Freshwater.'

I followed this Darth Vader clone as he strode through my house. I huffed and puffed to show my annoyance, but the fact was, I felt sick at the prospect of my brother being butchered right in front of my eyes.

He peered under the dining table. He looked behind the armchairs. He checked the loo and hall cupboard. Bloody hell, he was thorough. He mounted the stairs slowly, like he was listening for the sound of Freddy's knees knocking.

Crap! The bed in the guest room was bound to be a mess with Freddy staying in it. How would I explain that?

He moved stealthily from room to room, peering under, in and around anything that might conceal my brother. My heart was beating so hard in my chest, I anticipated a seizure at any moment, and considered faking one as a diversion. Finally, he pushed the door open to the guest room.

I held my breath.

He walked in and I followed.

The bed was piled with clothes. My clothes. The summer clothes I'd put away in the wardrobe till next year.

No evidence of Freddy at all. No rucksack. Nothing.

Jeez, my brother was smarter than I realised.

'Have you finished?' I asked.

He eyed the blanket box on the landing and pulled it open.

Don't look up, I thought, as much to myself as to him. If I looked up it would immediately transmit where Freddy was lurking.

He looked up. He looked back at the blanket box and closed it. He stood on it. He popped open the hatch to the attic and released the ladder.

Off he went, one rung at a time.

He spotted the light switch and flicked it on.

He disappeared. I didn't follow.

I waited and offered up silent prayers to any deity with a listening ear.

There were creaks and rustlings. I anticipated an 'Ooof!' at any moment.

My finger hovered over the 'Call' button on my phone believing there must be an ambulance out there with Freddy's name on it.

The guy's voice called down, 'Who's the painter?'

'What?'

'The artist who did these flowers. They're good.'

'My grandmother.'

More creaks.

Any moment now…

A biker boot stomped onto the top rung. Slowly, the guy descended and paused.

I held my breath. Freddy must have made a noise.

After an eternity, the guy carried on down the ladder.

'You tell that little shit of a brother, I'll get him. You hear?'

'But who are you?'

'You don't need a name, Gigi. You just tell him.'

I followed him down the stairs and outside. His gazed shifted to my studio.

The door was open, but I hadn't been in there all day.

He looked at me and back at the studio before marching through the door. I guessed it was too much to hope he'd pay top dollar for one of my angels.

'This is what you do?'

'Yes.'

After surveying the work table, the shelves and the sculptures, my next real and present fear was that he might vent his anger on my sculptures. Hours of painstaking work could be laid waste in a matter of seconds. 'Do you like sculpture, too?' I asked, rather feebly.

He looked at the footprints in the clay dust.

Bugger!

And made a beeline for the large kiln. As he pulled open the door, Freddy lurched at him from inside, screaming like a banshee.

Or maybe that was me.

He had a modelling knife in one hand and a wooden rolling pin in the other. But he was no match for a Macau gangster. Within seconds, Freddy was pinned to the floor by a hand around his throat and fourteen stone of biker on his chest.

The rolling pin had been tossed one way and the knife now resting in our visitor's hand, was angled at Freddy's eye. 'I hope you haven't forgotten our deal,' he said through gritted teeth. 'By Friday.'

'I'm getting it. Tell him, Gigi, tell him!'

'Yes, tell me, Gigi.'

It would have been easy to hammer the oaf in the kidneys with a stoneware angel. The sculptures were by my side, and he had his back to me but it didn't seem morally right to injure a man with a heavenly creature. Or maybe I was just chicken.

'We're selling this place to raise the money,' I croaked. 'The estate agent put it on the market at a silly price. It should sell very quickly.'

'Whose house is it?'

'Mine.'

'Really? Well, fancy that.'

I stared at the modelling knife pressed hard against Freddy's temple. Lucky for Freddy, it was as blunt as a butter knife, but it could still puncture his skin if forced. I watched it move as the guy called me over.

'Stand here, Gigi, and I'll tell you what I'm going to do.'

I moved into his sight-line.

'I'm going to take your brother back with me, and I'm not going to let the little creep out of my sight until the contracts are signed. Right?'

'But...'

He got up and hauled Freddy to his feet. 'If you behave yourself, Freddy, nothing need happen to you.'

It was made crystal clear to me, by both of them, that my cooperation was essential for keeping Freddy whole.

'Just as soon as this place is sold and the funds are in our account, you can have him back.'

'Thank you.'

'Till then, you'd better get onto that estate agents and make it worth their while to shift this place – and quick.'

I rather thought two percent of the sale price should be incentive enough but I didn't argue.

He turned to Freddy. 'Next time, maybe you won't get so flash at the gambling table.'

'Don't blame him,' I snapped, 'It wasn't his fault.'

'Really? So who was it slapped a picture of Willow View on Black, and yelled, "Shit or Bust?" Huh?'

I looked at Freddy. His momentary stillness was the only confession I needed.

'You bet your inheritance on a spin of the roulette wheel?' Silence. 'Is that even legal?'

Bikeman laughed.

Freddy's shoulders drooped.

'I don't get it – you guys have the deeds to Willow View. Why am I selling this place?'

'Ask Little Big Shot, over here.'

'Freddy. Tell him about the syndicate.'

His head turned away.

'Yes, tell me about the syndicate, Freddy,' sneered Bikeman.

Freddy said nothing.

'Would that be the syndicate that loaned you two hundred grand? C'mon, Freddy, you and I both know creeping round the loan sharks in the city doesn't amount to any kind of syndicate. You just got big ideas and greedy – making promises and hustling cash at every turn.'

'Freddy?'

'I wanted to set up a business, okay? I wanted to show Dad I could do it on my own. Do something right.'

I let out a wail. 'You don't do it like that! You don't hit the casinos to make money.'

'It works!' he yelled defiantly.

'Oh yes, I can see that.'

'It did. I made ninety-thousand in my first week.'

'How many weeks were you there?'

He didn't answer, but I knew it was less than a month.

'So the debt is all yours, Freddy?'

Again no answer.

Bikeman just sat there, nodding his head slowly.

My brother, never known to make a sensible decision in his life was all in.

And I was stuffed. My home had been gambled away.

Cheers Freddy.

It's odd how, faced with something so catastrophically bad and so grotesquely unfair, my mind and my heart seemed to freeze. It was just too much. Too much to lose and too much to take in.

'So, what happens now?' I finally managed.

Freddy shrugged.

'I'm not asking you!' I snapped.

Bikeman leaned against the table. 'Right now, I'm taking Freddy and you're selling the house. Just about as fast as you can.'

I threw a bit of a wobbler, then. In spite of Bikeman's assurances, I still didn't like to see my little brother being taken away – however lame-brained and misguided he might be, not to mention the source of all this trouble. Bikeman gripped me by the wrists, how grateful was I it wasn't my throat, pushed his helmeted head toward me and said, 'You have my word, once the funds are transferred, your precious brother will be back here.'

Something in my body language must have sneered back at him, because he loosened his grip ever so slightly. 'Gigi, I could've really hurt him back then, and I could've really hurt you, but did I? Did I?'

I may have shaken my head.

'That's because it would have made things even messier, wouldn't it?'

I stared into his narrow, black eyes, thinking how like onyx they were – dark and hard.

'This way, it's just a clean, fair transaction. A settling of debts. My guys get paid, you two go free.'

'I deserve to be free anyway,' I squeaked.

'You're collateral in the deal.'

'How do I know you won't come back for more? How do I know you won't pursue me and my brother for years to come?'

He laughed. 'Because you, Gigi, are insignificant to us, and Freddy's just whitebait in a sea of sharks.'

'So I won't have to spend the rest of my life looking over my shoulder?'

'Not if Freddy stays out of our way.'

I glanced across at Freddy, who was rigid with concern.

He held up his hands. 'Never again, Gigi, I swear.'

'Promise me.'

'I promise.'

'Anything like this happens again…'

'It won't. Never.'

Bikeman relaxed his hold on me. 'Sweet. Now, let's go.'

Freddy wasn't even allowed to grab any of his belongings. 'Best you feel you've got something to come back for, eh? Including your sister. That way, you won't be tempted to do anything stupid, will you?'

He handed my brother a helmet before making a phone call. I didn't understand a word of it but I got the gist. It sounded like: 'I've got the little fucker and I'm bringing him in.'

As soon as they'd gone, I locked and bolted the door, ran to a notepad and scribbled down the bike's registration number. I might still use it. Once Freddy was safe, I could turn the information over to…

What was I thinking?

How much of a hornet's nest might I be stirring up if I involved the police? Freddy had acquired those debts and debts had to be paid. In any case, the Macau Mafia would undoubtedly run rings around the Met.

No. I would only use those number plates if they made an unwelcome return in the future. Once Freddy's debts were paid, all would be well.

Wouldn't it?

I shuddered.

Chapter 36

When I discovered the Virginia Creeper trellis was fractured in more than one place, I worked out that Freddy had eschewed the attic, in favour of the less obvious kiln hidey-hole. He must have climbed down from the spare room while we were mounting the stairs. The newly-replaced sash window had slid noiselessly up and down, giving him a near-perfect escape. If he'd been just a bit smarter, he'd have legged it across the field to the stable and hidden there or, better still, sprinted off into a distant field and waited it out. However, I actually believe he hadn't wanted to leave me all alone. He wasn't big on loyalty, unless it was heading in his direction, but I flatter myself that I've been the one constant supporter in his life, and maybe – just maybe – it mattered to him that I might actually be in danger myself.

I hadn't seen or spoken to Luke since the For Sale sign went up. Maybe he was distancing himself on purpose. Maybe he'd decided I wasn't worth wasting time on.

Maybe he'd developed feelings for me and was guarding himself from further hurt.

Who was I kidding?

He was more likely hoping for a nice, independent new neighbour who would leave him to run his own life in peace.

In the meantime, I busied myself packing and labelling boxes. Again. Boxes only recently unpacked and consigned to the loft.

Tess scheduled a few viewings, over the coming days. It seemed making Bluebell Farm *Bargain of the Week* on their website had generated interest. Of course it had, it offered beauty, peace and comfort at a rock-bottom price.

For each viewing, I made myself scarce; a walk to the beach, coffee with Megan, a bus trip into Ryde. I wanted to squeeze the last drop of juice from of my time there, and not spend it smiling politely at people who wanted my house. I regarded them as cuckoos ousting me from my nest. Unfortunately, there came a day when it was hurling with rain and Megan was working so I opted to stay in the studio and busy myself with a small sculpture of a cherub. In a world crumbling to dust around me, it was soothing to model something innocent.

I caught sight of Tess greeting a family in the courtyard and ushering them quickly through the kitchen door; a couple in their thirties with twin boys.

Good, they hadn't seen me. I didn't have to wave and encourage them in. No, Tess could earn her commission while I burnished my cherub's bum.

Even so, I couldn't help wondering what they were thinking of the house and how they were reacting to the décor and the garden. Were they picking up the wonderful vibe of Nanna's energy, which those walls had absorbed over the last fifty years?

When the rain was particularly heavy, there was a kerfuffle as Tess and the family hurried across the courtyard and straight into my studio.

My sanctum.

The nerve of it! I don't think I hid my irritation very well.

'Sorry to disturb you,' Tess said. I'm sure she wasn't. 'Just having a quick look in here, we've been talking about turning this into a gym.'

'Fantastic,' said the mother. 'Look, James, it's perfect.'

'Not bad.'

Not *bad*? I wanted to shout. Not *bad*? They'd be bloody lucky to have it.

The boys, who I judged to be about four, shot passed them and peered at my cherub in wonder. 'What are you doing to his bottom.' said one of them, leaning perilously close.

'Sh! Arthur. It's art,' their mother explained.

'Well, what are you doing to his art, then?' he asked.

'And his willy,' said the other one, as they examined it, still fascinated, while I gritted my teeth. 'Look!' he squeaked, suddenly clocking a group of angels in the corner and making a beeline for them.

Instinctively, I reached out and clutched at the hood of his top before carnage ensued. At which point, their mother had the sense to intervene, and snatched up her boys' hands to drag their reluctant little bodies back towards the door and away from this mad sculptor. 'Come on, let's move you boys away.' There was an edge to her voice. I'm guessing it had something to do with my nearly garrotting her son with his own hoody cord.

Her husband hung around to inspect the electric points and the light fittings. 'Yes we have those on the Isle of Wight,' I was tempted to say. Eventually, he nodded at me and left with Tess.

I stared at them, and felt the joy of my recent past leaking from my life. I sensed an inevitable shift from my home to theirs; of that I was sure.

Twenty-four hours later, we had our offer. Bluebell Farm was sold subject to contract. Tess started to tell me about the buyer.

'Don't,' I said, holding my hand up to her. 'Please, I can't bear to hear it.'

She pulled a sympathetic face. 'Well, I'm sure they'll take care of it.'

I nodded. It's not like they were going to be the custodians of it for my return. The dream was over.

Thanks to Freddy, the Gill-Martin island inheritance was toast.

Tess had suggested the buyer might make an offer for the furniture, if they were planning on it being a second home. 'It's very tastefully done,' she said, 'almost too good for a holiday home.' But she'd been right. Four days after her visit, we received a derisory offer – twenty grand below the asking price – for the house and furniture.

'No way!' was my initial reaction. 'The sitting room furniture alone cost nearly ten.'

'They're cash buyers,' she said, 'No chain.' Which pretty much sealed the deal.

Some of my belongings were still in boxes from my arrival in the summer – stuff I hadn't needed yet. Now I was packing again, except this time, without a single shiver of excitement and definitely no lunatic grin on my face.

Chapter 37

'I'd love to have your cats,' Megan insisted, as she pressed a lump of clay into a rough petal shape.

'You're not worried they might smother Mackay or worse – feed him dead mice?'

'Nope. I was brought up with cats, ferrets and budgerigars. Didn't harm me,' she said, crossing her eyes.

'Will your mum mind?'

'She'll love them. In fact, she'll want to keep them but I promise you can fetch them whenever you like. In the meantime, you can have visiting rights.' She held up the flower she was forming. 'Waddya think?'

'I think it's a really good rose.'

'Bugger. It's meant to be a water-lily.' She laid it back down. 'Shame you're going to miss the Christmas Festival. Can't you come back for it?'

The Christmas Festival was the samba band's last big gig until the spring. All our practices were focussing on it. I shook my head. 'I've found a job at the V&A Museum.'

'Great!' She looked excited for me.

'It's just working in the gift shop over Christmas.'

'You never know what it might lead to.'

'Exactly. Maybe when Christmas is over, I could pop back and see you.' I was saying this to her benefit. To be honest, I was terrified any return would be painful. I'd never stayed anywhere on the island except the farm. The idea of visiting for a weekend and sleeping on Megan's sofa-bed would just hammer home how much I'd lost.

'I'm counting on it. And I have a vested interest…'

'Go on.'

'I'm seriously hoping you'll return the favour and invite me up to London.'

'Oh, Megan, of course I will. That totally goes without saying.'

It wouldn't be until I had a place of my own, though. There was barely enough space for me in Fran's box room, never mind guests.

Freddy fired off a text to tell me his debts were settled and he was a 'free' man. Lucky him.

A week later, he called to tell me he'd managed to find himself a job in London, working for the father of one of his old school friends. 'Starting at the bottom of course – making phone calls, chatting up people, getting the sales guys in front of the big boys.'

'Telesales?'

'Pre-sales, yes, but I'll get to go out and show them our wares. Dazzle them with technology.'

'What kind of technology?'

'Lighting installations – fancy stuff.'

'Good. It'll be great for you, I'm sure.' Of course, I was pleased for him. He was my brother, I wanted him to do well. All the same, it was clear to me that our conversation was a little taut.

'And I'll be great for it!' He sounded wildly positive, a flash of the old Freddy glimmering through the haze of bitter experience. I hoped it wasn't an act.

'How's it going so far?'

'Great. I think I'm a natural salesman.'

'That's good to hear.'

'Listen, Gigi, I need to come over to pick up a few

things from the cottage. Our friends from Macau aren't interested in my personal effects. When are you staying till?'

'Second week in December.'

'I'll try and make it over before you leave. It'll be a flying visit, I don't want to start taking holiday so soon just for a few bits of furniture'

'Of course you don't. It'll be nice to see you.'

I, on the other hand, had agreed to throw most of my furnishings in with the house sale. I had nowhere to put them, and the new owners were happy to offer an extra grand to cover the contents, which was a very sick joke bearing in mind what they'd cost a few months ago.

My finances were slightly improved, thanks to the sale of Bluebell Farm. Freddy's debts were a few thousand short of the sale price so I got to keep the change. I bought a low-mileage van. What it lacked in glamour it made up for in functionality.

My sculptures, materials and equipment were going into storage. I had no idea how long they would be there – months, maybe years even, but they were things I had to hang on to. I knew I could go back into the property business, but officially, I still had six months to prove myself to Dad. Despite everything that had happened, I wasn't prepared to give in, yet. Just as soon as Christmas was over, I planned on finding a daytime job and some studio space to rent. Anywhere, I wasn't fussy.

I'd already off-loaded most of my mugs, plaques and dragons to island shops – on sale or return. It seemed I'd been right about Christmas interest – they weren't exactly selling like salted caramel muffins but they were selling well enough for a couple of shops to ask for more. So I'd been burning the midnight oil, and capitalizing on my last few days with an operational studio to meet their demands.

How crap was that – seeing my work succeed, only to be forced to close down production?

In the meantime, I was moving in with Fran.

Two days before I left was Cat Eviction Day. At least, that's how it felt.

I'd hidden their crate in the shed, so as not to spook them. To a cat, crates and vets had an uncanny synchronicity. I carried the more tricky Gaudi under my arm to the shed. The moment he saw the crate, his legs locked against me, and his claws anchored themselves into my sweater. Now he was a rigid structure impossible to post through the tiny opening.

'Damn!'

As I tried to move him towards the crate, my sweater tented out as claws hooked tightly onto it. Fast as I teased the one foot from the fabric, he stabbed it back into another place, and punctured my flesh.

'Gaudi, you're not helping!'

There was only one thing for it. If the cat wouldn't let go of the sweater, he could bloody well take it with him. Using my free arm, I dragged the sweater over my head, emerging to lock gazes with a cat, who was seriously pissed off at having been out-witted.

I wrapped the fabric around him but he yowled and thrust his hind legs towards me, his needle-like claws hooking through the fabric, again, and into my belly.

'Calm down, Gaudi. We're not going to the vets.' Just the mention of the word and he was thrashing some more.

'Gigi?' Luke was standing outside the shed. 'D'you want a hand with that?'

'Oooff!' I looked over the squirming creature and into Luke's amused eyes. An autumnal gust whipped around my bare back and shoulders. I really should have thrown that greying old bra away.

Luke didn't wait for an answer but stepped forward, turned the crate on its end and held it between his legs. Then he wrapped his hands around Gaudi and my sweater. 'Sorry, old fella, you might as well relax.' Together we fed the cat through the crate's opening and secured the gate.

'Thanks,' I said, acutely aware of the goose-pimples springing up like a rash over my body. Question was, should I sashay back to the house, like Beyoncé on heat, or scamper off, giggling like Barbara Windsor in a Carry-on film?

Luke chuckled, 'Good job he only had a hold of your sweater,' and tipped the crate back onto its base. 'Will the other one be that difficult?' He stood up and looked directly into my eyes, quite deliberately not studying my lace-clad hooters.

'Ah, no, Rodin is much more compliant,' I said, and made what I like to think was a regal retreat. I grabbed a jacket off the coat-peg in the kitchen and pulled it on.

Rodin was oblivious to Gaudi's ordeal and allowed me to carry him out to the shed, where Luke was waiting with the crate. Once the two were contained, he said, 'I just came over to ask if you've made any plans for your last night on the island?'

An excited little fairy fluttered in my chest. 'No.'

'Ava's back for the holidays. She thought you

351

might want to come over for something to eat.'

The fairy flopped. Of course. What on earth was I thinking? Stupid Gigi. 'That's a lovely idea. Thanks.'

'Okay, well, any time after seven.'

'Great.'

'Now, anything else you want a hand with?'

'Nope. That's it. I need to take these babies to their new home.'

He crouched down and peered in at the two faces peering out. 'See you, guys. Be good for your mom!' Then he was off.

On my final full day, I watched Freddy drive into the courtyard in a rental van. He was only over for a few hours; hours in which I really hoped to see a change in him, a maturity and an assurance that this crap was well and truly over. And I did. Sort of.

Whilst I couldn't ignore the life-long tug of familial recognition urging me towards him, the fury of what he'd done to my life suddenly flared. It obviously made him hesitate in his approach. The look on his face was sheepish, just like when he was a child caught doing something wrong, but there was a strained and worldly look in his eyes, like he'd opened Pandora's Box and closed it again in terror – never to recover from the vision within.

He stood in front of me. Troubled. Older. 'I'm really sorry, Gigi. I'm a shit brother.'

'Freddy, you said, "Never again". Tell me you meant it.'

His voice was intense. 'I meant it. Truly. I meant it.' There were tears in his eyes. I hadn't seen those for a very long time. The familial tug won out over the flare of anger. I hugged him hard, and released all my pent up anxiety in a sob.

After a few moments I stepped back. 'You look smart.'

'I dropped in on Simon. He lent me this stuff.'

'Oh.'

'You never told me you and Rupe were over,' he added.

'It didn't seem important, at the time.'

'I'm sorry, Sis. I didn't mean to fuck things up between you two.'

'You didn't. Not really.'

'When are you off?' Freddy asked.

'Tomorrow. The removal van took most of my stuff, this morning. I've just got my sculptures and a few other bits to go.'

He glanced over at the studio. 'Never got a buyer for the big stuff, then?'

'Fraid not.'

'What would you charge for them?'

I shrugged. It seemed academic, right now. 'In terms of hours and materials, about six hundred each would cover it. If I could just get recognized, I could charge more.'

'One day.'

'One day.'

So much had happened and there was so much unchartered territory ahead of us. In years to come we might look back on this whole period as character-building, the best thing that ever happened to us. Perhaps.

'Gigi, I will make it up to you. I promise.'

I smiled. 'Just so long as it doesn't involve gambling, pornography or extortion.' It was a major milestone that he finally showed some sense of responsibility.

'Come on,' I said, 'there's stuff I need to do. You get over to Freshwater and I'll see you...when?'

'I'll call you.'

Chapter 38

'Your place looks so sad now it's empty,' Ava said as she stirred the rich savoury casserole of meat bubbling on the hob in Luke's kitchen. She was making tacos, her current culinary party-piece. Sitting there reminded me of my uni days, and the flat I'd shared with The Divas. The main difference here, was no champagne on ice or smoked salmon blinis from the deli down the road.

Luke was in his study, working on edits for his book and Chuck lay in the hallway outside his door.

'I hope you like your new neighbours. They have cute twin boys.'

Her eyes brightened. 'Really, how old?'

'Four, maybe.'

'Oh, that kind of cute.'

'Sorry.'

Placing taco shells onto an oven tray, she called to Luke. 'Dinner in five!' then turned back to me. 'So it's all change for you. Dubai next year, that'll be so amazing.'

I nodded. No need to fill her in on the detail. 'What do you plan on doing when you finish your degree?' I asked.

'I'm not staying here. It might suit Luke but you must admit, when you're young free and single, this isn't exactly the centre of the universe, is it?'

I chuckled. It was the centre of my universe, once. Newport didn't exactly have Regent Street shops, and buses didn't pass my door every few minutes but the island had beautiful scenery and the freshest air I'd ever breathed. I could trace my contentment here right back to childhood. Summers that lasted for months. Walks through trees and along beaches that threatened minimal pollution. I travelled without fear of some sweaty guy pressing his package into my back on an overloaded tube train, and the peace...you needed triple-glazing in London to even approach the kind of peace I found here.

Living on the island had been like being on permanent holiday, with a little creative activity thrown in. I'd had it tough, I'll admit, but the problems hadn't been insurmountable.

'So where will you go?'

'There's a research programme in Holland I'm interested in. I can do a month there next summer – no pay, just accommodation – if I like it and they like me, I'm hoping a place will open up for me. That would be so cool.'

'Keep thinking that way, and it just might.'

Wow, wasn't I sounding like trust in the Universe worked? Truth was, I felt just a tad sore with the Universe at that moment.

Chuck shifted in the hall as Luke came out to join us.

'So, what does the project entail?' I asked her, determined to keep the focus off me. The less my life came under scrutiny, the better. I hated lying but exposing the truth would have been even worse. It was deceitful, I know, but rather that than face their reaction. I'd been through enough, thank you very much, and figured a little white lie here, and a few concealed revelations there, would spare me the open shame and indignity of dirty linen aired in public.

I was conscious of Luke grabbing himself a can of beer from the fridge while Ava ran through a précis of the science project. I'm sorry to say I barely registered a word she said. Just twenty-four hours from now and I'd be back in London and Bluebell Farm would begin its long, slow journey into the recesses of my memory. I did manage to add, 'Sounds like that kind of challenge could really shape your career.'

'And get me out of this God forsaken hole.'

Luke rolled his eyes at me as he poured me a glass of wine. I grinned back. We were in full agreement when it came to the island.

The tacos were delicious and spicy as hell.

'Whoar!' Luke said, after coughing and taking a slug of beer.

'Jeez!' I croaked, reaching for my wine.

'Good, are they?' Ava asked, wrapping her lips around a fork full of spiced beef, and nodding her approval.

We ploughed on, chomping, whooping and spluttering, interspersed with the odd swig of cool fluid. Eating them helped take my mind off my impending misery. Although I could only manage to eat one and a half while Ava and Luke stormed through a full two each and debated sharing another.

'Tell you what,' she announced. 'Let's leave it to mature overnight and have it with jacket potatoes and yoghurt, tomorrow.'

'Good shout,' Luke agreed, and felt a pain pinching my chest at the knowledge I would be miles away tomorrow.

'Minghella's finest for dessert,' Ava announced. 'Which would you like, Tropical Coconut, Old

English Toffee or Blackcurrants and Cream? Or all three. There are no laws with ice cream.'

'All three, please,' I grinned.

'Me too,' said Luke.

'Shall I serve it up or just stick the tubs in the middle of the table?'

'Oh no,' Luke said, getting up to find some bowls. 'We have a guest.' He returned with bowls and a large metal ice cream scoop. 'And that's exhausted my waitering skills – ladies, help yourselves!'

The cool ice cream was bliss on my chilli-inflamed palate. Notes of blackcurrant whispered reminders of glorious past summers.

I looked around wanting to capture the image for future viewing – a new memory to treasure: Ava's eyes closed with the ecstasy of a mouthful of Tropical Coconut, Luke's hum of endorsement and both of them oblivious to my inner turmoil. Whereas Chuck sat beside me, his head tilted and his eyes peering up at mine.

'Hey, Chuck, no begging,' Luke said.

Chuck looked quickly at Luke and back at me. I stroked his head. I would miss this lovely, brown eyed body of canine comfort.

Stop it, Gigi. That way, misery lies! I told myself.

The Universe had a different plan for me. Great things lay in store.

I had to believe that.

'So, what time are you off in the morning?' Luke's question derailed my train of thought. Good job too.

'About ten, I'm on the eleven o'clock ferry.'

'Do you need a hand loading up your van?'

'The big stuff went with the removal company. It's just my sculptures and personal stuff to go.'

'Okay, I'll pop over first thing. I don't have any lectures till the afternoon.'

'I'll come and wave you off,' Ava announced.

'You reckon you'll be up by ten?' her brother asked.

'Course. After those tacos, I reckon I'll probably be up before nine.'

We laughed and I took this as my moment to leave. I stood up. 'Thanks for dinner but I'd better go, I still have stuff to do.'

'Sure thing.'

Luke stood too. Even though I only lived a hundred metres away, he always saw me home in the dark. I'd given up trying to talk him out of it. In any case, I rather liked it – knowing he had my back.

Ava gave me a hug and Chuck trotted up to the door with us. Luke grabbed the lead and fixed it to the dog's collar. 'I'll take him round the field.'

We walked towards Bluebell Farm in silence. Only as we started up the drive did he speak. 'I hope all goes well for you in your new life.'

'Thanks,' I said forcing brightness.

'D'you know what? I think you could make a success of anything you had a mind to.'

I swallowed back the tide of emotion forcing its way into my throat, and nodded. There were only a few more steps across the courtyard to my kitchen door. I could hold it together till then. 'I hope so.'

'You have that same plucky streak your grandmother had.'

'Thank you.' I had the key in my hand and was focusing on the lock, preparing to line them up. As the two converged successfully, I felt a rush of guilt and sadness. I owed this guy more than a hurried goodbye. It's not like this was the end of a really dodgy date.

I stopped, and turned around, not totally sure what I would say. He was a few paces away from me.

'Okay?' he asked, like he always did. In the beginning, he'd say, 'I'll wait till you're inside and the door's locked,' but it had ceased to be necessary after the second or third time.

I pulled a wide kind of smile – the one you make to seal the tear ducts. 'I'm okay.'

'I'll see you in the morning, then,' he said, matter-of-factly, and turned away.

Wait! I wanted to shout. Aren't you going to see me through the door and wait till it's locked?

But I didn't, and he didn't. In the silvery-blue light from the security lamp, I watched as he strode easily down the drive and away from me.

Sniffing back tears of disappointment and sadness, I let myself into Bluebell Farm for the very last time.

Chapter 39

I hadn't slept much. Nearly everything was packed. All I had to do was load up some cases and my sculptures, and I was ready to go. I'd spent the previous afternoon wrestling with rolls of bubble wrap and unco-operative angels. I'd left them in a very uncelestial group inside the studio.

I was just into my second cup of coffee, when Luke appeared at the window. I waved him to come in.

'All set?' he asked.

'All set,' I replied and stood up. 'I thought we could put the sculptures in first, then I can pack around them with bedding.'

'Okay. Ready to do that now?'

'Yep.' I'd learned it didn't pay to put off unpleasant jobs – just like ripping off bikini wax, you scream 'Geronimo!' and do it.

We went out together.

Half-way across the courtyard, I stopped, causing Luke to bump into me. I didn't need to go any further to see the studio was empty.

Barren.

Abandoned.

Nothing remained of my handiwork.

Slowly, I continued forward, as if it were just a trick of the light and I would see those robust, stoneware structures materialise like mountains from the mist.

But no.

I tried the handle. The door was locked.

'What's up?' Luke asked.

'They're gone.' I whispered, leaning my forehead against the door.

He came alongside and peered through the floor-to-ceiling window at the empty studio.

'But where? Who would…?' he paused. 'Forget it, you don't have to tell me.'

Only two other people had a key to that studio – the estate agent and Freddy. It didn't take the mental dexterity of Einstein to know Freddy would be behind this. 'How much d'you think they're worth?' he'd asked me. It hadn't occurred to me he might be calculating the value for himself.

Why hadn't it occurred to me?

To think I'd believed he could change.

I felt the warmth of Luke's hand on my shoulder, as he gave it a sympathetic stroke. 'I guess it's too much to hope your brother was trying to help you out?' he offered.

'Yes. Too much.'

My instinct was to call Freddy but after a brief mental battle, I dismissed the idea.

I turned around and leaned my back on the studio door. 'I guess that's just the cases and boxes to pack, then,' I said.

'No! Wait a minute.' Luke's hand was now holding my shoulder and his head was almost level with mine. 'This is theft, Gabriella. I know he's your brother but that work was hugely important to you – not to mention, valuable. You can't just overlook it.'

Yes I could. That's what I did for Freddy, or maybe what I used to do. 'What's your suggestion, Luke – call the police? Would you call the police on

Ava if she did something wrong?'

He gave my shoulder a final squeeze before putting his hand in his pocket, and stepping back. 'Did you know I once caught him trying to steal from Una?'

'No.'

He shook his head. 'Sorry, I didn't have to tell you that.'

I shrugged. 'Freddy's never been a paragon of virtue.'

'You can't let him get away with this.'

'I can if I want to, Luke.'

'Gabriella, he's stolen your work, and what do you think he's going to do with it, huh? Sell it for some other crackpot business venture?'

The Macau Mafia must be on his case again. More debts. Hadn't Freddy learned his lesson?

I pushed myself away from the door and moved past him. 'Let's get the other stuff packed, and then I can go.'

'That was your work!'

I kept walking.

'Why would he do that? Is he on drugs?'

'No.'

He moved swiftly in front of me and held his hands out. 'Be honest with me, Gabriella, please tell me you didn't sell this house for Freddy?'

I focused on the stitching of his shirt front.

'You really did that?' He let out a sigh. 'Gabriella, when is it going to stop?'

I honestly didn't know the answer to that one, although I was coming pretty close to it.

'What do YOU want? What's good for Gigi? Sooner or later you have to stop making sacrifices for

363

your brother.'

I looked up. 'What, like you did for Ava? She told me about the amazing job you gave up in Canada. She says you could have been a real hot-shot in that fuel company you worked for, if you'd stayed.'

'What?' He glared at me beneath a heavy frown. I had the distinct impression I might have overstepped the mark. 'Ava is my responsibility. Back then, she was just a kid at school and I needed to be around for her. Hot shot, indeed. What a great brother I'd have been, leaving her alone for days at a time while I flew off to oil sites. Yes, Gabriella, I gave up a great job but only to give her a more settled life, okay?'

I felt my skin burn with shame. I had even less right to criticise him than he had to pass judgement on me. What's more, I also knew he'd had his heart-broken – which was quite likely the real reason for leaving.

He continued. 'Ava's worth putting first because she's honest and smart, and she has a great future, whereas Freddy...' He threw his hands up and shook his head. 'Freddy is a waste of space and you know it.'

I gritted my teeth. 'He's still my brother.' I also wanted to say he'd had a raw deal too, but there didn't seem any point. We locked eyes, like a couple of cage fighters waiting for the first move. I could see he was absolutely boiling. I shouldn't have called him out on leaving Canada. His situation was entirely different but, equally, he had no right to tell me how to handle my brother.

Finally, he stepped back and raised his hands dismissively. 'Okay. You do what you think is right,' but it was said with very little conviction.

'Yes. I will.'

I walked around him, back into the house for the rest of my stuff. Stuck on the fridge door was a flyer advertising all the exhibitors at the gallery for the coming months – including me. I gasped. 'Oh, no!'

'What?' asked Luke behind me.

So, he hadn't gone, then? I went over and took the notice down.

'Your exhibition, right?'

I nodded.

Luke swore. 'Gabriella – Freddy must've taken your stuff in the last twelve hours. He can't have sold it yet. Call the police!'

I turned on him. 'Stop it will you! Just stop it!'

'You don't have to press charges but at least they can apprehend him, and you can get your stuff back.'

'No!' I would not put Freddy in mortal danger.

Luke pulled a phone from his pocket. 'It's the sensible thing to do, Gigi. If you don't call them, I will.'

'Don't you dare!' I yelled, holding out my hand, as tears sprang from my eyes. 'Don't do it! Just don't!' I clutched at the hand holding the phone. He glared back at me, his mouth open as if prepared to give me another argument. 'Please,' I said quietly. 'Don't.'

He snapped his mouth closed and lowered his hand but the look in his eyes was searing. Sampson on battery acid, Ava had joked. I let go of his hand and wrapped my arms across my chest. He returned the phone to his pocket, shaking his head slowly in disbelief.

I assumed he'd leave but instead he turned and lifted one of the boxes off the kitchen table.

'You don't have to do that,' I said, and sniffed noisily, wiping my eyes with the back of my hand.

365

'You'll be done quicker if I help.'

He couldn't wait to see me gone.

It took us less than ten minutes to load my remaining possessions into the van, and it was all done wordlessly.

I glanced at my watch. Nearly nine o'clock. Maybe, if I went now, I could catch the ten o'clock ferry. It was a quiet time of year so unlikely it would be full.

'I'm thinking of taking an earlier ferry,' I said aloud, as I watched Luke close the van doors.

'Good idea,' he replied with unsettling finality.

'Say goodbye to Ava for me?'

'Sure.'

I looked around, which was probably a mistake. 'I'll lock up.'

Luke waited by the van. I could practically sense him holding his breath in anticipation of my departure; I could picture him letting out a massive sigh of relief and jogging down the drive, before pausing, once, to kick his heels in celebration.

I sighed myself, as the lock clicked into place. I swallowed, turned and headed towards him, my hand outstretched like a salesman. 'Thanks for all your help.'

He frowned at my hand and at me.

Stupid Gigi. I pulled it back.

Shaking his head, he stepped forwards, opened his arms and drew me into the biggest hug of my life. 'I wish you nothing but the best, Gabriella.'

I was floored by the unexpected switch from anger to compassion. The anger was easier to cope with. The emotional wrench of leaving seized my heart like cramp. Layered over that, was the sickening fear of what Freddy might be mixed up in.

This was not how it was meant to be.

I clenched my teeth together, and squeezed my eyelids tight. If I didn't muster some self-control, I'd be no use to anyone.

I tried to concentrate on superficial things. All I could focus on was Luke's warmth, and that he smelled of clean laundry and wood smoke. His cottage had a lovely brick fireplace – not as grand as the one in the farm but cosy. I shut the image down and replaced it with the clinically white fireplace at Fran's flat. The one with the imitation fire that sprang to life at the flick of switch. Instant heat. Who needed logs and embers and soot?

I pushed myself away from him. 'Thanks, Luke. You really have been a great neighbour.'

'You too. And keep in touch, let me know how you're doing.'

'Thanks.' I opened the van door and climbed in, pulled on the seatbelt and started the engine.

Go! Leave! I silently urged Luke, as he stepped back and watched me. I gave him a brief smile. 'See ya!' I said pulling the door closed.

I drove smoothly away from him, paused between the gate posts and headed onto the road. 'No looking back, Gabriella,' I said aloud as I drove away. 'All things happen for a reason. The pipe dream is over. Your new life starts here.'

I kept up this pep talk until I saw a field ahead dip away, and the sun break out over the Solent. A huge sob caught in my throat and I had to pull over.

Heaven only knows how long I sat there as misery pumped through me. Suffice to say, I only caught the ferry with minutes to spare.

** *Winter* **

Chapter 40

Oxford Street is spectacular leading up to Christmas, and so is Covent Garden with all its lights and shimmering baubles the size of planets. London is exactly the place to go for a girlie shopping spree. You can take selfies under the enormous, glittering trees and sip mulled wine at one of the Christmas Markets. Yes, London is a-throb with festive cheer.

What a pity I wasn't quite feeling it.

In fairness, Fran had gone out of her way to make me welcome. 'Babe, I know things didn't quite work out the way you wanted but I'm so glad you're here.' I'm guessing the look I gave her was a touch on the frosty side because she held my hand and said, 'I don't mean, "your loss is my gain," well, not exactly. I mean, I love you to bits and, whilst I know this isn't what you planned, I don't want you to feel unwanted here.'

Freddy was keeping a very low profile. I'd left several messages, begging him to tell me where he was and what was happening. All I got were texts saying things like, TRUST ME. I'M NOT AS BAD AS YOU THINK.

'What d'you reckon he's up to, Fran?'

'I think he's desperate for you to still love him, in spite of everything he's done.'

'But where is he?'

Dad asked the exact same question when I met up

with him. He was now back at Gill-Martin Property – a much scaled down business compared with when I left it. We sat, formally, in his office. This was his way of controlling the dialogue. I'd tried to persuade him to meet me in a café but he'd insisted on the office. 'And get your brother here, too!'

If only I had that much control.

I braced myself for a serious grilling, by necking a large vodka and tonic in the bar opposite.

At first sight, Dad looked older. He'd lost weight, which was a good thing, but it made his face thinner. To my relief, he came straight over and hugged me tight. 'Darling girl, it's so good to see you. The last few months have been quite an ordeal.' He released me and stepped back. 'And for you too, I imagine.'

I could feel a lump forming in my throat. I nodded.

'I see Freddy's late, as usual.' He gestured to the leather sofa. 'Here, sit down and we'll have some coffee while we wait. Then you can tell me some of the better things that have happened since I last saw you.'

'That won't take long.'

'Oh?'

As I replayed in my head all the dreadful events, in an effort to pluck one or two good ones out, emotion got the better of me. 'Bugger!' I said, as my self-control took a back seat.'

'That bad?' he said, sitting next to me and placing an arm around my shoulder. 'Do you want to start without Freddy.'

'I don't think he's coming.'

Dad sighed. 'Then you might as well tell me everything.'

I stared at the coffee cup in front of me and began. It wasn't easy, and I didn't share every disappointment, just the top-line bullets. He wasn't the kind of dad who enjoyed the finer details of friendships and lost opportunities.

Finally, he said, 'You didn't deserve that.'

'No, well…'

'Just as soon as we get the business back on its feet, you'll be earning good bonuses again. Then, in a few years, if you want to buy a little place on the island, you can.'

I blinked as I looked at him. 'Bonus?'

'Of course. There are some opportunities in the pipeline. I know it might be a bit harder after the Spanish debacle to persuade people that Gill-Martin Property is still sound, but we've done it before, we can do it again.'

My chest felt suddenly heavy, like anchors had been dropped. I swallowed. 'Dad, I know this is going to sound like absolute madness to you but I don't want to come back to work here.'

The frown was scary. 'You're working in a gift shop, Gigi.'

'Dad, you gave me twelve months to prove myself. I have six months left.'

He chewed his lip and studied my face. 'Fine, you do what you want.'

I waited for the lecture. Nothing. 'Is that it?'

'That's it.'

'Okay.'

'Gigi…' he put his hand over mine. 'I learned a very humbling lesson, this year. It reminded me of something your grandfather once said to me, which was a very long time ago. He said, "It's not having what you want, it's wanting what you have." It's only now that I understand what he meant. And I think you do too – you wanted what you had, and it was taken away from you. What kind of a father would I be if I stood in the way of you trying to get it back?'

I smiled and looked around the room. 'Who are you and what have you done with my dad?'

He smiled too. 'Good luck with it, Gigi, and when we're back on our feet, if I can help you, I will.'

'Thanks, Dad. I'm hoping you won't have to.'

A few days later, Fran asked me to meet her, after work, at a new restaurant in Soho. 'Why?' I asked, 'What are we celebrating.'

'Oh, nothing…It's a friend's place. It's opening this week.'

'On a Tuesday night?'

'Why do you have to be so suspicious?'

'I don't have to be – I just am.'

'Will you or won't you be coming?' she asked, rather sharply.

'I'll try.'

'It would really help me out if you did,' she said, softening slightly, 'I promised him I'd gee up some business.' My heart sank. Restaurants in Soho weren't cheap.

So on Tuesday, we met after work at Oxford Circus. She looked very relieved to see me. 'Who is this friend with the restaurant?' I asked as we headed off down Regent Street.

'He's more of an acquaintance really, a business contact. Nice guy.'

'What kind of food is it?'

'Oh, er…I'm not sure.'

'What's the restaurant called?'

'Ellis something.'

'You don't know?'

'I'll recognise it when I see it.' She was walking very quickly. 'Good day at work?' she asked, glancing at her watch.

'Quite busy. Are we late?'

'No. I don't think so.'

We took a left and ploughed on, dodging Christmas shoppers and, in my case, building up quite a sweat. Eventually, after consulting the map on her phone, we turned into a side street and up ahead was a glittering sign: Elysium – Fine Dining.

'Looks very smart,' I said, wondering if I could get away with just a starter.

'Through the doors I could see a few people milling about but hardly heaving for an opening night. The lighting was dim, rather like a posh cave with fairy lights. As the door opened, I stopped dead.

Freddy was standing at the front desk, and not alone. An older man stood next to him.

I held Fran back. 'What's going on?'

She reached for my hand. I wasn't sure if it was a supportive gesture or a restraining one. 'Nothing bad, I promise you.'

'Who's the guy with Freddy, his pimp?'

'No, I think that's the owner.'

'You think? You said you knew him.' I looked at her anxious face. 'What's going on?'

Freddy looked very pleased with himself. Based on experience, it didn't bode well. My heart was racing – and not just from my recent speed-walk.

He came towards me but something about my body language must have been repellent because he didn't attempt to hug me.

'Gigi, I want you to meet Wilf Hunt.'

The question, 'Why?' was on the tip of my tongue but being discourteous doesn't come easily to me.

As soon as the introductions were done, Freddy could barely contain his excitement. He clutched at my arm. 'Gigi, this is the best thing, I've ever done. Ever in my life.'

'Well, that's nice to know,' I said, currently underwhelmed. I looked from him to Fran.

'It's okay,' she said, 'I think you'll be okay with it.'

'With what?' I said, very sharply. I wasn't madly keen on surprises, especially ones involving my so-called best friend and my errant brother.

Freddy took my other hand. 'Come in and see.'

Beyond the dimly-lit entrance, we entered a glowing sanctum with tables meticulously set for dinner. There were shallow alcoves on the walls, and in each alcove, an angel. My angels to be precise – illuminated beautifully to show off their attitudes and their forms. I gazed from Morael to Balthioul and across to Damiel.

They could only have looked more beautiful in a church.

'Well?' asked Freddy, desperate for my approval.

I looked at him. 'What did you do, Freddy?' I asked, convinced he must have robbed a bank to invest in a restaurant like this.

'You know I work on lighting installations, well we do other stuff too. I thought it was worth a punt.'

'A punt…with my sculptures? Why didn't you just ask, instead of buggering off with them?'

I knew that sheepish look of old. 'I wasn't sure I'd be able to pull it off but I had to try. I owed you that much. And I knew you wouldn't trust me to take them if I'd asked.'

'Dead right! So what do you call stealing them and ignoring my calls – therapy?'

Fran was closing in on me, conveying her calmest demeanour.

I was seriously pissed off.

Wilf put a hand on Freddy's arm. 'May I say something?' he asked me, with a beseeching look. 'Your sculptures are exactly what I needed to complete the décor. I was planning on using screen-prints but your brother's suggestion was inspired. And, if you're in agreement, I'm willing to pay eight hundred pounds for each of them.'

I made a quick calculation. Freddy had quoted more than I would.

'Erm…'

'Freddy has also explained to me that you might not be in agreement and, if that's the case, I'll go back to plan A, and once the prints are ready, I'll return the sculptures to you, and agree a fee for the temporary use of them.'

Freddy was visibly willing me to accept the terms. A very small part of me was still mad at him.

I was scowling as politely as is humanly possible.

'There's more,' said Freddy, unable to keep it to himself. 'Wilf has two other restaurants opening up, in Manchester and Bristol, they won't be finished till Spring but he's planning the same kind of décor there.'

I looked at Wilf, who nodded. 'He's right, If you're up for it, I'd like to commission more angels.'

Fran squeezed my hand.

I considered the offer. 'There's only one problem,'

I said, 'I have no studio. My kilns are in storage.'

Wilf held up his hand. 'We've thought about that. I have a warehouse in north London. There's an area we can cordon off, install your kilns and any other equipment you require. I just need you to say yes, and we'll get it done.'

There had to be a catch. My brother was involved.

'Can I think about it?'

'Of course. But if you decide to come on board, I would love the photographer to get a shot with you and one of your beautiful creations.'

'Tonight?'

He shrugged. 'Only if you're happy. We can always arrange another shoot.'

He gestured into the restaurant. 'Tonight we are open for suppliers and business associates. Perhaps I can offer you a glass of champagne?'

I looked at the people standing around. They weren't conspicuously dodgy and I didn't spot any tattooed necks above expensively tailored jackets. In fact, across the room, I realised top TV chef, Julio Mendes, was studying the menu.

'Champagne would be lovely, thank you.'

It became clear Wilf was an influential man in the food industry. Restaurants were just one avenue he was pursuing. He'd made his millions refurbishing restaurants and furnishing hotels. Now, he was taking everything he'd learned from years in the trade and combining it with his vision for a great eating experience.

The food was delicious – beautifully presented, like miniature works of art; Jackson Pollock sprays of jus across the plate and Mondrian linear parcels of delight. At the end of the meal, Wilf stood to thank his guests and to introduce the kitchen brigade. 'Please, welcome my son, Aran Hunt and his team, Juan Pablo, Lucy, Oscar and Emile.'

Aha! So this was a family business. Julio Mendes stood to applaud. 'He trained Aran,' Freddy confided. 'Bet he wishes he hadn't let him go, now.'

As the applause died down, Wilf continued. 'Many of you have been admiring the décor, in particular the beautiful angels you see around the walls. Please, allow me to introduce to you the wonderful and talented artist, Gabriella Gill-Martin.'

Freddy hooted and clapped.

I raised my hand a rather pathetic, sub-royal wave.

'Stand up!' Freddy nudged me.

'I can't,' I grunted.

'Go on,' Fran put a hand beneath my elbow.

I managed a half-rise-half-bow, like I was suffering from a bad bout of wind, before plopping back into my seat.

Looking around at the smiling faces, and sensing the waves of good feeling, I made up my mind and leaned in towards my brother, 'Freddy, I utterly condemn your methods but I do appreciate the motivation behind it.'

'You'll do it?'

'Yes.'

He swung an arm around my neck and hugged me to him. 'I'm not going to let you down again. Promise.'

I'd heard that before but I smiled anyway. 'Good.'

'Marvellous, I'm so pleased,' Wilf said when we told him my decision.

'Just one thing,' I said before any contracts could be drawn up or signed. 'I'd like to exhibit the new angels before they're installed – is that okay with you?'

'Why not?' he asked, possibly considering the publicity factor. 'No problem whatsoever. Now, can I persuade you to have your picture taken?'

'Sure,' I said. 'Fran, how do I look?'

'Gorgeous, darling. A spot of lippy and you're good to go.'

Freddy didn't stop grinning for the rest of the night. Finally, he'd done something he could be proud of.

Chapter 41

I was back on the island. Back at Bluebell Farm, pulling prize-winning carrots from the vegetable bed. Carrots with fluorescent green leaves and copper-coloured shafts.

'Fancy coming over to Compton for a walk, blow the cobwebs away?' asked Luke, his sun-browned skin crinkling appealingly at the edges of his eyes.

'Love to.'

'I'll point out the strata in the cliffs and you can guess just how long ago they were formed. Or we can just walk hand-in-hand through the surf'

'Bliss.'

'You'd like that?' he added quietly, moving closer.

'I'd love it,' I said, tilting my head up for the kiss I knew would be heavenly.

'Too bad,' a voice said.

Luke had morphed into Rupert. Rupert was laughing at the shock he'd given me.

My throat began to ache and my chest tighten.

'No!' I yelled.

'What is it. Babe?' Fran was sitting on my bed, pushing the hair back off my face. Gradually, my eyes assessed the room around me.

'Sorry.'

'That's okay. Bad dream?'

I nodded. It was a recurring theme. 'Usually, all the windows are breaking and I can't seem to stop them. The doors won't lock and I just know someone or something is coming to get me, but this time…'

'What?'

'This one was different. Luke was there.'

'He's the one coming to get you?'

I shook my head. 'He was the only nice part about it.'

She looked thoughtful. 'Are you in love with him?'

I could feel myself frowning. There was no point loving Luke. He would never reciprocate. He was too wounded by his past. Plus, I wasn't really on his intellectual level and considering everything he knew about my family, was probably a total liability in his eyes. I lay back. 'Just in love with the island and everything it meant to me, I guess.'

'What was he doing in the dream?'

'Offering to show me cretaceous rocks.'

'Really? That's a euphemism on a whole new level.' I smiled.

She looked at the bedside clock. 'Happy Christmas, sweetie.'

'Happy Christmas!' we hugged. 'It's so kind of your parents to invite me.'

'Darling, you know I gave them no choice. At least I have a hope of actually enjoying Christmas with you here.'

'And Alissa?' This was the first time I'd mentioned her since I'd moved in.

'I hear she's blooming. And good for her.'

'D'you mean that?'

'I do. She's got most of what she wants in life. And there is something else…'

'Go on…'

'I've met a girl called Jessica…'

'Aha! Tell me more!'

'It's early days yet.'

'But there's a spark?'

'Firecrackers.'

'Really? So, if Alissa were to walk in here, right now, what would you say to her?'

Fran sat up. 'I'd say, "Where did you get a bloody key from?"'

I grinned. It was good to see Fran on her way back to happiness.

The week after Christmas, my new studio was up and running. I had a corner of the warehouse, partitioned off with mobile fencing. My kiln was inside another fenced off corner, with a lockable gate to prevent any risk of tampering by nosy staff, and my tables and tools were in place.

Great...ish.

At the risk of sounding ungrateful, it was kind of weird to be a one-woman production unit in a warehouse full of catering gear and furniture. Especially when I discovered I would be the only person on site, most of the time.

Still, no distractions.

No view to speak of, either.

And no company.

But plenty of time to produce fourteen new angels.

✶✶ *Spring* ✶✶

Chapter 42

My return to the island conjured up a whole cocktail of feelings that were making me queasy. Never before had I felt such dread as I drove off the ferry.

I should have been celebrating. This was my first full exhibition since my degree show but back then, everyone who came to view was either related to, tutoring or boozing with the students. This time, I was facing a commercial show, to which Wilf – my lovely sponsor – had invited local celebrities, everybody from his southern counties network and a couple of journalists. He'd even chartered a swanky yacht – the no mast, no sails, pink-champagne-on-tap variety – to bring his cronies over.

Not that the show was the biggest threat – although a critical review would undoubtedly shatter my already fragile self-esteem. No. It was returning to the scene of my greatest failure.

Until now, I'd resisted all invitations to visit. I had, instead, cajoled Megan to come and see me in London for a weekend, while Fran was away. I'm sorry to say, I was less than the best hostess – dragging her to my 'studio' one afternoon to watch me work. I was shamefully overdoing the 'I'm too busy to leave London' charade. She didn't complain, bless her heart, but that might have been because she was just deeply grateful to be away from the responsibilities of motherhood or else she was hiding her boredom better than I was hiding my displacement activity. Either way, I owed her an apology.

And then there was Luke.

I was desperately hoping he would come to see my show. I was also dreading how I might react if he did. The drama of our last conversation – scratch that, our last argument – was a distasteful memory. It was like an angry little worm in my brain, chomping at my conscience. Just occasionally, to counter-balance this memory, I would recall The Hug. The hug that told me he did care in some small way. And after wallowing in the memory of that hug and what might have been, I'd shake myself and file it under No Regrets.

Who was I kidding?

At six o'clock, as the doors opened for the private viewing, I could feel the tempo of my heartbeat – it was doing a samba all of its own. I couldn't even bear to sip the complimentary champagne Wilf had provided, convinced as I was it would be back up in a second.

Wilf wrapped a bracing arm around my shoulders. 'Spectacular, my love. Good enough for Westminster Abbey, if you ask me.'

'You're very kind. Not sure everyone will think that way.'

One minute Freddy was busy blowing invisible dust from the crevices of the sculptures, the next he was squaring up the pamphlets on the stands.

Wilf had brought a photographer. No surprises there – It hadn't taken long to discover he was an expert at generating hype. But what if the world at large and, in particular, the art world viewed my exhibition rather like the Emperor's New Clothes? If that were the case, I could be hyped right back into obscurity.

Sonia, Fran and her stunning new partner, Jessica, were first through the doors. I'd blagged passage for them on Wilf's yacht so they were already pretty wonky from the free bar.

'Darling, fanTAStic,' Sonia said, bashing cheeks with me. 'Spent the last hour chatting up Julio Mendes,' she whispered. 'Bit of a dish himself.'

Behind them came a bunch of Wilf's cronies. There were so many of them, I wondered the yacht hadn't sunk. Pretty soon, they were all back-slapping and flute-bashing with bonhomie. I felt I was observing it all from somewhere outside my skin. It was like watching a reality TV show, only not mine.

Fran came alongside and hooked her arm through mine. 'Whose party is this?' she asked, touchingly miffed on my behalf.

Very soon, a journalist from the *Isle of Wight County Press* arrived, followed by a crew from *Hampshire and Isle of Wight TV*. Wilf seemed to know them all.

Eventually, Fran managed to talk me into a glass of champagne. 'Babe, everyone's really impressed. I heard the woman with the blue-rinse up-do saying she wants to commission a tableau for her garden – which she insisted on calling her jardin. How pretentious is that.'

'She'll just be saying that – people do,' I said. 'It won't happen.'

'I think it might,' Jessica purred, in a very sexy Irish accent, 'She's the owner of Le Jardin in Kent. It's a spa – costs a couple of grand to stay for a weekend.'

'Damn!' said Fran, 'I wish I'd been nicer to her.'

Sonia drained her champagne flute and asked me, 'Would it be very naff to get a selfie with you and that fit-looking angel over there?'

'For your information, angels are supposed to be sexless.'

'He hasn't met me, yet,' quipped Sonia.

'They're lacking in gender. They're just beings.'

'How dull.'

We posed by Dagiel, the angel with dominion over fish 'Dinky, isn't he,' she grinned. Even on the display plinth, he only came up to her chin. 'Pretty though.'

Fran took a couple of pictures.

'Now me on my own with him,' Sonia said, steering me away.

'Nothing cheesy or remotely pornographic, please,' I begged.

'Spoilsport,' she said, standing demurely to the side. 'Does this work for you?' She looked beyond us to the doorway. 'Oh, hello! Don't look now but a devine hunk, definitely male, just entered the gallery.'

Fran turned.

'I said "don't look!" Hubba-hubba. I think I may have spontaneously ovulated. Definitely twelve out of ten on the Throb-ometer. Gigi, give it a second, and you look.'

Fran turned back. 'I think I know him.'

'You do?' Sonia asked, brightening. 'Have I met him?' Her eyes were moving back and forth while she tried to remember.

I giggled. 'Stop it! The suspense is killing me, I'm going to have to take a look.'

I turned, casually scanning every face in the room until my eyes came to rest on him. He was tall and broad-shouldered with unruly black hair, the kind of hair that sprang into a gentle curl the moment it got wet – and tonight there was a light drizzle in the air. It was the kind of hair he'd need to tie in a ponytail if it were longer.

'Is he off the telly?' Sonia asked.

He was wearing a dark green plaid shirt with jeans, and the beard was gone – only the shadow of stubble remained.

'Gigi, where are you going?'

Yes, where was I going? I was pretty sure the door in the opposite corner would be open. Maybe I could gather my thoughts out there.

It was locked.

I looked carefully around, there were a dozen or so people between me and Luke. He was with Megan and Ava. Despite my anxiety over seeing him again, my heart squeezed with happiness, knowing they were there for me.

Yes, they were. So what the hell was I doing skulking in the corner?

'Shape up, Gabriella!' I could hear Nanna's voice in my head. It's what she used to say when we were children, and mucking about.

Sonia was already on the case, introducing herself – no doubt with a 'Don't I know you from somewhere' opener. Yep. There it was – the penny dropping. Her mouth popped open and she seized his arm in recognition. Then, together, they scanned the room in search of me.

Be normal, I told myself as I approached. He's just an old neighbour. Keep it light.

Ava, hugged me immediately. 'This is really fresh,' she said. Next was Megan and finally…

Luke hugged me to him and murmured 'Congratulations' in my ear. Well, maybe not in my ear, that makes it sound more intimate than it was intended.

'Thank you all, so much, for coming,' I said as I pulled away.

I couldn't stop beaming at them – nerves and delight working hand in hand. 'It's so good to see you again. I've missed you.'

I was avoiding Luke's face. He must have thought I was very rude, so I forced a look in his direction and nearly lost my breath completely. Sonia was right, he was hot. Too hot for me. The hermit had been supportive and kind. I could handle that. Now Luke was off-the-scale gorgeous, and totally out of my league.

Not, it seemed, Sonia's. She immediately assumed the role of tour guide. 'Let's do the exhibits together, while Gigi meets the rest of her public.'

'Can't you come too,' Ava said, linking her arm through mine, 'I kinda like being seen with the artist.'

I caught Luke throwing her a look.

'What?' she said. 'I'm a huge fan, almost her biggest.'

'It's okay,' I said. 'I'd love to. I was beginning to feel like a spare part, anyway.'

Sonia had already struck out towards one of the celestial groups.

'What do you think of Luke's new look?' Ava whispered.

'Nice. He looks smart,' Two totally inadequate adjectives.

'Megan said it was a tough job but hugely rewarding.'

Of course, it would be Megan's handiwork. I swallowed. 'She survived the force-field then?'

'I think he might have switched it off,' she winked.

So the trip to Canada had made a difference.

Sonia was pointing to angel Ruhiel, and loving the limelight. 'He has such a look of compassion, don't you think? Sorry – *it* has a look of compassion – apparently we mustn't allocate gender to angels. They don't have sex.'

Luke peered at the information card below the sculpture. 'Ruhiel, angel of the winds. Seems there's an angel for everything. Got one for palaeontologists?' He was smiling at me. The twinkling eyes hadn't changed. I just wasn't used to seeing them in such a handsome face. Which was bizarre, because his face hadn't changed at all, it was more like the hedgerow had been cleared to improve the view.

'Over here,' I said, my tongue suddenly sticking in my mouth. I led them to exhibit number four. 'Meet Araqiel, who's said to have taught mankind the signs of the earth. Will that do?'

Luke studied the sculpture and, in particular, the ammonite I'd modelled and placed in the angel's hands. 'Perfect.'

I blushed. I felt like the last contestant standing on *Take Me Out* – the one girl truly interested in Luke. Unlike *Take Me Out*, the ammonite didn't have a bright blue light.

'Isn't she amazing, our Gigi?' asked Sonia, crashing the moment, followed immediately by Wilf, gently touching my elbow.

'Excuse me for butting in, there's a journalist here from *Art Style Magazine*. She only has twenty minutes.'

389

'Of course,' I said. 'Excuse me.'

The journalist was charming but evidently busy. She reminded me of a harassed GP I had when I was at college; talking rapidly and moving me on to the next point while I was still wrapping up the last one. Both left me feeling a reluctant kind of gratitude that they'd even bothered to see me, and wondering if I'd done myself justice. The only difference being, my health – hopefully – wouldn't suffer as a result of *Art Style* getting it wrong.

Across the gallery, I could see my little posse of friends. Luke was flanked by Megan and Sonia, while Ava was busy studying the exhibition pamphlet. I could also see Freddy, shooting the odd glance in her direction. I crossed my fingers against any altercation between him and Luke.

'Gabriella?' the journalist was peering at me intently.

'Sorry – sorry. What was that?'

'Will you continue with the angel theme, or develop more along the dragon, fantasy line?'

'That's a very good question. It's the anatomy of creatures that fascinates me, real or fantasy. I like to describe attitude in their figures; portray gestures, invest character – if that makes sense?'

She nodded, and scribbled something down. 'So you won't be turning your hand to inanimate objects, then?'

'Not at present.'

'Great. Well, that's all I need. Good luck with the rest of the show, and sorry this was so brief.' She stuffed her book into her bag, shook my hand and made for the door, arriving at it just as my father walked in.

'Sorry I'm late, darling. The train was delayed outside Godalming. I had no idea I was on the slow one; stopped every-bloody-where!' Poor old Dad, he wasn't used to public transport.

'But you're here, that's all that matters.'

'Are you going to show me round?'

'Of course.'

I led him over to the first group, conscious that Fran and Jessica had joined forces with the others. Now and again, I glanced over to where Megan and Luke stood slightly apart, chatting easily together. And why wouldn't they? They had a lot in common – both single and living within ten minutes of each other. Plus he was practically a single parent himself. And look how she'd managed to turn him from hermit to hottie.

My heart lurched.

I loved Megan. She would be seriously blessed to link up with Luke, and he would make a fabulous step-dad for Mackay.

A hot dizziness swooped through me, like I was hurtling down the steepest side of a roller coaster. Visions of me and Luke tumbled into the distance, as images of Megan and Luke accumulated rapidly in their place. I put my arm through Dad's to steady myself.

Freddy came over. He and Dad had been reconciled after his success securing me the contract. It was like he felt he'd earned the right to face Dad again.

'Alright, Dad? She's done really well, hasn't she?'

'She certainly has.' He looked at me. 'I'm very proud of you, darling.'

I soaked it up. 'Thanks, Dad. But you know,

Freddy helped make it happen, in an odd sort of way.'

Dad rolled his eyes, but rested a hand on his shoulder. 'Could you try and be a little more orthodox in future, son?'

Freddy nodded. I think the word, 'son' had rather thrown him.

I hugged them both, and caught Luke's eye momentarily, before he returned his attention to Megan.

Wilf joined us. 'I'd like a picture, Gigi. Do you mind?'

Why would I mind? He was my biggest customer. In any case, it was good to be busy. It kept me away from Luke without appearing rude.

Unfortunately, Luke wasn't quite thinking along the same lines. As Wilf and I posed next to Theliel, angel of love, I was aware of Luke loitering beside the next exhibit.

As soon as we were through, he wandered over to me, one hand casually in his pocket, the other clutching an exhibition leaflet.

'Want me to sign it?' I joked, very badly.

He smiled. 'Not unless you want to.'

'No. Sorry. Just a bit out of my depth here.'

'I wanted to apologise,' he began.

'Oh?' Did he consider it a crime to fall for Megan? Could he tell I was upset?

'For tearing into you about Freddy, before you left.'

'Oh.' I shook my head. 'Totally understandable. I was pretty pissed off with him, myself.'

'I know, but I was out of order.'

I shrugged. 'Friends do that, don't they – look out for one another?'

He studied me for a moment. 'I'm glad you see it that way.'

'Sure.' My breath was all over the place again. 'Nice to see you here with Megan,' I blustered. 'And Ava, obviously.'

'Ava's always telling me I need to get out more.'

'I like the new look.'

'Another edict from Ava.'

'Makes you look much younger.'

'Apparently.' I swear he blushed. 'So, what's next for Gigi?'

'Good question. Wilf isn't planning on opening any more restaurants for a while and, between you and me, I think he's done with the heavenly diner theme. So I'm hoping the publicity will do me some good, and I can set up a proper studio, somewhere else.'

'In London?'

'Not with property prices the way they are. No.'

'Would you ever consider moving back to the island?'

Something in my heart tightened. That dream had failed me once, I didn't feel it was wise to go back. Especially not if he and Megan… I looked across the room. She and Ava were giggling together like old friends. 'I'm not sure it would work a second time.'

'No? I thought it really suited you, here. In spite of everything, you really seemed to…' he looked away for inspiration and then smiled, '…come to life in the face of adversity. If that doesn't sound too patronizing,' he added, looking into my eyes for approval.

'No, that's okay.'

'And I hear the Dubai plans are toast.'

I must have been going crimson. 'Er, yes. That's over.'

'You never really wanted to go anyway, did you?'

I wrinkled my nose. 'Was it that obvious?'

He was smiling. 'You mean, did I spot the way all the light went out of your eyes when you talked about it? I'd say so.'

He was studying my face now, and his smile faded. 'So would you consider coming back to the island? You used to say it was like all your planets lined up when you were here – all your kinks and wrinkles ironed out. That's gotta be good for something, huh?'

He remembered that?

I watched the way his face changed subtly as he waited for my response. I just wished I could construct a coherent one, I was blown away that he remembered how I felt.

At my silence, he said, 'You know, after seeing your dragon sculptures, it got me thinking and... I was thinking your skills would really lend themselves to modelling prehistoric creatures. Fossils show all the structural detail but you could create something solid and active. Fossils on their own do look kinda – dead.' I saw him swallow before he rambled on. 'They can do 3D modelling on computers but it's not the same as actually having something tactile. Is it?' He gestured a solid shape with his hands.

Despite all this dinosaur stuff, I could tell there was something else he was trying to say, and my heart bumped.

He shrugged and ran a hand through his hair. 'It's probably not really your thing, is it? Sorry, just an idea.' He pulled a face, like he'd made an epic blunder.

394

My heart bumped some more. I smiled. 'Dinosaurs with attitude?'

'Maybe not. Sorry.'

'No, no.' I placed a hand on his arm and several emotional volts shot through me as his body stilled. 'I think it's a cool idea. Really.'

He glanced at my hand on his arm and back up at me. His smile was warming my soul. 'You do?'

'It would need some pretty thorough research, though.'

'I could help you with that.'

'It would give me good reason for coming back to the island, wouldn't it?'

There was a moment's stillness between us. 'Would it change things, in any way at all, if I said I'd like you to come back?'

The earth began spinning at warp speed and my whole life flipped in a different direction. 'Luke, if you're saying what I think you're saying…'

I felt his hand gather around mine. 'I'm willing to give it a go if you are.'

I could feel the smile stretching my cheeks. 'One hundred percent, I want to give it a go.'

'You do?' He nudged closer.

'Absolutely.'

'Then I'm the luckiest man on the planet.'

'I'll remind you of that when there's clay in my hair and under my fingernails.'

'You're worth it.'

Finally, his lips met mine, and I felt all my inner kinks and wrinkles start to relax.

Somebody really famous must have arrived, because from across the gallery came a whole load of whooping and clapping. We pulled back to see who –

but it was just Ava, Megan, Fran and even Freddy, cheering us on.

'Bout bloody time!' yelled Ava.

'Go for it!' yelled Megan.

Fran just blew me a kiss and Freddy held his hands up in applause.

Luke grinned at me. 'Wow! That was a popular move.'

I giggled. 'Who knew?'

He wrapped his arms around me and pulled me close. 'So, which angel do we have to thank for this, then?'

I thought for a moment. 'I'm not saying she's an angel yet…but this could be Una Gill at work.'

'Well, she only ever wanted the best for you.'

'Nanna was an excellent judge of character.'

Thank You!

Thank you for taking time to read *Gigi's Island Dream*. If you enjoyed it, please consider telling your friends or posting a short review. Word of mouth is an author's best friend and much appreciated.

Thank you, again,

Rosie Dean.

Acknowledgements

I have a number of lovely people to thank, who helped me on research. As they say on the talent shows, *In No Particular Order*. Isle of Wight's own Fossil Man, Martin Simpson, who clued me in on palaeontology stuff; Jeremy Cornish of Wightlink Raiders ice hockey team; Georgia Newman at Quay Arts and Charlotte Hodge-Thomas for insights on the island Art scene; Babette Bishop who educated me on merkins and allowed me to use her name; finally, Dave Jones and the Raw Samba gang – I had a fabulous evening bashing a tamborim and getting in the groove – you guys rock!

Huge thanks to: my editor, Hannah M Davis, whose insights are spot on; Julie Cohen for her invaluable guidance; my beta readers, Noëlle Chambers, Lauren Broderick and Carolyn Gray; and Marie Macneill, Giselle Green, AJ Pearce, Liz Harris and Cara Cooper for input along the way.

I want to mention Isle of Wight eateries: Ganders, Olivo in Ryde and Solent View café – whose lovely food has sustained me on many occasions.

Finally, massive thanks to: Joe Brown for his cover designs; my family for their support and inspiration; and to you, dear reader, I hope you enjoyed the journey.

Millie's Game Plan

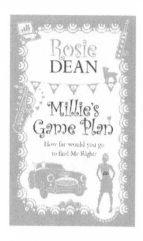

Does your life lack fun and love? Does your mother fix you up with her priest's middle-aged nephew?

Millie's does – so she takes a grip on her own future and draws up a plan to find Mr Right.

When the first guy to float her boat, Josh Warwick, doesn't match her wish-list, she moves on to wine merchant, Lex Marshall, who ticks all the boxes - he's sexy, rich and unable to keep his hands off her. But when Millie faces danger and betrayal, she wonders if her dream man might not be Mr Right after all.
So, who will be...?

"Loved it, loved it, loved it." Best Chick Lit

"Author Rosie Dean's debut book is a hit!"
Stephanie Lasley – Kindle Book Review

Chloe's Rescue Mission

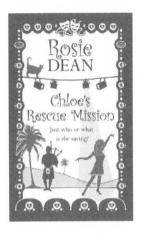

Can Scottish leisure tycoon, Duncan Thorsen, help Chloe save her family's crumbling theatre?

Can she resist his notorious charms?

And just how much exposure will satisfy the paparazzi's lust for headlines?

Chloe is about to find out...

'Rosie Dean is fast becoming one of my most favourite romantic fiction writers'
Heidi at CosmoChicklitan

5/5 'kept me smiling throughout'
Shona at 'Booky Ramblings

Vicki's Work of Heart

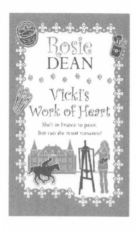

What if you found yourself stranded at the altar, knee-deep in your absent fiancé's gambling debts?

Vicki Marchant, humble art teacher and jilted bride carries on with the reception because she likes a good party. Then she seizes her freedom and leaves teaching to paint – in France.

It's her time and there's nobody to get in the way of her ambition. Definitely, no men…

She learns two things: some men are hard to resist and her judgement of them is still on the dodgy side.

'A beautiful and emotional story' – *CosmoChicklitan*

'The book is a sheer joy to read' – *Best Chic Lit*

Born in Derby, Rosie Dean has been writing stories since she was a little girl. She studied ceramic design – gaining a 'degree in crockery' as the man-in-her-life likes to call it – which she put to good use as an Art & Pottery teacher.

After moving into the world of corporate communication, to write training courses and marketing copy, she finally gave it all up to write fiction, full-time.

Rosie is lucky enough to live partly in the UK and partly in southern Spain.

www.rosie-dean.com